Bridles of Poseidon

Bridges DelPonte

This novel is a work of fantasy fiction. All of the characters, organizations, and events portrayed in this novel are either products of the author's imagination or are used fictitiously.

Cover image credit: DeepGreen/Shutterstock.com

To Divemaster Dave for sharing his enduring love and sense of wonder for the beauty and mystery of the underwater world

ACKNOWLEDGMENTS

I wish to thank and acknowledge my wonderful critique readers, Charlee Allden, Caroline E. Olson, Jean Osborn, and David W. Riddell for all of their helpful comments, insights and encouragement on this novel. I also wish to thank members of the Jacksonville Science Fiction and Fantasy Writers Workshop for their review of the initial three chapters of this manuscript. Last, but not least, I appreciate the Florida Writers Association for selecting *Bridles of Poseidon* as a finalist for the 2012 Royal Palm Literary Award (unpublished fantasy).

To learn more about Bridges DelPonte and her writing, visit her web site at http://www.bridgesdelponte.com.

Chapter 1

Aquan didn't flinch as his needle repeatedly punctured her right hip's smooth fair skin. Each jab felt no more bothersome than a cleaner shrimp on a whale's belly. Minor stuff compared to her shuddering pain when transforming.

"So what brings ya to Estonia?" asked Wazza, a talented tattoo artist.

"Just bumming around, backpacking everywhere."

No need to tell him that she spent over two days tracking a camouflaged Hydromorph until it disappeared in this tangle of medieval alleys. Or that before dawn she tagged dozens of bus shelter posters with green spray paint, blotting out cartoon images of helpless mermaids in those silly Sea Captain cologne ads. Aquan knew she could kick any sailor's butt.

"What's ya favorite so far?"

Thinking about her travels, she envisioned steam rising off Kilauea's orange molten lava flows at daybreak, violet and blue splashes of aurora borealis shimmering across a midnight sky in Canadian wilderness and chorus lines of ferocious hurricanes churning up seas between Africa and North America. With so many natural wonders, it was hard to pick just one.

"Body surfing at Kirra Point, off Australia's Gold Coast."

In an instant, she remembered her thrilling tumble with a pod of whistling dolphins in chilly midnight surf at Kirra Point. Kirra. Such a musical name with Aboriginal roots. Aquan often chose it when she shape-shifted into female Surface Dwellers.

"Cool."

She heard the Ceremonial Conch's first blast, but ignored it for now. Wazza turned up his grainy bootleg copy from last year's Punk Song Festival as he continued to outline her intricate design. Tapping his vinyl chair cushions to pulsating trance music, Aquan loved any rhythmic sounds, from a harp's soothing strings to a thumping battery of Black Drum fish. His needle's persistent buzz and those throbbing techno beats almost drowned out her aunt's disapproving voice echoing in her head.

"You may walk amongst Surface Dwellers, but you must not become one of them," said Aunt Sofronia.

Her aunt often chastised her for lapsing into human casualness and forgetting her ancestral traditions. Tattoos were strictly forbidden. And that's why Aquan wanted one to mark the start of her first season. With his hand mirror, Wazza showed her the initial dark contours of her tattoo. Her eyes flashed with delight as she gazed at her parents' interlocking symbols, a trident and a shield. She knew her scales would conceal this design, so no one in Rapture's End had to know.

"When you come back, I'll color it in. For now, keep it clean. Use antibacterial ointment for any scabbing. And don't go swimming."

Fat chance, she smirked. Aquan planned an early dip to refresh her shape-shifting powers before high tide ended and then resume her Hydromorph search. She threw on her long black coat, an array of paralyzing and lethal darts and a compact spear gun hidden within its folds.

Turning up her collar against a cool afternoon breeze, she prowled Tallinn's Old Towne with its crooked cobblestone streets as a lanky Finnish day-tripper with shoulder-length blond hair and pale blue eyes. She easily mingled with thousands of twenty-something Finnish tourists who poured off Helsinki ferries looking for cheap shopping and cheaper partying. Except Aquan raced a school of brown trout across the Gulf of Finland to hunt for a sea imp.

Near a brick marketplace, Aquan caught a whiff of Hydromorph stink, a mix of decaying seaweed and dead mackerel. Her heart beat faster as she trailed its rotting stench. Tourists and backpackers strolled through food and craft stalls unable to smell or see this Hydromorph, camouflaged to blend in with its surroundings. Aquan watched it sift through Baltic antique treasures and salvaged artifacts at long tables and display cases for several hours. Her joints ached as she longed to swim and rejuvenate her transformative powers, but she couldn't chance losing this creature again. At sundown, it left the market empty-handed.

Taking a seat at an outdoor café, Aquan sipped a Saku beer

while locals and tourists chatted and bounced to Estonian pop music. She noticed this imp's occasional flickering as it paced back and forth in a dingy alley next to the shuttered marketplace. As darkness enveloped Tallinn, a second Conch blast reverberated in her ear. Time was getting tight.

A half-hour later, Aquan saw it scurrying toward an isolated loading dock. She followed it and then hid behind a stack of grimy wooden pallets. Shedding its camouflage, this yellowish gremlin materialized with its huge frog-like eyes on each side of its tiny head. Speckled barnacles and knots of brown seaweed covered its arms and spindly fingers. It cracked open a glass vial with its jagged teeth and drank a liquid smelling of saltwater. Shivering and grunting, the creature turned into an electric eel. It slithered through a mouse hole in a rear dock entrance. A Hydromorph could shape-shift with its sea water potion for about thirty or forty minutes on land.

Grimacing, Aquan chirped a bird call and transformed into a Sea Martlet, fluttering through a gash in a second floor window. Sensing its clumsy moves with her sonar, she flew down a flight of stairs. Under dim emergency lights, Aquan spied it lurking around as a Surface Dweller. It broke a glass display case and reached inside to grab an amber-encrusted talisman.

"Stop, thief!" yelled a security guard.

The Hydromorph turned around slowly, recoiled and then sprang at the guard as an electric eel. He tried to fight it off with his club, but it jolted him into an unconscious state. Returning to human form, it grabbed the man's night stick to strike him dead.

"I wouldn't do that," said Aquan.

She stepped out of the shadows in her female form, her spear gun pointed at it. Stuffing its stolen amulet into its mouth, the imp converted back to an eel, too narrow for her spear gun. Aquan chased after it and flung a slim dart tipped with diluted box jellyfish venom. Screeching as her dart pierced its skin, the dazed Hydromorph became temporarily paralyzed. Its right cheek bulged with its filched charm.

"Who sent you here? And why are you stealing this?" demanded Aquan.

It kept silent.

"You're only stunned. I know you can still speak. Where are your accomplices? Grabbing other gems?"

The Hydromorph refused to reply.

"Tell me or I'll feed you to Selkies," she warned.

It coughed and spit out an amber talisman.

"Better to die as seal bait than face my Margrave's wrath."

"Millions of sunken gems litter our sea floor. I can't believe he ordered you to shoplift this crude trinket."

"One can't steal what is already my Margrave's property."

"He owns nothing, but his exile." Aquan seized the eel and it squirmed furiously in her hand.

"Then consider it a gift, Triton. A cursed message to your House from ours. Prepare for the Vanquishment."

It wheezed and then liquefied into saltwater rather than face any further interrogation. Another foolish believer in that Exori myth, Aquan thought, as its watery remains dripped through her fingers. She picked up the antique ornament with its three amber stones and intricate markings from a small yellow puddle. Why would it sacrifice itself for this simple object? Aquan glanced at a typed description inside its display case.

"Decoration of unknown origin. (Possibly Vineta?) Underwater salvage. Gulf of Finland."

She wiped the pendant with her coat hem. Strange visions flashed across each amber. In one gemstone, she observed a murky image of her mother, Evadne, sobbing pearls into her outstretched hands. It saddened Aquan to see her crying as her mother knew so little joy in their short time together.

Flickering mist veiled its second stone. Aquan heard a furious roar of an enormous wave surge. Cold dread gripped her as screams of terrified Surface Dwellers filled her ears. She grabbed her chest and steadied herself against a brick wall.

Its third amber displayed a crystal clear image of a catamaran named *Calusa* bouncing in white-capped waves. Under a full moon's bluish glow, a woolly Portuguese Water

Dog barked and leapt with its webbed-feet on deck as this vessel drifted in turbulent seas, torn from its anchor. A pungent odor churned in violent winds followed by a thunderous boom and a soaring funnel of fire. In this vision, Aquan drank in her own tears as roiling flames consumed *Calusa*. Suddenly, she awoke with a start from her visions. Confused, she decided to immediately return home to seek guidance.

High tide was nearly over and her body started aching. Thick beads of sweat washed over her as she fought to retain human form. Mopsus warned her about cutting her twenty-four hour clock too close. She could skip one high tide, but not two, to retain her powers. Aquan stumbled toward an abandoned commercial pier away from Tallinn's noisy weekend revelers. Certain she stood alone, she slid into brackish harbor water under a full moon's glow.

For a moment, she relished feelings of primal ecstasy as cold seawater splashed across her skin. She sang softly to distract herself from those initial stabs of pain. Unlike her fellow Archigens, Aquan knew both the joys of quivering cool saltwater through her gills and inhaling fresh air into her lungs. Diving deeply into the bay, her fish tail reemerged and mother of pearl scales climbed up to her waist. Her thick locks, a mocha shade of beach dunes at dusk, drifted past her waist and tickled her glacier blue skin. She secured the amulet in her deep waist pouch beneath her shimmering fish scales. After refreshing herself for nearly an hour, she transformed into a Killer Whale to race home before a third and final blast.

Chapter 2

Towering undersea mountains dwarfed even Aquan in her whale form. Six gill sharks patrolled these craggy ridges, changing colors to mask their stealth pursuit of hapless squids and lumbering sea turtles. Hordes of wrasse fish nibbled Aquan's whale blubber looking for any irritating parasites. She dipped down into sable fields of cooled magma teeming with rainbows of schooling fish and crawling crustaceans. Purple sea fans and pink-tipped sea worms undulated in shifting currents as she approached a gaping trench at the end of these volcanic fields. A soft glow from bioluminescent organisms marked a restricted entry into Rapture's End, dwelling place of the major Houses of Archigen, descendants of Oceanus.

Aquan swam through a network of subterranean caves and shimmied past spiky stalactites, still concealed from Surface Dwellers' primitive echo sounding tools. Raynord's brigade of steel gray Timarchs, centaurs blending exquisite and powerful elements of human torsos and sea horse tails, guarded key corridors into Rapture's End from renegade Exoris. He heard Aquan's familiar clicks and whistles and lowered his spear gun, waving her through his checkpoint.

"Welcome back, Aquan," said Raynord, in responsive Archigen whistles and grunts. His seal brown eyes softened as she neared him. "I knew you'd be last to appear. A minute later and you'd be locked out of Convocation. And shunned for a century."

Aquan would have happily endured a century of isolation to miss this three-day celebration of her cohort's first mating season, but she didn't say so.

"I owe it to my aunt to be here," she replied.

Aquan liked to annoy her aunt with her minor rebellions, like chopping off her long sandy locks leaving only a stubbly blue buzz cut or the increasing number of piercings on her nose, belly button and ear lobes. This tug of war between her freedom to roam land and sea and her duty to obey Archigen customs remained as unrelenting as ocean waves beating against a rocky coastline. But to be shunned was even too radical for Aquan.

"The rest of your group is already preening themselves for Convocation. Especially Thalassa."

"Your sister does enough for both of us. Besides I'm not one for preening."

"You don't need to," Raynord said.

He looked directly into her eyes and Aquan fought off an unexpected flush of red.

"Can I talk you into joining our Timarch House tonight for an evening of sporting events?" he asked.

She knew Raynord, a swift swimmer and an accomplished spearman, hoped his certain victories might spark her devotion. But Aquan didn't want to mate this first season with anyone, prizing her freedom to explore the Earth. Besides, a century represented but a ripple in the ocean's eternal drumbeat. Why rush into mating while so many adventures awaited her?

"Thank you, Raynord. Tonight, my House is holding a ceremonial evening hunt in honor of all Tritons reaching their first season. Strictly a family gathering."

Aquan knew he would be disappointed, although most Archigen females would be happy to have Raynord to themselves. Thalassa rushed toward them.

"Where have you been? I was so worried about you after the second blast when you didn't show up. I'm sure you must be on some important mission. But I couldn't bear not to see you for a whole century," said Thalassa. Aquan found her friend's chattiness oddly comforting. "What took you so long?"

Before she could respond Thalassa twirled around. "Don't I look fantastic?"

Crushed pink sand rouged her dove gray cheeks and tiny orange sea anemones dotted her flowing turquoise locks. Her curved sea horse tail was scraped to a polished silvery sheen. A necklace of Fijian black coral with matching black coral century bracelets accented her slender neck and wrists.

"No one can compare with you, that's for sure." Raynord laughed and shook his head.

"As usual, no words of encouragement from big brother."

"You are perfection," said Aquan.

"No truer words have ever been spoken." Thalassa's crystal blue eyes sparkled happily as she found all compliments were music to her ears, even solicited ones. "How was your trip?"

"Lots of cool music and other interesting stuff."

"Is that why you nearly missed our Conch's final call?" asked Raynord.

Aquan was taken aback by Raynord's directness. Thalassa quickly squeezed between Aquan and Raynord.

"And maybe none of your business." She hooked her arm around Aquan's and led her a few feet away from Raynord. "Been dying for you to get back. I've, I mean, we've got something for you. You must promise to love it and wear it forever."

Before Aquan could protest her enthusiastic demand, Thalassa presented her with a small item wrapped in a soft jellyfish sack.

"It's from our mother. But I helped pick it out."

Aquan gasped as she found a delicate bracelet of exceptional Hawaiian coral. Its golden hues danced across its rippling textures. A century bracelet remained a traditional gift between mother and daughter at Convocation, but Hawaiian coral revealed a truly distinctive choice.

"Our mothers were like sisters, Aquan. Just like me and you. We wished Evadne was here to celebrate this special time with you." Thalassa gave Aquan a loving embrace, something she had never known from her mother. "Mother wanted to present it to you personally, but got called away to handle some last minute details for Convocation."

"It's stunning," Aquan replied. "Tell Aunt Clarissa I love it. I'll come to thank her in person after tomorrow's hunt."

"I'll let her know," said Raynord. "And we'll be looking forward to your visit." He smiled broadly.

Suddenly Raynord snapped to attention as Pilot Commander Aries approached them.

"At ease, Captain," he said. "This message is for Aquan. I've received emergency orders from our Elder Council for her to report immediately to Quartz Hall."

*****

Aquan wriggled her sleek fishtail and her scales glinted with blue-green and red glimmers from bioluminescent fish and plankton lining a long passageway to Quartz Hall. Glowing blue and jade anemones encircled a final entry tunnel to this great assembly hall. The largest underwater cave in Rapture's End, Quartz Hall was an ideal place for ruling Archigen Elders to meet confidentially, away from other sea creatures and potential Exori attacks. Entering a watery vestibule, she donned an aquamarine squid skin robe to mark her maternal Triton family with a white seaweed sash for her father's Archigen roots. The Lineage Monument marked unions between major Archigen Houses bearing cracks and wear from many millennia of descendants. She placed her hand over a set of chiseled Triton and Archigen coats of arms, a trident and shield, her parents' rare union, to signal her arrival. For a moment, Aquan touched her hip with her hidden tattoo before enormous mother of pearl gates slowly creaked open.

Soft aromas of fragrant sea grasses filled her nostrils as Aquan swam inside the chamber's still waters. Charcoal silhouettes of pointy stalactites hung a hundred feet above her in its rock ceiling. Council members swayed with their fish tails twisted around cooled lava benches decorated with abalone shells and ocean jasper in a columned amphitheater. Some representatives were dressed all in white to mark their pure Archigen lineage while others wore colorful robes and sashes of other major Houses. She noticed several elders of her own House of Triton dressed in aquamarine, including her Aunt Sofronia who drifted forward to greet her.

"Peace to you, daughter of Archigen and Triton." Aunt Sofronia offered Aquan a sprig of sacred red algae. "Hallowed be Eternal Concordia."

"And peace to you, Triton Elder Sofronia." She bowed her head and consumed it. "Hallowed be Eternal Concordia."

As they bowed once more to each other, a gray funnel of steam and silt arose out of a volcanic rock cavity in Quart Hall, briefly obscuring Aquan's view. An ashen eddy touched down next to Aquan. A breathless Mopsus materialized wearing a ruby sash of the House of Tiresias over his white robe. He shook his scaly dark blue body to loosen any sediment from his garments, like a wet dog trying to dry off after a bath. Sofronia scowled at him as Aquan suppressed a giggle. Her good-natured tutor carefully primped his headdress of scarlet sea worms and picked a few strands of seaweed from his long green beard. Mopsus had trained Aquan for decades to do combat as different life forms and to understand complex Archigen lore and alliances inscribed in the Sacred Songs.

"Forgive my interruption and tardy entrance. But it isn't easy to arrive here quickly from our kelp fields. And what is a return home from a surface mission without kelp soup?" He bowed ceremoniously with a wink to Aquan. "Have I missed much?" he asked, hoping to annoy Sofronia for a moment longer.

Mopsus may have enjoyed playing a bumbling fool, but everyone knew he wasn't one. Aquan marveled at his gift of prophecy, his ability to harness biolumens to light Rapture's End and his skill in fashioning magical tools and weapons out of scavenged objects.

"Aquan has just arrived," said Sofronia. "Please be seated for her report."

Mopsus wriggled over to the gallery and squeezed his portly form into a front bench. Sofronia took her place at a moderator's podium in front of the chamber.

Aquan then described her surveillance efforts in Tallinn, her encounter with a Hydromorph and its theft of an obscure amber amulet. When Aquan held it up, she sensed a flash of recognition mixed with apprehension amongst some Elders. She handed the talisman to Sofronia who scrutinized it in her palm. Her aunt wrinkled her brow with concern. Sofronia then handed it to her fellow Elders for their examination.

"The imp spoke of the Vanquishment, liquefying itself rather than face his master's wrath."

Aquan then described her three visions. When she finished, Council members sat in silence.

"Thank you for your report, Aquan," said Sofronia. "We will deliberate about your observations. Unfortunately, you may have to cut Convocation short. Return to your House this evening and await further orders."

"Yes, Elder Sofronia," she said.

As she bowed, Aquan could barely contain her excitement about an important mission, but a chance to avoid Convocation and inevitable family pressures to select a mate only made it sweeter. Aquan quickly exited Quartz Hall, its immense gates slamming shut behind her.

Sofronia sighed and turned to face her fellow Elders. "The final blast of the Conch has barely died out under a full moon and high tide. I didn't think this would start so soon."

"The Margrave knows he only has until the next full moon's rise to complete the Sequencing or else he'll have to wait another century. He's not wasting any time," said Elder Polemus. "I'm sure he's commanded his allies to search for them for hundreds of years. Lying in wait until this moment."

"He's not hiding anymore. We've received word from a Timarch outpost that two dozen Hydromorph spies emerged from waters near Tasmania," said Commander Aries.

Whistles and grunts erupted among council members. Sofronia banged a purple coral gavel against her podium calling for silence. She nodded to Camulus, chief security advisor, from the Houses of Hadros and Archigen.

"One Hydromorph in Tallinn may be a warning, two dozen Hydromorphs is a provocation we cannot ignore," said Camulus. He shook his webbed fist. "The Margrave cannot be permitted to challenge his exile or those of his Exori rebels so boldly. This is a call to war!" His brown freckled horn jutting out of his forehead turned a bright yellow in anger.

Several Council members slapped their fishtails or clapped their flippers in approval.

Elder Eirene rose from her bench. "No Exori rebels have breached Obzula Ridge since their deportation. Only a few of his harmless drones have broken through to our seas. And Aquan has routinely chased them away in the past. Let us act with prudence and be certain of their intentions before calling for battle."

"Prudence or foolish pacifism? Why not just wait for the Margrave and his rebels to appear on our doorstep before we act?" he replied.

"Perhaps these Hydromorphs are rogues acting on their own without his approval, without his knowledge," added Elder Derseum.

"Hydromorphs don't make plans. Those drones only follow his orders," said Elder Polemus. He twitched his seal-like snout and whiskers. "I agree with Camulus. We should strike early and forcefully against them. We need to root out any remaining Exoris and their allies."

"And lose precious Archigen lives because of a handful of strays?" replied Derseum. "Without clearly knowing their motives?"

"He can only project his power through his drones for a day or so before they die on land. Martyrs to his foolish cause. We should not act in haste," said Mopsus.

"Aries warned us of his growing provocations throughout this past lunar phase. Next thing we know there will be Exori rebels massing on our borders," said Polemus. "This offense demands immediate action!"

"Any steps we take may only be defensive," said Eirene. "The Sacred Songs demand it."

"Before we can make any rational decisions, we'll need more information. Aquan will be dispatched to Tasmania with Mopsus's usual tools to conduct surveillance," said Sofronia. "How quickly can this be done, Mopsus?"

"I've already started to assemble a full complement of paralyzing and deadly neurotoxin darts. With tranquilizing ones for any pesky Surface Dwellers. I should be done with my work by morning."

"Good. After our Triton hunt, she will be dispatched to Tasmania in the morning." Sofronia looked out at the assembly. "Fellow Archigens, this period begins a perilous time for all of us."

"We knew this day was coming," said Eirene. "Ever since her birth."

"If you recall, not all of us thought raising her amongst us was the best course of action." Camulus snorted his disdain through his horn.

"It was this Council's decree after much debate and reflection," said Sofronia.

"Ridding ourselves of Evadne's spawn would have avoided this threat. Protected all of our children from possible enslavement or even worse, complete destruction," said Camulus.

Mopsus pounded his fist on his bench and glared at Camulus. "You sicken me with your calls to infanticide, to war."

"Allowing one young Archigen to decide our entire nation's fate is utter madness," said Camulus. "I still think I was right."

"It is far too late to revisit that decision now, Camulus," said Sofronia. "You know well enough that without her presence the Margrave would have attacked decades ago."

"Mopsus, do you have any prophecy for us on this matter?" asked Eirene.

He placed his fingertips on his dark blue forehead and closed his eyes for a moment, then slowly reopened them.

"Not anything specific right now," Mopsus said. He looked squarely at Camulus. "But nothing pointing towards global cataclysm or national downfall. I counsel patience. Only time will tell us more."

"A commodity we have little of," responded Polemus.

"I'm confident that Mopsus has trained Aquan well. As the Sequencing begins, we must initiate steps to defend ourselves, if necessary. My fellow Archigens, we must be vigilant, yet united and confident of our final victory."

"Let's hope you're right about how it will all end, Sofronia," said Camulus.

Camulus marched out of Quartz Hall followed by Polemus and other disgruntled Elders. The sweet scent of sea grasses now gave way to the rank odor of fear and dissent.

*****

That evening, the House of Triton welcomed Aquan and her first season cohort with a celebratory nocturnal hunt in Bliss Valley. Nearly four hundred members of her House flooded their ancestral valley swishing their strong glistening tails, their shrill hums and whistles swallowing up its stillness. After about twenty minutes, Aquan found herself quickly exhausted to her core and unable to concentrate on hunting. She wondered if her extended transformations and lengthy journey were to blame for her sudden fatigue. Shimmying beneath a deep, rocky shelf, Aquan gazed at her golden coral bracelet and slipped into a meditative trance to recharge her energies. In her daydreaming state, she envisioned flashes of *Calusa* again. Under a full moon's bright light, a catamaran drifted aimlessly over a series of deep swells, its mascot barking and jumping on its upper deck. She clearly smelled gasoline and heard thunderous explosions. Once more, Aquan drank in her own tears as roaring flames swallowed up this ship. Suddenly, she heard her mother's voice cry out in anguish, jolting Aquan awake. Her head accidentally knocked into a ledge above her. Thinking she had fallen into her dreams for only a few minutes, it must have been much longer. Stillness engulfed Bliss Valley, her House's ceremonial hunt seemingly over.

She looked around her resting place and noticed a peculiar dark mist encircling her. It rushed in and out with each ocean swell. Aquan squirmed out of her resting place and into the open vale. Rubbing her sleepy eyes, she spied what appeared to be large clumps of seaweed or squid drifting in the sea. Drawing closer, thick clouds of black blood drifted in swirling currents. Her agonizing wail shook every reef and ridge of Bliss Valley. Hundreds of butchered Tritons floated dead in their ancestral waters.

Chapter 3

The Council decreed three days of mourning and postponed Convocation until a final Triton burial procession to their Memorial Grotto. As tradition required, mystics of the House of Ambrose with their soft tentacles tenderly wrapped slaughtered Tritons in pressed sheets of green sea lettuce. Elders of each House witnessed this Solemn Enfoldment. Aside from Aquan, only Sofronia and two other Triton Elders, who hadn't participated in last night's hunt, remained alive. Although she heard a Black Conch's somber bellow, Aquan didn't attend this ritual. She couldn't bear to further witness the virtual extinction of her maternal House.

In solitude, Aquan wandered swaying fronds in a dense sea kelp forest, even ignoring Thalassa's whistles and squeaks. She found solace in revisiting the same refuge where her mother mourned Aquan's father's untimely death. From Aquan's earliest childhood memories, Evadne placed a necklace of saltwater flowers at their Ancestral Caves every month to honor her mate, Phorcys, but she seldom spoke about a father Aquan never knew. As she watched sea calves grazing on fluttering fauna in ocean meadows, Aquan felt agonizing waves of grief roll in with each passing swell. Remembering that Hydromorph's curse, she trembled with grief and guilt thinking her actions caused or contributed to this massacre. Vivid flashes of Triton carnage and fierce flames of revenge ripped through her thoughts. She tried, but couldn't sleep.

Rhythmic thwacks of a cutting tool against a kelp trunk echoed in the forest. Aquan glimpsed Mopsus pruning his beloved stalks with a shark tooth blade. He called out to her without turning away from his labors.

"Aquan, there's no need to hide your sorrows from me. It looms over our sea forests and meadows like a heavy fog."

Grabbing hold of a stalk, she steadied herself but didn't respond.

"I'm so sorry, dear Aquan, for your losses, your pain." Mopsus continued to whack several coarse stalks. "Tomorrow is our burial procession to your House's Memorial Grotto."

"I know," she replied.

"Sofronia needs you by her side."

"I'll be there."

"Elder Council has replaced Aries with Raynord as Pilot Commander. He wants a Timarch platoon to escort you and any Triton Elders to and from our Ancestral Caves."

"What good is security now?"

"You know Raynord would summon all forces of sea and sky to protect you."

Aquan shook her head and began to swim away.

"I've been thinking about your talisman," Mopsus said.

"It's not mine."

"Well it's meant for you."

Aquan stopped and turned. "How can you be sure, Mopsus?"

"Because only your visions appear in each stone, no matter who looks into them. Ask your aunt or any Elder Council member. They've all examined it."

"Who cares about visions?" Aquan said. "I only want to know who murdered my House and why." Her icy blue skin turned scarlet with rage. "Right before I tear them to pieces."

"Vengeance won't bring them back to life or bring their killers to justice."

"Justice? Those Exori assassins are long gone. Back to their underworld."

Mopsus fell silent and put down his blade.

"I'd hunt them down myself if the Elders would let me breach Obzula Ridge."

"Too dangerous, Aquan. No place for you or any Archigen."

"How do you know? Have you ever been there?"

"Once. Long ago to drive him and his conspirators into banishment, into an eternal midnight near scalding vents at our Earth's crust."

Mopsus shivered visibly at his memory of that remote region.

"Then you know how to get there. Show me, Mopsus."

"Don't be too anxious to meet the Margrave. He's

incredibly powerful within his domain. We do all we can to keep him in exile."

"So what about that talisman? Can you explain my visions?"

"I have my theories, but we should discuss them privately." Mopsus nodded at a school of barracudas darting around forest stalks. "Over a pot of boiled kelp soup."

*****

Mopsus placed a tangled kelp bundle into a net basket and pressed it into a hot gas vent bubbling in the center of his cave. He brushed aside several crabs from his worktable as Aquan wrapped her tail around a heavy volcanic rock bench. Mopsus poked at his basket and a salty scent of stewing kelp filled his chamber. Aquan noticed a beat up diver's watch, a small carved mirror peeking out of a velvety pouch and four corked vials of green granules on his workshop table.

"Are these for me?"

"Yes, special tools and some further instructions for your high priority mission."

The thought of doing something, anything, to escape the dark pall that hung over Rapture's End momentarily lifted Aquan's spirits. Staring into his cave's boiling vent, Mopsus raised his scaly blue left hand signaling a call for silence. Aquan knew not to speak until his soup was served as Mopsus disliked any interruptions in his personal cooking habits.

"A perfect caramel color," he muttered.

Mopsus pulled out his basket from the roiling vent and arranged steaming clumps of kelp in black limpet shells. He placed them on his worktable along with orange scallop spoons and sat across from Aquan.

"What is so critical about my mission?"

"Taste it first, then we'll discuss it."

Aquan quickly shoveled a spoonful of kelp into her mouth, chewed and gulped it down fast.

"Okay. What are the Elders' orders?"

"Do you like it?"

"It's fine. Now please tell me about my mission."

"What do you like best about it? I added something special

into my usual seasoning."

"Ah, you'll drive me crazy, Mopsus."

"Take another bite. See if you can guess it."

Aquan groaned and dipped her shell spoon into her bowl, scooping up another mouthful. She shrugged her shoulders in surrender.

"I put in a pinch of black sea salt. Makes a big difference." Mopsus smiled with bits of caramel-colored kelp stuck between his front teeth. "A really big difference."

He continued munching on his portion before letting out a loud, satisfied belch. Aquan stared at him, shaking her head in disbelief.

"What?" He methodically scraped every bit of kelp from his bowl.

"You torture me."

"Perhaps I'm trying to teach you some patience. Always in a rush, you young Archigens. Emissary or not, there's more to life than rushing around on missions."

"Mopsus," sighed Aquan.

"Don't be annoyed." He loudly slurped up some of his kelp broth. "I'm getting around to it."

Mopsus rose from his table and pushed aside a set of green seaweed curtains hiding a rear chamber. He pulled out a tiny wooden box. Sliding open its cover, he held up the amber amulet attached to a long silver chain.

"A lovely silver necklace from her majesty's *Sussex*. I found it shipwrecked off Gibraltar."

Mopsus placed this salvaged chain around her neck. The amulet gently clung to her chest like a starfish on a sandy sea floor.

"Your charge from our Elders is to find out why it was stolen. The Margrave must believe it holds some special power or else he wouldn't send any of his spies to fetch it. You must discover its power and see if there are any more of them."

"They could be anywhere. And could mean a million things."

"You have only until next full moon to complete your task."

"A month is not very long. Why so little time?"

"Some Elders are agitating for war. They would only agree to hold off during this lunar cycle. Your determinations may help stop a terrible war. Otherwise, many Archigen lives may be lost."

Aquan instantly thought of Raynord. He had been like an older brother to her and his loss would crush Thalassa and her mother. She couldn't bear any further mourning at Rapture's End.

"That Hydromorph spoke about the Vanquishment. Do the Elders think it has something to do with that Exori myth?"

"Myth? I'm not so sure about that."

"You can't believe any of that, Mopsus," said Aquan. "It violates Eternal Concordia."

"I'm not a true believer. Yet even myths don't survive without some grain of truth. Another Great Flood is always a possibility."

"Just wishful thinking by blood-thirsty fiends. They slaughtered my House without an ounce of remorse. Killing billions of humans would be easy for them. Except how would they do it?"

Mopsus frowned and moved uneasily on his bench.

"Remember, you stand between the Exoris and war-mongers on our Council."

She wrinkled her ice blue nose and peered into the gemstone, glimpsing her same visions.

"Do you understand what these visions mean, Mopsus?"

"Not for sure. But I think each seems to point to a distinct period of time. Murkiness enveloping your mother's image suggests a shroud of past memories. A wavering image of an angry surf suggests an uncertain future. Your vision of *Calusa* appears quite sharp. Our present is often our clearest path."

"But the roaring sea feels so real, like it's happening now. There have been lots of earthquakes and tsunamis recently. Maybe it's warning us about another pending disaster, Mopsus."

"It's possible. But Timarch scouts signaled that *Calusa* is cruising the Tasman Sea, not far from where a dozen Hydromorphs breached its surface. An unlikely coincidence."

"Are these Surface Dwellers on our side or are they Drowners?"

"We don't know. It's a research vessel from Key West, Florida. You'll need to engage them to find out."

"How will I get aboard their ship?"

"You're a clever girl. I'm sure you'll think of something."

Aquan didn't enjoy lying, but it came with the territory of being a shape-shifting Emissary.

"Are those for me?"

She pointed to several assembled items.

"Yes, I've tweaked these lost items with this mission in mind." Mopsus held up a battered diver's watch. "I found this one off the coast of South Africa. Wonderful diving if you don't mind Great Whites occasionally chomping your toes."

"How does it work?"

"Click on this red button and it will stop time. You can move about during these frozen periods, while others around you can't. Push on this green one and time will resume. You can also set it for a specific time period."

Aquan picked it up and strapped it on her wrist. "I'm guessing there's a catch."

"Yes, the Time Merchants are a stingy bunch. They gave us only twenty-minutes of suspended time, not a second more. You can use it more than once, but once twenty minutes are exhausted this watch will be good only for telling time, not stopping it."

She reached for his ornate mirror and Mopsus gave a playful slap to her hand.

"Careful. This one requires special handling. A fragile memento of *Santa Maria*. Columbus never really liked her. She ran aground near Haiti. I found this lovely pocket mirror in its wreck."

Mopsus slipped it out of its embroidered bag and turned it over. He read its inscription. "*Amor vincit omnia.*"

"What does it mean, Mopsus?"

"Love conquers all."

Mopsus looked momentarily lost, perhaps recalling a mate from an earlier season. Aquan rolled her eyes.

"Sounds corny."

"Don't be so dismissive of a great, fervent love. Someday your heart will burn with an unrelenting passion for another."

"Does it smooch my opponent to death?" Aquan smacked her lips several times.

"No, little upstart. Gaze into it and speak its inscription. You can physically be in two places at the same time. Only your essence holding this mirror can look to see what your twin is doing. Not the other way around."

"Will I be able to transform in both places?"

"Yes, but you cannot shape-shift as often or as long. When you split, you must refresh yourself every high tide, not every other high tide like you do now. You risk your life if you don't refresh in every twelve-hour cycle in both places. It will operate only five times for you. So make them count."

Mopsus gingerly pushed it back into its pouch, cinching its cord.

"Handle it with care. You don't want to get yourself in twice as much trouble."

"And those vials?" Aquan pointed to three small glass tubes on his workbench.

"Ah, yes. Green sand. Very rare. Olivine minerals from basalt lava. Collected these samples in Guam. I've mixed them with some other chemicals. Break each tube and spray it. You can turn anyone into any sea creature you want. Hopefully, something small and harmless. The grains won't work on crustacean shells. They're too hard to penetrate."

"If I do that, how long will their transformation last?"

"Maybe an hour or so, depending on the tides and moon. If it's a high tide and a full moon, they could be stuck in that form for three or four hours."

"Mopsus, you're an amazing genius." She patted his back.

"Of course, I am."

"I've put together your normal pack of paralyzing and deadly darts for Exoris and tranquilizers for Surface Dwellers. I've also created a more compact, collapsible spear gun for your cartridges. Plus my usual healing elixirs and seaweeds. They fit within your pouch or you can use this rugged little backpack on shore, if you like. Found it on a Micronesian reef."

"When do I begin?"

"Tomorrow. After the procession to our Ancestral Caves."

Aquan felt a wave of sadness overwhelm her once more.

"How will I know when my mission is over?" she asked.

"When you think you're done."

She sighed. "Do you always have to speak in riddles, Mopsus?"

"Only when I have no answers."

*****

At dawn, a Black Conch's morose tones echoed in Rapture's End. With Aquan by her side, Sofronia and two remaining Triton elders led a funeral procession from Bliss Valley to a cluster of dark volcanic rocks at the Ancestral Caves. The Elder Council selected thirty members from each major Archigen House to escort enfolded Triton bodies to their crypts. A teary-eyed Thalassa headed up a group of young mourners representing each first season cohort. Thousands of Archigens lined a route through Rapture's End in silence, releasing hundreds of garlands of white and pink sea flowers. A wreath for each murdered Triton now making a transcendent journey to Musterion, to a new afterlife with the Infinite Dreamer. Aquan looked up as floral chains filled the sea above the solemn procession. A battalion of Timarchs kept watch while forces were doubled at every border of Rapture's End in case Exoris tried to capitalize on this solemn moment.

Raynord stood guard at the Ancestral Caves' entry and bowed his head as Sofronia and Aquan entered a web of catacombs encasing Archigen remains for millions of years. Scents of sacred red algae filled their gills as they paused at Aquan's parents' burial chambers.

"Dear sister," Sofronia said.

Aquan attached a flower garland to a memorial stake at each of their tombs and ran her fingers over carvings adorning her parents' burial chambers. She reflexively touched her right hip bearing this same outline. As they entered a separate burial chamber, Sofronia gasped and squeezed Aquan's hand at the sight of 379 new tombs carved into the Tritons' Memorial

Grotto. Sofronia cried as Aquan put her arm over her aunt's quaking shoulders to console her. Aquan couldn't cry for cold barricades of anger and vengeance now firmly guarded her grieving heart.

"You're all that's left of our future," whispered Sofronia.

Aquan watched in silence as Elder Ambrosians solemnly placed each swathed Triton into their craggy burial vaults for the next three hours. She couldn't mourn them now. Her mind blazed only with thoughts of how to exact her pained revenge on the Margrave.

Chapter 4

It was 4:00 a.m. and Dr. Jennifer Ortiz remained wide awake. Her body clock was struggling to acclimate to Tasmania from her Florida time, not to mention booms of thunder and angry waves tossing *Calusa* that night. In the catamaran's center main deck, she frowned thumbing through several pages of data her new research assistant, Rick Emerson, generated a week after a ferocious tsunami. She wondered if they needed to take more water samples from different depths to explain this recent beaching. It was rare to find one giant squid, but when two colossal ones washed ashore still entangled in each other's nearly hundred-foot long tentacles, it provided a rare opportunity to prove her theories correct. These passionate lovers were covered in sucker marks, with an amorous male biting a female's crown with his beak. Tassie newspapers dubbed them "Romeo and Juliet" and every Hobart restaurant and fish market proclaimed southern calamari as an ultimate aphrodisiac.

Looking through a digital microscope, she squinted at water sample slides and twirled her auburn ponytail. Fidgeting with her computer monitor, she adjusted its image resolution to display textured and 3-D versions of her specimens.

"Finding any for mutating microbes?" asked Cutter. He yawned and scratched his thick sun-bleached hair making his way along his boat's center well.

"None of this makes much sense. Rick didn't find any elevated toxins so it's gotta be some new microbe that caused this stranding. Or maybe we need more varied depths for our samples."

"Or Jenn, maybe sea quakes are causing it like Stevenson always claimed?"

"Thanks for ruining my night." Jenn put the slide back into its case.

Cutter laughed. "I'm just yanking your chain. In my completely biased opinion, Stephenson is a total asshole."

"Yes, but an asshole who's being nicely bank-rolled by a

reclusive zillionaire. Let's hope his science stinks as much as his personality. Wanna take a look?"

"Not me. I'm out of that damn business. Besides you don't want to taint your findings with my crazy ideas."

"You know I still value your opinion."

"I doubt any Institute rep would be happy to hear that. And you can't afford to lose your grant money. Besides I need that cash to keep my baby afloat." Cutter patted one of his ship's walls. "Salvaging wrecks and leading dive trips alone ain't gonna do it."

She sighed knowing Cutter remained a gifted marine biologist, despite his feuds with the scientific community and his father, the Director of Key West Oceanic Institute. Jenn thought if Cutter could only have given up those foolish aquatelligence ideas, he would have been a superstar researcher.

As his ship rocked, Cutter teetered over to a head and slammed its door shut. Jenn often wondered how he managed to keep his ship running with up-to-date gear. He must have some generous patron. Ugly local gossip whispered speculations about shady Caribbean drug runs or illegal treasure-hunting. But Jenn refused to believe any of it, her scientific objectivity no match for her unspoken desires for his company. She wasn't ready to throw in the towel yet on Cutter, despite her mom's nagging to settle down with a nice Cuban boy back home in Miami.

Gypsy's sudden howling interrupted rhythmic smacks of waves against *Calusa*'s hull. Jenn popped her head out its main bulkhead sliding door. A waning full moon bathed *Calusa*'s swaying top deck in a bluish glow. Cutter's Portuguese Water Dog raced back and forth on the ship's starboard side.

"Shhh. Quiet girl, quiet," she said.

But Gypsy continued to yap, jumping up and down on her webbed paws. Jenn knew Gypsy didn't normally get agitated without a good reason. A patch of dark clouds slid across the moon, swallowing up *Calusa*'s deck in darkness. Jenn tore off her latex gloves, grabbed a flashlight and then pulled herself up the cabin steps topside.

"What's wrong, girl?"

She tottered across its deck as Cutter's vessel heaved up and down. Occasional flashes of distant lightning illuminated a roiling sea. As she reached out to pat Gypsy's wooly chocolate brown coat, Cutter's dog scrambled on to a rear diving platform and splashed into the water.

"Gypsy! Gypsy come back here."

Jenn wasn't afraid she'd sink as Gypsy's breed served as net retrievers and trusted companions to fishermen for centuries. But she worried that the dog's curiosity might lead to a lethal meeting with a jellyfish or a sea wasp. Following Gypsy with her flashlight, she was relieved when she dog simply used her nose to nudge a large piece of bark toward *Calusa*. Jenn ran her light across a length of driftwood covered with clumps of seaweed. She thought she spied something ensnared in this flotsam, perhaps a leatherback sea turtle or a barramundi.

Taking hold of a boat hook, she twisted its middle channel and stretched it to its maximum length, poking at seaweed clusters in hopes of freeing a trapped animal. Missing twice, her third try latched on to a corner of twisted wood and seaweed. Jenn screamed when she uncovered an unconscious young woman ensnared in its debris. Standing on *Calusa*'s dive platform, she tried to pull the woman closer with the hook. A rogue wave slapped the boat hard and flipped Jenn into a cold ocean.

Icy shivers raced along her backbone as salty water raked across her throat. Jenn became disoriented underwater, unable to distinguish inky sea from dark sky. Pushing out sea water through her nostrils, she squeezed her eyes shut and then opened them as brine stabbed her eyeballs. Glimpsing misty streaks of moonbeams above, she stroked and kicked hard to reach the surface. Her head popped above water and she coughed several times, spitting out bursts of sea water. Jenn's hands trembled with adrenaline as she grabbed hold of a piece of bark. Feverishly, she fought to untangle the woman as ocean currents pulled at them.

"Gypsy, Gypsy!"

Cutter's dog swam to Jenn and she seized her collar still clinging to the castaway. Gypsy barked as they battled against sea swells toward *Calusa*. She called for help hoping Cutter or Rick might hear her cries over roaring waves and thunder claps. With each of Jenn's frog kicks, ocean currents continued to drag them farther away from the catamaran. Saltwater stung her eyes and blurred her vision.

She motioned for Gypsy to go back on her own. "Go Gypsy. Get Cutter!"

Gypsy swam back to *Calusa*, her yelps filling the air as she tread water off its stern. Rough waves pushed more brackish water down Jenn's throat and she began to gag, but wouldn't let go of the woman. As several clouds parted, she made out dorsal fins of two bull sharks gliding through glimmering moonlit waves. She kicked harder and stroked with all of her might toward Cutter's boat, but made little headway. Her futile efforts quickly sapped her strength as currents yanked her away from *Calusa*. Jenn's mind raced with fear, but wouldn't let go of the injured woman.

"Catch it, Jenn!" cried Cutter.

He tossed a life ring on a rope to Jenn. She couldn't reach it, but Gypsy paddled toward it and dragged the preserver to Jenn. While Jenn gripped the woman's shirt, her other arm clutched this sea ring. Cutter and Emerson reeled them back to the boat. Reaching down, Emerson pulled Jenn on to the dive platform. Cutter grabbed his diver's knife and cut the unconscious woman loose from a mass of seaweed and palm tree bark. Hauling her aboard, they noticed a rucksack still strapped to her back. Ready to resuscitate her, they realized she was still breathing normally. Emerson brought up survival blankets while Gypsy shook herself dry, clenching a piece of driftwood in her teeth.

Jenn surprised herself by bursting into tears once she realized that they were both safely on deck. In the past six years, Jenn had never given any sign that she wanted an ounce of assistance from anyone. For once, she let Cutter wrap a survival blanket around her shoulders.

"You okay?" he asked.

"I'm fine. Just thought we were shark bait for a minute there."

Quivering, she smiled through her tears. Clouds rolled in and darkness once more covered Cutter's vessel.

"Let's get below so we can see what we're doing," said Cutter.

Emerson raced for towels as Cutter carried the unconscious woman below deck, placing her on vinyl cushions in a cabin seating area near his ship's galley. The rescued woman appeared to be of Aboriginal heritage with velvety dark brown skin and long curly hair. Athletic and leggy, she wore only a T-shirt with a Sydney 2000 Olympics logo on its pocket and a pair of battered denim shorts.

"She's not cold at all. Should be freezing. Her body temperature seems fine. No signs of hypothermia," said Jenn. "How can that be?"

"What was she doing out there?" Emerson asked.

Gypsy dropped a chunk of driftwood at Cutter's feet.

"Maybe fishing or boating accident," said Cutter. He dabbed her skin with a towel.

"We're nowhere near any islands," said Emerson.

"She could've been on a boat and got knocked overboard. We better check in with AMSA about any missing boats or persons," said Cutter.

Emerson examined a slice of driftwood. "It has got some kind of milky ooze on its sides."

Cutter ran his fingers across its sticky surface. "Feels like breadfruit to me."

Both Jenn and Emerson looked at him skeptically.

"I did a charter for *Expedition* magazine. A photo shoot on outrigger canoes. This milky stuff is probably breadfruit latex. Traditional boat caulking."

"Do you think she really could have tumbled out of an outrigger way out her, Cutter?" Jenn asked.

"Maybe. Or perhaps during the tsunami, she got pulled out to sea, Jenn."

"I guess she could stay alive without food or water for about a week or so," said Jenn. "Drifting out here like a leaf."

"Can't open up her backpack. Its zipper's stuck on soggy canvas," said Emerson.

"Hang it up to dry. We can check it later for any clues about our mystery woman. I'll call it in," said Cutter.

He got up and headed for *Calusa*'s bridge deck. Jenn waved off Emerson so she could remove this young woman's soaked T-shirt and shorts. She saw an ornate tattoo outlined on her right hip, perhaps a tribal marking, Jenn thought. She dried her skin with a towel and placed one of her floral beach wraps around her. Jenn couldn't unfasten a silver chain with amber stones from her neck as its clasp seemed rusted shut. A coral bracelet failed to budge from her wrist, too. Placing a pillow under her curly brown hair, Jenn covered her with a thick lamb's wool blanket. As she walked back to Cutter's bridge deck, Jenn heard him swearing at his radio.

"Damn it, too much interference from this lightning. This mess will have to wait until tomorrow morning," said Cutter.

Over the next half-hour, they commiserated in whispered tones about how this woman ended up in the sea. Pretending to be knocked out, Aquan wondered if they were Drowners, humans lured into Exori alliances with promises of vast stores of gold, gems and other riches from ancient shipwrecks. Blinded by greed, Drowners always ended up fish food, submerged undersea once the Exoris no longer needed them.

Eventually, her new hosts called it a night and drifted off to their cabins to sleep. While they snoozed, Aquan tightened Jenn's wrap around her body and crept up to *Calusa*'s wheelhouse. She looked around its control deck for any clues as to their activities. She pulled out a ship's logbook. In the past year, *Calusa* made numerous runs to Caribbean islands along with two trips to the Galapagos and several excursions to major ports in Central and South America. Its GPS travel history showed no unusual recent trips, mostly short shuttles between Hobart and various open ocean spots in the Tasman Sea. Clicking on their satellite phone, its call log indicated that four of their last five calls were dialed to Key West Oceanic Institute. The fifth telephone number was listed as private. Aquan's radar picked up someone stirring in their sleeping quarters beneath her. She shut off their phone and listened as someone clambered up to topside.

Aquan popped open a control deck hatch and slowly stuck her head out. She clearly made out a Pteron, a saffron-colored sea horse fluttering its hummingbird wings, in the misty darkness. This Exori messenger hovered above *Calusa*'s rear deck. Part of the ship's wheelhouse roof and massive mast hid most of the Surface Dweller from her view. This Pteron stuck its long snout toward an obscured figure to deliver its master's secret instructions. Aquan peered into the darkness trying to identify which human listened to its message. After a few seconds, the Pteron flew off and then dive-bombed into a wave. She heard footsteps padding across the upper deck heading for a center bulkhead, leading below deck. Aquan scurried across Calusa's main deck and quickly laid back down on its cabin cushions.

Moments later, she sensed a Surface Dweller leaning over her while she pretended to sleep. Rough hands touched her amulet against her skin for a moment. As a Surface Dweller moved away and headed to a lower deck, Aquan blinked open her eyes. She couldn't see which one of them crept in these shadows.

Chapter 5

As streams of hazy sun filtered through main cabin windows and open hatches, Aquan heard two Surface Dwellers murmuring as they stood over her. She abruptly pretended to gasp for air and flail her arms as if struck by a seizure. These two humans tried to hold her down and calm her as she screamed for help.

"It's okay. We don't want to hurt you," said the man. With ruddy cheeks and a dark beard, Aquan knocked his tortoise rim glasses off the bridge of his nose.

"Where am I?" she cried.

"It's alright. You're on a research vessel from Key West Oceanic Institute. We only want to help you," said a female Surface Dweller. Her anxious dark brown eyes were shaped like almonds. "I'm Jenn Ortiz and this is Rick Emerson. You're on a catamaran, *Calusa*. We found you floating in the sea last night."

"What's your name?" asked Emerson.

Continuing her ruse, she took a long, thoughtful pause and stammered, "Kirra, I think."

"Do you know your surname, your family name?" asked Jenn.

Aquan pretended to scan her thoughts for an answer, but delivered none.

"I don't know."

"Are you feeling alright?" asked a third Surface Dweller.

He slid down stair railings leading from his control deck. He wore a surfing T-shirt, long khaki board shorts and tan deck shoes. His steel blue eyes peeked out from ruddy, sun-tanned skin under a Fighting Conchs baseball cap. Surprisingly, Aquan found his physical appearance somewhat appealing.

"This is Dave Cutter, ship's captain," said Jenn.

"I—I feel okay," Aquan said. She tugged at her beach wrap. "Thank you so much for saving my life."

"I called it in and AMSA has no information about any missing people or overdue ships," said Cutter.

"Do you know how you ended up in the ocean, Kirra?" asked Jenn.

"I don't know. I can't remember."

"Interesting necklace you got here," Cutter said. He pointed at her talisman. "Got any engraving on it that might help jog your memory?"

Although she knew there was none, she turned it over to confirm it for him. These Surface Dwellers continued to pepper her with questions for another ten minutes, but she feigned ignorance on her family ties, personal history or professional life. Although Aquan could intuit the motives and actions of simple sea creatures, like Hydromorphs, she found human feelings and behavior often challenging to decipher. They tended to display uncertainties and inconsistencies, their emotions often at odds with their conduct. She sensed a mix of concern and distrust amongst them. Cutter's voice became increasingly irritated with her weak responses. Finally, he walked over, took her backpack off a wall hook and handed it to her.

"You had this with you. Maybe you'll find some answers inside."

Aquan took hold of her pack and slowly unzipped it. She didn't want to share all of its contents with them. Staring inside, she pulled out a thin red wallet she found on a sandbar last year. Aquan opened it up.

"A few Aussie dollars, but nothing more," she replied.

"You might want to dump your whole bag out and maybe we can piece things together for you," said Cutter in a no-nonsense tone. He folded his arms firmly over his broad chest waiting for her to comply.

Aquan froze for a moment. She thought about Mopsus's dive watch and other supplies inside, but hoped she might stall them without wasting any of his precious tools. Cracks of gunshots pierced the silence.

"What the hell?" said Cutter.

Gypsy began to dart around and bark while Cutter yanked up a cabin seat cushion and pulled out a lock box. He threw it open and grabbed a handgun and three clips, tossing a second gun to Emerson. He bobbled Cutter's spare gun in his hands.

"What do I do with this thing?" Emerson asked.

"Look menacing," said Cutter.

Jenn grabbed Cutter's gun from Emerson and told him to radio AMSA.

"Be ready to start those engines," Cutter added. "Gypsy, stay."

He scooted his dog under a galley table before heading topside. Jenn trailed Cutter toward the rear upper deck stairs. Aquan threw on her T-shirt and shorts and then opened her backpack clapping on her diver's watch. Pulling out sections of her spear gun, she quickly assembled her weapon. While Emerson nervously radioed for help, Aquan shimmied out a pilothouse hatch and climbed out on to the forward deck. She leaned low and tight against *Calusa*'s wheelhouse windows. Cutter peered out a main bulkhead door and spied a small speed boat with five armed men headed for their vessel. The men wore bandannas tied over their nose and mouth and dark sunglasses to mask their identities.

"Indonesian pirates," he said to Jenn. "What are they doing this far south?"

"Surrender ship and maybe you live," yelled a pirate over a dented bullhorn.

"Yeah, long enough to collect a ransom for our corpses," Cutter said, under his breath.

"You got five seconds. Or you dead, Cubano," he said.

"Cubano?" whispered Cutter as he crouched next to Jenn.

"It can't be me," Jenn replied. "Not exactly my kind of crowd."

He shrugged. "We can't let them board. When they try to tie up, we'll blast them. Otherwise, we're dead meat."

The pirate's captain started a lethal countdown over his bullhorn. Before he reached three, his speed boat sidled up to Cutter's vessel. One pirate fired a few warning shots from a pistol as two others grabbed hold of the starboard railing and began tying up to *Calusa*. Cutter rolled out on to the aft deck and fired at them, wounding one pirate who fell back into their speed boat. A second one, wearing a blue bandanna, returned fire as Cutter tumbled behind a metal deck box. Jenn fired two shots in the second assailant's direction. He ducked down into their speed boat, holstered his pistol and then yanked on an AK-47 slung over his shoulder. Pulling it into position, he let loose a spray of gunfire.

A third pirate jumped aboard and crawled along *Calusa's* deck railing, heading for its flybridge roof to shoot down at Cutter and Jenn. Aquan aimed her spear gun and shot directly into that pirate's shoulder, spinning him around. Her spear point's paralyzing toxin took immediate effect, his rifle now discharging wildly as he tumbled into the ocean. Their captain fired in Aquan's direction and she ducked behind the wheelhouse. She winced as his shots shattered two wheelhouse windows spraying glass pebbles over Emerson trying to fire up *Calusa's* engines. He screamed and clambered for cover under a chart table. Aquan saw two remaining crew members clamber on to the aft deck with AK-47s. These pirates whooped in unison as they started to spray Cutter's deck box and Jenn's hiding place behind a main cabin bulkhead. Aquan knew that their pistols were no match for these pirates' firepower. She couldn't let them be killed, especially since she hadn't learned their role in her mission yet.

Reluctantly, she pressed her watch's red button and all went still, except for waves smashing against both boats. She ran over to each of pirate and grabbed their AK-47s, popping out their clips and discharging any remaining bullets. Aquan tore extra clips out of their shirt and pants pockets, dumped their ammunition into the ocean and returned their guns to these immobilized pirates. She checked out Cutter to make sure he was uninjured. Diving into the water, she plucked out an unconscious pirate and put him on their speed boat's bow. She emptied their remaining weapons and collected clips from this wounded pirate and his captain tossing them into the sea and placing their empty weapons back into their hands. Wrenching a boat key out of its ignition, she threw it into the water, too. For a moment, she glimpsed a print out with a photo of *Calusa* and its registration numbers along with a fuzzy picture of Cutter, taped to their speed boat's dashboard. Aquan grabbed this print out and stuffed it in her back pocket. Before charging back to her original position, she untied and shoved the speed boat away from *Calusa*. She hit her watch's green button, allowing time to resume after two minutes and twenty-one seconds had expired.

Two pirates continued their yelling, but were shocked into silence when their weapons no longer fired. They hit the deck and reached for their extra clips, but found none. Their captain tried to fire at Aquan, but his gun clicked empty. He ran and tore a weapon from the wounded pirate's fingers and tried to fire it, but still no luck. As their captain barked orders, the baffled pirates started to edge back on to their boat. Two of them jumped from *Calusa* on to their ship. Aquan smirked as she saw another pirate rush to their ship's helm, frantically searching for its ignition key. She heard the captain swearing in Indonesian as their speed boat floated away. One final pirate dove into the water and began swimming frantically toward his gang's drifting craft. Cutter slowly got up from behind his bullet-riddled deck box and scratched his head as he watched them gliding away from his boat.

"What happened?" said Jenn.

She stepped from behind the center bulkhead door.

"Be damned if I know," said Cutter. "One minute they're blasting us, the next they're bolting outta here."

"Looks like they ran out of ammo," said Aquan.

She stood on the flybridge roof, resting her spear gun on her hip.

"Pretty handy with that, Kirra No-Name," said Cutter.

"Thanks," Aquan said. "Who knows, maybe those same pirates attacked my boat? I guess I'm lucky to be alive, too."

"Maybe," said Cutter, sizing up Kirra. "Maybe not. Either way we're heading back to Hobart now."

He ducked below into the main cabin out of Aquan's view and human earshot.

"Good shooting," said Jenn to Aquan.

"Thanks. Glad I could return the favor this morning," Aquan said.

Jenn followed Cutter below deck.

"That story doesn't wash. Who's floating around with a collapsible spear gun?" whispered Cutter turning to Jenn. "Bet she set us up. Faked that rescue. A nice diversion while her pals paid us a friendly visit."

"She didn't have to help us, Cutter. But she did."

"Yeah or double-crossing them by settling some old scores. Either way, don't take your eyes off her. She might slit our throats if we turn our back on her. When we get back to shore, she's off this ship and somebody else's problem."

Chapter 6

Calusa cruised past a cluster of convict-made sandstone and stucco buildings. A small crowd had already gathered at Sullivan Cove's docks. Word traveled fast about a research vessel plucking a mysterious indigenous woman out of the sea and fending off an Indonesian pirate attack. Local Tassie TV stations and several newspaper reporters were almost giddy about their good fortune, another great story just as public interest was waning over those giant squid beachings. A police sergeant, three constables and two marine safety officers stood on a marina ramp while an ambulance and two police cars were parked on an adjacent service road.

"Looks like we've got quite a welcoming committee," said Cutter.

"Do you think they'll impound your ship?" asked Jenn.

"A castaway, pirates and bullet holes adds up to a maritime investigation," said Cutter. "Let's hope all this attention gets my boat fixed cheap."

"And fast. I hate to think how much this delay is going to cost us in research time and grant money," said Jenn.

"We can always take our water samples to Tassie University's labs if we can't do testing on *Calusa*," said Emerson. "Maybe stay in their dorms and hang out with cute coeds."

"Yeah, Emerson," Cutter said. "You can amaze them with stories of your heroics this afternoon,"

He guided his catamaran into an end slip. Marina staff rushed over to help tie *Calusa* down to dock cleats.

"Any familiar faces, Kirra?" asked Jenn.

She shook her head no, cinching her backpack strap tighter over her right shoulder. As they disembarked, a police sergeant met them in the middles of a gangway under a gush of camera flashes and TV lights.

"I'm Sergeant Skabo, Hobart Police. We're glad you made it back to port safely. Good on ya for saving a young woman and fighting off those pirates, captain," he said, clipping off each word ending with his sharp Tassie accent. He heartily shook Cutter's hand. "If you please, we'll be taking you three to our local station so you can give the grim and gory to us. Maritime safety has got to impound your vessel until a preliminary investigation is complete."

"How long?" asked Cutter.

"We'll work as fast as we can, mate," said Skabo. "Our paramedics will take your young castaway to Royal Hobart Hospital for a check-up. We'll get her statement later with assistance from an Aboriginal culture liaison officer. No worries then, alright?" he said, as if any of them had any choice in this matter.

"What about my dog?"

"You can take her with you, Captain."

Several constables held back a growing crowd trying to snap a photo or catch a glimpse of an indigenous storm survivor and any telltale signs of a pirate gun battle. Reporters yelled out questions in vain hopes of getting a first meaty quote. Aquan smelled the rank odor of two Hydromorphs. She scanned this pack of onlookers for hints of their camouflage. Before she could speak any parting words to *Calusa*'s crew, two paramedics led Aquan into an ambulance and slammed shut its heavy doors. The ambulance hit its siren and pulled out of the marina as she watched police officers escort Cutter, Dr. Ortiz and Emerson into a waiting police car.

Aquan frustrated local doctors by refusing to let them examine her, even when a cultural liaison tried to intervene. She might look like a human, but her internal biological structure would make medical history, and three big stories might be too much for Tasmania's local media. A constable stationed outside her examination room wouldn't allow her to be discharged until one of Sergeant Skabo's officers took her statement. Ten hours later, she was released from Hobart's hospital around 8:00 p.m., but warned not to leave Tasmania until both police and maritime investigations were finished. The liaison officer gave her two vouchers, one for food at Salamanca Place and another for three nights at Darby's Youth Hostel. With her photo splashed all over Aussie papers and TV broadcasts, local officials assumed her family or friends would step forward soon to claim her.

Aquan walked back to Sullivan's Cove and found *Calusa* awash in halogen lights as maritime safety officers scoured every inch of her deck for clues about the attackers. Aquan headed to Salamanca Place hoping to find a sushi place, but all its shops were closed. Once more she sensed a Hydromorph, and ducked into an alley. She peered around an archway and caught a glimpse of sandstone block moving ever so slightly. Aquan stepped out with a dart poised between her fingertips. The Hydromorph realized she spotted it and ran, flashing its camouflage from sandstone block to pink stucco, and then back to sandstone block again. Seeing two drunks stumbling toward her, Aquan stopped her pursuit. No need to get any Surface Dwellers entangled in this situation. Besides, a second Hydromorph might be waiting to ambush her. Time to change her appearance to confuse them.

It had been nearly twenty-two hours since her last dip in sea water so she decided to refresh her transformative powers before making a switch. At a remote end of a deserted pier, Aquan looked around and then dove into Sullivan's Cove. She reverted back to her Triton form as saltwater rushed through her gills. Swimming in the harbor, she observed a school of spotted handfish strolling with their leggy fins on its sandy bottom. Their scurrying steps would warn her of any potential dangers. She decided to rest until dawn with clicking chants of distant bottlenose dolphins lulling her into a dream state of sleep.

*****

As morning sun glinted off the bay, Aquan emerged as a red-headed Bridget O'Neill, a freckle-faced marine biology student from Boston, bumming around Australia for a year. With students on semester break, Tasmania University's marine biology department was happy to pay a small stipend plus a dorm stay for a graduate student willing to work in its modern labs, especially one with an encyclopedic knowledge of Tassie aquaculture. For the next several days as Bridget, Aquan regularly observed and interacted with Jenn and Emerson at their temporary lab and visitors' dormitory. She admired their long hours put into rigorously testing water samples from stranded squids and evaluating microbes in hopes of finding lethal toxins or infectious bacteria.

In light of her visions, Aquan frequented the marina to gauge progress on *Calusa* repairs and maritime investigations. She wondered when she might make a connection between this ship and her mission. Following its captain seemed to make the most sense for now.

Cutter spent his days supervising mechanical work and arguing with marine inspectors and insurance adjusters about damage payments. At night, he mostly hung around Hobart's casino and local pubs until very late. As Hobart's newest maritime hero, Cutter never seemed to lack for company or a cocktail on someone else's tab. Aquan found Cutter easy to track since Gypsy often stood guard outside his usual watering holes. While Gypsy chomped on dog food or slurped water out of a plastic bowl, Cutter sloshed down beers, played pool or plunked on booze-soaked piano keys. Once Cutter turned in, Aquan snuck around spray-painting moustaches and beards on wooden mermaid statues and maidenheads at local taverns before slipping into an early morning sea to revitalize herself.

While tracking him, she realized someone else was observing Cutter, too. A chubby black man with a large belly hanging over his belt and a battered fedora hat, seemed to be following Cutter at a safe distance. He diligently clicked photos and punched information into a smart phone. Two nights ago, she saw Cutter duck behind a dumpster and wait for this man to walk past his hiding place before heading off in another direction.

This evening at closing time, Cutter left *The Drunken Skipper* alone for a change. He staggered down several marina docks with Gypsy by his side. As he turned a corner, Aquan sensed two Hydromorphs not far behind him. She kept her distance to avoid tipping them off, but Gypsy barked and growled as the dog sniffed their presence.

"Quiet, girl, quiet," said Cutter.

He pat Gypsy's side and stumbled along a tangle of narrow

lanes away from Sullivan's Cove and past Battery Point to the outskirts of town. He turned down a dark passageway toward flickering neon lights for Darby's shabby youth hostel. A handwritten sign in an office window read "Backpackers Welcome. No Sleeping Bags Inside." with a red slash through a poorly-drawn picture of a bed bug. Cutter banged its front door and a sleepy attendant appeared in its entryway.

"God, not you again. She ain't here," he said, yawning.

"Youuuu sure, pal." Cutter slurred his words.

"Never checked in, mate."

"You better not be lying." Cutter grabbed hold of the attendant's shirt collar.

"You're drunk, mate. Frog and toad." He shook himself free. "Hit the road."

The owner slammed his door shut in Cutter's face. He pounded on the hostel door several more times.

"Kirra, Kirra!!" yelled Cutter. He kicked it and then tumbled on to the cobblestone street. "Kirra."

Gypsy licked his face and barked in these creatures' direction. In the evening still, Aquan heard tinkling of discarded glass vials and then saw empty saltwater tubes rolling toward an alley gutter.

"I'm right here, Cutter," said one Hydromorph.

One imp had transformed into a copy of Kirra. He propped himself up on his elbows and rubbed his eyes.

"Kirra?" Cutter asked. "Are you one of them?"

That imp deliberately transformed into a walrus, then a sea dragon, a starfish, and back again to Kirra.

"Yes, I'm one of them."

A second Hydromorph assumed Jenn's appearance. "You were right, Cutter. Sorry I ever doubted you or your theories."

"We have lots of work to do. Let's go back to *Calusa*," said the Kirra Hydromorph.

These two shape-shifters helped to lift Cutter to his feet.

"You're beautiful," said Cutter. He stared at a Kirra look-alike and stroked her soft curls. He reached out for her talisman. "I've seen this before, you know."

Aquan observed these creatures dragging Cutter away

from *Calusa* with Gypsy trailing behind them. She then spied that pudgy black man striding towards Darby's, luckily having missed any displays of shape-shifting. As he scurried past her, Aquan flung a paralyzing dart at this nosey Surface Dweller, striking his left calf. He moaned and then crumpled on a stone sidewalk. Discarded beer bottles clanked as Aquan dragged him into a nearby alley. She pulled a business card case out of his jacket pocket reading "Ernest Tuttleberry. Paramount Life and Casualty Insurance. Fraud Investigator" with his contact information. She stuffed his card in her backpack and stuck one empty beer bottle in his hand and another into his coat pocket. Local constables would look after him.

Following at a safe distance, Aquan caught up to the Hydromorphs yanking Cutter toward an empty strip of beach. They dropped him at a Sea Monk's feet, his pale green skull poking out of his tonsured hair, his claw-like fins clasped as if in prayer. He wore a hooded cloak made of charcoal black scales. A Pteron was perched on his left shoulder.

Cutter looked up and squeezed his eyes shut, then open again. "There are more of you?" he asked.

"You've disappointed us, Dr. Cutter," he said. His red eyes glowered at Cutter.

Jenn Hydromorph pulled Cutter's head up by his hair, and this Sea Monk struck Cutter's face with the back of his claw.

"We thought you'd lead us to her by now. At this pace, we'll never finish in time."

"Finish what?" asked Cutter. Blood rolled down broken skin on his left cheek.

"Don't trifle with me. She dropped right into your lap, amulet and all."

"I don't know what you are talking about."

"You try my patience, Dr. Cutter." The Sea Monk leaned right into Cutter's face. "One final time, where is she?"

Cutter laughed and spit blood into his face.

"I'm the last thing you'll see before you and your precious theories gasp their last breath," he replied.

He reached up his clawed arm about to slash Cutter's throat with his jagged talons. As Bridget, Aquan shot a deadly spear point into this Exori monk's forehead, cracking through his skull in two. Groaning, he fell back into a mound of sand with a thud. His Pteron screeched and flew away while Kirra Hydomorph camouflaged itself and Jenn Hydromorph changed into a sandworm, burrowing a beach escape tunnel.

"Stay down, Cutter," she yelled. "Don't move."

Gypsy ran along the beach and barked at an unseen presence, a camouflaged Hydromorph. Aquan froze and waited for it to give away its position.

"C'mon, Gypsy," she said. "Go get it, girl."

Gypsy tracked its trail along the shore. As Aquan stood poised with her spear gun, she heard a sandworm wriggling beneath grains of beach sand toward her. Gypsy suddenly lunged at an invisible creature. Aquan shot a venomous spear point right past Gypsy's paws, liquefying a camouflaged Hydromorph into a puddle of seawater.

Its peer burst out from its underground hole at her feet, spraying sand into Aquan's face. She dropped her spear gun, trying to rub sand out of her eyes. It transformed from sandworm into a giant two-headed Sea Scorpion with iron spikes protruding from its enormous pincers and poisonous needles lining its six legs. Cutter fired two shots from his pistol at the creature, but his bullets bounced off its armor-plated back. This creature flipped its paddle tail, swatting Cutter ten feet in the air.

Aquan spun around and fired a spear that bounced off its hard-shelled body. Leaning back on its paddle tail, the creature whirled around and pounced, slicing through her pant leg. Aquan cried out in pain. It tried to grab her with its razor-sharp pincers and she transformed into a giant Moray Eel and slithered away wounded. An iron quill from one of its huge pincers slashed into her tail pinning her down. Balancing on its paddle tail, the creature smelled black blood from her wound and sensed an easy kill.

As it rose up to shred her with its other pincers, Cutter got up on one knee and fired directly into its soft underbelly. It shrieked and tried to twist away, but Cutter got off four clean shots. Green blood spewed from creases in its stomach.

Flailing, it toppled forward and its iron lances stabbed into the ground around Aquan. The Sea Scorpion froze suspended over Aquan, then liquefied drenching Aquan in seawater. This gush of seawater sealed her wounds and refreshed her strength. Turning back into Bridget, she got up and ran over to Cutter.

"Are you alright?"

He nodded as he backed away, pointing his pistol at her.

"Stay right where you are, Red."

Gypsy howled as it sniffed at saltwater puddles at Aquan's feet.

"I don't want to hurt you," she said.

"Is this real or a nightmare?" Cutter slowly backed away from her.

"Both."

She flipped a paralyzing dart from her back pocket into Cutter's arm. He winced and then collapsed on to the beach. His pistol fell out of his hand. Gypsy whined as she poked him with her nose.

"Don't worry girl, he'll be alright," she said, calmly.

Was Cutter a hopeless Drowner or an unwitting pawn? Aquan would have to wait and see. She needed to get him out of here quickly since any Sea Monk possessed the ability to regenerate three times in his life and might be rejoining them at any moment. Leaning over Cutter, he reached out for her amulet necklace dangling above him as he lost consciousness.

Chapter 7

Jenn stood on *Calusa*'s aft deck as Cutter trudged up a dock ramp, looking like he had been tumbling all night with boulders in a clothes dryer. A swathe of gauze covered ten stitches on his chin and partially hid a purplish bruise on the left side of his face. Cuts and scrapes crisscrossed Cutter's forearms and legs. Blood spatters dotted his Ron Jon T-shirt and his khaki shorts torn on the right side. He held a melting ice pack to the side of his head as Gypsy shadowed him.

"What happened to you?"

"A concussion is the worst of it. But you should see that other guy."

He pushed past her and lurched below to *Calusa*'s center deck. Cutter headed straight for his galley and rummaged through its cabinets, looking for something to deaden his aching injuries and that killer hangover. He slammed a bottle of aspirin on his galley counter and then tossed his ice pack into his mini-fridge and pulled out a cold Cascade beer. He dumped several aspirins into his palm and popped open his beer can.

"You really shouldn't be doing that if you suffered a concussion," said Jenn.

"Here's to the hair of any dog that bit me." He raised his beer can and washed down his pills with a long swig of beer. "Or whatever whacked me over my head at that beach."

"Somebody mugged you last night?"

"Actually several somebodies and a few somethings."

He paced around his boat's center well and gulped down beer.

"Was there more than one person?"

"More like several species."

"What? Did you report this to the police?"

"Nope," Cutter said.

"Why not? They may have been accomplices of those pirates."

"Why not? Why not?" he said. "Because if I told them what happened they'd take me right from their royal hospital to their royal loony bin."

He guzzled down his beer, crushed his can and angrily tossed it across the main deck.

"Then at least tell me."

She gently touched his arm and motioned for him to sit down. He didn't. Frustrated, Cutter angrily ran his fingers through his hair several times and continued to pace.

"I know how much you love to hear about aquatelligence."

She said nothing, but Cutter read her disbelief in her eyes.

"Which part do you want to hear about first? A killer sea creature dressed like a monk, a flying sea horse with hummingbird wings or that gigantic scorpion. Or how about those creatures morphing between mythical sea monsters and human forms? All looking for amber amulets, like Kirra's necklace."

"Cutter, drinking too much might have made those hallucinations seem very real."

"Last night went way beyond even my wildest theories."

"They're just stories, Cutter. Your grandfather's lively imagination."

"You're starting to sound like my dear old dad. Next thing you'll be firing me, too."

"You're a great captain. I want to help you work through this," she said.

"If you want to help, then get Maritime Insurers to pay my claim for that pirate attack. They're denying my claim and are calling for a full maritime investigation which should be done about two years from now. " He stopped and stuffed sheets of paperwork into her hands. "Or else figure out real fast how we're going to pay $25,672 in boat repairs."

"I'll try to talk to the Institute about an advance on our quarterly grant funding."

"Yeah, like my Dad is so ready to lend me a hand."

"He might as long as you keep it to a pirate attack and don't tell him your story about those beach creatures."

"My story? Story?" he snarled. He staggered past Jenn and headed for a lower deck. "Be sure to close the bulkhead behind you."

He disappeared slamming a door to his sleeping quarters shut.

*****

Appearing once more as Bridget, Aquan entered data from Jenn's latest samples into her computer in a lab cubicle. She kept her ear buds in, but muted Alexander Laing's fiddle-playing music to eavesdrop on Jenn's conversation with Emerson.

"How's Cutter doing?" Emerson jotted down some notes on a spreadsheet. "Ready to take *Calusa* out again?"

"The insurance company's not going to pay for his boat repairs. They denied his claim until an extended maritime investigation is done. And Cutter got beat up on a beach last night."

"You're kidding. Did he get badly hurt?"

"A mild concussion. Ten stitches on his chin. A bunch of cuts and bruises. He'll be okay."

"What happened?"

Jenn pulled Emerson farther away from Bridget's cubicle, although she could easily detect their hushed voices.

"He blamed it on aquatelligence, Rick," she whispered.

"Oh God, not that crazy grandfather story about Aquatelligence again. Wasn't it enough that it got him booted from the Institute? We should be looking for another captain. One with a working boat and a grip on reality."

"He's a great captain. Remember he helped save our lives in that attack."

Emerson looked down, clearly looking sheepish about his own behavior during the pirate assault.

"Did he say what attacked him?"

"A variety of real and mythical sea creatures and shape-shifting humans."

"How much *did* he have to drink?" said Emerson, with a chuckle.

"It's not funny. He really believes intelligent sea life attacked him. Transforming before his eyes."

"Why did these sea monsters supposedly attack him, Jenn?"

"Claimed they were looking for some magical amulets, similar to Kirra's amber necklace. Remember, she had an unusual talisman on her silver chain."

"That's crazy." Emerson shook his head and adjusted his glasses on the bridge of his nose. "What's next, alchemy?"

"I know, I know, Rick. I'll check in on him tomorrow when he's had a chance to sleep it off. I've got some calls in to the Institute for emergency funds. Let's get back to work. We've lost enough lab time on this trip already."

Aquan felt a bit distracted for the rest of her morning. What if anything of value could she report back to Mopsus and her Elders? All of these humans seemed aware of stories of her kind with only Cutter truly believing they existed in some form. But none of them spoke of the Margrave, Exori rebels or any Vanquishment. They all knew she wore an amber necklace, but appeared clueless about its potential powers. If that Pteron was delivering instructions to any of them, they were all doing an excellent job hiding its true intentions.

After lunch, a university secretary poked her head into Jenn's temporary lab. "Dr. Ortiz, you folks oughtta take a look at what's on TV?"

Jenn and Emerson rushed to a student lounge and Aquan tagged along. Emerson cupped his hands and booed, while a couple of graduate students hissed when Dr. Stevenson's face filled up their TV screen. Stevenson, a celebrity marine biologist, showed more interest in amassing broadcast time and headlines than undertaking pain-staking, mundane research. Jenn seethed as Stevenson stood next to an Indian news correspondent, each strand of his thick salt-and-pepper hair perfectly tousled for his close-up with a lizard-like grin pasted on his thin pale lips.

"Archeologists have long asserted that Shore Temple of the Seven Pagodas, a last remnant of seven original temples, and its surrounding rock sculptures are sole survivors of an ancient city swallowed up by the sea. Today this tide has taken another group of victims, three giant squids beached on its shores. We're fortunate to have Dr. Archibald Stevenson, Professor Emeritus at California's Marine Biology Center, to help explain to us why this has happened. Dr. Stevenson, what do you believe has caused this unusual stranding?"

"Sea quakes, earthquakes originating undersea, are a clear cause. First, Tasmania. And now, India. Each suffered a sea quake, followed by giant squid strandings."

Stevenson turned and dramatically pointed to four giant squid strewn across Mahabalipuram's beach. A camera slowly panned its shoreline and giant squids were strewn on sandy mounds near ornate Shore Temple. A series of small stone bulls decorated its ancient walls. Temple spires and domed pyramids of reddish stone poked above a small group of locals wandering around decaying squid carcasses. In the distance, one could make out Five Rathas, two-story carved monoliths of flying chariots, which Hindu gods raced into the Bay of Bengal.

"I believe it is irrefutable that sea quakes are causing these magnificent creatures to strand themselves. Bogus theories about shifts in electromagnetic fields or mystery lethal microbes are bandied about, but are largely unproven."

"Dr. Stevenson, what do you say to critics of your theory?" asked another correspondent.

"It's not easy being a scientific pioneer. But I relish every opportunity to help our world better understand these maritime puzzles. Including my own colleagues in this field." He winked with a haughty grin on his face.

"That pompous ass," said Emerson.

The news broadcast ended with a quick close-up on sculpted reliefs at Shore Temple. We've got to go there," said Jenn. "We need to take water samples and cultures from those beached squids as soon as possible for microbial anomalies."

"But what about *Calusa*'s repair bill?"

"We'll fly up now and Cutter can follow us later. I've got good contacts at the marine institute there. They can help us with lab space until he joins us."

Aquan wondered what to do next. Jenn and Emerson were heading for India while Cutter remained here. She needed a quiet place to think so she headed for a dark basement. Gazing into her amulet, *Calusa*'s image still remained clearest in one of its ambers. Splitting herself between India and this research vessel would demand more saltwater dips during each high tide. With both locations so close to the sea, she felt little risk in cutting her transformation time periods in half. Reaching inside her knapsack, she pulled out the mirror Mopsus had given her and looked at her reflection.

"*Amor vincit omnia,*" she said.

Shivers engulfed her body as one essence floated off to India to track Jenn and Emerson while Kirra remained in Tasmania keeping an eye on Cutter.

Chapter 8

After his beach attack and his colleagues' abrupt departure, Cutter largely secluded himself on *Calusa,* forbidden to leave without full payment of its repair bills and approval of maritime investigators. A local grocery service left food on its aft deck every couple of days for about a week while Gypsy roamed Hobart's streets of on her own. Three times, Aquan stuffed copies of articles on Tamil Nadu, and once even a music CD of rhythmic Kongu Nadu drumming she found soothing into his grocery delivery bags.

Time was ticking away so after midnight, Aquan stole across swaying dock ramps and found a lone constable guarding *Calusa.* Before he could even speak, Aquan flung a tranquilizing dart into his calf and he fell unconscious at his post. She quickly untied lines of *Calusa* from nearby steel cleats. Boarding Cutter's ship, she carefully pushed open its bulkhead door and slid down a railing into its main well. In its dim lit galley, she looked around and didn't see either Cutter or Gypsy. Its center cabin reeked of moldy leftovers and dirty laundry. Rumpled clothes, half-eaten plates of food and empty beer and soda cans littered its floor. She went below into a portside hull and crept along a low narrow corridor to Cutter's quarters. Cutter snored loudly as she gently opened his cabin door. Gypsy scratched out from under his bunk and began to bark rousing Cutter.

"What are you..."

Before he could finish, Aquan leapt forward and stuck Cutter with one of Mopsus's tranquilizing darts. Gypsy continued to bark and snarl until she shuddered and transformed into Jenn. She flipped on a light and looked around for Cutter's boat keys, finding them inside his Fighting Conchs baseball hat.

She headed topside and started up *Calusa*'s engines in their lowest gear, barely gliding forward out of its slip toward open ocean. About a half-mile out of port, she cut its engines and clambered up topside. She strode to its bow, breathed in and out deeply, and raised her hands palms up by her sides. Thankfully Mopsus often quizzed Aquan on traditional incantations and worldly wisdom handed down by centuries of globe-trotting Emissaries in their Oceanic Scrolls. One day, she would enter her own secrets into its chapters. She chanted a song of praise for Dynamene, a Nereid possessing a powerful ability to manipulate sea currents. Within a few moments, Aquan spied her riding her pink Bottlenose dolphin as Dynamene hurtled toward her.

"Peace to you, Princess of Our Vastness," said Aquan.

"Hallowed be Eternal Concordia, Emissary." She sidled up to *Calusa*.

Her long black hair covered her pale green skin as she stroked her dolphin's dorsal fin. Aquan knew that Nereides were vain, fickle creatures who saw no shame in allying themselves with different feuding Houses, and sometimes even Exoris, depending on their mood. Aquan wasn't certain she could count on Dynamene's aid.

"Why do you call to me, Emissary?"

"I'm on a critical mission for my Elder Council and humbly beseech you to help deliver me quickly to Shore Temple, Princess."

"Discard this clunky human machine and we will play on gentle waves lapping Bengal Bay by morning's light."

"Unfortunately, I must use this vessel so I ask for your help, hastening these currents to accelerate our trip."

Dynamene rode her dolphin around Cutter's catamaran, clicking her tongue as she sized it up.

"It will take a great deal of my energies. I do hate to be weary myself," she said, sighing.

"Ah, then perhaps those rumors are true," said Aquan. "I beg your forgiveness, Princess."

"What rumors?" snapped Dynamene.

"I'm not sure you want to learn of such cruel gossip."

"Gossip about me?" She frowned and clenched her fists. Does it involve Halia?"

Aquan knew of Halia, her youngest sister, who liked to clash with her older sisters for dominion and enjoyed stirring up giant rogue waves and erratic sea currents to bait them.

"Some say that perhaps a younger, more energetic Nereid should control our sea currents. One in her prime who won't tire so easily," said Aquan. "But I believe they're wrong. Only Dynamene with her supreme beauty and unmatched intensity should rule."

Dynamene cried out in disgust. "Halia and her sycophants."

"If you help me on my mission, Princess, only your name will ring out in Quartz Hall. I'll proclaim your might and majesty to all of our great Archigen Houses," said Aquan. "Glorious chants and echoing praise to Dynamene will deafen any rival's ears."

"I will prove those rumor-mongers wrong. Unfurl your sails and it will be done."

Aquan headed to *Calusa*'s helm, pressed its automated sail controls and set its course. Dynamene clapped her hands three times and then she and her dolphin dove beneath rolling waves. Winds howled and a once glassy sea swirled with fierce currents jerking *Calusa* forward. With Dynamene's mighty surge, Cutter's catamaran would arrive in India in two or three days. Aquan splashed into this heady undercurrent before high tide ended. Halia's surges pulled her alongside *Calusa* as she drifted back into her daydreams to restore her shape-shifting energies.

In early morning hours, she climbed back aboard as Kirra and headed to *Calusa*'s wheelhouse to chart their progress. Against the back of her neck, Aquan felt a gun's cold steel. She raised her hands above her head.

"Give me one good reason not to blow your head off."

Cutter tossed a paralyzing dart on to an adjacent chart table.

"Because I paid for your boat repairs, Cutter."

Aquan wondered if she could stop time on her dive watch before Cutter squeezed its trigger.

"One minute an abandoned indigenous woman, then a pale red-head, and now a generous sponsor with more than twenty-five grand to spend on my boat. How do I know you're not some evil shape-shifter that's going to kill me in my sleep?"

"I would've done it already. Besides I don't know if you're a Drowner, in league with that Sea Monk and his friends, with a plan to kill me."

"A concussion and stitches. Doesn't sound like old friends to me." Cutter racked his gun's slide.

"Maybe Cutter, you're a Drowner who double-crossed them?"

"Yeah, more like you set us up for your pirate friends and decided to shoot them rather than split any loot. Part of your own little double-cross."

"What kind of girl do you think I am?"

"I'm not so sure you're a girl at all. A powerful sea organism. Maybe even a fabled mermaid?"

Aquan bristled at that word. "A sailor's fantasy. I'm no dainty nymph."

"I know that already from our beach brawl. But what did you do to get those creatures on your trail?"

"They like my jewelry." Aquan dangled her amulet on its chain. "Just like you do."

"Turn around," said Cutter. "Slowly."

Aquan turned and faced him. Cutter was unshaven, his eyes red with exhaustion, his gun pointed right at her face.

"Keep your hands up where I can see them. Why are they after that amulet?"

"I don't know. They must think it has some value, some power. Perhaps your grandfather understood its worth."

"Keep him outta this." Cutter pushed the muzzle harder against her back. "You own it. Why don't you tell me all about it?"

"It's not mine, Cutter."

"You stole it then."

"No, I retrieved it from a Hydromorph."

"A Hydromorph?"

"One of those shape-shifters who nabbed it from an antiques market in Estonia."

"Why?"

"I don't know, but perhaps you do. What do you think makes them so important? So worth stealing, Cutter?"

He deflected her question. "Who do you work for?"

"The good guys," Aquan said.

"And who are they? The same ones speeding my boat along your route, practically breaking any speed records."

"I think Jenn said you called it aquatelligence."

"Don't mock me."

"I'm not."

"Then what are you? And why are you looking for more amulets?"

Aquan thought this Surface Dweller asked too many questions. As an Emissary, she might break a few minor rules, but followed her Elder Council's orders on missions without asking so many probing questions. However, she needed to walk a tightrope between revealing too much and not disclosing enough to encourage Cutter in order to complete her mission. She said nothing and shrugged.

"Aren't you worried that I'll let our world know about you, your kind?" asked Cutter.

"From what I hear, you've already made a name for yourself by telling too many people about us. And nobody believes you. So I'm not too worried."

"Why should I help you?"

"Because I'm the only one who knows you're not crazy. Did you like those reading materials I put in your bag about that Hindu temple, Cutter?"

"Been too busy to read."

"From the looks of things, you must be too busy doing laundry? Or is it washing dishes?"

"Why should I care about some shrine in India?"

"Because you want to know more about these amulets, too."

"What makes you think that?"

"I know you recognized it after Jenn plucked me out of the Tasman Sea. And you came looking for me at Darby's hostel because of it."

Cutter glared at Aquan, and then reached for and scrutinized her amulet around her neck. She noticed his breathing quicken, betraying a hint of both excitement and apprehension. He still clutched it and pressed his gun harder into her forehead.

"Do you own one, too, Cutter?"

"Not big on jewelry, but I need to get to India fast. And you seem to have useful friends."

Not the answer Aquan was looking for to further her mission. But if he was a Drowner, he wouldn't reveal anything too quickly. He slowly let go of her amulet and dropped his gun by his side.

"I won't kill you today. But then tomorrow's a new day."

Chapter 9

For the next two days, Cutter took his meals alone and spent his time behind his quarters' closed door or in the solitary hush of his dimly-lit wheelhouse. She wondered about Cutter's reticence as they worked *Calusa* with few words passing between them. Not that she minded long stretches of quiet, for she preferred whistling trade winds and rumbling waves to aimless chatter. But Cutter initially asked her nothing about his theory of aquatelligence. Maybe he didn't know what questions to pose or was afraid of her answers. She tried to grasp his feelings or figure out his thoughts as his ship creased through waves. Yet Surface Dwellers were not like simple Hydromorphs or prickly sea urchins, their complex minds and emotions resisted easy interpretation. His handgun stuffed into his waistband reminded her that Cutter didn't trust her and she must remain wary of him as a potential Drowner, too.

In her cabin, she seldom found any rest at night in her human form as she wrestled in her dreams with ghastly visions of her slaughtered Triton family. She wondered if her aunt suffered nightmares in her grief, too. Sometimes she listened to Jenn's music on a device she left behind with playlists heavy on bossa nova and Jamaican mento. Other times, she slipped into the ocean while Cutter slept, hunting game or racing with sharks in darkened waters. Once, she believed that she sensed the essence of her mother in the churning waves, lulling herself into a sleepy trance to restore her shape-shifting abilities. One evening, awoken once more by another nightmare, she got up and noticed Cutter sitting dazed in his wheelhouse as *Calusa* rushed along Dynamene's swift currents.

"Which of your pals is doing this?" asked Cutter. A half-drunk bottle of Jack Daniels bounced on his knee.

"A Nereid friend is helping us."

"Nereides are made up. Greek myths."

"Always a few kernels of truth in myths." She smiled thinking of Mopsus's reminder to her over a pot of boiled kelp.

"How many other kernels are for real in your world?"

"Many."

"How did the Greeks know about you?" Cutter took a health swig from his bottle.

"They were great sailors. Like the Phoenicians and Egyptians. It was inevitable that they would happen upon us, then weave their stories to try to explain us."

"If that's so, we should stumble upon your people more often now. We've got much more sophisticated tools than they did." He pointed at his GPS and fish finder screens.

"They posed little threat to us. But centuries ago, our Elders decided we must move to deeper depths to remain hidden. We've always been written off as myth. That's been good for our survival." She noticed a sudden flash of recognition pass across Cutter's face. He seemed to understand this already. "Have you ever come across my kind before?"

"My grandfather was a fisherman. He said he saw things out at sea. Told me all about it when I was a kid. My dad called him a confused, old man who drank too much and spent too much time hauling in fishing nets." He appeared lost in thought. "So why did they send you?"

"Some of us are destined to serve this way."

"What way?"

"As an Emissary."

"Is that your name?"

"No, my name is Aquan and my role is an Emissary with an ability to transform. Moving between sea and land. Between Surface Dwellers, like yourself, and my people." No need to tip him off to her shuddering pain or tidal needs with each transformation.

"Into anything?"

"Mostly sea creatures and Surface Dwellers." She thought it best not to tell him that she could transform into any living thing that had evolved from fish, meaning any amphibians, reptiles, birds, or mammals, and even creatures Surface Dwellers believed were only mythical beasts.

"For how long?"

"It varies depending on the lunar cycle. Being in saltwater continually renews my abilities." Aquan didn't wish to tell him more since he might use it against her someday.

"And what are Emissaries supposed to do?"

"We try to maintain equilibrium between land and sea. Eternal Concordia for our Infinite Dreamer."

"Who?"

"The One who is and always will be."

"Maybe you haven't noticed, but you aren't doing a very good job keeping things in check. We're destroying your oceans." Cutter took another hit from his bottle. "That Dreamer oughtta fire you."

His heretical retort angered her, but she didn't show it. No Surface Dweller would get the better of her.

"Emissaries have existed since the dawn of time. We've recognize your careless ways. But we aren't allowed to interfere with your development."

"We may develop you folks right out of a home."

"Our Infinite Dreamer is more optimistic about your ability to be creative, to learn from your mistakes."

"Believe me, we're slow learners," he said. He sized her up and down and pointed at her talisman. "Why are you looking for more of those amulets?"

"I'm not sure. I'm trying to find them before our enemies do. They seem eager to kill for them so they must be very valuable."

"You don't know why you're putting yourself on the line while everybody else is safely back home?"

"It's not my role to question our Elders' rulings."

"If my ass was in a sling, I'd ask a lot more questions."

Aquan didn't like his badgering, but realized he made a good point. For decades, she'd obeyed her Elders' commands about her surveillance operations. Her biggest rebellions were cutting her hair, getting piercings and putting a tiny tattoo on her hip. Was it wrong to find out if this mission was really worth risking an all-out war with the Exoris or even risking her own life? Aquan might disobey some old-fashioned prohibitions, but her sense of duty to her House and her fellow Archigens would not allow her to probe or contradict a direct order from the Elder Council.

Suddenly she smelled them, hurried out of wheelhouse and clambered topside.

"Hey, where you going?" Cutter called after her following on her heels.

Standing on *Calusa*'s dive platform, she noticed movement under a waning gibbous moon. She reached down and picked up a jagged brown piece of a large fish scale, its putrid oily odor filled the air.

"Gorgons," she said.

"What's a Gorgon?"

"Something we don't want to run into. The only thing it likes more than killing things, is eating them."

She examined the edges of Cutter's dive platform and saw no claw marks. Scanning a cloudless sky, she did not detect their enormous bloodshot eyes with their laser-like night vision. Listening for any whoosh of their dragon-like wings, she heard nothing. Aquan only encountered a Gorgon once before in her travels. Five years ago, from a safe distance, she spotted one Gorgon tearing apart another with its bronze talons and tusked mouth, its fiery ruby eyes glowing in delight.

Mopsus warned her to stay away from these voracious beasts, often pets of the Margrave, for fear they' would ensnare her in their swirling, eel-like manes and gobble her down as a tasty appetizer. Since they prowled in a maul of four or five, it would take several well-armed Archigens with lethal neurotoxins to bring them down. She decided not to swim tonight to avoid wandering into their pack. Gorgons were territorial creatures, not likely to roam far away from their realm. By daybreak, Cutter's boat would be out of this maul's region and she could refresh herself.

"What's wrong?" asked Cutter.

"We're in dangerous territory. Bring Gypsy inside. Best to stay below deck until morning," she said.

It must have been her serious tone, because for once Cutter had no sarcastic reply or barrage of questions as he whistled for Gypsy to follow them below.

Unfortunately, at dawn, she discovered more aggressive signs of Gorgons, several brownish scales on *Calusa*'s top decks, some claw marks on its boat rails and an occasional whiff of their rancid slimy scales. These continuing signs of their presence both puzzled and concerned her. She didn't dare go swimming even though she needed to refresh herself soon, especially since dividing her essence meant shortening her tidal times in half. Instead, she reluctantly dumped a few buckets of sea water over her body, hoping they would help extend her transformative powers. Aquan grabbed a boat hook and yanked a slick knot shed from one of their manes from the water.

"What's that?" asked Cutter.

"Piece of a Gorgon's mane."

"What does this creature look like?"

"Long headdress of slithering eels. Enormous bronze talons. Sharp tusks in the corners of its mouth. Bloodshot red eyes. Stinks worse than any oil spill in summer's heat."

"Your basic nightmare," said Cutter. "Will this work?" He held up his handgun.

"Maybe, if you shoot its head a dozen times. But you'll never get that close. You'll slow it up if you hit one of its wings."

"This damn thing flies, too?"

"Yes. Huge dragon-like wings." She let remnants of its mane slip off her hook and back into the sea.

"I've been in every ocean in this ship. And I've never seen one of them."

"Gorgons are nocturnal with extraordinary night vision. They'll see you long before you glimpse them and they don't leave survivors behind. This pack's been tracking us day and night, which isn't their style." She assumed the Margrave must be directing their actions, but no need to disclose that to Cutter.

"How can you tell?"

Aquan showed Cutter scrapes on his boat railing and decks and pulled out several scales she collected. Cutter tried to reach for one of its scales and she popped them back into her pocket. She didn't want to supply him with any physical evidence of aquatelligence.

"Luckily, Gorgons have tiny brains. They don't understand

machinery, so they'll be timid at first about taking any ship on. But they're patient. Hoping to catch us off-guard topside. Or dangling our feet overboard some night."

"Can these Gorgons kill you? Your kind?"

"Yes, especially if there are in a maul, a pack." Aquan realized she might need Cutter's help if they decided to attack. He could easily kill her with his gun, so why worry about explaining how to use her weapons. "Perhaps it's time I showed you how to use my spear gun."

She motioned for Cutter to go below deck. As she turned, Cutter plucked a couple of brown scales sticking to Gypsy's coat and shoved them into his cargo shorts.

"I've used spear guns before when I've gone spear fishing," said Cutter.

"This one's custom. Nothing else like it."

"Who made it for you?"

"My friend, Mopsus. A great craftsman." She wondered if Mopsus missed her as much as she missed him.

"Is he one of your good guys?"

"He's the best. Been looking after me for nearly a century."

"A century?" Cutter whistled. "That's almost seventy years older than me. Is that really how old you are?"

Aquan knew she shouldn't have said that, but got a laugh out of Cutter's shocked look. At one hundred years old, her physical maturity was more like a human at twenty- or twenty-one, although her decades of experiences made her wise beyond her years, at least sometimes. Cutter would be floored to know he'd be celebrating about one hundred thirty-two years in her world, roughly Raynord's human age.

"It's not nice to ask a woman's age," she replied.

For a moment, she thought she enjoyed their genial banter. Over the following hour, Aquan explained to Cutter about various kinds of neurotoxins and demonstrated how to rapidly snap each cartridge into place on her spear gun. She let him try it out with empty cartridges to help him get a sense of her gun's weight and recoil action. They went above deck and Cutter squeezed off several empty cartridges. Her spear gun's range and accuracy amazed him. After solitary years of practice, she enjoyed revealing her weapons to him and watching his excitement in practicing with them. She then let him toss some of her empty hand darts for use against smaller creatures and other humans.

"Flick them in your assailant's direction," she said. "You don't need to have perfect aim. If it's alive, they'll usually find your target."

Cutter took several practice throws at his boat bumpers, hitting their center each time.

"You've obviously played darts before," she remarked.

"My misspent youth. Chucking darts at local pubs on Duval Street in Key West for a free drink or two. Or three," he said, laughing.

She found herself smiling for the first time since that terrible night. As he continued to practice, she felt strong cramps in her arms and legs. While Cutter practiced with her darts, she dragged a plastic bucket over rolling waves and patted water over her body with a sponge. Her skin tingled and burned with heat as she wrung sea water out of her sponge on to her skin. Pulling practice darts out of his boat bumpers, Cutter grew serious for a moment. "Have you ever killed a human with these weapons?"

"No. It goes against our beliefs to kill Surface Dwellers."

"But not to kill those other monsters on the beach."

"We kill other sea creatures for survival, not sport."

"Have humans ever killed your kind?"

"Yes, mostly through carelessness, rather than intention. Like polluting our fishing grounds. Smashing their missiles into our sea beds."

"Why don't you fight back against us?"

"As more advanced beings, it is not our way," she said.

"I don't get it. If somebody threatened me or my family I'd kick their butt."

In due time, she planned to kick some Exori butt and maybe even finish off the Margrave to defend her people from further massacres. "It's getting dark. We're not safe out here."

Aquan placed her spear gun and cartridges on Jenn's lab table along with an array of paralyzing and deadly darts needed to fell a Gorgon. Cutter nodded his approval. Aquan returned to her quarters to lie down as her cramps grew stronger.

"Since you showed me how to use your stuff, how about I make us some dinner?" asked Cutter. He secretly slipped two Gorgon scales he snatched from Gypsy's fur into a plastic specimen bag. He didn't get a reply. "Or do you even eat cooked fish. I've got raw fish if that works better for you."

Again no reply.

"Hey, do you want dinner or not?" he called out.

Cutter heard strange gurgling and clacking sounds coming from inside Aquan's quarters. He knocked on her door and she didn't respond. He slowly opened it and saw her writhing on her bunk. A tentacle brushed up against his arm as Aquan turned into an octopus, then transformed into a sea goat, bleating as she swished her fish tail, followed by a squawking Pteron hovering over her bunk. Soon her transformations sped up so quickly that Cutter could barely identify each one, a manic kaleidoscope of sea creatures, real and mythical. Eventually she returned to her Kirra form. She broke into a cold sweat and fell from her bed on to the floor, vomiting black blood and panting for air.

"Oh my God. What's happening?" asked Cutter.

"Water," she sputtered, her chest heaving. "Sea water."

Cutter dragged her to *Calusa's* upper deck. Her legs flopped under her and Cutter carried her to the swaying boat's dive platform. She sprang from Cutter's arm, like a thrashing trout escaping a fisherman's clutches, and vanished under a surging current. Cutter ran aft and flipped on his boat's spotlight. Shining it across the waves, he couldn't see her. He called out her name but only a roaring sea responded.

Chapter 10

At Tamil Nadu, Aquan manifested herself as Rajneet Jagtiani, an Indian journalist, reporting on developments in these most recent giant squid beachings. Over decades of shape-shifting, Aquan found that pretending to be a reporter often gave her easy access to people and places. Surface Dwellers tended to be quite eager to share their stories. As Rajneet, she also managed to insinuate herself into Dr. Stevenson's media-hungry camp and observed Jenn and Emerson carrying out their sample collections on the beach once they arrived. She contacted each of them for an interview and sought regular updates about their activities. While she gleaned routine information from both sides, she kept a careful look out for any Exori renegades or Drowners.

After a daily swarm of tourists departed, this Mahabalipuram site returned to its natural serenity. A blazing sun and oppressive daytime humidity gave way to orange and purple hues of sunset and cool ocean breezes. Aquan felt a sense of peace as Rajneet quietly wandering ancient Hindu structures. She picked up a tourist brochure near a cluster of holy monuments. Aquan read about Pallava kings commissioning hundreds of promising apprentices at a royal sculpture school to chisel out intricate rock-cut cave temples, colossal stone chariots and gigantic sculpted reliefs of Hindu mysticism. Listening to an incoming tide's music, she marveled at octagonal domes sitting atop a five-story stone pagoda of Shore Temple. Aquan passed through its reddish stone pillars sprouting out of carved stone lions guarding its entryway, and ran her fingers softly over ornate reliefs to honor Hindu gods and herald royal achievements.

Not far from this temple, she noticed about eight or nine reporters gathering near a spot where giant squids beached themselves. Pulling out her notebook and hand-held tape recorder, she reluctantly left the tranquil shrine and headed for Dr. Stevenson's weekly briefing. A make-up artist blotted Stevenson's face with a powder puff while an impossibly skinny man fussed with Stevenson's hair until he achieved a proper of naturally rumpled perfection. Several bright lights illuminated Stevenson sitting in a high canvas director's chair. He nodded to a camera man for Scientific Adventure channel that sponsored his trip who counted it down.

"Ready on three. Three, two, one." He said. His camera whirred on to capture Stevenson's update.

"Ladies and gentlemen, thank you for attending my weekly briefing. I think you'll be pleased to know that my team has found further evidence that sea quakes cause these Giant Squids to beach themselves."

Dr. Stevenson's aides handed out slim bound notebooks with mind-numbing, detailed charts about seismic activity.

"These charts pinpoint a series of quakes that preceded this recent stranding," said Stevenson with a self-satisfied grin. "I have included an executive summary to help you work your way through them. In addition, we've found some critical data here to support our assertion. Please follow me this way."

Stevenson hopped off his chair and escorted a troop of reporters about a quarter mile away from a windy beach to an enormous carved stone relief of Arjuna's Penance on a low hill. Acting as tour guide, Stevenson described in rich detail an epic story of a heroic ascetic, Arjuna, witnessing the Ganges pouring down from the mighty Himalayas. A carved parade of flying celestial beings, meditating monks and enormous stone elephants accompany Arjuna on this colossal slab. Unexpectedly, Rajneet noticed that rotund black man from Hobart joining this group and taking photos of these temple ruins.

"As you can see, fissures in these carvings represent the Ganges River," said Stevenson placing his hands into a gap. "A little over three months ago, an archeological team led by Dr. Shom Gupta, undertook extensive measurements and photographing of all aspects of these ruins as part of a UNESCO World Heritage grant. If you look at pages ten through twelve of our study, you will see before and after photographs. There is extensive additional cracking to this relief between Gupta survey and its current state. Clearly supporting recent seismic activity leading to these Giant Squid strandings."

Aquan looked at his photos and noticed little difference. She saw Jenn and Emerson walking on a path alongside this relief each grasping a handle of a large wooden crate of capped water samples. That Hobart investigator stared at them and furiously jotted notes as they approached Stevenson's group.

"More importantly, there was an increase of 1.3 centimeters or one-half inch in each fissure," he said. Stevenson dramatically spread a tape measure over each fissure to demonstrate his point. "Such sudden changes in such a short time span can only occur after significant seismic activity. Once more pointing to sea quakes as causing this squid beaching."

Several reporters snapped photos and studiously wrote down his declarations as his videographer continued to shoot film of this announcement. As Jenn and Emerson made their way around the back of the group, Stevenson snapped his fingers and one of his aides handed him another notebook.

"Looks awfully heavy," he called out.

Jenn and Emerson stopped. He worked his way through his gathering and dropped a notebook on top of Jenn's sample box. "A little bedtime reading, Dr. Ortiz."

"I'm sure it will put me to sleep," said Jenn.

She and Emerson continued to lug their crate. Stevenson scowled as bored journalists laughed in agreement.

"Dear Dr. Ortiz. I know it can be so frustrating to realize that you've wasted your career on a dead end theory. Now with all that grant money drying up, it must be quite daunting."

Jenn kept walking, pulling her crate and assistant behind her.

"Thank you, Dr. Stevenson. We've got plenty of grant money," she said.

"So much that you're bumming a ride with that quack, Cutter? Is he still phoning home to parrot fish?" Stevenson laughed and his aides obediently chuckled in chorus.

Aquan never liked Stevenson's arrogant swagger or his smug dismissal of her kind, but as Rajneet she couldn't correct him now. Before Jenn had a chance to reply, Rajneet heard a soft tinkling of test tubes vibrating in their crate of samples. In a moment, the ground beneath everyone's feet began to vibrate and then violently shake, knocking two reporters on to a sandy dune.

"Aftershock!" yelled a journalist.

Waves of undulating sand followed. Fearing a tidal surge, panicky reporters ran for higher ground, a ring of upper dunes supporting a parking lot. One reporter tripped over Jenn's crate, knocking her test tubes into a sand mound. Jenn kneeled down and tried to salvage several test tubes.

"Jenn, leave 'em behind," hollered Emerson.

He grabbed her right arm, but Jenn pulled herself away. She stubbornly stuffed sample tubes in her shirt and pants pockets.

"Go, Rick, I'll be fine."

"Jenn, there's no time for this," Emerson said.

He pointed toward a massive twenty-foot high wall of water rushing towards them. Jenn and Emerson tried to escape for higher ground, but Aquan knew this roaring surge would swallow them up in an instant. Hitting her diver's watch red button, everyone around her froze in place. She raced towards an angry surf. Diving in, she turned into Parata, a sea monster with a cavernous jaw deep and strong enough to gulp down an entire ocean three times a day. Underwater, she opened her gaping mouth and sucked in sea water, her lower jaw ballooning as she consumed this localized tsunami.

After eating up eighteen seconds of time, she clicked her watch on to allow time to resume and to give Jenn, Emerson and several reporters a chance to flee to higher ground. Aquan belched out a series of swells and turned their force towards a distant horizon. Only gentle, low waves lapped up against the shoreline and shallow torrents of saltwater splashed through these historic monuments. Two reporters wept openly out of sheer relief that these rogue waves had not drowned them. Jenn hugged Emerson in relief and gratitude.

"I think I owed you one from that pirate attack," said Emerson.

"Great television. I hope you got that," Stephenson shouted. He pointed at a shaking camera man.

"No clue, man. No clue," he replied. Gasping for breath, his camera rested on his lap, his shirt drenched in sweat.

"We should go in case there's another aftershock," Jenn said to Emerson.

Panting reporters along with Jenn and Emerson anxiously hurried to their cars. As they headed for their borrowed van, Stevenson called after them. "Sea quakes, Dr. Ortiz. Sea quakes."

"Ignore him. It's just a coincidence," said Emerson.

Jenn nodded as she pulled a few rescued samples out of her pockets. Yet they both knew that too many coincidences were adding up to a perception that Stevenson's theory was indeed correct, further eroding their position and much-needed Institute support.

"Too bad Cutter's not here. He would've had a sarcastic reply," said Jenn.

"He'll be here in a week or so to cheer you up," said Emerson.

Little did they know that *Calusa* sailed only a few hours offshore on Dynamene's swift currents.

Chapter 11

Aquan dissolved back into her Triton form as she plummeted through watery depths, sucked down by some unseen force. The ocean reeked of Gorgons as she was drawn deeper, oily strands from one of their manes grazing her face and body. She tried to swim away, but her arms and tail fell limp, too weak to halt her rapid descent or to escape their clutches. Several spear cartridges shattered the water's surface nicking one Gorgons' wings. Its pained grunt reverberated in wrenching riptides churning around Aquan. A wounded Gorgon sank past her while two others streaked toward her. Their thick manes enveloped her and squeezed her fading life from her. In their unrelenting grip, Aquan and these two Gorgons continued to plummet into an unknown vortex. A high-pitched Bosun's whistle pierced the waves and these Gorgons immediately released Aquan and disappeared into a dark void.

Her listless body continued to spiral down through dense plumes of white ash and scalding steam from a rumbling underwater volcano. This submerged volcano spewed molten sulfur flares, cooling within seconds into exploding fragments of black rubble whistling past her. Whirlpools of dead fish killed by this volcano's toxic gases swirled around her as packs of hungry sharks and Goliath groupers feasted on their carcasses. She choked on noxious fumes, fighting to regain her physical strength to avoid smashing into rocky chimneys spewing giant boiling mud balls and disgorging black plumes of steam. Her silvery scales throbbed, her skin blistered as she hurtled toward intense heat from a volcano's scalding vents.

In a stifling funnel, Aquan heard her mother's voice chant, "Return to me. Return to me," as she blacked out.

She awoke dazed on a scorched bottom of an ocean volcano's dead chimney. A shaft of murky light glinted through its jagged, cone-shaped opening about a half-mile above her. Aquan could only hear muffled, distant rumblings of its central vents. Too weak to swim back through its stack's crown, she slipped into a trance-like state to heal and refresh herself for nearly twenty minutes.

When she blinked her eyes open, a funnel cloud of white ash formed a billowy image of her mother, Evadne, floating above her. Grief and joy mingled in her heart, longing to be reunited with her deceased mother for so many decades.

"Mother, I've missed you so much."

"I grieve for you, my dear daughter. And for our House of Triton. I hope we will gather together with our people soon."

"Has that time come for me to join you in Musterion?"

"Not yet, my child. Your life flow persists and must continue. But I mourn our people and feel your heavy sorrows for our House."

"Those Exoris will pay for what they've done to us."

"Our enemies are much closer than Obzula Ridge."

"Where are they so I can exact our retribution?"

"It's not yet time for vengeance, Aquan. First you must fulfill my prophecy."

"What prophecy?"

"My visions of a true Eternal Concordia. Fulfill my prophecy and I will return to you."

"But how?"

"Return to *Calusa* for this Surface Dweller is your unsuspecting guide on your journey," said Evadne. "Fulfill my prophecy, daughter of Triton and Protosian."

"Protosian?" asked Aquan. "What is that?"

Evadne's ashen figure stretched out her hand to her daughter. "Fulfill my prophecy."

Aquan reached for her mother's grasp, but Evadne's wan reflection dissolved into tiny dust particles, carried upward in swirling currents. Pallid embers of her mother's likeness lured her, and she followed their flow, swimming through an opening in a chimney vent. The massive volcano no longer belched searing vapors or molten rock, but silently presided over a desolate field of barren chimney vents, as if lifeless for centuries. She pushed aside her confusion and sadness and turned into a spinner dolphin.

*****

Calusa's rumbling engine and distinctive chatter from crusty barnacles clinging to her starboard hull made it easy for Aquan to find her way back. Approaching the surface, she spotted three Gorgons clamping their sets of bronze talons on the ship's railings. Two creatures seized the front railings while a third gripped its rear diving platform. Flapping their huge wings, they lifted *Calusa* out of the water. She heard its engine sputter as its propellers whirred in the air. They swung Cutter's boat back and forth and loud crashing sounds of glass and plates reverberated below deck. All three creatures snorted, their bloodshot eyes blazing with pleasure.

Aquan convulsed and then shot out as a Lusca, a gargantuan octopus. Shrieks from her enormous beak shook pierced the air and one startled Gorgon loosed its grip from *Calusa*'s front railing and tried to fly off. The ship lurched to its side as one of her enormous tentacles swatted this fleeing Gorgon, decapitating it. Another Gorgon kept one claw on the ship's railing and swiped at her with its talons.

Angered, Aquan attacked this second Gorgon and wrapped two of her tentacles around it, emitting poison from hundreds of her suckers. As it screamed in pain, she snapped its body in half, its orange blood exploding across the sky. A Timarch spear whizzed past her head lancing a third Gorgon right through its heart. It collapsed toward the sea, releasing its hold on Cutter's ship. As *Calusa* plummeted, Aquan caught its bow railing with two of her tentacles and wrapped two more tentacles around its stern. She slowly lowered it back into swaying sea currents.

Aquan hummed as she shivered and shape-shifted into Kirra. Climbing back aboard *Calusa*, she looked across a cloudy horizon and glimpsed watery trail marks from a Timarch sea chariot. Raynord must have been shadowing her return, probably at Mopsus's behest. Aquan noticed a huge spider web crack in one of the pilothouse's front windows. She pressed her nose against a cracked pane. Amidst shards of broken glass and a pile of charts, Cutter was lying still beneath his chart table.

Racing her way below deck, she picked her way through its trashed lower deck and found Cutter unconscious, his T-shirt soaked in blood. Gypsy whimpered and licked his face. Aquan ripped his shirt open and discovered deep serrated wounds from a Gorgon's talon across Cutter's right shoulder and upper back. His body burned with fever and his breathing was slow and erratic. For a moment, thoughts of his possible death alarmed her. She had never caused any injury or death to any human during a mission and she wouldn't let it happen now.

Aquan raced to her sleeping quarters, kicking aside a jumbled mess in her path. Yanking out her backpack from under her bunk, she grabbed Mopsus' medicinal seaweed and elixirs. She didn't know if they worked on humans, but she had to try. Returning to the pilothouse, she gently draped and pressed dark green seaweed on his wounds. Cutter's first aid kit contained a roll of gauze, and she wrapped it around his shoulder and back to secure Mopsus's seaweed to his wounds. She tilted his head back and poured a small amount of her tutor's liquid potion into his mouth. He swallowed and coughed some of this healing syrup up before becoming still again. As she cradled his head in her arms, Aquan wondered if he could really be an Exori ally after all. She carefully put his head back down on to his ship's floor.

Returning to Cutter's quarters, Aquan searched for a pillow and blanket. She slowly pushed open its door. All kinds of marine biology texts and books recounting sea adventures had tumbled out of shelves lining his cabin's walls. She pulled open built-in drawers looking for a fresh blanket. In one drawer, she found a fleece blanket folded around a weathered leather scrapbook. Aquan placed his album on his disheveled bed and took a blanket and pillow back to his wheelhouse. She put a pillow under Cutter's head and covered him with his fleece blanket. Gypsy curled up beside him. Stroking his brow, she ran her fingertips over his blond hair as he rested motionless. Aquan unexpectedly found herself drawn to Cutter as she studied his features.

A whiff of a Gorgon burned in her nostrils. Sniffing around, she discovered two Gorgon scales in Cutter's T-shirt pocket. Seizing both specimens, she looked around for any others. Turning into a perch, she flailed about until several scales fell off. Returning to her Kirra shape, Aquan substituted two perch scales for Cutter's Gorgon specimens and put fish scales into his T-shirt pocket. She tucked away his Gorgon scales into her backpack.

Letting Cutter sleep, Aquan returned to his quarters and hunted around for any more hidden Gorgon samples, but found none. As she was about to return Cutter's scrapbook into its drawer, her curiosity took hold. Leafing through it, she saw photos of Cutter with other humans. One looked like Cutter as a boy with an elderly man, holding a large fish on a fishing boat. *Calusa* in white paint was hand-scrawled on its port side. Maybe his grandfather. In another youthful photo, Cutter wore a black graduation robe and clutched a rolled diploma in his hand. She flipped through a few more pages and then glimpsed a photo of a Cutter kissing Jenn's cheek. Maybe they had been mates in the past. A yellowed newspaper article fluttered out of one of its pages. She read a Miami newspaper headline, "Florida Diver Missing at Dos Ojos." A story blurb told about a diving accident off the Riviera Maya coast. She heard Cutter groaning, so she slipped the article back into his album and quickly put it away.

When she returned to Cutter, he still remained feverish. She hoped Mopsus's remedies would help heal him. All she could do now was watch and wait. And patience remained her least favorite virtue.

*****

After a half-hour, she left Cutter's side and got busy clearing away smashed glass and tumbled charts. For a couple of hours, she swept up broken test tubes and dishes, put toppled lab instruments and notebooks back into their cabinets, and placed cans and foodstuffs on to the galley shelves. Exhausted, Aquan decided to return to her cabin. She pulled out Mopsus's mirror and gazed into it.

A reflection of her second essence in India appeared. She watched Rajneet transform into a rare golden-tipped Imperial eagle. Swooping over Shore Temple, her black eyes scanned its ruins and spied movements of three Hydromorphs wading in semi-submerged monuments.

Aquan whispered, "Stay on guard and wait for me. I'll be there soon."

The Imperial eagle screeched in agreement, soaring high over Hindu monuments.

Chapter 12

As Calusa cruised into the Bay of Bengal, Aquan sat quietly beside Cutter. He wrestled with fits of chills and fever for over three hours, but slept quietly now. The rushing currents dissipated to a gentle drift that guided the boat into a peaceful cove. She climbed topside and stood on the ship's bow.

"All praise to Princess Dynamene," she sang out.

She sensed Rajneet's Imperial eagle gliding toward Cutter's boat. Aquan knew she might be in two places at once, but she couldn't exist as two separate beings in the same place and time. Aquan flung her arms open under a shimmering third-quarter moon. The golden bird shrieked and then it instantly dissolved into the air. She breathed in deeply as salty sea air mingled with her own essence and then filled her lungs. Aquan shuddered and then once more became one.

Aquan went below and dropped anchor in this calm harbor. Checking on a sleeping Cutter, she put an extra blanket over him and filled Gypsy's food and water bowls. She grabbed her spear gun and cartridges and dove into the water. In her Triton form, she rapidly swished her silvery fishtail, skimming through receding waters and circling partially submerged Shore Temple and Arjuna's Penance. Her radar picked up clumsy splashing and grunts of Hydromorphs, but couldn't see them as dark waters enveloped these submerged stone monuments. She swam past stone temple lions and sensed more activity near waters swirling around the stone relief of Arjuna's Penance. An earlier narrow fracture in a Ganges River carving had cracked open more than three feet wide.

She dipped into a gaping cleft which suddenly gave way to a roaring waterfall which descended into an enormous underground cavern. The powerful waterfall pushed her into a whirling torrent, its undertow pulling her into a wide gash in a cavern wall. She silently floated in a stream for several hundred feet when she picked up a pinging of a metal tool chipping against stone. Ducking underwater, she noticed a greenish glow of biolumen sticks and heard low grunts of

Hydromorphs in a rocky corridor ahead. She let a current sweep her past this trio on an upper ledge. Two yellow gremlins furiously chiseling into a rock wall under a greenish haze. As they faded from view, she grabbed hold of a rocky outcropping and climbed out as Kirra, her spear gun loaded.

A man-made stone path lined this corridor, adorned with more Hindu reliefs, escape passages for the temple priests or the royal tutors during emergencies. These imps remained so absorbed in their work that they didn't sense her approaching them. Through a slit in a rocky archway, she watched them pounding beveled blades into a stone relief while a third pushed sand and loose rocks away. At one point, one Hydromorph screamed in pain as its mallet struck one of slim fingers. Its partner pushed it aside grabbing its hammer and continuing to bash a metal blade into stone. The injured Hydromorph sat down on a stone path and continued to whimper while two other imps kept working.

About five minutes later, one Hydromorph growled for its accomplice to stop hammering. It reached inside a relief and pulled out a silken pouch. A brief scuffle broke out between them over possession of this small bag, until a larger one wrested control of it. Opening it, this imp held up a gleaming amber amulet over his oversized head, identical to Aquan's talisman around her neck. All three Hydromorphs grunted with delight. The biggest Hydromorph directed its partner to a nearby stream to sip saltwater before turning into a Painted Stork. The large imp dropped its pouch into this stork's bright yellow beak before the creature flew off. This imp then slurped seawater and transformed into another Painted Stork, leaving a pouting Hydromorph to remain nursing its injured finger.

Aquan needed to improve her odds so she flicked a paralyzing dart at this imp. It fell into this underground stream and was swept deeper into this cavernous cleft. She then turned into a Painted Stork and followed the other two Hydromorphs. Outside, a Sea Monk stood on top of Arjuna's Penance, a Pteron resting on his right shoulder. A thick scar on his forehead confirmed that this creature fought with Aquan and Cutter in Hobart.

"Well done, my pets." He cackled as he reached into the first stork's throat pouch to pull out a sack. He tore it open and held up an amber gemstone. "The Master will be pleased."

The Sea Monk tossed raw fish heads out of his black robe pocket and two Hydromorphs, no longer Painted Storks, dove hungrily for these scraps. Aquan hesitated and this Sea Monk immediately realized she wasn't a Hydromorph. He swung at her with one of his claws, nicking her left wing. She immediately turned into a Bengal tiger and pounced upon both Hydromorphs eviscerating them in an instant. The Sea Monk clapped his claw-like fins and bellowed a Hindu incantation. The ground rumbled as five gargantuan elephants, each ten feet tall, thundered out of a cracked stone relief and stampeded through a series of partially submerged monuments. Avoiding its nimble tusks, Aquan's Bengal tiger leapt on one of the elephant's rear, clawing its fleshy rump. It bellowed in pain and then shook her loose from its leathery hide.

She tumbled and another elephant's huge padded foot nearly crushed her head. A third elephant's trunk struck her, flinging her fifty feet across these ruins. In her tiger form she hit a stone relief hard and fell into a churning eddy that pulled her into a pounding surf. Aquan returned to her Triton form in time to see rampaging elephants tearing through bay currents to trample over her.

Fiery lava-tipped arrows rained down on these marauding elephants as two dozen Timarch warriors in silver chariots, commanded by Raynord, raced beneath watery torrents. Frightened, several elephants blasted their trumpets and reared up on their hind legs. Disoriented, these elephants began colliding with each other. As these creatures smashed into one another, they crumbled into stone dust and bay swells carried their sandy remains out to sea.

A enraged Sea Monk howled and reanimated a dozen lions guarding Shore Temple. He changed them into Sea-Lions with upper bodies of lions with fierce saber teeth and powerful paws, their lower bodies turned into sea serpent tails. These Sea-Lions chased Raynord's charioteers underwater. Raynord and several other warriors swung their chariots around to fend off these Sea-Lions with arrows and spears. Raynord felled one growling lion about to attack a fellow Timarch's chariot. Raynord's chariot struck this wounded beast, upending it and throwing him into another fierce Sea-Lion's watery path. Its paws began to maul Raynord and Aquan shot this attacking creature with her spear gun. Timarch forces continued to battle these Sea-Lions when they all immediately turned into stone dust. The Sea Monk disappeared, having escaped with an amber amulet.

She rushed to Raynord's side in the ocean shallows. Deep gashes lacerated his body, his cobalt blood slowly drained into rushing currents.

"Aquan," Raynord gasped.

"Don't speak. Save your strength." She clutched his hand.

"Forgive me. Forgive me."

"There is nothing to forgive." She cupped her hands around his bloodied face. Raynord yielded to her tender touch, something he yearned from her for decades.

"Failed you," he groaned.

"No, you saved my life."

"Forgive me." His chest heaved with labored breaths.

"Be still now, Raynord," she whispered. Aquan wiped blood from his lips. "Don't worry. I'll retrieve that amulet."

"Innocents to slaughter." He reached up his hand to brush Aquan's cheek. His eyelids and wounded gills fluttered like butterfly wings trapped in a net. "Mopsus knows."

"Shhh, shhh. Keep your strength for our trip home."

"All is treachery." Raynord sighed as his body quivered in pain. Salty undertow washed over his wounded body.

"Think only now of your return to Rapture's End. To a hero's welcome," she said.

He began to cough up more blood and his breathing became more labored.

"Take your commander immediately to Rapture's End. I'll join you soon with a potent elixir," she told one of his lieutenants.

Aquan knew she ought to chase down that Sea Monk, but she couldn't leave either Raynord or Cutter in their injured states. She transformed into an Imperial eagle once more and flew back to Cutter's ship. He slept quietly as Gypsy snoozed by his side. She touched Cutter's forehead and his fever was subsiding. She grabbed hold of one of Mopsus's healing elixirs from her backpack and took hold of his enchanted mirror.

She gazed again into it, chanting *"Amor vincit omnia."*

One essence remained by Cutter's side while another rejoined Raynord's troops, whisking their injured commander back to Rapture's End. Despite her mission's urgency, she believed Raynord's safe return home trumped any hunt for amulets. She applied Mopsus's remedies to him as his troops returned to Rapture's End. And perhaps Cutter was right. Time to ask more questions of her own.

Upon reaching Rapture's End, Aquan had little opportunity to demand any answers as she found herself under interrogation before her Elders. No welcoming sprig of sacred red algae from Elder Camulus who now served as moderator in Quartz Hall, replacing her Aunt Sofronia secreted away for her protection.

"Aquan, perhaps Elder Mopsus failed to impart to you the seriousness of this mission. Why have you failed your duty and come back without any more amulets or any better knowledge of their power?" said Camulus.

He glared at Mopsus, sitting solemnly in a silent assembly of Elders.

"Raynord was gravely injured in a battle with Exoris. I thought it best to bring him aid and accompany him home safely for further medical treatment."

"Pilot Commander Raynord performed his duty to aid you as needed to promote discovery of these amulets and their significance. Your duty was to continue your mission, not to let another amulet slip through your fingers."

"Raynord and his family are very close to me." She clutched her coral bracelet from Raynord's mother, Clarissa. "Don't Archigen values of loyalty and friendship surpass a search for trinkets?"

"Not when they endanger the overall security of our entire Archigen society. Raynord and his troops well understood all risks involved in their duties. But they acted to protect our Houses. You have done the opposite by abandoning your mission for one soldier."

"But how do we know if these amulets even pose a danger to Rapture's End? We don't know if these gems are worth risking any of our people's lives or even those of Surface Dwellers."

"How dare you, an Archigen barely into your first season, question orders coming from our accumulated wisdom as your Elders?" thundered Camulus.

"I don't question your authority or wisdom. I'm trying to better understand my mission. In a dream, my mother spoke to me about fulfillment of a prophecy. Is that part of my mission?"

Indignation rippled throughout Quartz Hall.

"The Margrave is a master of deceit, using his powerful intuitive abilities to confuse you. Your mother sleeps in eternal peace, in Musterion. Didn't it occur to you that the Margrave is trying to distract you from your mission? Misleading you with false visions of your mother and lethal threats to your friends?"

Had she been foolish to return to Rapture's End? Maybe the Margrave was trying to dupe her, twisting her thoughts with phony visions and fake claims of an unfinished prophecy. Aquan glanced toward Mopsus, who continued to stare straight ahead. He must be angry at her for using up his mirror and elixirs to help Raynord, rather than accomplish her mission. Aquan stood in silence, crest-fallen over her public disgrace before her Elders.

"The Council has determined that completion of your mission is essential and must be done by our next full moon. That's all you need to know."

"I apologize to you Elder Camulus and members of this Elder Council." Aquan quickly spit out her apology. She didn't really want their forgiveness, but couldn't stand to be trapped there for another humiliating moment. "I must've fallen victim to the Margrave's deceptions. It won't happen again."

"Your apology is accepted. Now you're to immediately return to complete your mission. You may not return until you've recovered that lost amulet or any others that exist, and determined their value to the Margrave."

Aquan left Quartz Hall dejected. She shouldn't have listened to Cutter or ever thought of challenging the Elder Council's orders. The Margrave must be laughing himself silly over her blundering. As she swam away from Rapture's End, she heard a familiar high-pitched whistle and saw Thalassa racing toward her. Embracing, she saw her friend's eyes were red and swollen from tears for her seriously injured brother.

"Are you leaving so soon?"

"Yes, the Council has decreed it."

"You don't look very happy. Not like you usually do when you're heading out for a mission. What's wrong?"

"I got into lots of trouble for returning without finishing my mission. Pretty embarrassing."

"Bunch of old cranks. Jealous of you, I bet."

"Even Mopsus isn't speaking to me."

"That doesn't sound like Mopsus," said Thalassa. "Chalk it up to mood swings."

"Thalassa," sighed Aquan. "I know you're trying to cheer me up, but it's not really working."

"You saved Raynord's life with those medicines. He might've died if you hadn't insured his safe return. His wounds are very bad, but slowly improving. I'm glad you disobeyed their dumb orders." A trembling smile crossed her lips.

"If it wasn't for Raynord, I'd be fish food for a deadly Sea..." Aquan stopped midsentence, knowing that she shouldn't disclose any more details of her Council mission to anyone, including to her best friend.

"It's okay. I understand. But hurry up and finish this thing. And then return to us." Thalassa squeezed Aquan's hand tightly.

Aquan tried to smile, but simply nodded. She changed into a muscular Mako shark, in part for its tremendous speed, but mostly because it came quickly to mind. She couldn't bear to be herself for a moment longer.

Chapter 13

Calusa was gone, no longer anchored near Shore Temple. Her primary essence had Mopsus's mirror and backpack, so she needed to reunite with it. Aquan stood on the beach and concentrated. In a few minutes, winds howled and she breathed in her other essence and learned of Cutter's recovery. He had departed to a boat mooring adjacent to a nearby marine college. Relieved, she swam through partially-sunken ruins and squirmed back into a fracture in that Ganges River relief. Floating along its narrow passageways, she more closely examined these Hindu reliefs. One showed a thriving port city with seven splendid temples on its shoreline, another presented a long procession of religious pilgrims bowing before majestic figures on thrones with seven temples on the horizon. A third, more detailed panel displayed a Hindu God, Vishnu, half-man and half-boar, cradling a young woman in his arms, heroically rescuing her from a demon conjuring up a cataclysmic flood to submerge her. She remembered seeing a larger version of this relief when she strolled among Shore temple's ruins awaiting Stevenson's press conference. Aquan tried to think what might link this site and its history to her amber from Tallinn.

Diving back into the surf, she hurried toward Mahabalipuram's marine college. Near its school, she picked up a discordant chorus of prattling barnacles and a fishing rod clicking as it trawled for its catch at dusk. She poked her head above the surface and noticed *Calusa* tied up at an adjacent slip. Peering up, she observed Cutter sitting on his diving platform with a fishing pole, chomping on a cigar. His wounds, no longer bandaged, appeared to be healed. He flirted with two young coeds, regaling them with his Indonesian pirate story. Aquan grabbed hold of his line and gave it a solid tug. Cutter almost fell off his chair.

"Got a big one," he said.

Gypsy barked and jumped around. Giving his line an even stiffer pull, Cutter clambered to his feet and rapidly retracted his line. She yanked it several more times giving him a good fight as these young women cheered him on. Then with one sharp jerk, Aquan pulled him right off his boat into the water. The two young students doubled over in laughter, pointing at Cutter as he splashed around. He cursed as he hauled himself back on to his boat, his clothes and thick cigar soaked. Giggling, they scurried away to their evening classes.

"Are you okay, sir?" Aquan asked.

She stood on the dock as Rajneet.

"Yeah, I'm fine," replied Cutter sheepishly.

Not nearly as mortifying as her rebuke in Quartz Hall, but a good start thought Aquan. She strode toward the school's library hoping to access its computers. That strange little man loitered near its entrance and continued to watch Cutter from behind a carved column.

*****

Rajneet popped in her ear buds and listened to Telugu cinema music as she spent four hours checking out obscure references online and combing through stacks of maritime history books in a library carrel. Delving into Indian and Estonian sea lore, she hunted for any link connection between Tallinn and Mahabalipuram. The only truly fascinating information she found dealt with a tale of ancient sea gods envious of Mahabalipuram's splendor and arrogance conjuring up a tsunami to carry this grand port and six of its temples out to sea. She discovered articles on recent archeological efforts that recovered actual remnants of submerged temples to support this myth. Like Mopsus told her, myths are sometimes rooted in some genuine grain of truth.

Aquan felt a twinge of pain as she thought of him. Was he still angry with her? She hoped not. As she searched the Web, Tallinn claimed no folk tales of submerged temples or angry gods. Unlike Mahabalipuram, that city never witnessed any giant squid beachings or sea quakes either. Besides their histories as flourishing port cities, no other connections, real or mythical, materialized.

"Why does he want you?" She stared at her amulet, hoping for a simple Eight Ball response. But no luck.

"Library closes in ten minutes," a young man announced over a crackling intercom.

A school custodian dumped trash bins while another dusted a group of glass display cases near her. As she reached to turn off the computer, that inscription from the Estonian exhibit case popped into her head. She typed in one last query, "Vineta", and ran her eyes over dozens of hits. A contemporary Latvian painter. A group of print fonts for downloading. Sheet music for a trombone solo.

"Library closes in five minutes." The librarian repeated his warning.

Nothing promising until she stumbled upon search results for a Norwegian myth about resentful, blood-thirsty Norse gods who drown their rivals' disciples with tidal deluges and spare their followers on a mythical island called Vineta. She quickly typed in "Vineta myth" and a cluster of brief academic entries appeared about this archaic legend. A skinny, dark-haired student reached over and turned off her computer. Aquan pulled out her ear buds.

"I needed that," said Aquan.

"It will still be there in the morning," he replied, in a dour tone. "The Library is closed."

The student dutifully escorted Aquan and a few other stragglers out into the school's main lobby. She ducked into a ladies room, and found two young women chatting inside. One student, fixing her hair and make-up in the mirror, carried on an endless monologue about her boring professors. Her friend barely looked up from her volley of text messages over her cell phone. Aquan stepped into an end stall.

When they left, she hummed a Telugu tune as she shook and turned into a mosquito. She buzzed into a bathroom vent and flew out a library duct. Two custodians completed their cleaning tasks while several library staff reshelved books. Excited about her Vineta discovery, she hated to wait for them to finish so she continued through this duct system seeking out other computers. Jenn's voice echoed through an air vent and Aquan followed it into a college research lab. Jenn and Emerson spoke excitedly while Cutter peered into a microscope.

"There are traces of this type of bacteria, L11, in both our water samples and cultures from these stranded squids."

"Yeah, but are these levels high enough to disrupt their natural vibration sensors or make them sick enough to beach themselves?" asked Cutter.

"Not enough data to conclude that yet," replied Jenn.

"And did you find any of this L11 bacteria in those Tassie squids?"

"Not sure. We did find microbial anomalies that need more sophisticated analysis," said Emerson. "We don't have sufficient testing equipment here or on *Calusa.*"

"And even if we did, we don't have enough funding to do those additional tests right now. I'm projecting enough money to cover another week of sample collection and culture analysis. Then just enough left over to get us all back home," added Jenn.

"So what's your plan?" asked Cutter.

"I've contacted the Institute for emergency supplemental funding and reached out to some of our previous donors. We'll have to wait and see what happens."

"I'm getting a bad feeling about how I fit into all of this."

"This college will let us stay docked here without cost for another week or two, provided that we share our data and analysis with them, along with giving them some mention in our final report."

"And?" Cutter folded his arms and arched his left eyebrow.

"If you can stop billing our grant source for at least a couple of weeks, we can stretch our dollars until more funds come in. That would be a huge help."

"How about fuel costs, food, lodging? Where's that going to come from?"

"I'm hoping you might've set some money aside for a rainy day," said Jenn.

"You mean like actual savings?"

"Yeah. Like from your dive operations," said Emerson.

"Hey buddy. Do you know how to make a million dollars with a dive shop? You start with two million," said Cutter, in an agitated tone.

"What about other sources?" continued Emerson.

"Like what?" asked Cutter. He poked Emerson in the chest with his index finger.

"Well from what I hear you've got some interesting backers of your own."

"Rick, cut it out," warned Jenn.

"Oh yeah. What kind of backers?"

"Some people who don't like drawing attention to themselves. That prefer to pay you under the table. I mean, how else does a beach bum like you afford that boat?"

"I oughtta kick your ass, you little shit."

Cutter grabbed Emerson's shirt collar. They scuffled and a beaker and some glass tubes crashed to the floor. Emerson's eyeglasses fell off his face.

"Stop, stop," yelled Jenn as she tried to break them up. "This fighting won't solve anything."

Suddenly a college security guard stepped into their temporary lab.

"Is everything alright here, Dr. Ortiz?" he asked.

His hand rested on his nightstick. Jenn glared at Cutter and Emerson who dropped their hands by their sides.

"Thank you. It's okay. Just some heated debate."

He glared at Cutter and Emerson. "Gentlemen, let's be sure you keep it to a war of words." Nodding, he slowly exited their lab.

"Nice going. Let's try not to get ourselves kicked out of here," said Jenn.

She handed Emerson his glasses and motioned for him to leave.

"I'm sorry about that, Cutter. He didn't mean it," said Jenn, after Emerson's departure.

"Of course, he did."

"He's just repeating town gossip. A small dive operation and a pricey boat will get tongues wagging."

"I hope you don't believe any of it."

"Not a word." She gently patted his shoulder. "But if you can help us out in anyway, I'd really appreciate it. Even if you can help collect more samples while Rick and I keep evaluating these cultures. It might help move things along more quickly."

"I'll do what I can, for as long as I can. But I'm doing it for you, Jenn. Not him or the Institute."

She smiled broadly. "Thanks, Cutter. Thanks." She gave him a quick peck on his cheek.

"Just keep that asshole out of my way."

Always having to get in the last word, thought Aquan.

"No problem. Now I want to get your opinion on a couple more slides."

As Jenn continued to review samples with Cutter, Aquan flitted away. She buzzed into several more classrooms, but no computers. Returning to the Library, its lights were off so she zipped back to her computer carrel.

Reverting to Rajneet, she flicked on a computer and returned to her earlier search. Fabled Vineta, like Mahabalipuram, were both prosperous port cities, similarly wiped out for their arrogant misdeeds. According to the folk tale, Vinetan people ignored repeated warnings, feeling well protected behind twelve colossal fortress gates and unmatched military forces. One morning, a deluge swept them out to sea. Ringing bells from a town hall tower echoed in a dark abyss in the Baltic Sea, the town's sunken bell tower the only vestige of its once-thriving city. Perhaps each amulet was hidden in another submerged city, another daughter of Atlantis.

When Rajneet typed in Atlantis, there were millions of hits and hundreds of places claiming to be Atlantis. How would she ever whittle down that list, she wondered? She cleared her search box and sat for a moment looking blankly at its screen. Grasping her amulet, she looked once more into its gemstones to see if her visions changed. *Calusa* still remained her clearest image. She entered *Calusa* into her searches, but found only Cutter's web site for dive trips and salvage jobs.

Rajneet quivered and turned into a mosquito, escaping outdoors through a vent. Exhausted, she found a quiet stretch of beach and plunged into a gentle surf. As cool saltwater rushed through her gills, Aquan swam beneath a deep, rocky shelf in calm bay waters. As waves lapped against her hidden ledge, she gazed at her golden coral bracelet. Aquan slipped into a much-needed meditative trance to refresh her energies after so many rapid transformations.

In her daydreaming state, she envisioned *Calusa* once more. Gypsy yelping on its deck under a full moon as it floated aimlessly in stormy seas. A caustic gasoline smell stung her nose, moments before a deafening explosion. She swallowed bitter tears as flames engulfed Cutter's vessel.

Shaken by her vision, she squirmed out, thinking she'd fallen into her dreams for only a moment. Yet it must've been longer based as that evening's waning crescent moon moved its position in a starry sky. Hungry, she glided deeper to join a shiver of Tiger sharks on their nocturnal hunt. Over the past decade the popularity of sushi and sashimi made human food slightly more palatable. But few human foods beat hunting and devouring fresh raw prey. After feasting on Hogfish and tuna, she surveyed twinkling constellations and contemplated a galaxy of sunken cities. After counting two shooting stars, she glimpsed a Pteron streaking overhead. It startled her out of her languid state. That Sea Monk must still be nearby and she needed to find him now.

Chapter 14

Aquan tracked that pesky Pteron's flight and heard its splash as it plunged into deeper waters. A garden of spotted sea snakes, their bodies swaying, retreated into their sandy burrows as that creature zipped past them. It disappeared into a rusty skeleton of a sunken steel ship, *Delorosa*, its masts and hull burnt charcoal black from a fire. Two Manta rays glided over its rotting deck with splotches of brown, green, and maroon sea sponges. Small schools of pale pink Bombay Duck and silvery Ribbon fish darted in and out of its decaying portholes.

Circling this wreck, Aquan looked for a safe entry point. Clanking sounds of metal striking metal were punctuated with pained neighing from a distressed sea creature. She turned into a Ribbon fish and swam down to the wreck's bottom. That Sea Monk, with his scarred forehead, barked orders to three Hydromorphs struggling to restrain a magnificent snow-white Hippocampus. Its panicked gray eyes peered out from under its thick ivory mane. A heavy metal shackle was clamped to this sea stallion's pointed serpentine tail while heavy seaweed ropes were twisted around each of its hoofed forequarters. Aquan had only read about these stunning aquatic horses in her studies with Mopsus, but had never seen one. Their incredible speed and high strung dispositions made it tough to observe them. She wanted to tear its captors apart for mistreating this glorious creature.

"Be careful, you clumsy fools. We don't want to damage our gift for our Master."

Trying to quiet this animal, the Sea Monk offered it two purple sea apples. But this agitated Hippocampus continued to buck and whinny. He blew his Bosun's whistle in four shrill blasts, a different code than his earlier trill to call off those Gorgons. She still did not understand why he whistled their retreat during her blackout. But this time, a Moon jellyfish, with its gossamer bell-shaped body, pulsated horizontally through the water and unfurled its tentacles. Brushing its piercing tentacles across the Hippocampus, this translucent jellyfish repeatedly stung this magnificent steed as it fought against its restraints. The captive animal fell unconscious from these paralyzing punctures.

"Well done, well done, my angel."

The Sea Monk gently petted his pet jellyfish's bubble top. He released several mollusks from his hands. The jellyfish throbbed like a magenta lava lamp as it hungrily pulled in its delightful treats with its long tentacles.

"Bring our Master's chest," he called out.

Two Hydromorphs dragged out a weathered metal box, "Isthmia" emblazoned on its side. A Moray eel was wrapped tightly around it, baring its spiky teeth. It recoiled and loosened its grip in response to the Sea Monk's shrieking Bosun's whistle. He flung open this battered box and lifted out an intricately-carved golden bridle with sapphires and rubies on its cheek pieces. An amber amulet, identical to Aquan's gemstone, adorned a triangular gold plate in its brow band. She spontaneously touched her amulet to make certain it still hung from her neck. He placed this bridle over the Hippocampus's head and tightened its chin strap.

"Perfect, perfect," he howled with glee.

He removed it and placed it carefully into its Isthmia chest and his sentinel eel once more clenched it tightly. The sea floor shook with massive thuds. Aquan wriggled topside and spied twenty Hydromorphs escorting two yoked Behemoths, towards *Delorosa*. These enormous sea oxen took colossal strides with their elephant forequarters and hoofed hind legs. They snorted bubbles out of their scaly snouts. One Behemoth bore a large cage carved out of coral while its twin carried a Giant Clam in a canopied bronze litter. Both mammoths bowed down before the Sea Monk.

A dazed Hippocampus was unshackled and lifted into a coral cage by six Hydromorphs.

"Cover that cage with sailcloth," commanded the Sea Monk. "We want to hide our prize from prying eyes."

His claw tickled this Giant Clam while trilling his whistle. Slowly opening its mouth, five more Hydromorphs struggled to put his sea chest into this huge crustacean's mouth. It clamped down its shell over this box and its encircling eel. The Sea Monk then led a procession of twenty-five Hydromorph troops keeping watch. Aquan knew she couldn't take on a group this large, but must find a way to retrieve that amulet and free that Hippocampus.

*****

Swimming back to *Calusa*, Gypsy didn't bark as Aquan boarded Cutter's ship as Kirra. He trailed her as she crossed *Calusa*'s deck and slid down a banister to its main cabin. She crept around looking for her backpack, but couldn't find it. She headed below to Cutter's quarters and heard him snoring in his bunk. Slowly turned his door latch, Cutter's door creaked open. But she couldn't see her backpack in his darkened quarters, so she turned on a light. Shirtless, Cutter moaned and turned, tangled up in his bed sheets. Aquan noticed her backpack attached with a cable lock to his bed frame. She quickly unzipped it and pulled out two vials. Then she remembered Mopsus' warning that it wouldn't work on crustaceans, like that Giant Clam, so she put one back.

Keeping a safe distance, she journeyed back to *Delorosa*'s wreck and easily picked up their trail from swirling dust clouds from those plodding Behemoths. A torrent of sea creatures scrambled past her fleeing from these oxen's trampling path. With each mammoth stride, a thick fog of sand rose up and made it hard for Aquan to see ahead. As their thunderous jolts intensified, Aquan knew she grew closer to their convoy. She sucked in a minerals vial without swallowing it and changed into a black Gulper eel. She needed its incredibly large pouch-like jaw as well as its strong vision in murky depths.

Spying their procession, she slithered past several rear Hydromorph guards. This dusty silt storm obscured their vision as Aquan snuck into their coral cage for their paralyzed Hippocampus. Firmly winding her black whip tail around a cage bar, she spit out her green sand transforming their captive horse into a tiny Hermit crab. She unhinged her jaw and secreted it away in her mouth. Aquan darted from this caravan without any Exoris ever realizing their prize was stolen.

Returning to *Calusa*, Aquan hurried to Jenn's lab and spit the crab into a glass specimen jar. Pouring one of Jenn's sea water samples over it, its tiny antennae and four legs moved sluggishly. Puncturing holes in a plastic cap, she screwed it back on the jar. Aquan wanted to quickly find a tranquil hiding place for this creature where it could safely revert to its Hippocampus form.

"What the hell are you doing here?" Emerson's unexpected presence startled Aquan as he switched on a main deck light, a baseball bat in his hand. "Cutter, we've got a visitor."

Aquan slowly turned around, hiding her glass beaker behind her back. A bleary-eyed Cutter crawled on to *Calusa*'s main deck.

"Put that down, hero." Cutter grabbed his bat away from Emerson.

"What's happening?" Jenn yawned as she joined them in her lab space.

"Your research assistant almost smacked our new benefactor."

"Benefactor?" Jenn and Emerson asked in unison.

"Appears Kirra comes from a pretty wealthy family. Big in commercial seafood for centuries," Cutter said, with a wry smile. "They've been heartsick over her going missing from their family's processing vessel. When they saw her face on TV, they flew right down to Hobart. Paid for our boat repairs. And wanted to give you a reward for saving her, Jenn. She wanted to thank you and give you their donation in person. Isn't that right, Kirra?"

Aquan could barely believe how easily lies rolled off Cutter's tongue.

"Yes, it is. Never had a chance to thank you properly back in Hobart. I'm so grateful for your rescue and reuniting me with my family."

"Fifty-thousand should help keep things going for a while." Cutter grinned, enjoying every minute of Aquan's discomfort.

"That's right."

Aquan wished she could change into an electric eel and give Cutter a few blistering shocks.

"Thanks for being so generous. We could really use it. We're making some promising findings." Jenn excitedly shook Aquan's hand. "Perhaps I can tell you all about it at breakfast tomorrow morning."

"Sounds like a plan." Aquan carefully extricated her hand from Jenn's enthusiastic grasp.

"Okay, folks let's get some shut eye. It's been a long day."

"Now Cutter, before you head back to your bunk, I forgot my backpack this afternoon before I went touring. Where did you stow it?"

"Near my pilot chair. I'll show you," he said with a wink.

Jenn and Emerson trudged back to their quarters. When they reached his wheelhouse, Aquan punched Cutter's shoulder.

"What was that all about? A nice thanks for saving your sorry life."

"Hey, those Gorgi things practically killed me. Damaged my boat and Jenn's lab, too. Although you can barely tell I suffered a scratch. Whatever you put on me worked great." He rolled up his shirt sleeve, only a few minor scratches now visible. "They wouldn't have attacked my ship if you weren't on it. So it's a fair trade-off."

"And how am I supposed to come up with that donation?"

"Easy. If you are what you say you are, it'll be pocket change out of gazillions in sunken treasure collecting dust on the ocean floor. Or you might think about pawning that amber. Sure you'll get plenty for it."

"It's not for sale. What about yours?"

Aquan needed to know his connection to this gemstone. Cutter paused for a moment. No snappy retort, thought Aquan.

"Cat got your tongue?"

"How would I get my hands on a fancy piece of jewelry like that? I'm just a humble dive guy."

"Humble. This boat is damn expensive to own and operate, Mr. Dive Guy. Maybe yours fetched a good price at auction. Or in some black market deal or drug-run up to Florida?"

Cutter folded his arms and said nothing. Aquan sighed and pulled out her beaker from behind her back.

"Are there any large saltwater tanks at the marine college?"

"We got saltwater all around us."

"The open ocean isn't safe for it."

"For a little hermit crab?"

Now it was Aquan's turn to stay mum.

"A bit of aquatelligence," he said leaning in to her. "Why not leave your little pal on board so I can prove my theory to Jenn and Emerson?"

"No, they can't know anything about this. You'll be putting them in terrible danger. That Sea Monk will torture them, even kill them, to find out where it is," said Aquan. Besides, Jenn and Emerson remained on her list of possible Exori contacts. "We need a quiet, protected place, in sea water, so it can change back safely."

"Back into what?"

"I can't go into it with you now. We don't have a lot of time to act or it'll die."

"The school labs have plenty of aquarium tanks. Some as big as six by six feet."

"Not big enough, Cutter."

"For that little crab?"

"Trust me, I need something larger."

"I saw three outdoor pens for rescued sea life. On its north side."

"Do you know what's in them?"

Cutter scratched his head.

"If I remember correctly, one's got several injured dolphins."

"Too territorial and aggressive. Forget that one."

"I think some sick sea turtles are in a second one."

Aquan shook her head. "No, they might eat my little crab before it transforms. What's in their third one?"

"I don't know." Cutter shrugged. "We could reach it by boat tender. But going straight through their labs we'll reach it faster. I can get you in there with Jenn's access card."

"How are you going to get it from her?"

"Don't worry. She leaves it on a hook near her lab table. I'll lift it. You just worry about looking like her to get us past security."

Chapter 15

A nighttime security guard glanced up as Aquan, cloaked as Jenn, ran her access card through an electronic card reader. She set down her glass container on a lobby security desk and showed him her temporary identification card.

"Your assistant will have to sign-in our log." He pointed to Cutter. As Cutter signed in, the guard playfully tapped the covered flask on the counter. "What have you got there, Dr. Ortiz?"

"A little hermit crab with a lethal virus," she replied.

The guard quickly withdrew his hand from her beaker.

"Best to keep your fellow guards clear of my lab for a couple of hours, just to be safe."

He nervously nodded his approval.

As they walked away from security, Cutter whispered, "Don't take this the wrong way, but you got a mean streak. I'm beginning to think that's one of your more endearing qualities."

Aquan wasn't sure whether she should feel complimented or insulted as she followed Cutter to Jenn's temporary lab. They hurried through a maze of corridors, a rank mix of formaldehyde and fish odor wafted in the air. She felt nauseous rushing past labs filled with dead sea creatures suspended as specimens in tanks and glass containers. It made her dizzy for a moment and she stopped to catch her breath.

"Are you okay?"

"This place...." Her voice trailed off.

"We're almost there."

Cutter took hold of her elbow. He pushed past a set of glass doors to three open water pens. Low emergency lights dotted their walkway. In one darkened pen, an ailing dolphin squeaked and sidled up to their boardwalk waiting for a treat.

"Sorry fella." Cutter led her to a third pen on the far end.

"Hang on to this and let me check it out to make sure it's empty."

Aquan handed Cutter her glass jar and dove in, quavering and reverting to her natural shape. She swam around this pen's boundaries, her sonar searching for any movement in this enclosure. A wall of galvanized steel mesh facing the sea would keep out any ferocious predators from attacking rescued creatures. It was deep enough for the Hippocampus, too. All appeared still in this outdoor tank. But Aquan wondered how she would free it from this enclosure.

"We've got a problem," she said, surfacing.

"You're blue." His eyes popped wide at his first sight of her in Triton form.

"Let's talk color later. Right now, we've got a galvanized steel mesh cage attached to concrete footers. If I tear it out, it's going to attract too much attention. Especially if it takes out those other two pens, too."

"Can this thing jump or fly over that gate?"

"Nothing like that."

"What about some of that magic dust you used in Hobart? Change it into something else."

"I've already done that. A second transformation might kill it. It's been through a lot of distress already. It needs time to recover before it can be released into the open ocean."

"How long does it need?"

"More time than we probably have. That Sea Monk is bound to come looking for it once he realizes it's gone. He'll sniff out its musky scent. I gotta get it to deep water and as far away from here as I can."

"I've got my dive gear and an underwater torch from my salvage jobs. Should be able to score that mesh frame. Then you can change into something really scary and pull it away." He knelt down and handed down her beaker. "It'll take me about fifteen minutes to get my gear together and buzz over."

"Hurry, Cutter," she said, diving underwater.

She unscrewed its cover and watched the crab gently float out. This minute creature drifted in the pen for about ten minutes. Then it began to convulse and change color from red to orange, then pink and finally white. Suddenly, water churned and whooshed around her as the Hippocampus reemerged, descending lifelessly to the tank's sandy bottom. Aquan swam to its side and caressed its mane, anxiously waiting for it to start breathing once more. She put her mouth to its drooping ear and softly hummed a comforting ancient song. After several minutes, its nostrils twitched and it drew in shallow breaths. Its pointed fish tail flailed weakly, its eyelids fluttered open. Aquan pulled out clumps of sea grass clinging to the tank floor and slowly fed them to the recovering sea stallion.

As it munched on grasses, a buzzing sound of Cutter's tender motor alerted her to his approach. Three or four flashes of light bounced across the water's surface. Not a good time for lightning, Aquan worried. Cutter would be crazy to dive in and cozy up to a hunk of steel. But then she heard a splash and saw bubbles swirling from Cutter's tank. He wore a thick diving helmet with a dark welding screen attached to it. As he swam toward the steel mesh barrier, he pulled two cylinders, one acetylene and another oxygen with a cutting torch strapped to its side. Approaching this metal barrier, Aquan noticed Cutter held a diver's slate in his hands.

He wrote "Stand back, Shield eyes."

She gave him an okay sign and returned to the trembling Hippocampus's side. Cutter flipped down his helmet's dark visor. Aquan shielded the skittish stallion's eyes from bright white torch flashes as Cutter methodically scored the tank's mesh for about a half-hour. She continued to feed and sing as it began to slowly regain its strength. As she waited, thoughts tumbled through her mind about the meaning of these ambers, one taken from a display case in a Baltic marketplace, another hidden in a Hindu temple relief. What was that Sea Monk's fascination with his jeweled bridle? Why was Isthmia engraved on that sea chest? It made no sense for the Margrave to provoke a confrontation or massacre her family over a few ornaments. Aquan wished she could talk to Mopsus and get his advice, if he wasn't still too angry to speak with her.

As Cutter's torch went dark, she returned to the gate and Cutter held up a new message scrawled on his slate, "All done, what next?"

"Go, Cutter. For your own safety, take your tender and go back to *Calusa* so I can tear this out. Okay?"

He gave her an okay sign and she remained thankful that underwater he couldn't talk back. She waited to hear his tender buzz away before turning into a Tursus, a marine monster with a human torso and a walrus's head and hindquarters. She dug in her immense hindquarters and her huge human hands grabbed and shook the iron barrier. After this jolt, her massive walrus tail would smack against this rigid cage. She tried three times as lightning flashes illuminated the tank. On a fourth attempt, she battered this cage wall away from its frame and then leaned it against an adjacent rocky wall. The Hippocampus whinnied and bucked with fear as one of Aquan's huge hands scooped it up. Its sharp fish tail jabbed at her, but Aquan held fast until she reached the Indian Ocean's deep water. Releasing this magnificent horse, it neighed and then streaked away.

Aquan shuddered as her natural form reemerged. She watched the frightened Hippocampus disappear into a dark abyss of churning ocean flows. Exhausted from her rescue of this creatures and her rapid transformations, she drifted off into her dream state to refresh herself for an hour or so under a waning crescent moon.

*****

As sea currents pulled her back to Mahabalipuram, she sensed someone calling her name, first gently, then with increasing urgency. She tried to shake off her stupor and swim toward that voice, but she was too tired. Not until she floated close to shore did she feel that something was wrong. She followed jangling sounds from *Calusa*'s anchor chain and surfaced at its rear diving platform. As Kirra, she climbed on to Cutter's boat as it bounced gently in harbor waves. Cutter's wetsuit was slunk over a boat rail, his salvage gear in a mound on deck.

Going below deck, it all seemed quiet, too quiet. No barking Gypsy. No snoring Cutter. She sniffed for any lingering smells of a Sea Monk or Hydromorphs, but nothing. She found Jenn's lab remained neatly organized, her access card hanging from its hook once more. In Cutter's wheelhouse, his GPS glowed with a soft white hue marking his ship's location. She yanked her spear gun and some tranquilizing darts out of her backpack and crept below deck to their sleeping quarters. Slowly cracking open each door, their bunks appeared slept in with sheets rumpled from an evening's rest. Yet no one was aboard *Calusa*.

She headed above deck and stood on its bow, scanning the waters around her. Cutter's tender borrowed from the marine college was no longer lashed to his catamaran. Perhaps Cutter had evacuated them out of concern about the Sea Monk's potential return for his missing prize. She waited a half-hour and then heard a humming tender's motor. Around a rocky tip, Cutter sat in his motorboat alone as he pulled alongside *Calusa*.

"Where is everyone?" he asked, tossing her a boat line.

"I was going to ask you the same question."

She tied down his tender and Cutter jumped on to his dive platform.

"I got back from the pens and they were gone. Gypsy, too. So I went puttering around the cove trying to find them. Maybe that Sea Monk got back here quicker than you thought."

"I doubt it. They leave a pretty heavy stench behind. From what I can tell, it looks like they went willingly."

"At 3:00 a.m.? You might not put up a fight with a gun to your head."

"Or maybe someone looking for you."

"Me?"

Aquan pulled a print out from their pirate ambush out of her back pocket. "Those Indonesian pirates were gunning for you."

"No way." Cutter tore it from her hands. He scanned this sheet and shook his head. "Where did you get this?"

"From that pirate's speed boat. It was tacked to their dash. That assault was no accident. And he called you 'Cubano'."

"I don't know these guys. I swear. I have no idea why they're after me or *Calusa*. I'm not even Cuban."

Aquan sensed that he spoke the truth, so it was time to pry further.

"And I suppose, you have no idea about that chubby black man who's been trailing you."

"What guy?" The curl in the right corner of Cutter's lip gave him away.

"You know who I mean. You even ducked behind a dumpster to avoid him in Hobart."

Cutter folded his arms and then plunked down on one of his deck chairs. "His name is Ernest Tuttleberry. That jerk just won't leave me alone."

"Why is he following you?"

"He's a pain in the ass investigator."

"Investigating what?"

"Insurance fraud."

"Is that how you keep this thing afloat?" Aquan pointed to Cutter's galley and main cabin.

"That's what he thinks. But he's got it all wrong. Typical insurance guy. Happy to have you pay premiums, not so happy when they have to pay your claims especially when there's a big pay out. But it was all legit."

Aquan eyed him suspiciously. "Why should I believe that?"

"Because you oughtta trust me. I could've blown your cover weeks ago."

"True enough."

"Don't knock yourself out with gratitude." Cutter shook his head at her.

"So this guy wouldn't harm anybody."

"Least of all Jenn or even that idiot Emerson."

"Then where are they?"

"If it's not one of your freaks. And it definitely ain't Ernest. Then I've got no clue where they are."

They sat quietly as *Calusa* rocked languorously over bay waves. Suddenly, Gypsy's bark pierced the early morning stillness. They both jumped up and Cutter pointed his flashlight toward a nearby beach. His light caught his dog yelping and splashing in a gentle surf. They jumped into Cutter's tender and roared toward shore.

Chapter 16

Gypsy led them into a thicket of scrub pine fringing beach dunes and then up and down a series of small sand dunes. At one dune's crest, Aquan spotted glowing lanterns surrounding an encampment in a distant clearing. Six silhouetted guards armed with machine guns patrolled two large white tents.

"Kill that flashlight." Aquan yanked Cutter down into a small vale between dunes.

"What are you doing? Gypsy's getting away from us."

"I know where she's going."

"Where?"

"A camp."

"I didn't see anything."

"My radar and eyesight are far superior to humans. It's about mile ahead, north."

"What are we waiting for? Let's go." Cutter jumped up, ready to storm up another dune.

Aquan grabbed his arm. "Hold on. It's surrounded by armed guards."

"Can we take them with some of your darts and my pistol?" He patted his gun hanging from his hip.

"There are six of them, heavily armed so I doubt it. There might be more patrolling.

Besides we don't want to risk any harm to Jenn and Rick."

"Let's kill two birds with one stone. You shape-shift to save Jenn and Emerson and prove I'm not nuts."

"I don't want to kill anything if I don't have to." Aquan pondered their predicament. "I've got an idea." She pulled out Mopsus's dive watch. "Take this."

Cutter took hold of it. "How's this going to help us? Looks pretty beat up."

"Your friends may be in danger, so no time for explanations," said Aquan. "For once just go with it and don't ask any questions. I'll explain it later." She had no intention of explaining anything about this device to him. "I'm going to turn into a peregrine falcon and do a quick fly over to see what's happening. I need you to press this button when you first hear me cry out like this." Aquan let loose a falcon's piercing shriek.

"That's amazing." Cutter stared in disbelief.

Setting its timer for one minute and forty-five seconds, Aquan assumed that would give her enough time to survey the camp. "After I check it out, I'll fly back and let you know what I saw. Got it?"

"Okay." He unexpectedly touched her forearm. "Be careful. Falcon might be on today's breakfast menu."

Against her better judgment, she smiled at his concern for her safety and then burst into falcon form and whooshed away. Bay winds rippled through her feathers as she soared high in an early morning sky. She spied four more guards patrolling dunes and a huge yacht named *Gaia* in gold lettering, anchored about a half-mile offshore. As she neared their camp, Aquan made out a helicopter sitting about five hundred yards east from their tents with two more beefy guards watching over it. Screeching for her first time, a moment later everyone around her froze.

Swooping down, she touched down returning to her human form. She quickly entered one tent with two satellite dishes propped up on each side of it. Electronic gear filled this tent, including computers, radio equipment and satellite phones. Four staff inside wore camouflaged outfits and identification tags dangled from each of their necks. Their names were printed above a blue tripod logo for "Apollo International Ventures." She dumped out bullets from their pistols, cradled in each of their shoulder holsters, and kicked sand over them.

She strode to a second larger tent and removed cartridges from an entry guard's weapon gripped in his hands. Stepping inside, Aquan observed Jenn and Emerson seated on canvas director's chairs. Jenn held a tea cup to her lips. They sat before an elderly female with olive skin and a large beak nose and a dark mole on her sagging chin. Her graying brunette hair was teased up high on her head. With a theatrical flair, she wore heavy blue eye shadow, rosy cheek blush and ruby lipstick. Her orange and blue floral kaftan flowed over the sides of an ornate chair inlaid with teak and rosewood. A silver tea service brewing green tea simmered on a low table with two more tea cups and saucers and one large china plate of baklava and other light pastries. All of their facial expressions appeared calm and relaxed. It puzzled Aquan for their meeting appeared to be cordial, not hostile.

Aquan exited the tent and slipped to its rear wall just seconds before all around her jolted back to life.

"Oh my, I forgot what I was saying." The older woman spoke with a strong Greek accent. "The cruelties of age."

"I believe Countess that you were discussing an upcoming conference." Emerson reached down to pick up a slice of baklava.

"Yes, yes. Our conference sponsor, Mr. Papandreas, has asked me to invite you to join us at his Maritime Symposium Conference in the Canary Islands next month. Great thinkers in marine biology will be presenting papers there."

"We'd be honored," said Jenn.

"Mr. Papandreas has a great interest in your research on microbial bacteria and large mammal and sea creature strandings."

"I thought he was funding Dr. Stevenson's research efforts."

"He is. But prefers to keep a spoon stirring in every pot. For now, he also desires to provide a generous endowment for your projects on your research vessel. *Calusa*, I believe?"

"We're leasing that ship and its captain, Dave Cutter, who was, um, is a very promising marine biologist in his own right," said Jenn.

"You need not be concerned. We know of Dr. Cutter and his bizarre theories. But then my sponsor is a bit eccentric in his own right." Countess Daimonakis snorted and then slurped green tea from her cup. "He appreciates similar peculiarities in others. So long as they do not detract from our mission at hand."

"No need to worry about that, Countess. We have a very focused research plan."

"Good, Dr. Ortiz. Then expect a wire transfer of $500,000

from Papandreas Foundation into your research account tomorrow morning."

Jenn nearly spit out her tea and Emerson gulped his pastry.

"Where should I send my account information?" sputtered Jenn.

"We already have your account information and bank from your Institute. But be sure to send along a weekly report of your research findings as well as detailed descriptions of your travels. Due to ill health, Mr. Papandreas seldom leaves his home but enjoys reading about scientific experiments and exotic locales. Now off with you to your ship before your captain begins to wonder what happened to you. I look forward to seeing you next month at our maritime conference."

In a moment, two guards were escorting Jenn and Emerson over to a helicopter. It roared and kicked up a sandstorm as it whisked them off to *Calusa*. Aquan was about to transform back into a falcon when she heard a satellite phone beeping.

"Yes, they've just left," said Countess Daimonakis. "Of course, our little story went over quite well. A bit of flattery and a pile of research money tends to make academics deaf to rational judgment." She let out a deep, throaty laugh. "Let the Master know that our insider has maintained his cover so we continue to know their every move. If anything, her trust continues to grow in him which helps to insure our success. I'll keep you regularly informed."

Aquan heard Countess Daimonakis click off her phone and order her crew to pack up their tents for a return to *Gaia*. The cold sting of Cutter's treachery made her heart sink. She realized that he must be a Drowner, cozying up to here as the Countess's insider. At that moment, Aquan didn't know if she was angrier at him for being on the Margrave's payroll or herself for letting a Drowner get that close to her and endanger her people and mission. Floating dead bodies of her Triton family flashed before her eyes. What worldly treasures must they have promised him in exchange for his betrayal of her? She shoved aside her feelings and transformed into a falcon, reluctantly flying back to Cutter.

Once more in Kirra form, she grabbed Mopsus's watch out

of his hands and stuffed it back in her backpack. Aquan sauntered off toward their tender.

"What happened?" Cutter trailed her.

She couldn't bring herself to look at or speak to him. Her voice choked with rage as she marched back toward their dinghy. Cutter caught up to her and yanked on Aquan's backpack.

"Hey, slow down."

Aquan wanted to strangle him. Maybe she should have let him die from those Gorgon wounds, should have saved her elixirs and her mirror's magic for someone else, instead of this Drowner. He grabbed her arm and she turned into a hissing boa constrictor, poised to strike him with her razor-sharp teeth. Cutter fell back in surprise and then she changed into a scorpion crawling on his right foot.

"What's going on? Are you having another one of those creature fits again?"

As she rose up to sting him, Aquan knew she needed to take hold of herself. Her people were counting on her. She tried to focus on her dead family members and her Aunt Sofronia in mourning and not on Cutter's deception. *Calusa* remained in her visions so she must not burn her bridges with its captain and crew quite yet. But she needed to seek an expert's help on that bridle.

"No, I'm not having a fit" she yelled in his face, as Kirra again.

"So just another ugly mood swing?"

Aquan turned on her heel and proceeded to stomp back to the shoreline. "It looks like your pals decided to have a nice early morning tea with a potential sponsor without telling us or doing something reasonable, like leaving a note?"

"At 3:00 a.m.?"

"A bit of flattery and a pile of money tends to make academics deaf to rational judgment."

"What do you mean?" Cutter jogged to keep up with her.

She stopped and looked squarely at Cutter, barely able to swallow back her fury and disappointment in him. "Do you know someone named Papandreas?"

"Stavros Papandreas?"

"Yes, that's him."

"He's a real nut job. A reclusive multi-billionaire who owns lots of companies. Dabbles in funding scientific research. Including Stevenson's work on sea quakes."

"Seems he's betting on both sides. Decided to fund your friend Jenn's scientific research, too."

Cutter let out a low whistle. "Finally some good news. That oughtta keep my boat up and running and Gypsy and I fed for a few more months. So what are you so pissed about?"

As they neared the shore, Aquan stopped suddenly and swung around. She practically spit her words at him.

"I don't give a damn about microbes or sea quakes. Or all any of that silly research you do. All you and your experts know about the ocean would fit in a thimble. We've wasted precious resources and energy tonight on a wild goose chase."

"So what? For once nobody got hurt. All's well that ends well."

"I'm done wasting my time with you and your crew. Head back to *Calusa* by yourself. I'm going it alone for a while."

"I can't believe you're bailing like this. I thought you said we were part of your mission."

"I was wrong. You are a useless distraction."

"Me?" asked Cutter, pointing to himself. "I didn't ask to be part of this. You came on our boat. Brought all those freaks of nature gunning for us."

"Well guess what? You can go back to your miserable little life, skipper. I'm washing my hands of all of you." At least for now, she thought.

"What am I gonna tell Jenn and Rick?"

"Why not tell them a lie?" said Aquan. "You're good at that."

She turned back into a peregrine falcon and flew away, leaving a confused Cutter ashore with Gypsy beside him, barking in a dawn mist.

Chapter 17

The Antiquarian waited on a stone bench along Venice's Grand Canal. He adjusted his steel rim glasses and stroked his silver-haired goatee poking out of his red scarf. He pulled out a sketch book and a thin black drawing pencil. With her knapsack strapped to her back, Aquan as Bridget looked like any summer backpacker who crowded Venice's cheap youth hostels. She sat next to him pretending to puzzle over her tourist map.

"Why does the Adriatic flood Piazza San Marco every Spring, Signore?" she asked using a local dialect.

"To remind Venetians of how much they owe the sea." He did not looking up from his pad. "And the sea always collects on her debts." He continued to sketch.

"Hallowed be Eternal Concordia, Antiquarian."

"Hallowed be Eternal Concordia, Emissary. It's been too long. I thought I might have outlived my usefulness for my favorite clients."

"Never. Your family has always been of tremendous service."

The Antiquarian was a trusted descendant of Italy's DiGiacomo family, who for centuries possessed expertise in appraising Archigen treasures and appropriate discretion in disposing of them. Although they earned lucrative commissions from these artifacts, their loyalty flowed from a rescue in 1206 of the sole DiGiacomo heir from a shipwreck off the coast of Madeira. An aging Emissary took pity on a handsome young Venetian clinging to remnants of a ship's mast, its cargo of Italian antiquities bound for England sunken beneath storm-tossed seas. From that day forward, his family remained staunch allies, although they knew only a tiny slice of Archigen history.

"How's business?"

"Slow. But I have a feeling you're going to change that."

She smiled. "You know me too well."

"I'm at your service. Anything in particular you're seeking to put to auction?"

"Nothing right now. But I need your assistance identifying two unique items. One is an elaborate bridle."

"An equestrian bridle?"

"For a very special horse."

"Arabian?"

"No, a rare water horse. Our Greek friends spoke of it in their ancient tales."

He stopped sketching and lightly scrawled "Hippoc" on his pad. Aquan nodded.

"I glimpsed it in a murderer's hands. A gold bridle with sapphires and rubies on its cheek plates. With a unique amber amulet centered on a triangular gold plate in its brow band."

"What does this amulet look like?"

She pulled her amber talisman out of her T-shirt and let it dangle openly. The Antiquarian studied it for several seconds, then quickly took several cell phone photos and jotted some additional notes. When he was done, she secreted it away beneath her T-shirt.

"I may need a week or so to research these items."

"Sooner would be much better. For our need is critical."

"I will do my best."

"Might you know of a master craftsman who can assist me in crafting certain items?"

"Yes, I have someone in mind."

"This person must be very talented and discrete."

"Not to worry, Emissary. Venice is full of tight-lipped artisans."

"Good. Something for your trouble."

Aquan pressed five rare Roman coins into his palm. He glanced at them and his eyes opened wider.

"You are too generous. I'll do my best to expedite my research. Do you stay in your usual place?"

"Yes."

"Then expect to be contacted in my typical manner."

"Grazie, Signore."

For three days, Aquan walked to an amethyst street lamp closest to Rialto Bridge at dawn, but no signal from him. She found herself spending too much time thinking about Cutter and his treachery. She felt so foolish over letting her guard down for a Drowner. Why did she ever allow any feelings for Cutter to ever sprout? Yet trying to forget about him only seemed to generate more thoughts of him.

With each passing day, her heart sank deeper as she saw lovers stroll the Grand Canal's banks or embrace in ornately carved gondolas. She strolled restlessly along crooked alleys and hidden neighborhoods of Venice, staying far away from hordes of summer tourists. Under a new moon's darkness, she sat in a shadowy corner of Piazza San Marco hoping classical ensembles tossing open air musical challenges back and forth across this plaza might ease her mind. Yet as nights rolled on, she numbly tossed euros into their instrument cases, growing deaf to their beautiful melodies. Aquan sipped glasses of Chianti and nibbled on plates of calamari at lively outdoor cafes, but took no pleasure in these treats. Every other evening, she refreshed her transformative powers in the Adriatic, but felt no sense of rejuvenation. She didn't understand her own depleted energies or downcast spirits.

On a fourth morning, she discovered a tattered program of last season's program for *Rigoletto*, opened to Act III, resting at their designated lamp's base. Relieved, Aquan ducked into a narrow alleyway and plunged into a canal, swimming to the Antiquarian's antique shop near Campo San Maurizio. She climbed out at his shop's partially submerged loading dock. Pressing a hidden door buzzer, she observed a blinking red light and heard DiGiacomo's surveillance camera softly whirring. A minute later, a rear entry slid open and then abruptly shut behind her. Once inside, Aquan discovered the Antiquarian sitting behind a teak desk in his cramped backroom office. Dark circles rested under his eyes and his once trim goatee now appeared scruffy. Empty espresso cups, lopsided stacks of dusty books and lengthy computer print outs surrounded him. A tangy odor of slender brown Sigaro Toscanos, stubbed out in a brass ashtray, hung in the air.

"I hope you have good news for me, Signore."

"I have some news, but I'm not sure how good it is."

He invited her to sit down, removing two throw pillows

and a blanket from a red velvet divan where he must have napped.

"I have found nothing about your ambers."

Aquan sighed.

"But I did find numerous references to a jewel-encrusted bridle, both in Greek mythology and ancient art history texts. Most are grounded in Poseidon worship. Greeks believed he harnessed his team of four Hippocampi to pull his magical chariot. His galloping chariot generated roaring waves, daily tides and rumbling earthquakes in the sea."

The Antiquarian peeled back a yellowed page from a thick, leather-bound book and showed her some early Greek paintings. In one painting, Poseidon floods Atlantis as his sea horses tow an ornate chariot.

"According to myth, each horse represents a different direction on a nautical map's compass rose, covering every Earthly hemisphere. Poseidon could create a global deluge at a full moon, but only during rare cycles of extremely high king tides."

"Yet the moon is only full for an instant."

"Right, so Poseidon must be very precise in timing. His global ride starts as this full moon ascends east to west. Once a full moon reaches its apex during a king tide, it begins to descend and his bridles lose their power for another century. He has only succeeded once, leading to the Great Flood. And never managed this feat a second time."

"That story is only a myth, but this gem and that bridle I saw are real."

"Poseidon wasn't a myth, but a real god to Greeks. They fashioned enormous bridles out of devotion to him. Eunicus, the most skilled of all Greek silversmiths, crafted some bridles that still survive in fresco paintings at various Greek temples dedicated to Poseidon."

He showed her a color printout of two temple frescoes of Poseidon's enchanted bridles.

"That looks like the one I saw." Aquan pointed to a painting at Sounion's temple ruins.

"You may have seen a precious original. But it's likely a

copy. Less skilled artisans typically fashioned dozens of reproductions of major works for secondary temple sites."

"Did your research find any bridles still in existence?"

"A crumbling remnant of one bridle is on exhibit at our National Archeological Museum of Athens."

On his computer screen, he showed her a digital photo of a withered skeleton of a bridle from a museum's online database. The decrepit remains, laid out over a black felt stand, paled in comparison to the Sea Monk's exquisite treasure. Aquan frowned in disappointment.

"I reached out to my contacts who advised me about a second one. It has supposedly gone through numerous hands for centuries. Staying one step ahead of Greek authorities seeking to recover plundered antiquities. No one will confirm it, but rumor has it that another Eunicus bridle was sold at an invitation-only auction in 1928. It was supposedly a multimillion-dollar sale."

"Who bought it?"

"An anonymous collector."

"Any chance that your network might be willing to disclose his identity?"

"No luck on that. Confidentiality is essential in our profession."

"I'm very grateful for that. But it's not much good to me right now."

"I do have a possible lead for you. This artifact was initially shipped to Maison du Chappelle in Paris. One of the most revered antiques restoration houses before being sent to its new owner. Henri Broussard Chappelle is its current director. I've made his acquaintance at professional gatherings and I'll try to provide an introduction for you, if you like."

"Yes, please tell him of my equestrian streak, but don't let him know any more specifics. I prefer to discuss it with him directly. How soon can you get in touch with him?"

"I will e-mail him immediately and follow-up with a call this morning. If he has useful information, he may expect payment in cash to avoid any entanglements."

"Naturally." Aquan knew that she must wire the Banker in

Belgium to draw upon her accounts built up by centuries of Emissaries. "Has your craftsman finished his work?"

"He will need more time to finish."

"Alright. Please send whatever you have to my security box in Brussels. I will e-mail you my bank's address."

"I'll need your assistance in describing how you want to present yourself to Monsieur Chappelle, Emissary."

"You've met him. Any ideas on what will make him more likely to help me?"

"He's a Frenchman. So being beautiful, sexy and ridiculously rich will surely get his attention. Promises of a hefty commission will certainly keep it."

Chapter 18

The Antiquarian arranged for a limousine service to pick up Aquan from an opulent Paris hotel. Wearing stiletto heels and designer finery, Aquan did not enjoy playing a spoiled daughter of a newly-rich Russian oligarch with an unquenchable desire for all things equestrian. Any high-end Parisian art dealer would be familiar with most European royalty and notable families, but not necessarily emerging oil and gas Russian billionaires with shady business dealings and even shadier pasts. Savvy dealers would be happy to help a neophyte clean her family's dirty money with extravagant fine art purchases.

Hiding her pale features behind dark sunglasses, her thick sable fur coat reached mid-calf of her long, slender legs. Aquan reapplied her ruby lipstick as her driver rolled up to the tony Saint Germain address, nestled amongst luxury antiques houses of Paris. Chappelle's family coat of arms with its cobalt blue shield emblazoned with a golden eagle was sculpted into a stucco wall above a nondescript entryway.

Monsieur Chappelle's executive assistant, Sanjay, stood curbside to greet her. With a regal Brahmin bearing and impeccable Raj Hotel hospitality training, he opened her limo door and lent his gloved hand to her.

"Welcome to Maison du Chappelle, Mademoiselle Popovich."

"Thank you, Monsieur Sanjay."

She rested her hand on his forearm as she gingerly climbed out and he showed her into Maison Chappelle. A young woman scurried to collect her coat while another associate pulled back a red velvet curtain. Sanjay escorted her into a private salon, a mahogany-paneled room with thick woven medieval tapestries hanging from its walls. Lucienne Delyle's lilting voice singing "Luna Rossa" floated out of an oak phonograph's silver horn. Aquan relished the sounds of Delyle's velvety inflections accompanied by a tinkling mandolin.

Sanjay led her to an exquisite Louis XIV settee and placed a cushioned stool at her feet for her Louis Vuitton purse. Two large leather portfolios with gold trim rested on an adjacent burled wood table inlaid with mother of pearl. She looked around and noticed a large statue of Venus in one corner and what appeared to be an ornate Faberge egg raised high on a display stand. A brass pendulum of an English longcase clock rhythmically ticked off each second, its gilt dial adorned with a schooner sailing over a curling wave. Two large brass candelabras with flickering wicks stood guard on each side of the room.

"May I offer you a glass of champagne? Or perhaps a kirre?"

"I tire so of champagne," said Aquan, with a Russian accent. "Have you no vodka?"

"We have Jean-Marc XO, Mademoiselle?"

"Da, da. Straight up."

"It will be my pleasure." Sanjay picked up a telephone receiver mounted on a wall. "Please advise Monsieur Chappelle that Mademoiselle Popovich is here and please bring in our finest Jean-Marc."

A moment later another functionary appeared with a cart and vodka in a Lalique crystal decanter. The waiter poured several shots of vodka into a simple glass. Placing it on a silver tray, he held it out to Aquan who sized up its ordinary look.

"How am I to drink from diss?" Aquan snapped.

Sanjay stepped forward.

"As a fashion icon in your own right, we thought you might enjoy drinking from a glass from Madame Coco Chanel's estate."

"Chanel?" She examined this tumbler more closely. "I drink." Throwing her head back, Aquan plunked her glass down empty and it was quickly refilled.

Soft chimes rang and every associate snapped to attention. A stout, balding man, nearly as wide as he was tall, quietly padded into the room. His bushy black eyebrows framed his hazel eyes. His clean-shaven pink face seemed too big for his body. A purple silk handkerchief, to match his satin tie, peeked out of his suit jacket's vest pocket. His shoes were polished to a glossy black sheen. Reaching out both hands, he clasped her right hand, bowing slightly at his waist.

"If I had known such an exquisite beauty awaited me, I would have hung up on our Prime Minister much sooner," he said. Syrupy flattery easily flowed from his smiling lips. With a stern glance, his subordinates quietly disappeared. "Welcome Mademoiselle. I see you have liquid refreshment. Can I offer you anything to eat? Coquille Saint Jacques or perhaps a dish of fresh escargot?"

"No fish. Horses are my passion."

"Yes, Signore DiGiacomo told me of your interest in all things equestrian." He lifted the record needle and turned off his phonograph. "I have been doing my homework on equestrian finery."

Chappelle sat across from her on a chair with a crown and sharp beaks of eagle heads carved into its armrests.

"It has been my pleasure to research exquisite pieces of fine art, sculpture and saddles for your consideration. All from Europe's finest art auction houses."

He gathered up two portfolios and handed one to Aquan. She quickly flipped through her binder. Each embossed page contained a photo of an item and a brief discussion of its provenance and artistic significance.

"If I may, Mademoiselle?"

Opening up his identical portfolio, he droned about various investment benefits of fine art collections. Barely two minutes passed before Aquan interrupted him.

"Deez bore me."

Aquan shifted restlessly in her seat. She dropped her organizer on his desk with a thud.

"Mademoiselle, I apologize that my recommendations do not please you. How might I return a smile to your beautiful face? A sparkle to your turquoise eyes?"

She pulled the Antiquarian's color print out from her bag and handed it to Chappelle.

"I vant diss. From painting."

He stared at her paper and Aquan noticed his right hand faintly trembling.

"My dear, Mademoiselle. This is stunning. But it is unlikely that it ever existed. The Greeks were tremendous storytellers."

"Not story. Maison du Chappelle fix it."

"I don't recall our restoration of this exquisite artifact."

"In 1920s. I do homework, too."

"Those records may be hard to locate after all these years. With the war and all." A slight twitch tugged at the corner of his mouth. "I'm not sure we can locate this object, even if we do have a record of it."

"Maybe you ask grandfather."

"He's long deceased, Mademoiselle."

"But he tell you story. Or warn you."

Chappelle's pasted smile melted away and he gulped hard.

"I see hands shake. Lips tremble."

Rising from his chair, Chappelle walked over to his serving trolley. He poured himself a glass of vodka and took a long, deliberate swallow.

"I'm sorry, Mademoiselle, but I cannot help you."

"Then help with diss?"

Chappelle looked up from his glass. Aquan dangled her amber amulet before him. He slid a jeweler's loop out of his coat pocket and examined it. His breathing became labored and he lurched back into his chair. Sweat began to pour out. He mopped his brow with his handkerchief and reached for his telephone.

"Sanjay, close the shop and send everyone home. Immediately. I said, immediately." He dropped his receiver back into its cradle and sat silently for a few moments, lost in his thoughts. "They told me you would come someday, looking for it."

"Who?"

"My grandfather told my father. He passed this family story down to me."

"How they know diss?"

"The buyer made it a condition of our lucrative restoration of this artifact."

"Who was buyer?"

"My grandfather never met him. He always worked through intermediaries. They told my grandfather that bridle was to be kept in trust for a later descendant."

"Am I that one?"

"I don't know for certain. But you possess its missing amulet contained in our restoration specifications for the bridle. And that is enough to admit you to his next level."

"Next level?"

"Yes, please follow me."

Chappelle stood up and locked his salon from the inside. He then strode over to a statue, pressing a button secreted away on its base. A rear wall panel slid open. Pulling a rusty skeleton key from his vest pocket, he unlocked a massive oak door with enormous black iron hinges. Chappelle grunted as he pushed it open and flicked on a dusty wall switch. A string of scarlet emergency lights barely illuminated a dark stone tunnel. Silky cobwebs glistened in their soft red glow.

"Who make diss tunnel?" asked Aquan.

"The buyer secretly renovated an ancient sewer duct. Our family has maintained it for nearly a century."

The portly art dealer swept aside sticky webs and barely squeezed his round body through this corridor door.

"Please watch your step. This stone floor can be slippery."

Aquan slipped off her stilettos and trailed Chappelle in her bare feet. This cool damp cavity raised goose bumps on Aquan's human skin. As they inched forward, splashing sounds of lapping river water echoed in this pathway. Chappelle handed Aquan a handkerchief and raised his own to cover her nose and mouth as a stench of gutter water grew more powerful. This rough-hewn tunnel ended at a stone walk paralleling the Seine.

"What now?"

"I don't know, Mademoiselle. I have never gone any farther."

She looked around wondering why this trail ended so abruptly. Peering into the murky river, she could not see any underwater fissures in this stonework. Aquan edged along a rock path, her toes hanging over its lip, her finger tips skimming its back wall.

"Mademoiselle, your necklace," said Chappelle.

Aquan looked down and noticed an amber light pulsating from it. Her talisman burned brighter as rough granite gave way to a smooth chunk of wall. She discovered Chappelle's coat of arms scored into its polished stone.

"Monsieur Chappelle, diss vay."

He hesitated. "I cannot swim."

"Not to worry. I, strong swimmer."

With a shudder of apprehension, he sidled along the river wall until he reached his family markings.

"Place here."

Thinking of Lineage Wall at Quartz Hall, she took his hand and rested it over his family crest.

"What will occur?" he asked.

"I don't know. Maybe give us some clue."

She continued to creep along as her amulet's tawny radiance deepened. Ten feet ahead, she spied interlocking crests of her Houses of Triton and Archigen. Touching this symbol with her hand, Aquan and Chappelle covered their family emblems in unison. Their footpath rumbled and a rectangular doorway opened up between them. Her gemstones shimmered as Aquan walked along a narrow passage which opened up into a small amphitheater, a diminutive granite replica of Quartz Hall. A carved moderator's chair stood at the front of this assembly room, a round basin of river water in its center. Aquan wondered if Mopsus might appear in a steam funnel to guide her next steps.

"Remarkable," said Chappelle.

Aquan sensed movement in the chamber's well.

"Monsieur Chappelle, I think you should go."

"I've waited all these years for this mystery be revealed. I won't go back now."

He draped his handkerchief over a front row bench before sitting down.

"Please, for your own safety. Go now."

Yet as her warning escaped her lips, river water churned into a whirlwind, its roaring whoosh bouncing hard off these chamber walls.

"Mopsus?"

Aquan blurted out as she gazed into this eddy. This funnel rose up and suddenly wrapped around Chappelle, like a slithering snake. He cried out, his eyes filled with terror, as this water spout tightened around him. Soon his jaw became rigid and his eyes rolled back in his head.

"I knew you would come."

A deep baritone timbre emanating from Chappelle's lips shook this amphitheater, but it was not his voice.

"Who are you?" asked Aquan.

"I've been waiting for you. The Elders are so cruel for keeping us apart for so many years."

"Who are you?"

"Who would you like me to be?"

"Release him."

A bellow of laughter echoed in this chamber.

"Still fighting for Surface Dwellers. Very sweet. Although I must say you were pretty naughty to steal my beautiful Hippocampus. They're not that easy to capture."

"It can't be." Aquan was stunned that she hadn't sensed his presence. "You're in exile."

"I'm only physically under house arrest. But not mentally. And I've had lots of time to develop my mental powers beyond Obzula Ridge."

Rage coursed through her veins. "If you were here, I'd tear you apart for slaughtering my House."

"Destroying Tritons does not serve my interests."

"Destroying you serves mine."

"Such fierce passion. So much like your mother, Evadne."

"Don't ever speak her name!"

"There's no need to yell. Try communicating with me with your thoughts. Simply project your thoughts, your will through others as I do. Or hasn't Mopsus taught you yet?"

"I don't know what you're talking about."

"So much untapped power. But then they like things that way. I'll help you to reach your true potential. Then they will fear you, serve you. Join me and sit by my side as we reign over a new kingdom to come."

"I'll never join you."

"Never is a long time. I thought you enjoyed our game so far."

"What game?"

"Hide and seek. Much more fun than chasing silly Hydromorphs or Sea Monks. Don't you think?"

"What if I don't want to play?"

"If you don't play, then I win by default. If you stop looking, Eternal Concordia is up for grabs. And I'm way ahead of any competition."

"I know you're looking for this. And now I know why." Aquan clutched her amulet tight in her hands.

"Good for you. But I doubt you have the whole story. And I'd hate to spoil things or else you might stop playing. Our contest is only halfway complete and it's tied one to one. We get to keep whatever we find first. But I'll need all four when we're done playing."

"You'll have to kill me to get it."

"No need to be so difficult. Especially when we've just met. I'm sure we can make a mutually beneficial arrangement where you share yours with me."

"I won't share anything I find with you."

"Sharing can be such a sweet virtue. Besides I can be very persuasive."

"Why did you bring me here?"

"It is you who brought us all here, to this very moment. Yet we need to speed things up for my timetable. The Sequencing is only about two weeks away and there's a big planet to scour. So I'll send someone along to help."

"I don't need your help."

"I wouldn't roam too far away from your friends on *Calusa*. I'm sure Evadne's given you that advice already. She foretold it before you were even born."

"You don't know her. You tricked me at that undersea volcano. Propelling your thoughts to make it look like her soul was speaking to me from Musterion."

"Evadne doesn't sleep in Musterion. She exists in her own wretched exile. I suppose Mopsus forget to tell you about that, too."

Aquan knew this claim couldn't be true, but a sting of doubt unexpectedly pierced her heart. She often thought she felt her mother's presence through the years. But why would Mopsus and Aunt Sofronia tell her such a terrible lie? She must not fall into his trap, remembering Camulus's warning about the Margrave's ability to deceive. Her blood ran hot as she transformed into a Giant Puffer fish. The Margrave didn't respond or take any defensive steps. She realized he might not be able to see her, only speak to her through others. She unhinged her jaw and began to drain his gushing spout. His river column collapsed, dragging Chappelle into its eddy. She sucked in and then disgorged this center pool. Chappelle washed up on a stone bench at the rear of the amphitheater. Aquan rushed to his side.

"Prepare for the Vanquishment." The Margrave's words seeped out of Chappelle's pale lips.

Despite her efforts to revive him, a mix of river water and blood streamed from Chappelle's parted lips. His eyes spun back in his head and his body felt cold to her touch. Another Drowner paying a price for his family's alliance with the Margrave. Aquan dragged him out and sealed the chamber's entryway. Carrying him back his antique salon, she laid Chappelle on his settee.

"Forgive me, Monsieur."

Aquan closed his eyelids shut and then poured alcohol from the trolley's bottles out on to a rug and wall tapestries. Tipping over a lit candelabra, its orange flames raced across the floor and ignited its walls. As black smoke billowed in Chappelle's salon, Aquan grabbed a remaining candelabra and several liquor bottles. Hurrying to the end of Chappelle's secret passageway, she smashed any remaining decanters and tossed a second candelabra on to its alcohol-soaked path. Throwing Chappelle's skeleton key into the river, she dove in as a hungry blaze devoured Maison du Chappelle. As fire truck sirens wailed, Aquan headed toward Le Havre and out to open ocean.

Chapter 19

Like a child on Christmas Eve, Jenn barely slept on her canopied bed with its pressed European linens. She needed to pinch herself, having upgraded from her cramped quarters in *Calusa* to a waterfront suite at Hotel Royal Tenerife in a couple of days. Sipping coffee, she reviewed her notes for a hundredth time that morning in preparation for her afternoon presentation. Most academic maritime conferences were forgettable gatherings with minor scholarly rivals bickering over scientific minutiae in beige hotel ballrooms with stale bagels and wilting vegetable trays. But a Papandreas symposium was known in academic circles as an exclusive, lavish five-day affair for world-renowned maritime experts. Stevenson had attended them for years. Jenn knew she shouldn't measure herself against him, but to finally be invited meant she had arrived. She planned to capitalize on this opportunity to showcase her research. Maybe even shake a few more dollars out of that elusive money tree.

Jenn walked on to her balcony overlooking cobalt blue waters of port city, Santa Cruz. It sat at the foot of steep volcanic Anaga Massif Mountains. These majestic ridges stood shrouded in white contrails of morning mist. This world seemed like a dream to her. She spied *Calusa* sandwiched between over-sized yachts and research vessels docked at a local marina for this conference. She couldn't convince Cutter who was allergic to academic gatherings to join her at any sessions. But she left an extra badge at reception for him in case he changed his mind. Jenn knew Cutter preferred to hang out on *Calusa* and hob knob with other boat captains rather than captains of industry and über-wealthy maritime adventurers with slim scientific credentials, but incredibly fat wallets. All were looking to stake their claims on a next big maritime discovery. A knock at her hotel room door interrupted her musings.

"Oh my God. This place is unreal," said Emerson. His conference name tag hung from his neck while he clutched an overflowing canvas bag, emblazoned with "Apollo—Always One Step Ahead" in his arms. "This goodie bag is awesome."

"I'm sorry they didn't reserve a room for you, too."

"Don't worry. You've earned it after doing this work for years. I'm with the rest of the newbies at a nearby guest house right. Sort of an unofficial headquarters for all of us lowly research assistants. Lots of Canary Island cuties, too. So it's pretty cool."

"You got to help me with that." She pointed to a gargantuan gift basket of fresh fruits, savory snacks and a bottle of champagne. "I'm too excited to eat."

"Not me. I can always eat," said Emerson. He pulled out and peeled a banana. "How's your presentation coming?"

"I've got it all down. Our isolation of L11 microbes in those beachings should blow people away. Just tweaking it to make sure it pops, gets us attention from the right people interested in promoting our efforts."

"Hey, that half-million from Papandreas came at a perfect time."

"He's asked me to join his special VIP dinner tonight." Jenn smiled.

"Nice chance for you to rub elbows with those high rollers in yachts. You should see those ginormous boats. Some are so big they have to be moored out in the harbor. They make *Calusa* look like a dinghy."

Jenn laughed. "Don't let Cutter hear you say that or he'll make you walk the plank."

Emerson rolled his eyes.

"Have you run into Stevenson yet? He speaks at tomorrow's morning session."

"I narrowly escaped an encounter. Saw his film crew setting up last night in this hotel's lobby so I steered clear of them. Wanted to stay focused on our work and not get distracted by his sideshow, Rick."

"I'm sure he'll be gunning for you during your session."

"Yeah, I know. But I've got it under control. I think anyway." She took a long gulp of coffee.

"You'll do fine. Just remember to breathe and keep handing

out those business cards."

She nodded her head.

"We better get going. It's about forty-five minutes before opening session. The Opera House is about a ten-minute walk so we can take our time and enjoy a few sights. It might help me to burn off some of my nervous energy."

"Think Papandreas will show, Jenn?"

"It would be a treat to hear from him. But he hasn't been seen in public for ages. Let's keep our fingers crossed."

Jenn threw her computer bag over her shoulder and grabbed a juicy strawberry from her gift basket.

*****

Strolling toward Santa Cruz's Opera House, a fellow pedestrian in dark sunglasses and a gray suit, its buttons straining to hold in his round belly, stopped them.

"Excuse me, Dr. Ortiz, Mr. Emerson. May I speak with you for a moment?"

"How do you know our names?" asked Emerson.

He looked around and said in a low voice, "I make it my business to know each of my suspect's names."

"Suspects?" blurted out Emerson.

"I'm sorry. Who are you?" Jenn folded her arms and stared at him.

"Ernest Tuttleberry. Paramount Life and Casualty Insurance." He handed each of them a business card. "I'm a fraud investigator."

"What does this have to do with us?" asked Emerson.

"I noticed that you've been traveling quite a bit these days on a nicely-refurbished *Calusa*. That's what I wanted to talk to you about."

"You can talk to *Calusa*'s captain, Dave Cutter, if you want to discuss any insurance issues."

"Cutter's under investigation for insurance fraud and you may be illegally benefitting from his crime. That makes you accomplices. But if you cooperate my company might be willing to overlook your transgressions."

"Ridiculous. We've received a big injection of funding which accounts for our travel and recent boat improvements," replied Jenn.

"Funding from Mr. Cutter?"

"No, funds from generous and legitimate research sources."

"So you admit Cutter is not a legal source for funding."

"You're twisting my words." Jenn pushed past Tuttleberry.

"Now Dr. Ortiz..."

Jenn spun around and stood nose-to-nose with Tuttleberry.

"I know that Dave Cutter is a man of integrity. I won't stand here and let you sully his reputation. You can contact our university grant office if you want to know any further details. This conversation is over, sir."

She turned and sauntered toward the Opera House. Emerson hurried to catch up with her.

"Do you think there's any truth to it?"

"Cutter may be a lot of things, Rick. But a petty thief, no way. He stood so firmly by his principles that he lost his academic post. I don't buy his cheating an insurance company. I can't believe you'd think that for a second."

Emerson didn't reply. Jenn frowned and continued to march toward the conference hall. She knew that so many others doubted Cutter, from his aquatelligence theories to his ability to maintain an expensive research vessel on a limited income. Previously, Jenn worried that Cutter might be in with a bad crowd to keep *Calusa* afloat, but she just couldn't, or at least didn't want to believe that Tuttleberry may be right.

As they neared their conference, Jenn tried to shake off this encounter, marveling at Santa Cruz Opera House's unique beauty. She snapped photos of its magnificent stark white structure as cool morning breezes blew in from the sea.

"It looks like a gigantic wave, frozen over a building," said Jenn.

In its front plaza, Emerson and Jenn took turns clicking off photos of each other standing before its enormous curved arc cresting over pointed hatches which housed its auditorium and concert hall.

"Would you like one together, Dr. Ortiz?"

"Well hello, Ms. Jagtiani."

Aquan stood there as Rajneet once more, her reporter's satchel bulging over her shoulder.

"Please call me Rajneet."

"What a surprise. Are you here to cover this conference?" asked Emerson.

"Yes, the director of our marine college were invited to attend. I see you are to make a formal presentation, Dr. Ortiz. Quite an honor. With your permission, I hope that I might do a follow-up story on your team's progress for my newspaper."

"That's great," replied Jenn. "We've received an infusion of additional funding and we're really moving rapidly ahead."

"Terrific. We can talk later about a time that works for you. After your presentation, of course."

Emerson handed her Jenn's camera. Aquan fidgeted with it camera as she tried to line them up for a photo.

"A bit to your right so I can get the Opera House in, too. Okay now on three. One, two, and three."

As Aquan depressed the camera button, Dr. Stevenson walked right in front of Jenn and Emerson, his usual entourage scurrying behind him.

"Hey thanks for walking right into our photo," said Emerson.

"Oh, so sorry to interrupt your little tourist moment," said Stevenson, without a speck of apology in his voice. "Be sure to take a lot of good photos, Miss. It might be Dr. Ortiz's first and last chance to be invited to one of these." Stevenson continued into the Opera House.

"I ought to sock him in the nose," said Emerson.

"Don't worry," murmured Jenn. "I'll get my punches in when I present this afternoon. Sea quakes, my ass."

"Shall we try again, Dr. Ortiz?" called out Aquan. She snapped several photos. "May I take a few with my own camera for my story?"

Jenn smiled. "Absolutely, this time without any more ugly interruptions." She wasn't going to let either Tuttleberry or Stevenson ruin her day. A crowd of attendees soon began to swarm across the plaza as a fleet of long black limousines screeched behind Aquan and into rear entrance.

"It appears that our host may indeed be speaking at this year's conference. First time in at least ten years," said Jenn.

All three of them rushed inside to take their seats in a large auditorium. Aquan bid Jenn and Emerson good-bye and headed for the press gallery. She lifted her doctored press pass from a tipsy reporter wandering around a swanky casino's Black Jack tables last night.

The audience buzzed with excitement as house lights dimmed. A latecomer nudged Jenn in her seat. Annoyed, she looked up and saw Cutter's smirking face.

"What are you doing here?" she whispered as he took his seat. "I thought you hated these things."

"I loathe them. But through my binoculars I saw Papandreas sitting in a boat tender launched from his yacht. Had to see him for myself. Besides, think I'd miss out on you eating Stevenson's lunch at your presentation?"

He gave Jenn's hand a quick squeeze. She couldn't fight a broad grin from spreading across her face. Jenn was glad it was too dark for Cutter to notice her blushing.

Music began to play and an enormous screen slowly dropped down from a high auditorium ceiling. A short film chronicled a history of Papandreas family ancestors, successful ancient Greek ship builders and sea merchants whose interests were expanded for centuries. Today a vast modern empire of commercial, philanthropic and research interests thrived under the stewardship of Stavros Papandreas and his deceased father, Pasicrates. As the film ended, the audience politely clapped. House lights were only partly raised and a hushed silence prevailed.

A shriveled man, just an inch or two over five feet with trim white hair and thin moustache and wearing a charcoal Armani suit, slowly shuffled on stage. A young attendant wheeled a long oxygen tank behind him as he stepped on to a riser behind a decorated podium. His pale bony hand shook as he pulled a microphone closer to his lips.

"Good morning," he said. His gravelly voice boomed across the conference hall as if he every speck of energy in his emaciated form was summoned up to project his voice. "My dear friends of the sea."

The attendees roared their approval in applause.

"I come to you today almost unable—unable to breathe. Yet I'm compelled to speak a few words to you. Our time on this planet is short and mine has been greatly shortened by illness. I could not have imagined years ago that oxygen tanks I once used to scuba dive would now be my constant companions, keeping me alive on land." He motioned toward a softly hissing oxygen tank. "I call upon you to do what you can to better understand the mysteries of our seas, to protect her from mankind's excesses."

The audience once more broke into applause.

"This is a special year for the Papandreas Foundation as it marks its 500th year. A year in which I hope that scientists, like you, will help to reveal more of long-held secrets that our oceans so jealously guard."

Aquan's ears pricked up as she began to hear an undertow of soft clicks and squeals as Papandreas spoke. She looked around and it appeared that no one else could detect these sounds. Straining, she could make out a garbled hum underlying his spoken words. Aquan looked around but didn't see or sense a Sea Monk or Hydromorph.

"We know our sea levels continue to rise, and at this pace, our oceans will surely swallow this planet whole." His jolting coughs echoed into the auditorium's hushed silence. Waving off his attendant, he cleared his throat and continued. "Like the legendary Atlantis, this world is heading for catastrophe. Doomed to be swept away by relentless seas."

As his voice quavered in anger, those annoying clicks and squeals grew louder to Aquan. She couldn't decipher this unknown dialect.

"The human race has brought this tragedy upon itself." He shook a gnarled index finger. "Our weak wills and puny minds have failed to understand the limits of life on terra firma. Will there be a Noah to resurrect us from the sea's fury this time? Will there be a chosen few who might survive to rebuild our sinking world?" Papandreas paused and looked around, his face stiffened, his lips curled into a sneer. "Do you think you will be spared? Spared a certain destiny that humanity's ruinous ways have wrought on this planet?"

High-pitched clicks and squeals intensified and seared Aquan's ear drums. A dribble of blood flowed out of her right ear and on to her cheek. She wiped several splotches with a tissue and made her way out of her row.

"Recognize that time is surely not on your side. So enjoy this conference and any time on this Earth left to each one of you. Thank you."

Conference participants seemed momentarily stunned into silence by his somber rebuke, a final farewell not of sunny memories and future hope, but of harsh denouncements and an apocalyptic future. Papandreas shambled across the stage and conference attendees clapped their hands as he disappeared into the wings. Screeching sounds persisted until Aquan felt the hall spinning as she passed out near a press gallery exit.

Chapter 20

Aquan blinked her eyes open and was startled to find a pair of frog-like brown eyes peering back at her from behind thick eyeglasses resting on a long thin nose. He held a small glass ear dropper in his left hand and his wooden chair creaked as he continued to lean over her. She tried to get up from an overstuffed green couch, a pillow behind her head and under her feet, but her head continued to spin.

"Easy now, Ms. Jagtiani."

He gently placed his hand on her shoulder and eased her back down.

"Who are you? Where am I?"

"I'm Doctor Gugliano, Signora" he replied with a sing-song southern Italian accent. "Mr. Papandreas' personal physician. And you are in his conference hospitality suite."

"What happened?"

"You passed out at when Mr. Papandreas concluded his welcome speech."

"It is not often that my words evoke such reactions," remarked Papandreas.

Aquan slowly turned her head and saw their host sitting in a dove gray winged back chair. She instantly sensed he was an Archigen. A long slender oxygen tank hissed at his side.

"You are fortunate that my doctor always travels with me."

"Your ear was bleeding." The doctor motioned toward her right ear. "I've applied some drops to reduce any inflammation and placed some cotton in your outer ear to keep this medicine where it is needed." He held up a small medicine bottle. "Three more drops in your ear at bedtime and you should be fine."

She remained silent, sniffing for a camouflaged Sea Monk or Hydromorph, but nothing."

"You need not worry. My physician is trained to address our unique physiological needs."

"I'm not sure what you mean," said Aquan.

She glanced around his suite for her satchel of paralyzing darts. Her bag hung from coat rack in a rear corner of this room. Aquan wondered if she would be able to reach it, if needed.

Papandreas sighed and tapped his fingers impatiently on an arm of his chair. "Doctor, please leave us. Ms. Jagtiani and I need to speak privately."

As the door creaked closed, Papandreas got up and sat in Doctor Gugliano's vacated chair, wheeling his oxygen tank by his side.

"For many generations my family has longed for this day. Shape-shifting for centuries on this barren surface waiting for you. I hoped I would have a chance to meet you before I am released to Musterion."

"You must have confused me with someone else, Mr. Papandreas. I'm Rajneet Jagtiani, Mahabalipuram Times." Aquan flashed her press badge hanging from a lanyard around her neck. "But I would be happy to interview you for my paper. We reach a wide readership in India."

"I'm sure you are Rajneet today, Emissary. Perhaps we can sift through your bag and you can explain what's inside. Hardly a simple pen and paper of a news reporter. I know why you are here."

"I will play along if you wish, sir. Why am I here?"

"You are searching for the next amulet."

Aquan reflexively reached for her necklace.

"Do not worry. Your necklace is still there. I cannot take it from you. You must give it willingly."

"It is merely a family trinket. Why would I give such a trifle to a billionaire who could buy anything?"

"To reclaim your heritage, to revive our House of Proteus."

"House of Proteus?"

"The first Emissaries who transited between sea and land as you do now. Your forerunners." Papandreas wheezed for air.

"Mr. Papandreas, I'm not familiar with these names, these Houses."

"Perhaps not." He reached back and grabbed his oxygen mask dangling from his tank and inhaled deeply." But only an Emissary would have detected his speech intertwined with my conference address."

"I heard some high-pitched noises. Maybe some feedback from your microphone. Not any language I've ever heard before."

"It was our ancestors' dialect pricking your untrained ears. The tongue of your Protosian ancestors which you were never permitted to hear. He knew it would reveal your presence to me."

"I don't know what you are talking about Mr. Papandreas."

"I may be old, nearly 1,200 years old, but not an idiot, my dear."His laugh dissolved into a hacking cough, his face turning bright red.

"The centuries have been kind to you, Mr. Papandreas."

He grimaced and then looked squarely at her.

"Actually, quite cruel. I lost my true family. Just as you were robbed of yours. I can still remember my daughter's cries. Snatched away days before her first season. Your age, Emissary."

A flash of intense pain across his face made Aquan shift uncomfortably on his couch.

"I'm sorry about your daughter, sir."

"Since her death, I have wandered this surface, away from my ocean home for over 900 years. Along with a handful of once-young males, like myself, tattered remnants of our Protosian people."

"I don't know anything about a Protosian House."

"They were erased from our history. At one time, there were but two founding Houses, Proteus and Archigen, united under a shared family crest, a nearly identical outward physical form."

Aquan placed her hand on her hip, thinking of her tattoo of interlocking symbols of her Houses of Archigen and Triton.

"Through millennia, they intermingled and created our diversity of Archigen Houses. Over time, only Protosians evolved into shape-shifters. Once they had mastered how to change form, their Archigen kinsmen feared this mutation and their domination of land and sea."

Aquan doubted that Mopsus or Aunt Sofronia would have remained silent about an entire race of Emissaries, if only to protect her from their potential threat to her missions.

"How do I know if you're telling the truth?"

He closed his eyes and drew in a deep breath. Papandreas turned into Countess Daimonikas and then flapped around as beta fish a moment later. He then returned to his human form. Coughing, Papandreas and pointed toward his oxygen tank. Aquan reached out and pulled it closer to him. Papandreas grabbed his mask and inhaled fully three or four times.

"It takes a great deal of my strength to do that at my age."

"What happened to Protosians?"

"At one Convocation, Archigens invited Protosians to gather for a communal banquet and poisoned them. Those that survived were hunted down and butchered. No female Protosians survived and a few males escaped to land. They thought we had been stamped out. Yet, certain Archigen males with Protosian lineage could still randomly produce Emissaries, like you, with Triton female mates. With Protosian males in exile, the Elder Council banned all mating between Archigens and Tritons to stop further births of more Emissaries. Your mother, Evadne, and several other Triton females refused to abandon their Archigen mates with Protosian blood and paid a heavy price."

Aquan felt dizzy as her heart beat faster, her mind filled with questions. "Does my mother live?" Her voice faltered with mix of hope and despair.

"She was banished. I do not know where she was sent or what happened to her."

"What about my father?"

"He died in exile."

"Why not just return to Rapture's End to avenge these cruelties? Or do you prefer worldly power and treasures on land?"

He shook his head. "Our numbers are small and aging. We could never take on Archigen forces with our depleted numbers. They threatened our complete extinction if we dare return to our homes. We kept an uneasy truce, relying on Sea Monks and Hydromorphs to be our scouts. But the time has finally come for our revolt, and we are ready to free ourselves from our surface prisons." His face turned stiff and white, his hand started shaking. "By now, Mopsus must be 1,400 years. That Judas who betrayed Protosians. Turning his back on us."

"Mopsus would never betray anyone," blurted out Aquan.

"Your loyalty is his greatest power over you, his enduring chokehold over our House's dying embers. Your real ancestors are Protosians not Archigens. Cast out of their beloved sea. Our leaders exiled beyond Obzula Ridge for daring to defend our House, our ancestral waters."

"The Margrave and his Exori followers are not my family. They are my enemies."

Aquan tried to get up to seize her satchel filled with weapons. But her head fell back on to a small mound of pillows, banging furiously with pain. Her vision became blurry. A sharp knock on the door interrupted them.

"Enter," growled Papandreas.

Countess Daimonakis swung open his suite entry, standing in a long floral dress with an enormous floppy blue hat partially obscuring her face. She flicked off a wireless device clipped to her left ear. Her left eye peeked out from under her hat and she stared at Aquan.

"Pardon my intrusion. But your meetings and conference calls are beginning to back up. Your final instructions are needed for this evening."

"Yes, Countess. In another moment or two." Papandreas motioned for her to retreat.

"I will send for Phillip," she said.

The Countess slowly shut the door behind her, never taking her eye off Aquan.

"In all of these years, I have never been able to escape time's eternal drumbeat," said Papandreas, shrugging. "None of us can."

Unexpectedly, he clasped his hands tenderly over hers, his features softened.

"I do not mean to overwhelm you with these facts, Aquan. Think about what I have said. You have a chance to avenge your parents and your true people. I beseech you to search your own feelings. Ask yourself, Emissary. Have you ever truly felt that you are one of them?"

His question hit her like a hard, unexpected slap across her face. Aquan always prized her unique heritage. Yet why were there so few couplings between these two prominent Houses? She had always believed it to be chance. Aquan now wondered if it had been by design, to end any line of Emissaries. He seemed so sincere. But she knew that the Margrave and his Exori allies would do anything to discredit Archigens. She pushed aside her doubts and focused on her reason for seeking him out.

"Do you still have that antique bridle restored by Maison du Chappelle?"

Papandreas stroked his chin. "I'm holding a dinner for special guests this evening on my vessel. Will you join us?"

"Only if I get a chance to see it."

"Expect my launch for you and my other guests at Santa Cruz Marina. 8:00 p.m. sharp. Unless you prefer to swim out to my yacht."

"I didn't say I would attend."

A smirk tugged at a corner of his mouth. "No, you did not." He rose from his chair and nodded to her. "Until this evening, Emissary."

Chapter 21

Aquan's blue sari fluttered in balmy evening air as she arrived at the water taxi dock. Dissonant clanging of sail riggings mixed with a local Canarian's drumbeats. His friends swayed to his tajaraste music and tipped back Dorada beers. Still deeply troubled by Papandreas's claims, Aquan felt her step enlivened a little bit with this local music. Up ahead, she saw a gathering of four men and three women in formal attire. Jenn wore a soft peach gown with an Empire waist, her silky auburn hair twisted up in a French braid. She chatted animatedly, seemingly holding court as her fellow marine biologists quizzed her about her L11 microbe research.

"Good evening, Dr. Ortiz," said Aquan. "A beautiful evening gown."

"Your sari is magnificent. How are you feeling, Ms. Jagtiani? I heard that you fainted at this morning's opening session."

"I'm fine, thank you. An unfortunate mix of too much jet lag and not enough breakfast. I learned your presentation was quite a hit this afternoon."

"Yes, it was really gratifying. Obviously Mr. Papandreas thought so. He's been reading my research paper," she said. "He wanted a sample, but I told him my research might be compromised if any L11 samples left my lab." Jenn leaned in to Rajneet and whispered, "It was a last minute invitation so I had to run out and buy a gown this afternoon."

"It is quite an honor. I think he only invites a handful of conference attendees to dine with him on his yacht. And what's a private little Papandreas dinner without a little press coverage?" Aquan waggled her notepad.

Aquan almost didn't notice Dr. Stevenson brooding at the dock's far end without his usual entourage. His arms were locked over his perfectly tailored tuxedo as he cast his gaze out to sea, turning his back to his colleagues.

"Good evening, Dr. Stevenson. Any comments on Dr. Ortiz's remarkable findings about L11 microbes?"

"Flash in the pan," he replied dourly. "Much too early to tell if her claims will hold up under intense, long-term peer scrutiny."

"Will you continue to map out ocean fault lines and quake cycles for your sea quake theory? Or will you be involved in evaluating and challenging Dr. Ortiz's microbe discovery?"

"I'll leave it up to others to waste their time on testing her undeveloped guesses. My work will continue unabated." He grumbled and returned to scanning the dark horizon. "We'll see who walks off with a Nobel, Ms. Jagtiani. And that's all I have to say on this matter." He shook his index finger to punctuate his assertion.

The dock bobbed up and down as a sleek launch with its twinkling green and red running lights slowed down in the marina. Its uniformed crew flipped its bumpers over its sides, bearing Apollo logos. The tender gently thumped a pier edge as two crewmen scrambled out to tie its lines and spread a small Oriental rug on the gangplank's landing. As its crew helped guests to board, Cutter strolled casually out of the shadows wearing a tuxedo. His blond hair was slicked back and his men's cologne lingered in the air. Aquan felt her blood start to boil, wondering if he was meeting Papandreas to get his orders or inform on his friends.

Stephenson grunted as he saw Cutter approaching Papandreas's water taxi. "Obviously Mr. Papandreas has a sense of humor."

"Always a pleasure, Dr. Stephenson," replied Cutter.

Jenn laughed as Cutter stood next to her. "Nice shoes."

A pair of scuffed up dock shoes marked his only rebellion against that evening's formality. Even with his casual footwear, Aquan hated to admit that he did look quite handsome.

"This monkey suit was all I could get on short notice," he replied. "All you ladies look especially lovely this evening."

A chubby fiftyish female scientist in a screaming yellow chiffon gown giggled with delight.

"Cutter, this is Rajneet Jagtiani, a reporter for Mahabalipuram Times. Try not to say anything that will embarrass our project."

"Actually I've already met, Dr. Cutter near our marine

college. Soaking wet from a tumble into bay water."

Cutter stuck out his hand to shake hers. A gust of wind blew momentarily and her sari scarf flapped revealing her amulet. He tightly clasped her hand to signal his recognition.

"I thought you were doing some solo freelancing far away from our little group."

"Seems like I can't get enough of you and *Calusa*."

Aquan glared at him and clutched his hand so hard that she heard two of his knuckles crack.

"Looks like those water aerobics are really playing off, Ms. Jagtiani."

He returned her shake with an equally tight grip until they were locked in a bit of a contest, finally interrupted by Papandreas' launch captain. She released his hand and he frowned, rubbing his sore knuckles.

"Ladies and gentlemen, Mr. Papandreas asks your patience as we take a longer than usual route to *Athena*. We are expecting rough seas this evening and have anchored in a protected cove a bit further south. Please enjoy the light refreshments below deck with his compliments."

Generous platters overflowing with shrimp, mussels, lobster claws and Greek antipasti rested on starched white linen tablecloths under candlelight. Champagne glasses floated on silver trays balanced on fingertips of gloved waiters, hinting at a sumptuous feast to follow.

*****

On board *Athena*, Papandreas did not disappoint, offering up an eight-course gourmet dinner. He did not allow a plate to remain empty or a glass to stay dry in his gleaming cherry wood-paneled dining suite. His four-story yacht served as Papandreas' year-round home, office and research vessel. Although physically diminished, he retained a passion for knowledge and peppered his guests with questions exhibiting a phenomenal understanding of and insight into their diverse marine projects. He asked Jenn in intricate detail about her L11 microbe discovery.

"So Dr. Ortiz, do you believe L11 is from nature or of human invention?"

"I believe it is a hybrid. A naturally occurring bacteria that has mutated and become more lethal due to pollutants in our air and water."

"Have you been able to recreate it in your lab?"

"So far we have been able to replicate them briefly in our lab, but they dissolve in an hour or two. Further research will show whether our fabricated microbes will pose the same risks."

"So this L11 microbe is making whales and squids beach themselves?" Papandreas asked.

"It appears that high concentrations of these tainted microbes in certain oceans contaminate their radar. Impairing their delicate senses of direction and likely leading to these mass strandings."

"What levels of contamination must be present for such strandings?"

"We have done some early computer modeling, projecting L11 levels ranging from localized to globalized beachings of mammals and large cephalopods."

"Is global cataclysm likely?"

"Hopefully not. But extremely high concentrations of L11 might produce such horrific results. We'll need to study the further to determine if L11 is acting alone or whether other elements, like temperature or salinity, are factoring into these beachings."

"So you must admit that L11 concentrations could just be coincidental and not be a cause at all," A sneer jerked a corner of Stephenson's mouth.

"It's unlikely, but it could be possible, Dr. Stephenson," replied Jenn. "So our research continues, thanks to Mr. Papandreas." Jenn raised her glass to her benefactor.

"And Stephenson, you must agree that sea quakes might be a big fat coincidence, too," said Cutter.

He tipped his champagne flute in Stephenson's direction. Cutter then noisily sucked down an oyster and took a gulp of champagne out of his glass, never taking his eyes off Stephenson. All side conversations ceased and heads turned toward their end of the table. Mr. Papandreas eased back into his chair wearing a Cheshire cat grin.

"Well, Cutter, I'm surprised you've been following my work. I thought you had switched fields from science to science fiction," said Stephenson.

"Aquatelligence is more real than anything you're peddling as research," said Cutter.

Jenn glared at Cutter and gave his knee a sharp pinch under the table.

"At least I've retained my academic post to prove my theories and wasn't thrown out on my ear by my own father."

"You mean you actually know which traveling snake oil salesmen was your father?" asked Cutter.

Papandreas laughed. "At last, robust debate. I love it," he exclaimed. "Dr. Cutter, I must say that your theories are unorthodox, but certainly as plausible as any other untested scientific hypothesis."

"With all due respect, I cannot believe a man of science such as you, Mr. Papandreas, would give any credence to these fantasies," said Stephenson.

"Weren't notions of a flat Earth once accepted scientific theories while true ideas about our world and solar system were thought to be heresies?"

"Yes, but these earlier contrarians were men of science trying to dispel superstitions. They had some scientific evidence to support their hypotheses."

"Enough to get ex-communicated," said Cutter. "Besides we know a lot more about outer space than we do our own oceans."

"Perhaps Dr. Cutter someday you will return to your research. I think many truths about our diverse sea and planet have yet to be fully revealed. I'm sure Ms. Jagtiani will agree."

Aquan did not expect this sudden and bold remark.

"As a reporter, I cannot help but expect and hope for more scientific revelations as time marches on."

"True enough. And speaking of time, I believe I am overdue for a ship-to-shore call." He pointed to his watch. "Please enjoy your dessert and I will rejoin you for an after-dinner drink on the upper deck. It will only be a first quarter moon, but a clear night. We should be able to make out a candlelight procession to Basilica Candelaria to venerate these islands' patron, the Virgin Mary. Quite stirring, I'm told."

His attendant magically appeared at his side and escorted him along a portside corridor. As trays of ornately-decorated pastries and cakes were delivered, Aquan waited for about five minutes and then excused herself. She asked a waiter for directions to a ladies restroom which she promptly ignored. Her radar tracked Papandreas's light scuffing and his attendant's footsteps on the carpeted hallway. She heard a soft ping of an elevator bell sensing their movement two floors beneath her. Aquan crept through a labyrinth of corridors and clambered down steep ship steps. She finally reached closed mahogany double doors with dolphin-shaped brass handles. Before Aquan touched its handles, Countess Daimonakis pulled open both doors. She stood draped in another oversized red floral kaftan, her heavy make-up plastered over her face.

She nodded to Aquan.

"Welcome, Emissary."

The Countess led Aquan into a spacious cabin suite with two ultramodern s-shaped couches with a center glass cocktail table etched with a wave pattern. Three flat screen televisions tuned to different business channels and a long conference table with black swivel chairs were placed at one end. On its opposite side, a bank of four computer monitors blinked on a credenza behind an enormous rosewood desk stationed beneath an antique wooden maidenhead. A hissing oxygen tank was parked beside the desk, but Papandreas was absent.

"He will be with you in one moment. Please have a seat, Emissary."

She motioned to Aquan to sit on one couch and exited shutting the suite's double doors behind her.

Aquan took a seat and felt vibrations beneath her feet as the cocktail table slid right. A large glass display case rose through a floor opening. Peering into this case, she recognized another bridle similar to the Sea Monk's treasure in that Isthmia chest. Instead of rubies and sapphires, emeralds and black opals were set in its cheek pieces. No amber amulet adorned its triangular gold plate in its bridle brow band. As she leaned forward, her amulet slipped out of her silk scarf and dangled above this ornate harness. Her gemstone glowed and then pulsated emitting a low humming sound. Stepping back, its hum dissipated and his bridle ceased glimmering. Suspending her amulet above his harness again, it began to throb and buzz once more. Aquan moved away from Papandreas's display case and his harness fell silent.

"It seems pleased to see you." Papandreas stood next to her.

"I'm not so sure that I should be pleased to see it." Aquan stuffed her amulet back under her sari and backed away from his bridle. "Is this one from a temple at Corinthus or Skyros?"

"Rescued from Atlantis."

"Which one?" Aquan thought of her research on Vineta and Mahabalipuram.

Papandreas smiled. "Yes, so many have laid claim to her. Yonaguni in Japan. Tartessos in Andalusia. Souss-Massa is Morocco. Even archaic Guanche people of these islands claimed lineage to mighty Atlantis. And of course Shore Temple where you let that amulet slip through your fingers."

Aquan felt rage building inside as she thought of Raynord's near fatal wounds. She slammed his display case hard but her hand bounced hard off its protective coating.

"Before you hurt yourself, you may want to find out why I'm even showing this harness to you."

Aquan slowly picked up her fist, still glowering at Papandreas.

"It came from an archeological dig in Egypt, early 20th century when robbing graves of ancient kings passed for scientific pursuits."

"But Eunicus never lived outside of Greece."

"True. Yet his bridles passed through royal hands of many empires through war and plunder."

"How many of Eunicus's works survived?

"Enough. Their full promise unrealized until now. The power to recreate a Great Flood, an ancient deluge found in every culture. A global submersion of Surface Dwellers in an instant."

Aquan thought of her third vision and those terrified screams of Surface Dwellers. She feared her third vision might be a horrific premonition.

"The Vanquishment is a false prophecy."

"Not unless you decide to make it so. Our Protosian forefather drowned vain, haughty children of Atlantis for failing to worship him. Fate has once more given us a chance to devour arrogant Surface Dwellers who despoil our seas."

Papandreas pointed to her amulet around her neck.

"I won't help you to violate Eternal Concordia."

He leaned in close, his stale breath brushing across her cheek. "Return us to our rightful place, Aquan. Rule a future world in which saltwater reclaims every corner of our Earth."

"The Infinite Dreamer entrusts us to keep Eternal Concordia."

"What does keeping Eternal Concordia mean to you?"

"Preserving equilibrium between land and sea, between Surface Dwellers and Archigens. Our Sacred Songs decree it."

"Their meanings have been twisted. Nearly unrecognizable from their original cantos. Our earliest songs demand preservation of this fragile blue planet at all costs."

"You propose killing billions of Surface Dwellers to achieve your version of harmony. That's insane."

"Better their decimation than a complete ruination of Earth by them."

"Nobody's ever been right in their dire warnings about our world's end. Why believe it now?"

"Because it has been foreseen."

"By who?"

"Your mother."

"She never told me this. Evadne never warned me about these lost amulets or these bridles giving anyone this power."

"These potent gems are scattered to the four winds every century awaiting an Emissary to reset Eternal Concordia. At long last you are here, entering your first season. Poised to reclaim this planet for our sea." He clasped his hand over her forearm, his eyes wild with a thirst for revenge. "It will give you this power, Emissary. You can rule alongside the Margrave over this globe."

Aquan pulled her arm away from him. "I'll never join forces with him."

"You no longer need to be an errand girl for the Elder Council. They will bow their heads and fall to their knees before your throne, daughter of Proteus. Our House returned to its rightful dominion once more. You are our last, best chance to free us from our banishment before it's too late." Papandreas' thin voice cracked and he took several deep gulps of oxygen.

"The Infinite Dreamer promised to never allow another flood to destroy Earth again."

"But Surface Dwellers, like citizens of Atlantis, have failed to live up to their obligations to protect this world."

"It is not my place to judge them. I won't violate the Infinite Dreamer's sacred pact with them. Your dream of another Great Flood is nothing but a wild fantasy, a delusion."

"If that is true, then simply hand over your amulet and nothing will come of it."

Aquan turned away from him. "I will not test a divine pledge."

"Then perhaps a brief demonstration will show you that you do not accurately understand the Dreamer's real intentions. Please come with me."

Aquan reluctantly followed Papandreas to a private elevator that took them to an upper deck. He escorted her over to a gathering of the dinner guests sharing tiny glasses of Madeira port wine. Cutter and one Australian marine biologist chomped on fat cigars. Soft moonlight bathed this upper deck under a first quarter moon. Papandreas' guests squinted at several thousand dots of shimmering lights of pilgrims carrying candles. They walked along Candelaria's beach to its illuminated Basilica for its annual religious festival. Aquan felt it a moment before she saw it, a deep rumbling and then a series of roaring whooshes. Papandreas gripped Aquan's shoulder to prevent her from leaving *Athena's* deck. There were too many people around and too little time for her to transform. Aquan's throat closed up as she realized she would not be able to stop this carnage. Tsunami sirens screamed their belated warnings.

"Holy shit." Cutter dropped his cigar.

A second later, a colossal wave swept across the beach. Panicked shrieks of fleeing pilgrims filled the evening air. Squeals of twisting rebar and then thuds of concrete tumbling from basilica walls followed. Ringing bells from a basilica tower plunged into this angry surf. Growling waves swirled high swallowing up thousands of pilgrims and hungrily consumed an entire beachfront town in less than two minutes. These dark waters then receded, yanking battered village homes, smashed fishing boats and human bodies into murky depths. Shock froze Papandreas's guests as an eerie stillness fell across this devastated town.

"We gotta get below." Cutter pulled Jenn and other guests towards stairs leading to a lower deck for safety.

"See my truth," Papandreas whispered in Aquan's ear. "Know the Dreamer's will."

Trembling, Aquan stood speechless. She knew only one thing for certain; her mere existence caused another horrifying slaughter of innocents.

Chapter 22

The next morning, Papandreas postponed his maritime conference for three days as a somber pall fell over Tenerife. More than 632 people were known to be dead and about 1,500 more missing and presumed dead in Candelaria. Many thousands more were left injured and homeless, their community stripped down to heaps of stone rubble, twisted metal and demolished fishing boats. Aquan read about Papandreas' donation of ten million euros for tsunami relief and wished he'd choke on his own hypocrisy. Her disgust only grew as she observed Cutter ferrying medical staff and emergency supplies from Santa Cruz to Candelaria. But then he needed to maintain his cover and she needed to complete her mission.

Aquan received an e-mail from the Antiquarian that her package had been sent by courier to the Banker. She requested that the Antiquarian make the necessary arrangements for Nathan Ahava in the usual Brussels hotel. As Rajneet, her reflection could easily stay behind to report on the devastating tsunami while keeping a firm eye on *Calusa*. She then pulled the mirror out of its velvet pouch.

"*Amor vincit omnia.*"

*****

As Aquan tried to sleep, vivid flashes of Candelaria's tsunami and screams of its victims looped over and over in her mind. Restless, she got up for some fresh air on her hotel balcony and looked out over Brussels' cobble-stoned Grand Place. A rambunctious crowd of young people at a weekend beer festival stood in grim contrast to her thoughts about Candelaria's disaster. She watched revelers' cheerful faces as they moved from café to café and beer stall to beer stall tasting local brews. Last month, Aquan would have happily joined in with them before tagging mermaid maidenheads at local pubs until dawn. But not this time.

When morning came, she barely slept a full hour the night before. Yawning, she knotted her red silk tie and smoothed her pants. The Antiquarian had arranged for a tailored navy blue suit to be sent to her room. Her narrow rectangular glasses pinched her nose as she slicked back her sandy brown hair in a bathroom mirror. She hated to retire Mr. Moshe Ahava, a Holocaust survivor, who built a family textile empire after World War II and endowed his family's trust in one of Belgium's most prestigious private banks. Yet enough years had passed that she decided it was time to introduce Mr. Ahava's grandson, Nathan, to the Banker. Nathan, a successful London solicitor, would become a new executor for his family trust. Unlike other allies, the Banker knew nothing of Archigens, so no cryptic phrases were needed. Nathan's family already spoke the only global tongue that counted to the Banker, finance. Mr. Ahava and his family quietly deposited huge sums of money and rented a sizeable safety deposit box for nearly sixty years at his private bank.

"I am so sorry to hear about your grandfather's death, Mr. Ahava. He was a wonderful man." The Banker shook Aquan's hand.

"Thank you. My grandfather was truly one of a kind," said Aquan smiling.

The Banker ushered Aquan into an oak-paneled office where a young female receptionist placed a silver tray service of black currant tea and dark chocolate truffles on an ornate table next to a paisley guest chair. Aquan handed the Banker a leather portfolio with legal paperwork that the Antiquarian drafted with the help of one of his less-than-reputable contacts. As Aquan sipped tea and munched on a chocolate, the Banker squinted from behind a pair of thick glasses reviewing her thick wad of legal documents.

"Everything seems to be in order." He signed and stamped several documents. "I received a courier delivery for you yesterday and I had it placed in the safe overnight. My assistant will have it delivered to your private salon. Do you have your key, Mr. Ahava?"

Aquan pulled her key out from an inside suit pocket. "Yes, right here."

"Excellent. Please follow me."

The heels of his hand-made Italian shoes clicked on a marble floor as he led Aquan into a quiet bank basement. He punched in his code and pressed his thumb on a biometric fingerprint pad. A first set of glass doors swooshed open. A rotating video camera whirred from every corner. Behind another set of glass doors, a guard buzzed them in and Aquan signed in as Nathan Ahava. A second guard trailed them with a gleaming silver cart. They walked past neat rows of gilded safety deposit boxes nestled in individual slots, catacombs of centuries of hidden wealth. When they reached box number 2012, the Banker and Nathan inserted each of their keys into its twin locks and turned them simultaneously, freeing it from its secure place. A guard silently placed this long rectangular box on a cart and wheeled it into a windowless room. A sealed package rested on a marble table top with a cushioned chair pulled out for Aquan.

"Please take all of the time you need. You may dial seven on that phone if you need any assistance." He pointed to a slim black phone on the wall.

"Thank you," said Nathan nodding.

As the Banker departed, Aquan opened a package from the Antiquarian with a note of apology inside.

"Sorry. Only enough time for two."

She hoped for more but these two would have to do. Aquan slid both of them into her inside jacket pocket. Then she raised her box's cover where stacks of various currencies lined its inside, a small portion of converted proceeds from millennia of sunken treasure. Stuffing thirty thousand Euros into her wallet, Aquan had enough to make full payment to the Antiquarian's craftsmen and for her travel expenses.

Staring her amulet, she hoped it might give her guidance about where to go next. Her visions remained but one image containing *Calusa* seemed to be altered. Gypsy still barked on Cutter's storm-tossed deck but tinkling sounds of glass, not thunderous booms of an explosion, could be heard. She must leave it up to Rajneet to deal with any disturbances and keep focused on finding that next amulet.

As she hurried back to her hotel, she remembered

Papandreas told her that these stones had been dispersed across four winds. Her talisman had been recovered north from Vineta with another gem east from Shore Temple. Any remaining amulets must be somewhere north and west of the prime meridian. Yet with so many global spots claiming lineage to Atlantis, finding these amulets seemed like looking for a single krill in a blizzard of marine snow. Aquan needed to narrow down her options to improve her chances of finding these last two amulets before the Margrave.

Aquan had never called upon the Cartographer before and only knew about him through Mopsus's tutoring her on the Oceanic Scrolls. These earlier Emissary tales acclaimed his ability to interpret ancient maps when others believed in a flat Earth and major continents were unknown to each other. Slipping into the North Sea, Aquan joined a school of barking Soldierfish to disguise her journey to his home in Olympos.

Chapter 23

As dawn neared, Aquan caught sight of Chimera, eternal methane flames, spouting from Olympos's rocky Turkish coast. Swimming ashore on a deserted pebble beach, she transformed into Beate Gerhard, a six feet tall German backpacker with muscular legs and broad shoulders, carrying her trusty backpack. Her short wavy brown hair curled in summer humidity as she swatted away mosquitoes. Her khaki shorts and tie-dyed T-shirt clung to her sweaty body. Citrus and fig trees lined these steep trails and she snatched and devoured a sweet orange drooping from a low-hanging branch. A gently bubbling mountain stream served as her only companion for most of this strenuous hike with enormous boulders strewn across rutted trails. Crumbling Lycean and Roman ruins and a skeletal Vulcan temple peeked out of lush vines and scrub bushes, ghostly vestiges of ancient empires, once exalted then crushed in bloody battles. This serene pine forest eventually gave way to echoing shrieks of laughter and throbbing techno dance music floating down from bohemian bars and tree house youth hostels.

When she reached a main huddle of tree houses, the sun had risen and noisy partying had wound down. One passed out camper snored on a bench in a granite plaza and a small circle of hikers shared a joint around smoldering embers of a sandstone fire pit. A dirt path wound its way through a patchwork of rustic tree houses, some made of rough-hewn logs, others of simple pine clapboards. Each hostel reclined in sturdy pine tree limbs above her. As Beate, Aquan made her way to a more remote tree house camp where rickety log tree houses dangled precariously from thick tree limbs. She knocked on a sturdy wooden door of a ground level cabin flying a Turkish flag. A sleepy young man with a dark brown moustache and scraggly shoulder-length hair creaked his door open.

"All full. All full," he repeated. He yawned and pointed to a sign hanging in his window.

"Good morning, I'm Beate. May I please speak with Mr. Hephaestus?" Aquan asked in Turkish.

He shrugged his shoulders and then slammed his door shut. She knocked hard four or five times more until he opened it again.

"Do you know if Mr. Hephaestus moved? Where his family might live?"

"No, go try some other hostel owners. Maybe they'll know."

Aquan stopped at other registration cabins for tree house hostels but no one knew Mr. Hephaestus. Perhaps the Cartographer had moved to a nearby town. Or worse, maybe he died taking his secret treasure trove of maps with him. While pumping water into her canteen, Aquan tried not to think about that possibility and started to trek back to Olympos Beach.. Taking a detour to sit near a cluster of Chimera, Aquan hoped these flames that guided mariners for centuries might inspire her journey.

Resting, she heated a steel cup for tea over a small natural methane flame roiling out of split rocks. Looking out over a vast sea, a sense of hopelessness overwhelmed her. Icy fingers of doubt gripped her once more. Locating these scattered amulets in a couple of weeks seemed an impossible task. To think, she counted herself lucky to skip Convocation and now she felt beaten, her mission looking doomed to failure. If she could only talk to Mopsus or Aunt Sofronia for some guidance. But the Elder Council had forbidden her to return Rapture's End without bringing all of those ambers with her. Squeezing her eyes shut, Aquan tried to conjure up her mother's spirit to no avail. She gazed into her amulet and *Calusa's* image still burned brightest. How could she have been so stupid to let Cutter, a Drowner, distract her from her mission? Unexpectedly, the hopelessness of her mission engulfed her.

"Beate, Beate." A teen-aged girl ran toward her.

Aquan looked up as a girl with gleaming brown eyes and wide grin peeping out under a multi-colored cotton beanie. Her small chest heaved in and out of her floral T-shirt like an injured sparrow's quavering chest. Sweat glistened across her slender arms and legs after racing along this bumpy trail. She gasped for breath.

"I hear you are looking for Mr. Hephaestus."

"Yes, do you know where I can find him?"

"I'm Hephaestus."

Aquan looked this young girl up and down, wondering if she truly be the Cartographer so highly praised in the Oceanic Scrolls. Sniffing, Aquan did not detect a Hydromorph or Sea Monk only salty sea air.

"I know it's kind of hard to believe. But I am Fatimah, the only living descendant of Ahmet, known as Hephaestus. I'm really excited to finally meet you." She stuck out her delicate hand to shake Aquan's hand enthusiastically and continued to chirp animatedly. "My father and grandfather never had a chance to meet an Emissary. Only my great-great-grandfather, Serdar. I could almost burst. This is so cool," she giggled. "My grandfather was so sad when my parents had no sons. But my father taught me all about cartography. He told me that I'm a lot smarter than any boy in this region." She paused and drew a deep breath. "Oh wait, I'm getting ahead of things. You've got say your words first. My father made me practice my part every day."

Aquan smiled as Fatimah's chattiness reminded her of Thalassa, who must have already chosen her mate from a major House of Archigen. She longed for her friend's amiable prattle.

"What makes the waters of this Turquoise Coast so alluring?" asked Aquan.

"Cleopatra's lover, Marc Anthony, bestowed this shoreline upon her as a wedding gift. Her tears of joy gave this sea its aquamarine tinge," replied Fatimah.

"And why is its pounding surf so salty?"

"Because Cleopatra's teardrops of regret saturated its waves with bitter brine after her lover's betrayal."

Aquan's heart leapt with hope that not all was lost.

"Hallowed be Eternal Concordia, Cartographer," she said.

"Hallowed be Eternal Concordia to you, Emissary," gushed Fatimah.

"I'm sorry to show up so unexpectedly, but it's an

emergency. I need help to find two more of these." Aquan pulled out and displayed her amulet. "I don't know where to go next."

"Come with me," said Fatimah.

She led Aquan to a crumbling crypt shell with Aphrodite's face and a ship's hull carved into its stone walls. A gnarled web of fig tree branches shaded this burial site as twisted vines embraced an ancient sarcophagus. Aquan peered inside a rough hole punched through a front tomb wall. Centuries ago, pirates had pillaged any treasures from this crypt, but a red, blue and yellow tile mosaic of a compass rose remained largely untouched on its floor. Fatimah ran her fingers over this tomb's inscription.

"It's a sweet funereal epitaph. Please put your hand here, Emissary, and say it with me," Fatimah said.

She guided Aquan's fingertips over it as they recited its words together.

"His ship sailed into its final harbor,
With no hope of a sailor's wind, it journeyed no more.
The spirit of Captain Eudemos was extinguished,
His life as short as a wave breaking over a distant shore."

The Cartographer motioned for Aquan to crawl inside. Each pointed edge of this tri-colored compass rose separated to reveal an underground stone staircase. Summer's heat gave way to cool dry air below Captain Eudemos's crypt. Fatimah flipped on a switch softly illuminating a series of underground chambers. Each wall of these subterranean rooms bore royal symbols of a succession of ancient conquerors. A final chamber, scrawled with Neolithic creature and plant characters, contained hundreds of stacks of rolled maps secreted away in individual wall alcoves.

"Our family has been collecting and safeguarding them since ancient Egyptian times."

"How do you know which map to examine?" asked Aquan.

"Only ten of these maps relate to aligning Eternal Concordia between Earth and Sea. One map for each hundred-year cycle within a millennium."

Aquan recalled Papandreas's words about this cycle and her claimed place in it.

"Which one of these atlases applies to this cycle, Cartographer?"

"I don't know. You must choose it."

"But how?"

"I will take them out and you must decide which one is right."

While Fatimah pulled maps from their cubby holes, Aquan searched her memories for any teaching from Mopsus about maps. None came readily to mind. Fatimah carefully arranged ten maps in containers of stone, wood or animal hides on a large square table hewn from fig bark.

"Please select which map you wish me to interpret."

Fatimah took several steps away from this simple table. Aquan approached this row of maps, gently touching each map container and hoping for inspiration. Fatimah gave a reassuring smile as Aquan slowly passed by each map. She nervously reached out to touch a map wrapped in a gritty elephant hide, and then put it down. Leaning over a ninth map in a varnished ebony box, her amulet pulsed and vibrated as it had done with Papandreas's bridle. Aquan touched a tenth map in a stone container and her amulet fell silent. She then touched another map holder and her talisman remained still, only whirring to life over this ninth one.

"It must be this one," declared Aquan.

She cradled this ebony box in her arms as her gemstone continued to blink and drone. Fatimah placed cloth gloves on her hands and gingerly removed this map from its black container, unrolling it carefully on her tabletop.

"A beautiful parchment with hand-painted land masses," said Fatimah. "There are some Spanish notations at its edges." She peered through a magnifying glass at a weathered atlas. "Awesome," squealed Fatimah. "It's Alonso Sanchez de Huelva's map." She handed her magnifier to Aquan.

"Who was he?" asked Aquan, scrutinizing this colorful map.

"A great adventurer and ship's pilot who first explored the

New World for Europeans in the fifteenth century."

"I thought that was Columbus," said Aquan.

Fatimah smiled. "Yeah about twenty years later. de Huelva explored it first and drew this map. He fell ill on a return journey and stayed at Columbus's home in Madeira, spilling all of his adventures and showing his charts. He never recovered and Columbus wisely peddled his maps to Europe's royal families as his own creations. And the rest, as they say, is history."

"There are no longitude or latitude lines," said Aquan. "How did they find their way?"

"It's a portolan map for mariners with compass rose symbols designating currents."

Fatimah pointed to an enormous wind rose off Africa's southern tip and a dozen smaller ones dotting this map.

"It doesn't show all of today's land masses. Some of these place names are made up. How will I know where to go?"

"These nautical charts were mostly guesses, more art than science back then. But I can make some comparisons with modern atlases for you. Give you basic guesses of how they might line up with today's globe."

Aquan wasn't sure that rough estimates would be enough to locate two gemstones before another full moon in less than two weeks. Yet it was better than nothing.

"I found my first amulet here in Tallinn, Estonia and another one in India."

Aquan grimaced at having lost that one to the Sea Monk.

"Where were they precisely found, Emissary?"

"I don't have exact locations. One was in a Tallinn marketplace, but supposedly came from a submerged city called Vineta. A second gemstone was buried into a relief at Shore Temple in Mahabalipuram. Both places are linked to lost civilizations associated with Atlantis. I'm assuming these last ones will be, too."

"Each one was found near bays. Bay of Finland and Bay of Bengal." She pointed at each location. "One northeast, one southeast."

"They were tossed to the four winds. I think the other

amulets might be hidden in or near bays on northwest and southwest points on a wind rose. But which sisters of Atlantis? I don't know."

"There are so many possibilities, Emissary," said Fatimah. She puzzled over de Huelva's map for a few moments. "I have an idea."

She hurried over to another cubby hole and pulled out a roll of tracing paper, an over-sized beam compass and an enormous wooden protractor. Fatimah smoothed her tracing paper over de Huelva's map with its colorful contours still visible. Sliding her beam compass wide, she put its needle pin in a main compass rose's center and scribed concentric circles of equal distance from this central point. Aquan watched intently as she carefully etched twelve circles radiating from this wind rose.

Fatimah grabbed her protractor and drew lines from the Bay of Finland through a center spot in this main compass rose to a southwest corner and from the Bay of Bengal to a farthest northwest tip. She ticked twenty-four spots where lines intersected with her circles.

"Each 'x' is a potential site."

"That's still a large number. I only have about two weeks to find them, Cartographer."

"Your amulet, Emissary."

Fatimah pointed to Aquan's talisman. She removed her necklace and walked around this atlas swinging it over its crossed intersections. Her gem lit up as she dangled it over a farthest outer ring on a southwestern map edge. Fatimah circled that "x". Passing her amulet over its northwest quadrants, she shadowed marked intersections on Fatimah's concentric circles. Her amulet glowed and hummed when she reached a fourth circle's center. Fatimah circled that second location. Pressing down her tracing paper, Fatimah groaned.

"Neither of these named spots is connected to modern land masses. Please give me a couple of hours to calculate some possible coordinates, Emissary."

*****

Sand pebbles crunched under Aquan's feet as she walked to an isolated portion of Olympos Beach. Stripping down, she dove into breaking waves, relaxing in warm waters. Salty ripples tickled her nose. She swam into an underwater cave and fell into a restful trance. In her dream state, she imagined Thalassa and other young Archigens in a procession of her peers celebrating Convocation, their first mating season. Aquan envisioned Archigen parents escorting each young mate wearing their lineage sashes through a network of caves in Rapture's End, their pathways illuminated with green biolumens symbolizing fertility. A dozen Conches, one for each House of Oceanus, sounded off as young Archigens approached Quartz Hall and presiding leaders of their Houses.

In her reverie, she saw her Aunt smiling at Thalassa, anointing her forehead and wrists with oil from now-extinct baleen gray whales and crowning her head with a wreath of sacred red algae. All Archigen Houses would unite in a banquet overflowing with riches of the sea, their high-pitched whistles and clicks reverberating throughout Rapture's End. Then a final chorus of Conch blasts would free first season Archigens to pursue their desired mates.

Aquan envisioned Thalassa laughing and flirting with a handsome Archigen hunter and a muscled Brizon swimmer. Each potential mate flushed a series of camouflage colors in rapid succession to Thalassa's delight. A yellow fin tuna squirmed as the Archigen seized it as a delicious gift for her. Then the Brizonian swooped in and snatched this captured fish from his rival and laid his stolen catch before Thalassa. The two challengers began to wrestle swirling sand around them. A third male of Archigen lineage grabbed each battling rival by their tails and flung them across a gorge. Thalassa squeaked with delight.

Churning dust obscured this interloper's face as he clicked and flexed his sinewy biceps. He flapped his scaly tail creating such powerful currents that her other suitors became exhausted, like salmon swimming up steep mountain streams. This victor grunted and reached his hand out to Thalassa. She placed her algae garland over his head and he placed his wreath over her turquoise tresses. In Aquan's daydream,

Thalassa's mate turned and looked squarely at Aquan before stealing away with her friend. His face bore Cutter's likeness on a shimmering silver chest and rainbow fishtail body of an Archigen male. Startled, Aquan instantly awoke and resurfaced, dazed and gasping for air.

She swam out of this cave and played in currents with loggerhead turtles until orange and purple sunset painted the sky. In darkness, she returned to Captain Eudemos's tomb and found Fatimah putting away each map into its assigned nook. A small hand-drawn chart with longitude and latitude coordinates lay on her chart table.

"Emissary, I think I've narrowed it down to these two locations." Fatimah discussed her calculations based on de Heulva's map along with historic claims of a mythical Atlantis. "Your best bets are Bay of Tulum, off Mexico's coast."

"A seaside home of Mayan lineage, descendants of Mu," replied Aquan.

"Yes, a sister continent to Atlantis. Its ruins, the only surviving Mayan sea fortress and temple, sitting on a bay."

"Where is your second option?"

"Hope Bay, off Trinity Peninsula, in Antarctica."

"Antarctica? How could that barren continent ever be confused with Atlantis?"

"I had a similar reaction. But I went back into my grandfather's historical logs and he noted a Jesuit priest named Athanasius Kircher, an esteemed natural scientist and Egyptologist. Kircher produced an ancient Egyptian map linking Antarctica to Atlantis. He claimed Antarctica was once a tropical Utopia before it broke off from South America. It became submerged under glacial ice and sea water to become a frozen moonscape."

"It's still a lot of territory to cover to find two tiny amulets," said Aquan.

"I wish I could give you more precise coordinates. But these points are my best guesses, Emissary." Fatimah squeezed a hand-written chart into Aquan's hands. "I've also drawn latitude and longitude calculations of nearby coastlines. I hope they help direct your search."

"Now where to start, north or south?" Aquan wondered aloud.

"Our ancestors often looked to Chimera for guidance."

"Thank you for your help, Cartographer. Your father would be very proud of you."

Fatimah smiled and held both of Aquan's hands in hers. "Hallowed be Eternal Concordia. I wish you well, Emissary." She bowed at her waist. "I hope I can be of service to you again."

*****

Once more, Aquan trekked up to Chimera under a star-filled sky. Several groups of hikers gathered quietly around methane cracks, chatting and marveling at their constant blazes. A young man sat on a large boulder and played a brass shepherd's kaval, his fingers bouncing across its grooved air holes. Chimera flames seemed to dance to his lilting tune, their smoke snaking up to a little less than a half-moon. Aquan looked out over a calm sea, rubbing her talisman with her fingers. She tore an empty corner of Fatimah's chart and rolled it between her fingers. Placing this fragment into a Chimera flare, she watched it shrink and blacken. A bluish smoke rose from this burning paper gliding south in a mild breeze. She shuddered with thoughts of taking on Antarctica's frigid waters.

Chapter 24

Two polar bears fighting over a harp seal's bloody carcass offered a first telltale sign that Aquan approached sea borders to the House of Boreas. Briny Antarctic waters scratched through her gills and reddened her eyes. Splintered ice chunks drifting past her soon disappeared into a vast ice field. As its ice mantle thickened above her, a foggy haze was cast over swirling currents. Aquan never met a Borean but Mopsus spoke of their distinct culture during her years of training. North Wind females seldom mixed with other Archigen Houses, preferring to live amongst their own in an immense solitude of undersea glacial ridges and mountains. She retained her Triton form remembering Mopsus's teaching that their fierce Borean spirit of endurance was only bested by their insatiable curiosity.

Aquan felt uncertain about whether she should arrive armed with a gift of whale blubber or a loaded spear gun. She brought both, including a variety of neurotoxin darts secreted away in her pouch. At a distance, four Borean sentries patrolled frozen columns carved out of a glacial entrance to their nation. Their delicate white porcelain faces belied their blubbery thick skins designed to tolerate subzero temperatures. Their slender torsos gave way to powerful albino minke dorsal fins and tails. Their stark white locks of hair hovered like puffy cumulus clouds over their bodies and down to their fluke tips. They stiffened up and flashed their serrated steel claws when their hunting radar detected Aquan's movements.

Once they seized their jagged ice spears, Aquan reeled against a sweep of wintry currents to slow her advance and emitted calming clicks and squeals. She sat on a frosty ridge to await their sentry's interrogation. One Borean, with deep set gray eyes, wriggled toward her and clutched a spear. At a safe distance, she stopped to examine Aquan.

"Who are you? Why do you trespass here?"

Aquan heard cracking sounds as this Borean's youthful,

high-pitched voice bounced off a glacial shelf above her.

"I'm Aquan of Rapture's End. I come to pay homage to your queen."

Aquan jerked a seaweed mesh ball filled with whale meat.

"No one sees our queen of their own accord. She must summon you."

"Then a gift for you to allow me to visit your territory and await your queen's invitation."

"You cannot bribe me, Triton. Only Boreans may pass."

"Then I will become a Borean."

Shivering, Aquan transformed into a replica of this guard. Leaning back, this sentry let out a yelp of alarm, shattering some slender icicles hanging from a nearby ice ridge. This Borean guard shot away from Aquan, returning to her peers. Three guards then sped back, their spears in hand, while a fourth one headed for reinforcements within their community. Two of them dragged a fishing net spun from sturdy twisted strands of white Borean hair. Aquan heard a zing of an ice spear as it whizzed past her head, smashing on an ice chunk floating behind her.

Transforming into a Giant Magellan King Crab, Aquan clambered atop a nearby ice ridge. Another guard heaved her ice lance which shattered against Aquan's steely red shell. As they neared her, two other sentries slung their net over Aquan. Her razor-sharp pincers and spiny shell shredded their silken net as if it was a gossamer spider web. Stretching out her pincers, Aquan snatched up two guards and held them high above her head. Her loud chirps pierced the air as she rubbed her two rear claws against her shell sides. Flinging these guards, they tumbled and slid across this slippery glacial terrain. A remaining guard flung ice chunks which smashed into tiny ice cubes on her hard shell. Aquan scrambled across this craggy ice field toward the entry to Borean territory.

Six Borean archers and another two dozen guards greeted Aquan as she squeezed through a columned entry into their kingdom. Aquan groaned as two arrows pierced her soft underbelly, four others bounced off her casing. She swung around and backed into a group of oncoming Borean soldiers, protecting her underbelly from their arrows. Numerous Boreans jumped out of her way and several guards hollered in pain as her thorny ridges scraped against them. She swept through their defenses churning purple blood of injured sentries in their icy blue water. Suddenly, a thunderous screech scattered these attacking Boreans and a second shriek caused them to vanish into hidden defensive caves and ridges.

Aquan slowly turned around and found an Elder Borean, her snow white hair turned a steely gray, her porcelain features lost in weather-beaten creases. A long uneven gray scar was slashed across her skin, from her right cheek down to her shoulder, possibly from a battle with a neighborhood killer whale. She didn't don a spear, but her finger nails wore long steel claws with serrated edges for close, deadly combat.

"Reveal yourself, witch."

Aquan quivered and returned to her Triton form. "I am no witch."

"Then by what magic do you cast these spells?" she asked. Her tone indicated that she was used to demanding answers and getting them, immediately.

"It is not magic. I am an Emissary."

She sized up Aquan.

"Impossible. There have been no Emissaries for centuries. Not since the Great Insurrection."

Aquan had never heard of this event.

"I don't know about this rebellion. Only that I've been able to transform on land and sea since my birth."

"Prove yourself."

In an instant, Aquan turned into this old Borean and cackled before turning into a slithering yellowish brown eelpout, and then back to her own form. "No magic potions. No spells. Just me."

"Who are your people?"

"I'm Aquan of the Houses of Triton and Archigen." Aquan paused momentarily wondering if she should be saying Protosian instead. "Daughter of Evadne and Phorcys."

"I am Hecate, Queen's consul. House of Boreas."

"I must speak with your queen."

"No one may address Queen Chione, except those that she calls to her throne."

"I come on a mission vital to all Archigens. To preserve Eternal Concordia from perilous attack."

"No one may threaten Eternal Concordia."

"The Margrave and his fellow Exoris are moving beyond threats and are planning to create imbalance."

"That is heresy." Her nostrils flared. "So why do you come here? We are no friend of the Margrave."

"Fate has sent me here. Your Queen may be essential to stop his conspiracy."

She furrowed her wrinkled brow.

"Wait here and I will see if my Queen wishes any contact with you."

Hecate whisked away leaving Aquan drifting alone in an ice field. She felt several dozen pairs of eyes watching her as she swam past their territory entry to retrieve her net of whale blubber. She felt twinges of pain and looked down to see two gashes on her left side from Borean arrows. Reaching inside her pouch, Aquan pulled out a vial of Mopsus's healing elixir. Her bottle was nearly empty after she rubbed a few drops directly over her wounds. Most of her healing balm had been dispensed for Raynord's injuries, and Cutter's, too. Cutter. Her jaw tightened and her teeth ground as she thought of him. She hoped another tsunami would devour him just as it had drowned those innocent pilgrims at Candelaria. A half-hour later, Hecate returned with three armed Boreans.

"Our Queen will see you. Follow me."

Her Consul led Aquan across a mile of glacial mountains, some so high that they nearly touched lumpy undersides of surface ice packs. They entered a white bioluminescent tunnel burrowed into a peak, Aquan's fish tail flapping against its narrow contours. This narrow corridor opened into a flat plain at the foot of Queen Chione's blue ice castle chiseled out of a cavernous glacial mountain. Ice spears by their sides, Borean guards patrolled its semicircle entryway and archers with crossbows peeked out of every carved turret and tower.

"Quite a welcoming party," said Aquan.

"Our troops are always on high alert in case outsiders try to mount an escape attempt. We restrain many dangerous Archigens in this ice pack."

"I didn't know Boreans operated a prison."

"We prefer to say captive stasis." She arched her eyebrow in disapproval. "Until the Elder Council decrees their release, our detainees are kept in a constant dream state. Hardly cruel punishment compared to most earthly prisons."

"Who are these detainees?"

"Archigens who have committed serious crimes against their Houses."

"It must be risky to have these criminals within your borders."

"Our remote location and challenging environment make our territory ideal for security purposes. These stasis ice chambers are not near our core community, yet we remain vigilant nonetheless. Our Queen must be protected at all costs, especially at this time."

"Is this a mating period for your Queen?" asked Aquan, thinking of Convocation back home.

Hecate smiled. "Boreans share sensual pleasures amongst ourselves, but our Queen's reproduction is asexual. She is spawning our next generation for our community's hatchery."

The Consul's party swam through a fortress entry in this glacial mountain. Aquan craned her neck up to gaze at ice crystals sparkling from icicles as wide as tree trunks hanging from a distant, unseen ceiling. A broad pale green trail of glinting peridots covered a narrow walkway to an ice throne covered in shimmering diamonds. An ornate chair dwarfed two ten-foot long Weddell seals lounging alongside it, their yowls echoing in this desolate hall.

"Silence, children," she clicked. Hecate gently brushed their zinc-colored coats. "Feed them and take them up for some air." She directed a Borean guard. "Please wait here and give me your gift."

Aquan handed her tethered bait ball to Hecate who disappeared into an ice shaft behind her queen's throne. Two remaining guards nipped at Aquan's fish tail as she treaded water awaiting Hecate's return. Another hour passed and Aquan felt each thump of her heartbeat as critical time ticked away on her mission. Thinking she should depart for Mexico soon, the Consul suddenly returned.

"Our Queen will grant you a brief audience. But I will keep your visit short as she is greatly fatigued from two weeks of spawning. Speak softly and whatever you must report do so quickly."

Behind her Queen's throne, Hecate waved her hand across an invisible ice wall seam and it slid open for them. Swimming down another corridor, Hecate and Aquan descended into an antechamber. A dozen Boreans guarded its mouth and four more Boreans fell in behind them. Hecate once more waved her hand over some concealed monitoring device. Two Gothic ice doors on golden hinges slowly opened. A shrill series of pained clicks and squeaks stabbed Aquan's ears. She covered her ears as these piercing sounds continued.

"Her spawning calls can be sharp for those unfamiliar with Borean birth pangs," said Hecate. "Nearly 500 new Boreans will free themselves from their jelly shells in the next two months. Imagine how much pain our Queen suffers for her people."

Swaying purple and yellow fan coral partially obscured the Queen's birthing chamber, raised high on a frosty ice platform. Aquan first spied a curved tip of a sleigh-shaped bed made of blue and green striped glacial ice. She nearly gasped at a cocoon of silken cords crisscrossing their Queen's brilliant white torso, strapping her down on her left side to a rimed slab. Loose strands of snow white hair wriggled like tiny albino garden eels from her hair piled high on her head. Her arms and tail flailed violently as her anguished cries rang out in her birthing compartment.

The Queen's pale white face contorted with agony as three or four large milky pellets were deposited into a translucent egg sack. Six Borean sentinels surrounded this clear sack to protect her eggs. Her claws raked both sides of her ice bed. She panted and then her screeches subsided and her body fell limp, no longer pushing against her restraints. Several attendants comforted their Queen, rubbing her back and stroking her fish tail. Hecate motioned Aquan to come forward.

Aquan bowed as she approached. "Hallowed be Eternal Concordia, Queen Chione. Please forgive this intrusion."

"Hallowed be Eternal Concordia to you, Emissary." Queen Chione waved off an attendant trying to feed her some of Aquan's whale blubber gift. "We have only met one Emissary, nearly three centuries ago. Come closer. Let us see you clearly."

Her sparkling gray eyes seemed to look right through Aquan. She reached out and patted Aquan's cheek with the soft back of her clawed hand.

"Why does the Elder Council send a child to do its bidding?"

"I've reached my first season already, Queen," said Aquan.

"A whole one hundred years." The Queen threw back her head and let out a throaty laugh. Her attendants echoed her chortle with smirks and squeaks.

"I come in search of an enchanted amulet, like this one." Aquan held up her amber pendant. "The Margrave seeks another like it to destroy Eternal Concordia."

"It is not familiar to us."

"Is there any chance it may have been secreted away in Borean territory without your Majesty's knowledge?"

She narrowed her eyes. "Nothing occurs in our territory without our knowledge."

"Forgive my poor choice of words, your Majesty. But you are so young and it may have happened before your reign."

Queen Chione smiled flattered that the flower of youth still graced her appearance.

"All of our Borean stories and secrets are passed down from queen to queen since time immemorial."

Aquan couldn't hide her disappointment. "I am sorry that I interrupted you during this sensitive time, your Highness. I will take my leave and wish you hallowed be Eternal Concordia."

She bowed to Queen Chione. Dejected, she dropped her head and wondered if the Cartographer had miscalculated her location.

"And what of your mother, Evadne?"

Aquan looked up. "Sadly, my mother sleeps in Musterion, your Majesty. Buried in our Memorial Grotto at Rapture's End."

"That would be quite a surprise to that Timarch platoon which came to transfer her but two days ago."

Aquan's eyes popped open wide. "My mother? Imprisoned in stasis?"

"Yes, for some ninety years."

The Queen nodded to Hecate who waved her hand across an ice wall. A flickering image of hundreds of rows of ice blocks with Archigens encased in sea water was displayed. At one end of a row of ice tombs, Evadne floated in liquid stasis, her eyes open, but expressionless, her arms and fish tail limp. Aquan's heart nearly burst through her chest. She reached out to touch her mother's face in this vision.

"What was her crime, your Highness?"

"We are neither judge nor jury. We only carry out sentences until the Elder Council orders a release."

"Who took her, your Highness? Commander Aries?"

"We don't know what Timarch officer led the security forces, but an Archigen Elder directed their operations."

Instantly, Aquan's head swirled and pounded with a million contradictory thoughts. Her mother in stasis while she mourned her death since childhood. Her voice choked into silence for a moment with a mix of shock, confusion and disbelief. "Who—who was the Elder, your Majesty so I may ask him about her transfer?"

"We are not at liberty to disclose that," she replied. The Queen tore a slice of blubber from her servant's outstretched hands and devoured it in a single gulp.

"Do you know where they took her, your Majesty?"

"No, their leader did not share those arrangements with us."

"Please tell me what you can, your Highness. I beg of you." Aquan's plaintive squeak alarmed Hecate who grabbed Aquan's arm and pulled her away from her Queen's bedside.

The Queen's body stiffened and her face grimaced as she beat back a wave of contractions before wilting exhausted on to her ice slab again.

"Enough," said Hecate in Aquan's ear. "Her Highness needs to preserve her strength. Time to go, child."

Five Borean sentinels joined Hecate to remove Aquan from Queen Chione's chamber.

As she struggled against them, Aquan called out, "Queen Chione, help me. Please reunite me with my mother."

"Silence, girl." Hecate hissed and brandished her steel claws.

"As a compassionate Queen who now gives birth to her own children," cried out Aquan. Borean soldiers dragged her away from their Queen's ice platform. "As a mother of daughters! Would you want your daughters torn from your protection, Queen?"

As doors to her bed chamber were about to slam shut behind Aquan. "Wait," the Queen said. "We have not dismissed this Emissary yet."

Hecate nodded to her guards to release Aquan who rushed back to Queen Chione's side.

"We will help you today, not as a Borean queen, but as a mother. But you must do something for us first."

"Anything, Queen Chione," blurted Aquan.

"You must help win back our twin sister's freedom. Born three minutes after we first emerged from our shared egg. Zetes was kidnapped from our territory two decades ago."

"Who took her, your Highness?"

"Exori agents. The Margrave demanded our allegiance to ransom her. We refused so she has remained in his custody."

"Is she beyond Obzula Ridge?"

"She could not survive its boiling steam vents. But she is our twin and we sense that she is still alive."

"Do you know where she is imprisoned, Queen Chione?"

"We don't know where she is held. Perhaps if you have something he wants in exchange for her, she will be freed."

The Queen pointed at Aquan's amulet around her neck. Aquan didn't plan to give away her strongest bargaining chip to a Queen she didn't trust. "I can't give you this."

"Then we can't tell you about who took your mother away."

She looked down at her necklace and wondered if Mopsus had misinterpreted its visions. Her mother's pearl tears representing her current confinement. If her mother truly remained alive, Aquan couldn't let this chance to rescue her slip through her fingers. Slowly she unhooked her necklace and removed her amulet from its chain. Aquan allowed her fingertips to slightly tremble as she handed her talisman to Hecate.

"Seek out Elder Camulus if you want to discover your mother's whereabouts."

Aquan voice quavered. "Thank you, Queen Chione. Hallowed be Eternal Concordia."

She bowed solemnly to Queen Chione and sped out of her castle, expecting to be out of Borean territory well before any exchange of her amulet for Zetes could be set into motion. Aquan headed north and hoped to sense any movements of that platoon which snatched her mother. After traveling two hundred miles, she reluctantly realized that too much time already passed since their departure. Even her keen senses could no longer detect their path. She thought of returning to Olympos to seek further help from the Cartographer, but her mind raced with angry thoughts about being deceived about her mother's death.

Knowing her next destination should be Mexico to find that third amulet, her fury and bewilderment blinded Aquan to her mission. There was time before the next full moon and her rage pulled her back home. Besides, her mother's vision had spurred this fear of another Vanquishment and she needed her advice. To hell with any Council orders not to return without all four amulets. She must discover the truth without alerting the Elder Council, including Aunt Sofronia and Mopsus. But who could she trust to know and tell her about such sensitive information? Raynord. She remembered he begged for her forgiveness at Shore Temple. Aquan cringed at the thought that he participated in his grand deception. Or perhaps Raynord knew nothing and merely regretted not preventing her fellow Tritons' deaths?

With a Sailfish's lightning speed, Aquan raced to Rapture's

End to demand answers about her mother's sudden rebirth.

Chapter 25

As Rajneet, Aquan kept close tabs on *Calusa* in Santa Cruz. She noticed Tuttleberry continuing to stalk Cutter. A creature of habit, Aquan recognized that he seldom deviated from his daily pattern of activity during Papandreas's revived conference. At 7:00 a.m., he exited a rundown motel best known for its voracious bed bugs and buxom hookers. His baggy blue suit, unacquainted with an iron, jiggled as his rotund body waddled down to a tiny café overlooking a harbor marina. Sipping on his coffee and munching a bran muffin, Tuttleberry scribbled notes into a tattered yellow legal pad and whispered into a handheld recorder all morning long. He snapped photos with his cell phone camera of anyone visiting with Cutter, mostly Jenn or Emerson, during breaks from their academic presentations. His crooked dark sunglasses and battered straw Cuban fedora could not disguise a permanent scowl on his face.

At noon, he would lumber over to a dockside canteen truck and order a greasy cheeseburger and fries, sitting on a park bench with a direct line of sight to *Calusa*'s slip. He stayed there until sunset jotting notes and speaking into his recorder as Cutter helped with local tsunami relief efforts. She thought it must surely gall Tuttleberry to see Cutter's rescue actions having pegged him as a scam artist. Little did he realize that Cutter allied himself with terrible creatures that caused this horrific disaster.

Every evening, Tuttleberry returned to his café perch for quick dinner and then lurked around a marina gate waiting for Cutter to leave for his nightly ramblings. As in Hobart, Tuttleberry followed Cutter to sailor's taverns where he downed beers and shot pool with other local captains into the wee hours before stumbling back to his boat. Sometimes alone, sometimes with a new female friend. Aquan hated to admit that she felt a twinge of jealousy. She rapidly batted away these feelings, reminding herself that he served as a Drowner, an Exori puppet.

When morning arrived, Tuttleberry began is daily cycle

again. Aquan puzzled over his obsessive dedication to his fraud investigation since nothing of significance ever seemed to happen. There had to be more to this story than Cutter ever told her.

As the conference approached its closing day, Aquan noticed that Tuttleberry lurked in dusky shadows as Cutter pulled his catamaran into its slip at sunset, having completed another day aiding tsunami rescuers. Tuttleberry watched Cutter hosing down his boat and inched closer to a marina gate. He twice tried to catch a swinging gate from exiting boaters, but failed. Aquan wondered if he might finally try to confront Cutter on his ship. Although she hated to miss those possible fireworks, Aquan had already scheduled a post-dinner interview as Rajneet with Jenn. She headed for Hotel Royal in hopes of finding out *Calusa*'s upcoming itinerary.

After a final conference dinner, Aquan found a quiet corner booth at a lobby bar for her evening interview. Jenn sipped on a vodka tonic as she spoke excitedly about future steps in her L11 research. Aquan didn't enjoy alcohol, it dried out her gills, so she drank spring water as she took notes. Observing Jenn's animated facial gestures and expressive eyes, Aquan admired her enthusiasm for her project. Could she be a Drowner, too? Aquan doubted it.

"When do you return back to Key West to continue your research, Dr. Ortiz?"

"Our flight leaves day after tomorrow. I expect to be back at the Institute in about two days."

"And what of your floating research vessel, *Caboose*?"

"Actually, it's called *Calusa*," Jenn said.

"What a funny name? Does it mean anything?" she asked.

"Yes, it basically means 'shell-seekers'. An indigenous people who lived in our Everglades. They were decimated through a deadly combination of disease and warfare."

"How terrible." Aquan winced as she thought of her own Triton House's devastation.

"Unfortunately, we missed an opportunity to learn so much history swept away in those early Spanish conquests. Luckily, some researchers continue to try to piece together what remains of their society."

"When does your research vessel return to Florida?"

"It should take a few weeks for it to reach home port in Key West."

Scribbling in her reporter's notebook, Aquan knew she must speed up that timetable if *Calusa* was to play a role in finding a Gulf of Mexico amulet.

"Do you have any L11 microbes in containment on your boat?"

"We have shipped most L11 specimens back to our Institute for further study. Only a small number are locked away on board for follow-up work."

"I'd like to take a few photos of you on your research vessel working with your samples. They would be great for my article, Dr. Ortiz." Aquan hoped to glean something about Tuttleberry's visit or maybe even catch him arguing with Cutter.

Jenn paused. "I'm not sure if our captain, Dave Cutter, who lives aboard, is busy hosting guests this evening."

Aquan frowned in mock disappointment and dangled a juicy publicity carrot in front of Jenn.

"Oh, that's too bad, Dr. Ortiz. Photos always increase my editor's willingness to publish my articles." She closed her notebook and shoved it into her reporter's tote bag. "Without pictures, it will be difficult to squeeze in our interview with all of this pressing tsunami news. It would be fantastic to be able to bring more attention to your research and your Institute in my newspaper. It has an upscale, progressive readership that might be supportive of your project."

Jenn put down her drink. "Hmmm. I guess we could walk over and see if Cutter's boat might be available for some quick photos."

"Wonderful idea," said Aquan. "If we hurry, I can make an early paper deadline. Maybe get your interview published in this week's science section."

She quickly paid their bar tab and hustled Jenn to the marina, a fast ten-minute walk away. Near a dock gate, Aquan heard fluttering sounds of Pteron wings, but could not detect its location. Jenn entered her marina code and they walked along dimly lit planks as the dock swayed under their feet. Jenn climbed aboard Cutter's vessel.

"Cutter? Cutter?" she called out. There was no reply. She rapped on his boat's bulkhead door, but no response followed. "You're in luck. Guess he's not in so you can click away."

Jenn pulled out her bulkhead key, but found it was already unlocked. She slid it open and Aquan trailed her below deck. Dim emergency lights hummed in a still main cabin. Aquan sniffed a lingering stench of a Sea Monk a moment before Jenn flicked on a light switch.

"Oh my God," she cried out.

Aquan snatched a lethal dart from her tote and squeezed it in her hand. Shards of glass from broken test tubes littered the vessel's lab floor. Lab microscopes were toppled over and her research notes were scattered like confetti across her workbench. Jenn raced over to her specimen cabinet and punched in her security code. The door popped open and Jenn peered inside to find her limited onboard samples remained sealed and dated inside. Suddenly, Aquan grabbed Jenn's arm when she glimpsed a stream of blood snaking away from an edge of her lab table.

"There's blood, Dr. Ortiz. Quick, get help quickly," said Aquan. "I'll stay here to preserve this scene until police arrive."

As Jenn raced topside, Aquan looked out and spied curious boaters tumbling out of their vessels and gathering in small knots around *Calusa*. Aquan slammed the bulkhead door shut. Bits of broken glass crunched under her feet as she inched along Jenn's lab table, a lethal dart poised on her fingertips. Aquan readied herself to find Cutter dead or seriously wounded, done in by his association with Exoris. Grimacing, she discovered Tuttleberry, his throat slashed right through to his vertebrae, his rumpled fedora soaked in blood. A blood-stained galley butcher's knife rested near his body.

Aquan reached down and quickly removed Tuttleberry's recorder from his inside jacket pocket, stuffing them into her canvas bag. She couldn't find his cell phone at first. Looking around, it seemed to have disappeared. Dropping to her knees, she squinted and looked under Jenn's lab bench bolted to the ship's deck. His slim cell phone was wedged into a sliver of space between the table's base and Cutter's deck, an impossible spot to reach fast. Before she could shape-shift, squawking sirens announced the arrival of local police who swarmed over *Calusa*. Jenn and Aquan were taken to a police station to give separate witness statements. Despite their protests, its chief detective told them not to leave Tenerife until their stories were corroborated. As Aquan and Jenn signed out of a visitor's log, two officers were dragging Cutter in handcuffs into its lobby.

Jenn rushed up to him and one officer blocked her from reaching him. "Cutter, what's going on?" she asked.

"They think I killed Tuttleberry," he shouted over his shoulder.

Both officers pulled him through a fortified entry into a city jail. As its door banged shut, Jenn pressed her hands and face against a barred window.

"I can't believe any of this is happening." Jenn's face became ashen and she teared up. Cutter's no saint, he's certainly no killer, Ms. Jagtiani."

Aquan felt badly for Jenn, and may have underestimated her attachment to Cutter.

"You should contact your consulate immediately. They'll be able to assist you."

Jenn brushed aside a tear. "Thank you. That's a good idea."

She got directions from a desk officer before heading off to her national consulate.

*****

The following day, local news reported Cutter's arrest for Tuttleberry's murder. In various media interviews, area TV stations constantly replayed video clip of marina guests claiming they heard angry voices and breaking glass coming from *Calusa*. A police spokesperson stated that Cutter's prints had been found on a bloodied knife recovered from his boat. Things weren't looking very good for Cutter, and Aquan felt no sympathy for him. He allied himself with murdering Exoris who drowned hundreds of innocent victims at Candelaria and slaughtered her Triton people. She hoped his imprisonment would start a long, painful period of punishment for his crimes.

Aquan feared law enforcement inquiries would inevitably blow her Rajneet cover. She needed to refresh herself in saltwater and come up with a new identity, fast. Slipping into chilly Atlantic surf, Aquan heard a chugging yacht engine and caught sight of *Athena* steaming out of Santa Cruz harbor. She wanted to follow him, but she felt exhausted. Aquan emptied her mind and fell into a dream-like trance, awaiting her reunion with her mirror image traveling back from Antarctica.

Chapter 26

Aquan might never have discovered a hidden entrance into Rapture's End through Mopsus's workshop if not for her long-standing habit of violating curfew with Thalassa. Her special whistle to her best friend let Thalassa know their coast was clear to swim through this private shortcut. Burrowing into a patch of sand, Aquan scared a gathering of garden eels whose heads popped up and down like a carnival whack-a-mole game. She swam through a rock tunnel which emptied into a kelp storage cave. Aquan peered into Mopsus's workshop, but he was not there. In anger, she stuck two discharged darts into his work bench to let him know of her uninvited visit. She scooped up a handful of fresh darts before heading to the House of Timarch.

Transforming into Thalassa, she easily swam past several Timarch guards patrolling their House's entryway. She rushed to Thalassa's private chamber and quickly glanced inside, hoping to avoid disrupting any mating rituals. Aquan sighed with relief when she found it empty. She sensed someone moving in another cave in this honey-combed rock. A strong odor of healing sea kelp balm filled her gills as she darted through several corridors towards Raynord's cavern. He floated listlessly in a semi-conscious state, his eyes glazed over with a mix of pain and numbing medicine. Aquan reached out to touch his face, his steel gray skin burned with fever. He groaned, but didn't awaken.

"I'm glad you weren't one of them."

Aquan shivered and returned to her Triton form. It lightened her heart to know he wasn't part of Camulus's platoon who removed her mother from captive stasis.

"One of whom?"

Aquan spun around to find Clarissa carrying fresh seaweed to dress his wounds. Thalassa favored her mother's Galene looks, sharing a similar dove gray skin, thick turquoise hair and slender silvery fishtail. Yet Thalassa's gregarious and brash ways showed her paternal Timarch genes, clashing often with

Clarissa's more sweetly calm Galene manner.

"Clarissa, hallowed be Eternal Concordia," said Aquan.

"And to you as well." She suddenly embraced Aquan. "Thank you for bringing him home safely. Although Mopsus told me you disobeyed orders to do so. I thank you."

"I couldn't abandon him. He is like a brother to me."

"It's good he's in a healing state. He'd be disappointed to hear that. Raynord's still longs to be so much more." Clarissa smiled and began to remove blackened seaweed bandages from his wounds. "I would happily welcome you as a daughter into our family."

Aquan remained quiet as she helped Clarissa replace Raynord's depleted swathes.

"I'm not free to join with another House, Clarissa."

"Why not? You have reached your first season, just as Thalassa. She has many potential mates and so will you."

"I couldn't abandon the search for my mother while she still lives."

Clarissa continued to fuss over a seaweed patch on Raynord's side. He mumbled and grew restive as he wrestled with his painful wounds.

"Evadne lives on in all of us who remember her with fondness. She would be pleased if she knew you had a mate while she slept in Musterion."

"She does not sleep in Musterion. She's alive."

Reapplying a fresh seaweed patch, Clarissa said nothing.

"My mother has been trapped in stasis for decades. Kept from me all these years."

"Who told you this story?"

"Queen Chione told me that our Elder Council sentenced her to captivity. All of these years I thought she was dead. She came to me in a vision and I thought I must be dreaming. But now I know all of you lied to me. My Aunt Sofronia, her sister. Mopsus, my tutor. You, her best friend." She grabbed hold of Clarissa's forearm. "Why did you do this terrible thing?"

Clarissa gently slipped her arm from Aquan's grasp and returned to tending to Raynord's wounds, placing a final kelp plaster in place.

"You told me so many times that you were like sisters. Is this how you would treat your sister? Turn your back on her and let her languish in an eternal prison of ice. And then lie to my face. To me, whom you would welcome as a mate for Raynord, as a daughter in your home."

Unexpectedly, a plaintive wail seeped from Aquan's lips.

"Aquan, you must let me explain."

Clarissa placed her hand on Aquan's wrist, but this time she pulled away from Clarissa. "Explain or tell me more lies."

"Perhaps we should have told you sooner, but we thought you were too young to endure it."

"I'm not a child. I deserve to know the truth."

"You're right. Having reached your first season, you're old enough to know about your mother. But let's retire to my chamber and allow Raynord to continue to rest."

Clarissa gathered Raynord's old dressings from Aquan's hands and led her to a small chamber far from her home's communal center.

"I don't know if I ever told you this, but your mother and I used to disappear here when we played hide-and-seek with other Archigen children. And later on when we wanted a private spot to share our thoughts," said Clarissa. Sadness clouded her face as she ran her fingers over carved benches in the room. "Regrettably, the Evadne I once knew as a mischievous girl has long been dead to her people."

"Why? What did she do?"

"She mated against our laws."

"Banishment to eternal stasis seems too cruel. Would you want that for Raynord or Thalassa if they mated with a wrong Archigen?"

"I would if their only other options were a tortured exile and an ignoble death. Your mother was warned in advance several times. She knew she risked a severe penalty, but continued to mate with an unsuitable Archigen male anyway."

"You mean an Archigen of Protosian lineage."

"Yes, Phorcys of the Houses of Archigen and Proteus."

"My father," whispered Aquan. She thought of Evadne's frequent brooding over losing him and her weekly trips to lay flowers at his burial site during Aquan's childhood. "Papandreas, a Protosian who lives as a Greek tycoon, told me all about the birth of Emissaries, about matings of Archigen males with Protosian roots and Triton females. He spoke of a deadly Archigen massacre of Protosians."

"No, Protosians were not brutalized. They openly threatened Eternal Concordia and fomented civil war. Promising to wipe out every Surface Dweller with another Great Flood. They demanded that we defy our sacred duty to protect Eternal Concordia, the Dreamer's promise to never destroy humans with another cataclysmic flood."

"Why would Protosians who can transform on land and sea want to get rid of a surface world? It doesn't make any sense."

"Protosians were hungry for power and wanted to dominate our planet. Yet walking amongst humans, they realized they could never fully possess unfettered control over unruly Surface Dwellers. By annihilating them with another Great Deluge, Protosians could govern over a vanquished surface once this flood subsided. They planned to use their land base to mount attacks on Archigens until they reigned supreme over land and sea." Clarissa's face turned pale and she visibly quaked. "When our Elder Council refused to comply with Protosian demands, they brought civil war to our Houses. We acted in self-defense. Thousands of Archigens were killed."

"I don't remember this war."

"It happened before you were born, Aquan. Some Protosians fled to the surface. Others fought on and were ultimately exiled to blistering vents at Earth's core. At that time, exile seemed more merciful than murdering more of our kinsmen, regardless of their crimes."

"But Papandreas claimed he was banished 900 years ago."

"Battles between Protosians and other Houses have flared up for more than a millennia. Your mother became entangled in a more recent period of rebellion."

"How did my mother avoid exile beyond Obzula Ridge?"

"Your Aunt Sofronia and I begged for mercy as she was pregnant. Mopsus persuaded our Elder Council to let her come to full term in three years and to wean you for your first decade before serving her sentence in captive stasis."

"How is a lifetime in stasis compassionate?" Aquan's voice rose in disgust. "Forced to exist in limbo. Alive but unable to truly live."

Clarissa placed her hand on Aquan's shoulder.

"Many wanted her to be killed along with all of remaining Protosians, calling upon human allies to assassinate them on Earth's surface and Timarchs to decimate those remaining undersea. Others demanded she be exiled into a hellish darkness beyond Obzula Ridge. Stasis spared her from death or awful torture in that eternal darkness."

Aquan buried her face in her hands as divergent waves of anger at their deception and gratitude for their efforts to spare Evadne washed over her.

"Queen Chione told me that Camulus and Timarch troops took my mother from stasis. Where was she taken?"

"I don't know. I believe Camulus moved her to ensure your mother's and our collective security during this uncertain time. I can tell you that she won't be released until you have restored all four amulets to our Elder Council."

"I know he wants to use them to bring the Vanquishment to pass."

"Yes, the Margrave's power to set another cataclysmic flood into motion rises with each amulet he recovers. He will surely reset Eternal Concordia to obliterate Surface Dwellers. Unless you can stop him."

Aquan shuddered as she heard echoes of terrified screams at Candelaria, this tragic scene but a faint test of the Margrave's plan to wipe out all humans.

"Daughter of Triton, restore honor to your House and win your mother's release from stasis." Clarissa clasped Aquan's hands and then softly patted Aquan's Hawaiian coral bracelet on her wrist. "I beseech you to seek out these amulets before their power can be abused to violate our Sacred Songs, to flout our Infinite Dreamer's will. Reclaim all of those amulets if you wish to save your mother, to spare billions of humans." She bowed to Aquan. "Hallowed be Eternal Concordia."

"And also to you, Clarissa."

As Aquan left, Clarissa heaved a deep breath through her gills. She sat on a carved bench and thought back to her childhood, her kinship with Evadne. Squeezing her eyes shut, she shook her head over her friend's misfortunes.

"Forgive me, Evadne," she whispered.

"You would not need Evadne's forgiveness if you spoke the truth," said Raynord. He winced in pain as he struggled to swim into her chamber. "Did you tell Aquan everything?"

"Raynord, you must not strain yourself this way or you will never heal." She placed his arm around her shoulders and guided him to a nearby ledge.

"You didn't answer my question, Mother."

"I told her all she needs to know for now."

"That's not what I asked."

"Raynord, I have done my best to protect her. Thanks to those oils in her coral bracelet, she fell into a dream state during the Triton hunt. Otherwise, she would have been awake and out in the open in Bliss Valley, killed with her fellow Tritons."

"Did you blame their massacre on the Margrave, too?"

"We didn't talk about it. And you shouldn't speak of it. You must obey your loyalty oath to our Elder Council as Aries's replacement. We only discussed her parents and the amulets."

"Have you told her about her mother's role in the Scattering?"

"Under our Sacred Songs, I can't interfere. These choices must be Aquan's not ours, nor the Margrave's wishes."

"He is powerful. We can barely keep him at bay. But we expect Aquan to fight him on her own, Mother."

"Only she can defeat him as an Emissary. His ultimate downfall and our retention of Eternal Concordia is all that is required at this moment."

Raynord grunted his disapproval. "The Council will soon no longer need her alive to keep Eternal Concordia once he is destroyed. Who will protect her when this mission is done?"

"We don't know what will happen until after the Sequencing is over. There is no need to make hasty judgments.

Hopefully, Mopsus will think of something to spare Evadne and Aquan."

"If he doesn't, I will defend Aquan to my death." Raynord recoiled in agitation as his wounds throbbed and burned. "I swear it, Mother. She has done nothing wrong. You won't be able to stand in my way."

"Raynord, you can do nothing until you are fully cured. So rest my son and let's pray there will be no more killing."

As Clarissa soothed Raynord back into a dream state, she feared that her prayers wouldn't be enough.

*****

Before leaving Rapture's End, Aquan revisited Memorial Grotto and ran her hands over her parents' names inscribed on their tombs. She didn't understand why they would ever champion murdering billions of humans. But then she never knew her father and her mother always kept herself at a distance during their brief time together.

As she swam deeper into her Ancestral Caves, she stared at hundreds of her fellow Tritons' graves, fresh reminders of the Margrave's cruelty. Her passion for vengeance roiled within her and fueled her journey to seize another amulet and to defeat his ruthless march toward the Vanquishment. She transformed into an enormous Atlantic blue marlin for her trip to the Gulf of Mexico. Yet as she journeyed north, she suddenly reset her course back to Tenerife.

Chapter 27

Aquan hurried to Santa Cruz's grim central prison, Tenerife II. This island's glittering beaches and misty mountains gave way to barbed wire spun across high concrete walls. Its watchtowers kept silent vigil over a cluster of one-story stucco buildings with hundreds of individual cells with two bunks, one sink and toilet and no fans in sweltering tropical heat. Since Tenerife II held twice as many prisoners than its intended design, overburdened staff only briefly glanced at Aquan's business card before permitting her to visit her client. She lifted it from a friendly Madrid attorney at a hotel bar last night. The magical powers of a business card to open doors, even gates to a prison, never ceased to amaze her.

Signing into a prison visitors log, she asked in her best Spanish, "Has he had any other visitors?"

"At this point, no one is allowed to visit until we complete his initial processing, except you and a representative of his country's consulate," replied a guard. He had trim black hair and clean-shaven olive skin with a name plate reading "Palma". "After processing's done, he can get fresh clothes and weekly visits from immediate family during designated hours."

"When will his processing be complete, Señor Palma?"

The guard shrugged his response.

"It gonna take about twenty minutes to bring him here. He's confined in an isolation unit in North Facility with other new arrivals. It's farthest away from our visitor's center, so be patient. We're short on staff."

"No problem, I'm billing by the hour," said Aquan.

Palma laughed and mopped his sweaty brow with a handkerchief. He showed his identification tag to another guard behind a thick glass window who buzzed him into a staff passageway behind a heavy metal door.

As she waited for Cutter, Aquan closely observed their guard uniforms, including identification badges clipped to their shirt pockets and night stick holsters slung on their hips. About an hour later, she was shown into a bare holding room reeking of bleach cleaner. Cutter trudged in wearing handcuffs and a sour look on his face. Manacles on his feet clanked with each of his steps. His cargo shorts and T-shirt, stained with sweat, stunk from two days of wear. Palma sat him in a battered chair across a wobbly wooden table from Aquan.

"You have a half-hour, Señor Cabrera." Palma tapped his watch's face. "If you're done early, you call me." He pointed to an ancient intercom hanging near a doorway.

"Gracias, Señor," said Aquan.

After Palma exited, she nodded to Cutter.

"I'm Alfredo Santander Cabrera, your attorney, Mr. Cutter."

"I didn't ask for any lawyer." Cutter scratched at beard stubble on his chin.

"Your consulate sent me to represent you."

Aquan smoothed her tailored navy blue suit as she settled into her seat.

"I don't need a legal rep. I'm innocent."

"I wouldn't have any cases if it weren't for all of my innocent clients." She stroked her well-tended, dark moustache.

"I didn't kill Tuttleberry. There's a bunch of guys who can vouch for me drinking at Los Pescadores that night."

Aquan knew the joint, having tagged its mermaid sandwich board with black fangs and claws. "Drunk patrons are seldom reliable witnesses, Mr. Cutter."

"They got nothing on me."

"Local Canarian authorities impounded your boat and found plenty. Your fingerprints were all over the murder scene and murder weapon, a butcher's knife."

"It's my boat and my knife from my galley kitchen." Cutter emphasized "my" each time he used this word. "So my fingerprints should be everywhere on my boat and my knife."

Stubborn as always thought Aquan.

"Other boaters at Santa Cruz Marina overheard a noisy argument on your ship, Mr. Cutter. A dead body was discovered lying on your lower deck. Sounds like more than enough evidence for Spanish authorities to hold you for quite some time."

"I've argued with him before, but not here in Tenerife. But I never laid a hand on him. Even though he followed me around like a hungry tick on a fat dog."

"So you didn't have a confrontation with him on your boat?"

"No, I didn't. They've got it all wrong."

"Then who else has access to your vessel?"

"Besides me, there's Dr. Jenn Ortiz, a research marine biologist, and Rick Emerson, her lab assistant."

"Would either of them have a reason to kill Tuttleberry?"

"No way. Dr. Ortiz is a respected academic and a decent person. And I don't know Emerson very well, but he's a first rate wimp. I doubt he'd harm a fly."

As Aquan scratched out a few more notes she realized that Tuttleberry had broken his routine and that was his undoing, possibly surprising an Exori ally on Cutter's boat.

"You'll need to set things right, Mr. Cutter. These are very serious charges and it may take up to two years for local courts to try you for his murder. So unless you have years of life to waste in this prison, I suggest you work with me."

Aquan unzipped a leather portfolio and pulled out a yellow legal pad.

"Why would I want to kill that little turd?"

"Perhaps we can start with how you know this victim."

"It's a long story."

"I've got a whole twenty-five minutes left. Let's get started."

"He's a pain in the ass insurance investigator."

"What was he investigating?" asked Aquan.

"Insurance fraud."

"Casualty insurance on your vessel?"

Cutter ran his fingers through his hair. "No, life insurance."

"Life insurance?"

"I was a beneficiary on life insurance for my friend, Rodrigo."

"Tell me about this Rodrigo."

"We grew up together in Florida. His parents were killed in a car crash so he lived with his grandparents. While our granddads fished in their rickety trawlers, we got bored and started scuba diving. I fell in love with the underwater world and he got high on its dangers. Always had to ratchet things up to some extreme." Cutter paused and smiled wistfully. "We made big plans to start our own dive shop after high school. But my parents steered me towards college and marine biology and Rodrigo's grandparents moved to Miami. When they died, he got mixed up doing with some shady characters and landed in big trouble."

"What kind of trouble?"

"Doing boat charters for shifty customers. Instead of fishing for tuna, his passengers fished packages out of the water at different coastal drop sites."

"So he was a drug dealer."

"More like a water taxi for drug dealers. When he went to jail, a lot of folks wrote him off. But I knew he had a good heart, even if he could be a real knuckle head, a little too full of himself."

Aquan thought of Thalassa, good heart, big head.

"So why did Mr. Tuttleberry think you defrauded his insurance company?"

Cutter drew in a deep breath.

"About five years ago, I was bored to death in my PhD program. Tired of being cooped up in labs. Rodrigo was out of jail and back rebuilding his life in Key West. We decided to take off for Riviera Maya, Yucatan peninsula in Mexico. Bummed around as dive masters at tourist resorts. While we were there, Rodrigo got this crazy idea in his head about finding Mayan treasures."

Not so crazy, mused Aquan, knowing that ocean caves hid many sunken caches of pirate plunder and shipwreck fortunes, and hopefully, a third amulet.

"One trip, we took some experienced divers, doing nitrox tanks, for a night dive to Dos Bocas."

"Dos Bocas?"

"Yeah, a freshwater cenote near Tulum. The entire Yucatan peninsula is like Swiss cheese, a huge network of underwater sinkholes and caves. You gotta be nuts to go into its caves without being trained and certified. Rodrigo was pulling up the rear of our group. When that dive ended, he didn't surface. One diver told me she thought she last saw him flashing his light into an entrance to Devil's Pit."

Aquan took notes on her yellow pad. "What's Devil's Pit?"

"One of the deepest cave passages in that region. About four hundred feet deep. I had air left so I dove back in and headed straight for its entrance about a hundred feet down. Grim reaper warning signs are posted at its mouth. I figured he probably got curious and headed in, losing his way in its dark emptiness. I shot a couple of flares hoping he might see them and find his way back. It's crazy, but I started to feel my way inside, thinking I might find him and save him."

Cutter paused and Aquan noticed his voice quavering.

"They never found his body. A fisherman found one of his flippers mangled and sandwiched between cavern rocks a week later. Another found his dive light tumbling across a bottom of another cavern chamber."

He fell silent and Aquan didn't try to fill it with her questions.

"His grandparents took out hefty life insurance on him as a baby. He must have made me his beneficiary after they died. Tuttleberry thought we worked a scam, faking his death to soak up his life insurance money."

"How much was his policy worth?"

"Three million dollars."

Aquan froze and stopped taking notes, realizing the bases for Tuttleberry's dogged persistence.

"I used some of it to buy *Calusa* at a DEA auction and retrofit her for salvage and research operations. Never got around to opening that dive shop we always dreamed about."

"That sounds like three million reasons for you to want him dead."

"Why kill him? His company already paid off and Rodrigo's not alive. Tuttleberry kept thinking Rodrigo was going to show up in some remote location to split the pay out." Cutter sighed. "If only he could. I'd hand over the money in a second, to have my friend alive and well."

He blinked his eyes furiously to fight back a tear sliding to a corner of his eye. At that moment, Aquan knew that he must be telling her the truth. Someone else must have killed Tuttleberry or conspired to have him killed him and ransack Jenn's lab. But why, she wondered.

"Mr. Cutter, it was brave to try a rescue."

"It was stupid of me to try to find Rodrigo in an underwater cave. But he was my oldest friend. I should have died, too, if it hadn't been for...." His voice trailed off.

"If it hadn't been for what?" asked Aquan.

Cutter fidgeted in his chair. "Nothing."

"Mr. Cutter, I need absolute honesty if I'm going to be able to defend you."

"If I tell you, you won't believe it."

"As your attorney, everything you say is just between the two of us." Aquan pointed to Cutter then herself. "I can't tell anyone else. So let's hear it."

Cutter looked directly at her and spoke in a rapid fire clip.

"I blacked out in Devil's Pit. No more nitrox in my tanks. A creature, a form of mermaid appeared. Took me to the surface. Rescued me from certain death."

"At least we still have an insanity defense on our side, Mr. Cutter."

Frowning, Cutter shook his head. "Forget it. I knew you wouldn't believe me."

"What did she look like? I assume long hair, big breasts and scaly fish tail."

Cutter started to get up from his chair. "No need to mock me, wise ass. I've had plenty of people laugh at me for years."

"Sit down, Mr. Cutter."

"We're done here." Cutter called out for Palma.

"Was she wearing something like this?"

Aquan turned in her seat and slowly opened her suit jacket, pulling out her amulet from its inside pocket. Cutter's eyes popped open wide as she dangled it from its chain.

"You gotta be kidding me." He looked Cabrera up and down. "Why didn't you tell me it was you?"

"Because I needed to know your real relationship with

Tuttleberry. And I needed to find out why you recognized my amulet before on *Calusa*."

Cutter plunked down in his chair. "Nice get up. You had me fooled. Now what, lawyer?"

"I need you to show me where you saw that mermaid so I can locate her amulet."

"Did you ever find out why your bosses want it?"

"Yes, Candelaria is but a small taste of their power in the wrong hands. Put all four of them together along with a full moon and humanity will be wiped out in another worldwide deluge. There will be no Noah to spare your people this time."

Cutter let loose a low whistle. "Total annihilation by flood. Why?"

"Part of a civil war between my people for dominance."

"I thought you claimed your people were all about sparing life, acting only in self-defense."

"Most of us do believe that. But a small sect schemes for power and wants to rule this planet. Decimating humans is one part of their game plan."

"Can't you turn into something big and mean and bust me out of here right now?" Cutter motioned toward his cuffs.

"Let's shoot for something a little more subtle. Go back to your cell and I'll return for you after dark. Then we're out of here."

"How are we going to get aboard *Calusa*? It's gotta be crawling with cops."

"Don't worry. I have another of Mopsus's tools to help us." She paused, his name catching in her throat. Aquan wasn't sure she'd ever speak to or trust anything Mopsus told her ever again.

"Where's Gypsy?"

"With Dr, Ortiz."

"I don't want to leave without her."

Aquan rolled her eyes. "You got to be kidding."

"Seriously, I'm not going without my dog."

"Fine," said Aquan. "I'll tell Dr. Ortiz you asked me to retrieve her. Now lay low until I return."

*****

Signing out, Aquan asked Palma about the latest time she could visit her client.

"Six-thirty. Prisoners get locked up nightly at 7:15."

"Then I may see you again later today."

She smiled and took a good look at his face.

"Someone will be here. But not me. I'll be celebrating my tenth anniversary at Cuchara's tonight after my shift ends at six."

"Congratulations to you, Señor Palma. Best Canarian food on Tenerife," replied Aquan.

As she exited Tenerife II, Aquan knew that there were too many security precautions for her to quickly stop time and break Cutter out. She didn't want to waste what time she had left on her diver's watch. Better to come back after dark and change Cutter into something small and portable.

Chapter 28

In late afternoon, Aquan strolled down to Santa Cruz Marina. An armed policeman guarded *Calusa* to make sure no one tampered with its crime scene. Slips on either side of *Calusa* had been vacated and cordoned off to keep gawkers away. She noticed Jenn tie Gypsy's leash to a nearby park bench and then punch her access code into a marina gate. Walking up to the officer, Jenn pulled her passport out of her satchel and seemed to be trying to persuade him in broken Spanish to allow her on Cutter's boat. He kept shaking his head "no." She persisted and her face grew tense, but eventually he shooed her away like a pesky fly.

As she exited, Jenn plopped down on a stone bench and buried her face in her hands. Gypsy started barking as Aquan approached her as Cabrera.

"Are you alright, Señorita?"

"Terrible, just terrible," she replied, without looking up. Her hands and shoulders quaked.

"Are you sure I can't help you, Dr. Ortiz?"

She shot him an anxious stare. "How do you know my name?"

"I'm Dave Cutter's attorney. Sent by your consulate." Aquan handed her Cabrera's business card. "And this must be Gypsy." The lawyer patted Cutter's dog. "Mr. Cutter told me to expect both of you trying to board *Calusa*."

"Thank God." She grabbed Aquan's arm as if it was a life preserver on a sinking ship.

"Is he alright, Mr. Cabrera? They wouldn't let me see him."

"He's fine. A little tired and hot, but otherwise he's okay."

She sighed with relief, her face still strained with angst. "When will he be freed?"

"He's facing serious charges, Dr. Ortiz. It may take weeks before an initial hearing."

"I know he's innocent. He's my friend and I know he wouldn't kill anybody. I won't stop fighting for his release."

The fierce emotion in her voice confirmed for Aquan that

Jenn's feelings for Cutter were not merely platonic.

"Nor will I. I'm confident that I'll be able to bail him out very soon."

"What's going on with that policeman guarding *Calusa*? I couldn't help but notice your frustration with him."

"I've been trying for a day and a half to get back on Cutter's ship to retrieve my research notes, tools and water samples. Fortunately, I have most of my notes on my laptop and shipped most of my samples back home to my home base in Florida. But I don't want to leave valuable samples behind and they could prove hazardous."

"I'm sorry, Dr. Ortiz. But Cutter's boat will remain confiscated until this local homicide investigation is complete. Standard procedure."

"How long will that be?"

"Things move slowly here." Aquan patted Jenn's shoulder. "But I'll do my best to try to hurry things along."

"Glad to hear at least one good bit of news today."

"What else is happening?"

"My research assistant, Rick Emerson, is missing. Haven't seen or heard from him for nearly two days. We're both supposed to leave on a flight to Key West tomorrow."

"Are you sure he's not out having some holiday fun on the beach?"

"I wondered if he met someone or was playing a little hooky with other grad assistants. But he's been such a dedicated researcher. This conference is very important to him, personally and professionally. When he didn't show or contact me, I got worried so I went to La Mar Azul, a guest house where he was staying."

She handed Aquan a business card for his guest house with room #32 written on it.

"The owner told me he hasn't seen him in a couple of days. I've left messages on his international cell and texted him numerous times, but no response. That's not like him and I'm really alarmed since Mr. Tuttleberry's murder."

Jenn placed her hands over her mouth and shook her head with worry written over her face.

"No need to assume the worst, Dr. Ortiz." Although Aquan presumed that with a Sea Monk in town the local body count might inevitably rise. "Did you file a police report?"

"I tried, but he's an adult and it wasn't officially forty-eight hours yet."

"A lawyer at your side may help to get things started. Let's go together to file that missing person's report."

"Thank you, thank you," said Jenn. She clasped her two hands around Aquan's hands.

After helping Jenn file a missing person's report, she managed to convince Jenn to return to her hotel in case Emerson tried to reach her there. Aquan told her he would stop by this evening to pick up Cutter's dog for a local boarding facility so she could pack and leave for her scheduled morning flight. With a couple more hours before nightfall, Aquan decided to pay a quick visit to La Mar Azul.

*****

Laundry fluttered in summer winds above Aquan's head in an alleyway next to La Mar Azul. This five-story stucco guest house catered to young travelers and seemed a bit worse for wear in a neighborhood of cheap cafes and noisy bars. Aquan hid behind a dumpster and softly sang a local favorite, "Edad de Hierro", as she shook and turned into Emerson. She adjusted his tortoise shell eyeglasses and straightened his shirt and khakis he often wore, then slung her backpack over her shoulders. Aquan pretended to fumble with a map as she waited outside this yellow stucco building. When two tourists exited its rear door, she stepped inside before it slammed shut.

She crept slowly up the creaky wooden stairs to its third floor. A stale scent of a Sea Monk lingered in its hallway and she pulled out two deadly darts. Standing outside room number 32, she didn't sense any movement inside it. Aquan turned its brass door knob, but its door remained locked. She pondered whether to turn into a Tenerife Wall Lizard to crawl inside. A cleaning lady, her graying hair pulled back in a tight bun, rolled her cart outside a nearby room.

"Señor Emerson, where have you been?" she exclaimed. A worn plastic name plate, "Clara", was pinned to her faded uniform. "Dr. Ortiz came many times and our manager has been looking for you."

"Lo siento, Señora Clara. I'm so sorry. But I was staying with a lovely señorita at the beach. I lost track of time." Aquan dug into Emerson's khaki pants pocket and rifled through an outer pocket of the backpack. "And my wallet."

The cleaning lady wagged her finger in Aquan's face. "You must be more careful. Lots of crooks here to rob tourist money."

"I think she stole my room key, too," said Aquan. She continued to rummage through her backpack.

Clara put her hands on her ample hips and shook her head. "Tontillo. You are lucky to still be alive. A man was killed at Santa Cruz Marina this week. In cold blood." She unlocked his door with her master key.

"Muchas gracias." Aquan slipped two Euros into Clara's palm.

"You should let the manager know you are not yet dead, Señor Emerson." Clara shook her head. "Tontillo." She waddled into another room to complete her cleaning duties.

Aquan closed the door behind her, gripping a fatal dart in her hand. Emerson's room smelled of Sea Monk and Pteron odors, but she did not feel their presence. Its windows and shutters were flung open so his visitors could have flown into his room. She slowly crept into a narrow bathroom and yanked back its shower curtain, frightening only a tiny gecko crawling up its worn tiles. She tipped up the toilet tank's porcelain lid and did not see anything secreted away in it.

Returning to Emerson's main room, his bed was neatly made and ten Euro was left on his bureau next to a hotel notepad with "Muchas gracias, Señora!" scrawled on its top sheet. Pulling open each bureau and nightstand drawer, she found nothing. Poking inside his closet, only three metal hangers clanked on a closet pole. No luggage, clothing or shoes left inside. She scanned his room for blood stains or signs of a struggle, but none were visible. Sitting down on his bed, her mind began to race. Either Emerson had gone willingly with them or he was forced to leave with them. Neither option was a positive development.

Aquan spied a wicker trash basket in a corner of his room. She dumped its trash on to the floor. A conference program and Emerson's conference identification and lanyard spilled out along with other loose trash. Sifting through his rubbish, she discovered a half-used travel size shampoo bottle, a candy bar wrapper and torn remnants of his unfinished travel itinerary. She pieced its ripped pieces together and his return flight to Florida matched Jenn's planned departure. Aquan wondered if Emerson ever actually intended to return to the Institute. In a wadded up ball of toilet paper, she found an empty water sample vial, its identification label removed. Only sticky tape marks remained. Aquan shoved this empty vial into her backpack.

She peeked out the door to make sure Clara was not roaming around and then she slipped out a set of back stairs. Darkness had fallen in Santa Cruz and it was time for Attorney Cabrera to pay another visit to her new client.

Chapter 29

"Palma, what are you doing back here?" asked a guard behind a glass at a front desk.

"I almost made it home when realized I forgot my wife's gift in my locker, Monteiro. I'm supposed to take my wife to Cuchara's for our anniversary," said Aquan, transformed into Palma.

"Fancy, fancy. You going to get lucky tonight, Palma." Monteiro laughed. "Where is your security card?"

"Ah, I forgot it in my car. Gimme a break. Buzz me in quick or my wife is going to kill me if we're late for dinner."

"You're lucky we're short-handed. Can't afford to lose another guard, even a dummy like you." Monteiro buzzed Aquan in. "Take this temporary card and give it back to me on your way out."

Aquan seized a temporary security card and quickly made her way past an employee locker room and on to its northern facility. She nodded to a fellow guard patrolling a cell block.

"That American's lawyer is here to see him again."

The guard frowned and looked at his watch, 6:25 p.m. "Just under the wire. But get him back here by 7:15 for lock-up."

"No problem," said Aquan.

Aquan followed her fellow guard to Cutter's cell.

"Your lawyer's here to see you. Let's go." As Palma, she held a pair of handcuffs in the air.

Cutter jumped up and turned around as the guard fastened them around Cutter's wrists. Palma escorted Cutter out of his unit. As soon as they exited, Aquan clasped her hand over Cutter's mouth and pushed him behind a stack of concrete blocks.

Cutter struggled against her until she whispered, "It's me, Cutter."

"Holy shit. I never know when you're going to pop up," he muttered.

"We don't have much time. We gotta get out of here and head for *Calusa*."

"With all this security, how do you expect to get us out of here and on my boat?"

"I got a plan."

Aquan pulled out a vial of green sand from her pants' pocket.

"What's that?"

"Shhh. No time to explain. Just sit still."

She broke open her vial and sprinkled its powder over Cutter. Within three seconds, he shrunk into a Stripless Tree Frog. Aquan deposited him into her shirt pocket and buttoned it before striding back to its main building. As she handed her colleague back a temporary card, just as Cutter let out a gurgling burp. Monteiro glanced up at Palma.

"What was that?"

"I better get to dinner. My stomach is grumbling pretty loud."

Aquan rushed out and headed for Santa Cruz Marina. She unleashed Gypsy from a sidewalk bench near a marina gate. A single police officer continued to guard Cutter's vessel. Two nosy boaters with crab nets in hand milled around as a local TV camera crew set up their equipment for a murder investigation update. Local church bells clanged 7:00 and Aquan knew she needed to shove off soon before those prison guards realized their evening count was one short. In frog form, Cutter rustled in her shirt pocket and she couldn't afford to have him springing out in plain view. She pressed in his key code and hurried along bobbing planks with Gypsy dancing by her side.

"You must clear this dock." She flashed her corrections badge.

"How come?" asked one police officer.

"Official orders. We have a prisoner transfer from Fuerteventura coming in. No civilians or local police allowed here."

"I'm doing a live broadcast in two minutes. We'll be out of here soon enough," snapped a reporter. He adjusted his tie and smoothed back his dark hair.

"You'll have to tape it later. Come back in twenty minutes."

"I don't see any boat coming in yet. Plenty of time."

At that moment, the frog let loose another loud belch. Several onlookers giggled.

"Officer, escort these civilians away from this dock."

"I don't take orders from you." He unhooked his mobile radio from his belt. "Let me call dispatch to see what's going on."

Suddenly, a bulging frog leaped out of her shirt pocket, its size increasing as it hopped along dock planks. She yanked a crab net from a boater's grip and chased it along the dock's edge. Twice she swatted her net down but missed him as it hopped and grew with each passing moment. Aquan heard a whirring camera and saw his bright camera light follow her as she chased this ever-expanding frog. Running out of dock and her net was soon too small to capture it as Cutter would soon revert to human form.

"Are you getting that?" exclaimed the reporter.

"Absolutely," replied his camera man.

At the end of the dock, Cutter jumped into the harbor with an enormous splash.

"Cutter!" she yelled. But there was no reply.

Aquan hated to waste precious minutes on her diver's watch, but she had no choice. Clicking its button, all around her froze. She grabbed both pair of handcuffs from the officer's duty belt, hooking one pair to the reporter's ankles and a second pair linking together the two boaters' ankles. She pulled out Palma's pair hooking the officer's hands behind his back. She pulled his police radio and keys and tossed them into the harbor. From the camera man's shoulder, she wrenched away his camera and dumped it in the salty water, too. She snatched a life ring hanging on a dock hook and pulled it tightly over his head and shoulders.

Gathering up Gypsy in her arms, she carried him to *Calusa*'s main deck and unhitched lines binding Cutter's boat to its slip. Aquan fired up its engine and reversed it, bashing into two small tenders docked behind her. Pulling away from Santa Cruz Marina, she sniffed for frog scent. Up ahead, a gigantic frog floated on rolling waves. Aquan powered *Calusa* toward him, sidling it next to the stilled creature. Reaching for it with a boat hook, she finally snagged its hind leg and tugged it stern side. She groaned, dragging and lashing this fat creature on to the rear diving platform.

Opening *Calusa* full throttle, Cutter's ship creased across waves until the lights of Santa Cruz faded from view. Having lost sixteen minutes, fifty-four seconds of time, she clicked her diver's watch and time began its inevitable march once more. Singing a sorrowful Guanches' folk song, Aquan reverted back to Kirra and flipped on autopilot and hurried aft to the diving platform. Gypsy barked as a giant frog strained against its ropes, gurgling and burping constantly. In a flash, it reverted back into a soaking wet Cutter, who sputtered and coughed up water.

"What the hell do you do to me?" he yelled.

"Still no Prince Charming," replied Aquan. She stepped down and untied Cutter as *Calusa* sped along. "You can thank me later for saving your butt from prison."

Cutter trailed her as she clambered on to its main deck, rubbing his head and stretching out his back. "You gonna tell me what happened?"

"I turned you into a frog so I carry you out of jail. Like always, you couldn't sit still. I nearly lost you in the ocean."

"You turned me into a frog?"

"Yup, a Stripless Tree Frog who couldn't stop belching, to be precise."

As they reached his pilot room, Aquan began to punch coordinates into his GPS. Cutter clamped his hand over its touch screen to block her.

"Where are we going with my boat?" Cutter asked.

"A nice quiet place."

"It better be empty. Spanish authorities are going to put out an alert on us and on *Calusa*."

"I know. That's why we're headed for Tura."

"Tura?"

"Yeah, Tura Island. It's nearby. Moroccans and Spanish having been fighting over it for years. Pretty much a legal no-man's land."

He released his grip and then reached over to flick on his

marine radio crackling with static.

"Never heard of it."

"Mostly deserted, except for some goats. And smugglers doing a brisk business between Africa and Europe in light arms and drugs."

As she punched in coordinates, Aquan hoped that Battuta was still alive and able to work his magic for them.

Chapter 30

As darkness descended, *Calusa* glided into a harbor hidden between a set of jagged cliffs, bleached white through a mixture of intense sun and seagull droppings. They anchored off a sliver of craggy coast.

"I'll go ahead. On my own."

"I don't think going it alone with smugglers around is a good idea. You might need some help," said Cutter, loading his pistol.

"Not to worry. I'm visiting an old friend that smugglers will never find. It's better that you stay here to keep watch on *Calusa* or else it might not be here when I get back."

"Okay. Any trouble, I'll shoot up a flare."

Aquan strapped on her diver's watch and grabbed a few darts before diving into the sea. After refreshing herself in saltwater, she crawled on to Tura's rocky shore. Random bleating of goats punctuated sounds of slapping waves and gentle whooshes of wind blowing across this disputed island. Transforming into a snowy white goat, Aquan climbed steep cliffs toward sparse pastures. In eerie silence, she roamed until she picked up a soft snapping of tent canvas in the wind. She could hear him, but not see him. Aquan let loose a high-pitched bleat and then three more blasts until a small tent and campfire suddenly materialized beside a tumble of broken rocks.

A slight figure under five feet in height crawled out of his tent. His back and shoulders were hunched over as he gripped a crooked staff in his right hand. He threw an edge of his black haik, a Roman-style toga, over his right shoulder, jangling carved silver and stone talismans hanging from a leather cord. His sandaled feet trudged across a stony path, slowed from nearly ninety years traversing nomadic Berber outposts in Morocco, digging out a subsistence living. His narrow brown eyes, sunken in deep creases of his leathery brown skin, peered out from under his dark blue turban. Aquan ambled up to him, bleating more faintly, as he reached to gently pat her head.

"Where is your flock, goat?" he said, in his Tamazight dialect.

"Holy Man, we roam aimlessly in barren sea cliffs," replied Aquan, in his native Imazighen tongue.

"Have your brothers and sisters been lost to a watery grave in these storm-tossed straits?"

"Holy Man, we await a wise shepherd to lead us to safety," replied Aquan.

He stroked his long gray beard. "Then I will be your guide from this turbulent shore to Anzar's peaceful green pastures."

Aquan trilled a few notes and appeared as Kirra dressed in an off-white haik with a colorful floral scarf on her head. She clasped his hands in hers, "Hallowed be Eternal Concordia, Battuta. I'm honored to see you again."

He kissed her hands twice. "Hallowed be Eternal Concordia, Emissary. The honor is all mine. I didn't know if I should lay eyes on you again before my days ended."

"I desperately need your help, Battuta. Before dawn, I journey to the Gulf of Mexico and need fast, safe passage for my ship. Away from prying eyes of Surface Dwellers and scheming allies of the Margrave."

"When do you need to appear there?"

"I must arrive there in a day, maybe two at most. It is a large vessel."

"Yes, a catamaran with a human passenger. I saw it in my dream tonight. Do you wish for a lethal cloak, Emissary?"

"No, I don't want to harm anyone who comes into my path. I only wish to hide my ship from discovery."

He caressed his beard once more and nodded his head. "Come sit by my fire while I contemplate."

Battuta sat quietly and meditated under a nearly three-quarter moon for an hour. Then he took hold of a brass bowl and collected scrub grasses growing in stony crevices and mixed them with goat manure and desiccated pasture soils. He snatched a scorpion inching across a nearby rock and snapped it into two pieces, draining its poison and blood into his concoction.

"We must let those mingle for an hour or so." Battuta

placed his bowl next to the heat of his fire. "Come drink some fresh goat milk and tell me of your journey."

"Battuta, I don't want to burden or endanger you with any details of my mission."

"I understand that you must have your secrets, Emissary."

"I wish I possessed your wisdom. For my right path is still unclear to me."

"Wisdom may not be what is needed."

"Without wisdom, how will I know what to do next, Battuta?"

"At times, it is best to quiet your restless mind. Open your heart to many possibilities and let it carry you forward." Battuta softly placed his hand on Aquan's heart.

"I'm not very good at that. I like having a plan."

"Then perhaps that is the lesson you're being taught."

Aquan frowned and looked more deeply into his fire searching for answers.

"Let your mind move away from your mission for now. Tell me of wondrous places you have seen since we last met to ease your mind."

Aquan then regaled him with stories about a host of natural and man-made wonders in her travels. Questions tumbled out of his curious mind. His eyes crinkled with childlike joy drinking in her observations until his fire cooled. Aquan carried a torch and Battuta cradled his brass vessel in his arms as they climbed down to Tura's shore. Dancing flames from Aquan's torch illuminated Cutter standing guard on *Calusa*'s darkened deck, gun in hand. Aquan motioned for Cutter to bring the ship's tender ashore and he zipped to ashore.

"Battuta is a great holy man, a mystical Jamtan, Cutter. His powers will help us get to the Gulf."

Battuta scanned Cutter from head to toe and tapped his calves with his walking stick. He poked Cutter's shoulders and chest and squeezed each of his hands in turn. The holy man nodded.

"A good specimen. Strong body. Hands of a working man. A good mate for you."

"He's the boat's captain, not my mate," laughed Aquan.

Battuta's grin grew wider. "We'll see."

"What did he say?" asked Cutter.

"He's welcoming you to his island."

Before Cutter could speak another word, Battuta began to scrape his warmed mixture on Cutter's forehead and forearms and then repeated his actions with Aquan. Cutter wrinkled his nose at the smell of goat manure.

"That stuff really stinks," said Cutter.

"Take what paste remains in this bowl and rub it paste over your ship's bow and stern," said Battuta to Aquan.

"What will happen, Battuta?" asked Aquan.

"You and the ship will be cloaked in sea mist. Invisible to our physical world."

"How will it speed our trip?"

"Once you apply my balm, your boat will absorb powers of a Serra. It will fly high above any waves with its vast bat-like wings." He kneaded his Serra talisman on his necklace. "Once your ship touches down in Gulf waters, Serra's fish tail will swim to your destination. Your ship will return to its normal form and you will both become visible again."

Distant thumps of helicopter blades sliced through an early morning darkness. Search lights scanned outlying harbor waves.

"We got company," said Cutter.

"Spanish patrols," said Battuta to Aquan. "Looking for illegal smugglers. We must hurry."

"Any other instructions?"

"Yes, hang on to something below deck if you don't want to get blown into the ocean."

"Thank you, Battuta," said Aquan. "Will you be alright?"

Battuta smeared some of the paste on himself. "I will be but a passing cloud to them. Now go, Emissary."

"I'm sorry I cannot stay longer." She clasped his hands once more.

"Someday we will have eternity to stroll together."

Aquan grabbed his brass bowl and doused her torch in breaking surf.

"We have to apply this stuff to your boat, Cutter."

They jumped on to Cutter's boat tender and peeled toward *Calusa* and then hurriedly applied Battuta's paste to its stern and bow. Aquan and Cutter rushed to his wheelhouse and braced themselves in his bolted pilot chairs. Aquan peered out his pilothouse window and watched Battuta raise his staff and rub his talisman.

Military helicopters whooshed over, their bright lights whisking across *Calusa's* deck. As these helicopters swung around to take another look, loud sirens blared and muffled commands were barked repeatedly through a bullhorn.

"Is this gonna work?" asked Cutter.

Aquan smiled as Battuta evaporated from the shoreline. "Absolutely."

As her words escaped her lips, *Calusa* jolted forward and ascended skyward, stars rushing by them in long, white streaks. The naval helicopters were left to scan an empty harbor.

Chapter 31

Cutter's scuba tanks clanked as his rented Jeep sped along a bumpy sandy road leading to Dos Bocas. After a violent afternoon rainstorm, steam from humidity hung heavy in this dense tropical forest. Honeysuckle scents of passion fruit flowers tickled Aquan's nose. Cutter's excitement about their Serra flight to the Gulf gave way to quiet introspection as they drove deeper into the rainforest. Aquan wondered if he might be replaying his memories of Rodrigo's accident. Bright red and orange smudges of sunset burned across the sky as Cutter stopped at an entry gate. This tourist park was closed, but Cutter contacted an old diving buddy who knew a guy who knew a brother of a gate guard. For a small fee, this sentry happily unlocked his park gate for evening dive tours.

"Bueños noches," said a uniformed guard.

While Cutter counted out his cash, he flashed a Cheshire cat smile looking at Aquan as Kirra. He seemed particularly enamored with Kirra's long slender legs. Cutter threw in an extra fifty pesos to guarantee their privacy.

Parking his SUV in a dirt lot above a string of cenotes, Cutter swatted hungry mosquitoes as he sorted out his diving gear. Standing on a rocky outcrop, Aquan looked down on two wide mouths of freshwater cenotes. Under these crystal blue pools lay huge caverns leading to an extensive network of smaller tunnels and caves filled with rivers snaking out to the sea.

"I can see why Mayans thought these waters were sacred. So beautiful."

"So deadly," said Cutter.

He pulled out his full-length wetsuit.

"Are you up for this?" asked Aquan.

"Sure. No problem." Cutter didn't look up from his gear as he checked his regulator and hoses.

"Do you remember which cave your friend went into? There's hundreds down there. It might be easy to get them mixed up."

"It's seared into my nightmares. About a hundred feet down near a cluster of Mayan ruins. Has a big stop sign at its mouth."

"How long can you stay below?"

"About a half-hour travel time and then about twenty or thirty minutes bottom time. I've got to make decompression stops at sixty and thirty feet on my ascend." Cutter stuffed rope into his dive bag and snatched its handles. "Ready?"

"Can I help with anything?"

"Yeah, take that extra tank, will you? We're heading for that first cavern."

She hoisted tank straps over her shoulder and carried her back pack in her left hand. They picked their way along a rutted path to a mouth of a cenote. Manic flapping of bat wings echoed in its cavern. Aquan shooed away an iguana before resting Cutter's back-up tank on a wooden platform.

"On our way down, I'll tie off a spare tank at sixty feet on a guide line. Should give me plenty of air for decompression on my way up."

"Okay," replied Aquan.

As Cutter strapped his dive knife to his leg, Aquan pulled sections of her spear gun out of her backpack. She assembled it and loaded it with lethal darts.

"Think you'll need those?"

"Never know, Cutter. Rather have it in case things turn sour."

He grimaced and then snapped on his BC vest.

"Once we get to the cave, I'll wait for about fifteen minutes before I've got to turn back. How will I know if you run into trouble?"

"You won't. Just lead me there and worry about getting yourself back here. Take my backpack with you. If I don't surface in an hour, assume the worst and get away from here as fast as you can."

"I'm not leaving the park without you."

Cutter stopped and squeezed Aquan's shoulder. She felt a quiver through her body from his touch.

"You can't wait on me, Cutter. If I make it out, I'll swim

back to your boat by finding a cave that empties out into the sea."

An uncomfortable silence washed over them.

"So this could be good-bye."

He looked straight into her eyes. Aquan felt her face burn hot. She looked away and busied herself with clicking her darts into her spear gun.

"Don't get all mushy and sentimental with me, Cutter. Neither of us is any good at it."

"I'm more worried that you'll save our world and I won't get an ounce of credit," replied Cutter with a devilish grin. "And if you blow it, I'll be at fault for ending mankind."

"Don't worry. If this gets screwed up, there won't be much time left for anyone to blame either of us."

She laughed weakly, stumbling over her own bad joke. Aquan helped Cutter tighten his BC straps on his back.

Attached to a D-ring of his vest, Cutter flicked his underwater light on and off. He yanked on his fins and adjusted his mask. At the top of a rustic branch ladder leading to a lagoon, he stopped and turned to her.

"Good luck, Aquan. Thank Kadru for saving my life when you see her."

"For sure. I'll try to get back to *Calusa* by morning," replied Aquan.

Before taking a giant stride into the water, he gave her an unexpected kiss on her lips and splashed into a dark blue pool, disappearing beneath its glassy surface.

Aquan placed several darts in her pouch and hummed "Down by the Water" as she reverted to her Triton form and followed Cutter into the cenote. Its narrow mouth quickly opened up into a huge sandstone pit dropping straight down. Shafts of muted twilight streaked through its clear water. They descended past underwater stalagmites and stalactites which reminded Aquan of Rapture's End. At about sixty feet, Cutter fluttered his fins as he attached a decompression tank to his line. He gave Aquan a "thumbs up" and dove deeper.

At about eighty feet, a mysterious white fog floated beneath them, a strange cocktail of river water and decaying vegetation and minerals leeching from limestone walls. Aquan wrinkled her nose at a rotten egg stench from this moldering vegetation. They dropped through a wispy haze like airplanes dipping below thin cirrus clouds into a pitch darkness. Cutter flicked on his dive light illuminating his trail of air bubbles. Gurgles from his regulator broke a murky silence as he inhaled and exhaled.

They glided through a dead forest of submerged trees and scattered brambles. Tiny shrimp crawled over pottery shards strewn along its sandy bottom. Silver Tetra fish darted in and out of rubble of isolated Mayan ruins, many decorated with petroglyphs of sea serpents and sharks. Cutter motioned for Aquan to follow him behind a carved ruin depicting Descending God, a squat Mayan deity with a feathered headdress, diving toward Earth. Orange and red sponges clung to limestone rocks dotted with cave openings. Cutter pointed to a gaping hole with an ominous sign reading "Stop" and "Alto" with a crude painting of a grim reaper. He pointed to his dive watch, only five minutes of bottom time left for him. Flashing his dive light into this crevice, Aquan gazed into a black cave pit. She understood why Mayans believed these cenotes were portals to a feared underworld. Cutter tapped her shoulder and held up his diver's slate with "Good Luck" written on it. Aquan smiled and tapped his shoulder before she ducked into its entrance.

As Cutter's light faded from view, Aquan adjusted her eyes to peer across twisted cave contours in a still blackness. Her natural radar guided her deeper and deeper into this cave which suddenly thinned into a tight tunnel. Aquan collapsed her spear gun as her tail brushed along this rock channel's sides, knocking off several of her rainbow scales. This tunnel meandered about seventy-five yards and then split into two separate passageways. She froze for a moment wondering which burrow to choose and then decided to explore its left channel first. That tunnel zigzagged for several dozen feet and then curved up. Aquan surfaced in a dry cave with a crumbling set of columns. She spied broken ceramics and charred wood and more Mayan inscriptions on its walls. Examining a small heap of bones, she realized it must be one of many Mayan ritual chambers for human and animal offerings to their gods. Aquan listened for any sounds, but heard nothing, and did not sense any presence of a living thing. She dipped below its surface and retraced her path.

Swimming into the other tunnel, Aquan felt water currents gently pulling her forward. Fresh water gave way to a saltier taste and Aquan guessed this channel must ebb and flow with ocean tides. Her amber talisman started to glow, throbbing more intensely as she made her way through this channel. Two moss green scales floated and danced along Aquan's collar bone and she seized them. Their sheen looked like those of an Ophion, a half-human, half-sea serpent Archigen, ornery creatures known for their sharp fangs and even sharper tempers.

This burrow flowed into a large underwater chamber where she smelled sea salt and heard a distant crash of waves. Curled up in its corner, an Ophion female slept on a bed of green sea lettuce. Her long black seaweed locks were wrapped around her blue-green skin. Aquan noticed that her serpent tail had shed many scales, a sign of age or sickness. This Ophion's shallow breaths lightly flickered her gills behind her ears and her split tongue unfurled and rolled back with each breath. Aquan cautiously slid a paralyzing dart out of her pouch. As she drew closer, the Ophion slowly opened one of her beady yellow eyes and reared up to strike Aquan with her venomous fangs. Before Aquan could jab her with a dart, she recoiled into her corner.

"It is forbidden for you to come here, Triton."

"I'm come looking for an amulet, like this one," said Aquan. She held up her amber necklace.

"Sentinels should not gather together with their amulets. Obey our Sacred Songs. Return to your corner of the compass."

"I'm an Emissary."

She looked Aquan up and down, her eyes glowing like flames. "Prove it."

Aquan grimaced and turned into an Ophion before reverting to her Trident form.

"I am Kadru, House of Ophion and Archigen." She pulled back her thick, dark hair and revealed her own amulet, strung around her neck with a braided seaweed cord. Her amulet and Aquan's gemstone both reverberated in each other's presence. She bowed before Aquan. "Forgive me, Emissary. I had to be certain."

"Don't bow to me. I should pay homage to you."

"I am but a servant of our Archigen Houses. A Sentinel of a western compass point."

She sighed and quaked and several scales dropped from her body. Aquan guided her back to her cave nook to rest.

"I've never heard anything about Sentinels, Kadru."

"Nearly a century ago I was chosen to safeguard this amulet. Any females of each major House, life-givers of Archigens, may be called to serve in the Scattering. Nearly a century ago, we gathered when Mopsus prophesied a birth of an Emissary who could reset Eternal Concordia. None had been born for centuries."

Aquan knew she must be that Emissary and couldn't understand why Mopsus didn't tell her about these events.

"Guided by our Infinite Dreamer's will, we threw the dice of providence to determine who would serve as Sentinels, keepers of these powerful amulets. Protecting each stone fiercely like our own offspring. I was selected to seek out a western submerged city to protect that hemisphere from a flood, from the Margrave's thirst for another Vanquishment. Waiting for an Emissary to come to collect it and determine Eternal Concordia," said Kadru.

"Have you have been waiting here for a hundred years for me?"

"Yes, I was in my eighth season and could decline this duty. But I'm honored to finish out my life in service to my people. To preserve our Infinite Dreamer's promise never to allow a flood to devour this Earth again." She smiled, proud of her sacrifice, and flicked her forked-tongue in and out.

"It must have been lonely service."

"It is one I do gladly."

"Do you know who else was chosen as Sentinels and where

they are hidden?"

"No, we were chosen separately as part of the Scattering. If one Sentinel is captured or tortured by Exoris, she cannot identify any other Sentinels or where their amulets are located. Only our Elder Council knows the identity of our Sentinels, but not even where we hide. We independently decide which sunken city within our allotted hemisphere. There are hundreds of these cities within each direction of the compass."

Aquan didn't know how she would find that last gemstone. She might try to contact the Cartographer once again for more guidance.

"I found this amulet in a marketplace in Estonia. Another was buried in Shore Temple in India." Aquan winced as she thought about losing that amulet to the Sea Monk. "Why would those Sentinels let their gems out of their custody?"

"Perhaps a Sentinel was gravely ill, nearing death or about to be discovered. In her last hours, she might secret away her gemstone as best she could to keep it away from Exoris."

Aquan wondered what terrible fates must have befallen those Sentinels to force them to abandon their underwater refuges. Kadru unhitched her cord and handed her talisman to Aquan who placed it in on her chain alongside her original one.

"Thank you, Kadru for waiting all these years," said Aquan. "For fulfilling this harsh, solitary duty. You've earned your return home."

The Ophion smiled and shook her head. "I fear I'm too weak to journey to Rapture's End. Before you leave me, I plead with you to remember our Sentinel sacrifices." Kadru stared into Aquan's eyes, gripping her arm, before she slipped back on to her stone ledge. "Do your mightiest to keep Eternal Concordia, Emissary."

"I promise you that I will, Kadru."

She nodded her head and asked Aquan to stay with her until she drifted off to sleep. Telling Kadru about Cutter's gratitude for her rescue, Aquan remained by Kadru's side for about an hour until she fell into her final nocturnal trance. Gently covering Kadru in green seaweed, Aquan kneeled before her in thanks and wished her soul a swift journey to Musterion.

In a tapered tunnel leading away from Kadru's lair, Aquan followed currents toward the ocean. Under a waxing gibbous moon, Aquan swam along Tulum's coastal cliffs headed for *Calusa*. She turned Kadru's story over and over again in her mind. Mopsus had lied to her about her mother, about the purpose of her mission and about the power of these amulets. With his deceptions piling up, she grew more angry and confused. So distressed, she failed to notice a small power boat docked about a two hundred feet away, its tender sidled up to *Calusa*'s portside. Emerging as Kirra in a wetsuit, she found a loaded gun pointed directly in her face.

Chapter 32

In a late afternoon's sticky humidity, Jenn tromped up wooden steps to her Key West bungalow. She unlocked an oak door with a stained glass oval in its center. A mound of mail pushed through her door slot cluttered her front hallway. Exhausted from a flight from Spain, she dropped her satchel and suitcases on a hardwood floor. Instead of sorting through two months of mail, she kicked off her shoes and walked directly to her kitchen. Her neighbor left a note on her kitchen table reading "Welcome back. Nice bottle of wine in the fridge. Mojito's in your backyard. Only killed two of your herb plants. Jeremy." She flung open her refrigerator door and grabbed a bottle of chardonnay, leaving only an ancient baking soda box behind.

Her cell phone vibrated in her pocket and she pulled it out as "Mamá" flashed on its screen. At times like this, Jenn was glad that Key West was far enough away from Miami to give her some space from her hovering mother. Jenn knew she should answer it, but she wasn't ready to try to explain all that had happened in the Canary Islands. A tragic tsunami in Candelaria. Cutter, an international fugitive. Her research assistant, missing. Dozens of research samples, lost somewhere. Even her excitement over Papandreas's conference and his funding were drained from her. Settling down with that Cuban guy in Miami didn't seem like such a stupid idea anymore. She texted her mom about arriving home safely and needing to get her jetlagged body to bed.

Turning on an overhead fan in her rear screened porch, she plopped down on a lounge chair. Jenn held her Chardonnay bottle to her throbbing forehead before twisting off its cap. Too tired to bother with a glass, she took a long, hard swig from its bottle neck. Her tabby cat brushed across her leg and meowed loudly.

"Don't judge me, Mojito. I've had a tough week." Jenn picked Mojito up and stroked its furry back. "You're a little fatty," she said. "Jeremy's been feeding you too much while I was away. Your diet starts tomorrow."

Jenn took a few more sips of wine and her head bobbed back and forth as she fought off sleep. But finally she surrendered to a quick nap on her porch.

When she awoke, Jenn discovered Mojito licking a puddle of white wine. Jenn shooed her away from it and returned to her kitchen to grab paper towels. Her vintage Kit-Cat clock, its eyes and tail swishing back and forth, read a little after seven o'clock. As she wiped up spilled wine, her front doorbell buzzed several times. She made out his blurred figure through ripples in her stained glass. Taking a deep breath, she unlatched her door and reluctantly opened it. Dr. William Cutter, Director of the Key West Oceanic Institute, stood there with every silver hair on his head neatly in place, the creases of his khaki pants carefully ironed, and a navy blue jacket over his white button-down shirt without a wrinkle.

"Please tell me he didn't do it," he said drily, adjusting his half-rim glasses.

"Of course, not. William. Come on in."

Dr. Cutter scanned her mail scattered across the floor.

"I just arrived home. Excuse any mess."

He stepped over her mail and into Jenn's living room.

"Not as big of a mess as that son of mine has created. I've got FBI agents on my doorstep and hounding my staff for his whereabouts. A complete PR nightmare." He shook his head in disgust.

Jenn motioned for him to sit down on her floral couch near her living room fireplace. He sat stiffly on a cushion edge, his back ramrod straight.

"Do you know where he is, Jenn?"

"I don't. But I assume he's on *Calusa*."

"The FBI tells me that he broke out of a prison, and then overcame a police officer and a TV camera crew to escape. He's got to be working with somebody. Is Emerson with him?"

"No, he's still missing. I think your son may have teamed up with an indigenous woman we rescued in the Tasman Sea. Supposedly a daughter of some well-connected Aussie family."

"Let's hope she's got a solid alibi for him and a deep bank account. All of his accounts have been frozen, his credit card activity under surveillance. They'll find him once he tries to access any of them."

"That wouldn't be a bad thing. At least we'd know he's safe."

"I never thought his troubles would lead to this. Chasing those underwater fantasy stories, wrecked his academic career. Bumming around dive resorts, ends up getting Rodrigo killed. Now a murder charge is about to ruin his life."

She frowned and said nothing.

"Jenn?" pressed Cutter's father. "Is he back on that kick again?"

"He got banged up in a fight in Hobart. Told me about a confrontation with several sea creatures on a deserted beach."

His father huffed and stood up.

"Can't believe he's still even discussing that madness with anyone."

He wrung his hands and paced around Jenn's living room.

"I thought he might get back on track seeing you, a real scientist doing real marine research, not chasing crazy theories. I guess his lawyer can always claim insanity. That aquatelligence nuttiness might spare him from being locked up in prison for life."

"He does have a lawyer in Spain," said Jenn. She hurried over to her satchel and yanked out Cabrera's business card. "Mr. Cabrera was very helpful in filing a missing person's form for Rick, too. Maybe he's heard from him. Or has an update on Rick."

"He might be a decent starting point. I better go and give you a chance to settle back in. Besides I need to take a few donors out to dinner, calm them down before they pull their pledges over this disaster."

As he headed for her front door, he added, "By the way, good job on securing that Papandreas's funding. I heard he was quite taken with your project."

"He was very enthusiastic about L11 microbes and exploring how they relate to whales and other marine life standings. Unfortunately, some of those samples were stored on *Calusa*. But I still have my laptop data and a majority of my samples were shipped ahead through a courier service."

"Good. Some light at the end of this tunnel. Try to relax this weekend and see you on Monday, Jenn."

"Take care, William. I'll call if I learn anything about Cutter or Emerson."

As Cutter's father left, Jenn closed and leaned her back against her front door. For a moment, she couldn't shake her disappointment that William remained so concerned about the Institute's reputation and funding rather than Emerson's or even his own son's safety. Looking at letters strewn around her bare feet, Jenn collected them and dumped her stacks on a kitchen table. Tossing a frozen pizza into her oven, she rummaged through her correspondence. It was hard to keep her mind on these mundane tasks as she imagined horrible dangers facing her friends. After two hours of paying bills and sifting through months of letters and notices, she discovered a delivery receipt from a Spanish transport service. It indicated that her water samples and slides had been delivered to the Institute yesterday. Too restless to fall back to sleep, she decided to go to her lab and log in her samples. She threw her laptop bag over her shoulder and hopped on her scooter heading for her lab.

*****

Jenn slid her card key into a darkened employee front entrance at the Institute. Her flip flops clacked as she headed down a deserted hallway, overhead motion lights clicking on as she walked toward her lab. She punched in her code into a central key pad and sauntered through a series of lab modules where her colleagues researched a wide range of marine life. Suddenly, she stopped and puzzled over an aquarium of sea horses. All of them were floating upside down in their tank.

"Weird," she whispered.

As she neared her lab, Jenn could see one light had been left on and heard the familiar sounds of clinking test tubes.

"Hello," she called out, expecting to find a cleaning crew at work.

Entering her lab unit, Jenn discovered slashed plastic bindings and shrink-wrap piled on one end of a lab table. She examined a crumpled shipping label and recognized its name.

"My samples," she cried out.

Before she uttered another word, Jenn noticed motion lights turning on in an adjacent lab. Without thinking, she dropped her laptop bag and chased after a burglar stealing her life's work. Jenn quickly gained on him as he struggled to steer a dolly loaded with two heavy crates of water samples. When they reached a final lab, he was cornered unable to punch in an exit code and wheel his heavy cart around a tight corner simultaneously. Clad in black with a ski mask, he gasped for air as he clutched the cart's metal handle. A long steel lab bench stood between them.

"Don't come any closer or I'll smash these tubes to bits," he yelled.

"Rick?" asked Jenn.

"Stay where you are."

"I know it's you. Why are you doing this?"

Rolling up his ski mask, his glasses sat crooked on his nose. His face burned bright red, shiny with sweat.

"Jenn, for your own safety, you need to turn around and pretend none of this happened."

"What are you talking about?"

Emerson's chest heaved as he tried to catch his breath. "Sorry, Jenn. These samples are worth a lot more than you could ever imagine."

"No one is going to pay you for those water samples."

"You're wrong. Bioweapons are quite valuable to certain people."

"You can't weaponize those microbes. They're harmless to humans."

"Right, but that's not how they're going to be used."

"I don't understand." She furrowed her brow.

"It will take too long to explain and I don't have time right now." He stepped toward an exit key pad to punch in his code. "The deal is done."

"I can't let you leave here with those samples, Rick."

"You can't stop me," he replied. He pulled out a Taser from his windbreaker pocket. "I don't want to hurt you. So stay out of my way."

"Okay, I'm backing off."

Jenn raised her hands in surrender and took a step away from him. Emerson started to enter his code and Jenn pushed a lab table over on to him and his dolly. She dashed into an adjoining lab and punched in her code to escape, hoping to pull a fire alarm in the Institute's main lobby. As she neared its foyer, Jenn felt a painful sting of two barbs piercing her skin. A thunderous jolt of electricity burned through her body. She collapsed on the vestibule's cool tiles. Before passing out, Jenn looked up, her eyes popping wide open with strange hallucinations before she lost consciousness.

"Good evening, Dr, Ortiz," he said, standing over her still body. A Pteron screeched from its perch on a Sea Monk's shoulder.

Chapter 33

Quartz Hall reverberated with furious voices and angry stomps of Council members. Every Elder from each major House, not only their elected representatives, crammed its benches and quarreled over the fate of Aquan's mission. Only Triton Elders were absent, still secluded under protective custody after the massacre.

"Silence, silence," said Eirene, an Elder of the House of Lamia.

She occupied the spot behind a moderator's podium. Despite having the sharp teeth, dorsal fin and tail of a shark, Eirene tended to be one of the more deliberate, calm members of the Council.

"I call this emergency meeting to order. Mopsus, you requested this special session so you have the floor." Eirene nodded to him to proceed.

"I requested this emergency meeting to address a matter of grave importance. A serious violation of our Sacred Songs. Elder Camulus has interfered with the Sequencing's natural course of events. Without Council approval, he removed Evadne from Borean territory and relocated her in stasis to an undisclosed holding area. He did so in order to impact our Emissary's mission." Mopsus pointed directly at Elder Camulus in a front row bench.

"Outrageous." Camulus snorted and slammed down his webbed fist.

"His actions are a perversion of the Sacred Songs which require that we not influence or seek to change the outcome of the Sequencing process." Mopsus's booming voice bounced off every cavern wall. His scarlet sea worms sprouting from his head twisted and turned white with anger. "I move that Elder Camulus be expelled from this Council and confined to his House of Keras until the Sequencing is over."

"As our Council's chief security advisor, I am within my authority to protect this body and our Archigen people. I don't need prior approval to act in emergency situations when harm is imminent."

"Camulus is correct that he may act unilaterally in emergency situations as our chief security adviser," said Eirene.

Mopsus shook his head and stroked his green beard. "Imminent danger? Evadne has been in stasis for nearly ninety years for her crime. She doesn't pose any danger to this Council or any of our Houses. His actions are a blatant attempt to interfere with the outcome of a century's highest tide and fullest moon during the Sequencing."

"Don't lecture me, Mopsus, about interfering. You battled those power-hungry Protosians like the rest of us. You supported our ban on Archigen and Triton unions. You persuaded us to spare Aquan so you could spend a century trying to mold her into an Emissary who would choose to protect Eternal Concordia. You've interfered plenty," replied Camulus.

"All defensive strategies in response to known dangers. None were affirmative steps with unknown consequences that violate our Sacred Songs, Camulus."

Mopsus opened his lips to say more, but restrained himself. He didn't have enough proof to indict Camulus and his allies in the Triton massacre. He assumed these acts were final brutal attempts to murder Aquan and exterminate all remaining Triton females capable of giving birth to more Emissaries, and all conveniently blamed on Exoris.

"I disagree," said Polemus, a long-time ally of Camulus. "With Evadne secreted away, her sentence to stasis remains unchanged. But if permitted to remain in a Borean prison, Aquan would have freed her and that amulet would now be in the Margrave's hands."

"You don't know that outcome for certain," said Eirene. "You're only speculating about what Aquan might do."

"We have proof of her poor judgment already. Queen Chione reported that she exchanged one amulet to barter Zetes's freedom from the Margrave. Aquan recklessly and willingly surrendered her talisman, solely to learn who took her mother," said Polemus.

Members of the assembly buzzed with disapproval. Mopsus heaved a disappointed sigh.

"Do you think for a moment that once released from stasis, Evadne will not exact her revenge upon us? She will make certain that Aquan resets Eternal Concordia to call forth the Vanquishment or that Aquan gives him her permission to do so," said Polemus.

"Elder Polemus is right. Keeping Evadne hidden makes certain that there will not be enough bridle amulets in the Margrave's control before our next full moon. We'll avert a horrific global deluge and uphold our Infinite Dreamer's oath to Surface Dwellers," added Camulus.

"Our Sacred Songs are clear that only an Emissary can reset Eternal Concordia every hundred years. It is her decision, not ours. Her choice stands as judgment on whether we are worthy custodians of this global responsibility," said Elder Derseum.

"She may possess that power, but it doesn't mean that we must sit by like fools and do nothing to ensure a proper outcome," said Camulus. "We cannot passively resign ourselves and our futures to an insolent adolescent, spawn of a treasonous mother."

"Regardless of her lineage, she is an Emissary. Part of a long line of Emissaries that has bridged the gap between land and sea, humanity and Archigen," said Derseum. "Emissaries have always chosen the right path, protection of Eternal Concordia."

"Yes, but that was before insurrection split our Houses. We banned Triton-Archigen unions to prevent further breeding of Emissaries to avoid this danger. She is the first Emissary born since that civil war with the House of Proteus," said Polemus. "And she can't be trusted."

"We should have killed her when she was born and wiped out all of these risks," said Camulus. "Nothing says we cannot kill her after the Sequencing to prevent this crisis from every arising again. We should not spare her life while putting our entire nation at risk."

Polemus clapped his seal flippers in approval and others

roared their support with whistles and squeaks.

"Listen to yourselves," cried out Mopsus. "Scheming your way to eternal bliss in Musterion. Your craven thirst for eternal joy no better than Protosians hunger for power, for the Vanquishment. Did you ever think Aquan's journey might not be about testing her, but about testing us? Testing our fidelity to our Sacred Songs."

Mopsus beat his fist so hard on arm of his magma bench that a decorative abalone shell popped off and floated away. Silence fell across the assembly.

"You are so ready to condemn Aquan solely to spare your own lives, your own souls. Do any of you think you could do better under these circumstances? Would you want your own child to carry out this mission?" added Mopsus. "Look into your hearts and ask yourselves, will our Infinite Dreamer find descendants of the House of Archigen to be any less corrupt and murderous than our exiled kinsmen? Are we better or worse than those first malevolent humans swept away in that first flood? What we decide today will surely give us our answer and seal our fate."

"Fine sentiments from her hapless mentor. But you are wrong, Mopsus. We act only to keep our people safe and to do our Infinite Dreamer's will. For if she fails to maintain Eternal Concordia, then our Archigen people, not Aquan, will pay the price," said Camulus. "Each of you and your loved ones will suffer an eternity in darkness beyond Obzula Ridge while Protosians reign supreme." Camulus marched around Quartz Hall, pointing to different Elder Council members. "Do you want that? Or you? Or you?"

Several Elders shook their heads "no" while others called out a resounding chorus of "nos."

"I call for a vote on Mopsus's motion," said Camulus.

"Camulus has called the question. All in favor of Mopsus's motion signify by saying 'yea'," said Eirene.

Only Mopsus and Derseum cried out, "Yea."

"All opposed signify by 'nay'," said Eirene.

Quartz Hall boomed with "nays" echoing off its high ceilings.

"The 'nays' have it and Mopsus's motion fails." Eirene looked around the assembly, "Is there any other business before we adjourn?"

"Elder Eirene, I have a new motion to bring," said Polemus.

"Proceed, Polemus."

"I move that this Council approve of Elder Camulus's actions in removing Evadne and hiding her in a confidential location to help protect our Archigen nation. I ask that we reaffirm his authority to act as chief security adviser to safeguard us from threats, whenever and by whatever means necessary."

Numerous Elders clapped and whistled their approval seconding his motion.

"The motion has been made and seconded. All in favor signify by 'yea'."

The amphitheater erupted in thunderous "yeas."

"All opposed say 'nay'," said Eirene.

Mopsus replied with a solitary, "Nay."

"The 'yeas' have it and Polemus's motion passes. This meeting is adjourned," said Eirene.

Dejected, Mopsus remained seated as his fellow Elders exited Quartz Hall. It pained him to think that Aquan would so quickly forsake her training and so foolishly surrender one of her amulets to the Margrave. Had all those years of training been for nothing? Perhaps she did so deliberately out of shock over her mother's imprisonment or anger to repay decades of deceit. If he could only explain his deception and help her understand that he meant only to shield her from danger and anguish. Yet with Camulus and his allies in firm control, Mopsus recognized he could no longer protect her. For the first time since her birth, he truly feared for Aquan's life.

Chapter 34

Under a bright three-quarter moon, a man with a shaved head and five black teardrop tattoos on his face, one for each murder promoting him through his gang's ranks, stood on an edge of Cutter's dive platform. He clenched a semiautomatic pistol in his right hand, another gun poked out of his baggy shorts. Tattoo sleeves covered both of his muscular arms bulging out of his shorty wetsuit. Red-and-black lettering inked "Diablo" on his right shin. Another goon, with an ammunition belt slung over his shoulder, rested a tip of his AK-47 against Cutter's left temple. Blood trickled from a corner of Cutter's mouth and dripped on to his dive suit. His hands were lashed behind his back and zip ties were tightened around his ankles. Aquan decided that transformation at this moment might get them both killed.

"Hola, chica." He pulled Aquan aboard as Kirra. "Where are you coming from?"

"Swam ashore to check out Mayan beach ruins," replied Aquan.

"Not too safe swimming alone at night. Sharks love to feed on sweet meat." Diablo made loud chomping noises next to Aquan's ear. "Right, Chunk?"

A bear of a man with an immense stomach, Chunk laughed hoarsely inflating his pink flabby jowls. He gripped a rocket launcher with his meaty hands. Aquan heard sounds of someone stomping below deck, tossing items around and pounding his fists against *Calusa*'s interior walls. She wondered if Cutter's past had finally caught up to him at the worst possible time for her mission. Diablo shoved Aquan on to boat cushions on the upper deck.

"Be a good girl, now." Diablo grazed his gun's muzzle against her cheek. "Or we'll blow your boyfriend's head off."

"He's not my boyfriend."

"Maybe we'll all become your boyfriends before we're done here."

His men smiled and nodded their heads as Cutter struggled

against his bindings, spitting in Diablo's direction. Chunk shoved the butt of his launcher into Cutter's stomach. He grimaced and doubled over in pain. Gypsy howled straining against a leather leash fastened to a boat railing.

"Please don't hurt him. I'll try to help you find whatever you're looking for."

"Maybe you can help us." Diablo smiled and pushed his gun against her forehead. "We're looking for a stolen flash drive. It took a while for them to figure out who did it. By then, Rodrigo was already fish food. His gringo buddy here, long gone. That cartel boss put out a generous reward for anybody who tracked down his pal and returned that flash drive. Lots of important information on it. We're going to collect that reward. So I'll give you a whole ten seconds to cough it up."

As Diablo counted down each second, Aquan's mind raced with panic. She wouldn't be able transform before Diablo or his henchman squeezed their triggers. Aquan didn't want to risk getting Cutter killed or getting *Calusa* blown up.

"It's not on this boat," Aquan said.

Diablo pressed his barrel harder against her forehead.

"But I know where it is," she added.

"Good. I won't have to kill you just yet. Where is it?"

"In a dry bag with some cocaine bricks and cash hidden in a run-off pipe. Adjacent to that beach." Aquan pointed in the direction of Tulum's Mayan ruins. "I was coming back from checking out our stash. I forgot to bring a boat hook with me."

"Okay, you take me there now. And no funny business or else he's fish food."

"Alright, but it's too shallow for this ship. We've got to use your inflatable to carry everything back. We'll also need a boat hook to snag a guide line for our dry bag."

"Get up here, Oscar," yelled Diablo.

A fireplug of a man with dark curly hair and jack-o'-lantern teeth, appeared from below deck. A huge scar ran from his left temple to the base of his neck.

"Oscar, you're coming with us. You two stay here. Blanco, if he gives you any trouble, shoot him. Chunk, keep that rocket launcher handy. Vamos," he said to Aquan and Oscar.

Aquan stepped into their tender and Diablo followed right behind her. Oscar passed a boat hook to Diablo. Sputtering away, she lost sight of Cutter in a couple of minutes as they disappeared into darkness. Moonlight danced across tips of foamy waves cresting toward Tulum Beach.

"Slow down," said Aquan. "We're almost there."

"I don't see nothing." Diablo ran his flashlight across the water.

"It's right below where the waves are breaking. It's low tide. We'll need to swim the rest of the way."

"Go with her, Oscar," he ordered.

Aquan slid into the water and Oscar followed with boat hook in hand. A beam of light from Diablo's light bounced up and down as their tender rode the surf.

"Slow down," Oscar said, trying to catch up with Aquan.

"Almost there," she said, swimming in swirling currents. "Right below here."

Diablo positioned his light where Aquan stopped as Oscar caught up to her. Momentarily dipping underwater, Aquan trembled and changed into a sea wasp, its translucent bubblehead and tentacles swaying in ocean swells. Oscar splashed right into her invisible tentacles, pricking his skin several times. His agonizing shrieks did not sound human, but more like pained cries of a severely wounded animal.

"Oscar," called out Diablo. "What's going on?"

He ran his flashlight across the rolling surf and caught sight of Oscar's limp body reeling over and over in its waves.

"Where are you, bitch?" he said.

Diablo tore off his khakis and kicked off his water shoes. Hiding his guns under a tarp in his tender, he dove in with his flashlight. He swam toward the beach and found Oscar's boat hook drifting ashore. As Diablo waded in, he looked around wondering where Aquan had gone. Suddenly, he felt a half-dozen stings on his ankles and calves. Within two or three seconds, her venom paralyzed his muscles and his breathing became labored. He sank to his knees in the sand before several ocean swells knocked him over. Reverting to human form, Aquan dragged his stiffening body on to Tulum Beach.

Only his eyes could move, darting back and forth in sheer terror.

"Don't worry, Diablo. You might even survive," she whispered into his ear. "But it's gonna hurt like hell. Worse than a shark bite, sweet meat." She mimicked his earlier shark chomping sounds.

Aquan raced toward an overflowing trash bin near a beach parking lot. She yanked out a liner filled with trash and tied it off. Dragging it through the surf, Aquan tossed it into their drifting tender and climbed aboard cloaked as Diablo. Pulling their tarp around her trash bag, Diablo's guns clunked out onto the tender's floor. She grabbed them and whirred back to *Calusa*. As she neared Cutter's catamaran, Chunk anxiously waited on a rear diving platform, scanning the harbor.

"You okay, Diablo?"

"Bueno, bueno," Aquan replied in Diablo's form.

"What was all that yelling?"

"That girl and Oscar ended up shark bait."

Chunk and Blanco glanced nervously at each other.

"More for us." Aquan laughed and patted her tarp mound.

They all laughed as Aquan climbed aboard *Calusa*.

"You guys, take this stash back to our boat while I finish him off. Then come pick me up." She took Chunk's rocket launcher as he climbed into their tender. "And hurry up. This hour's drug patrol will be nosing around pretty soon."

As they buzzed away from *Calusa*, she strode slowly toward Cutter.

"You're lucky I'm tied up, 'cuz I'd tear you apart with my bare hands, Diablo," Cutter said.

"I'm going to shoot and you're going to fall down."

"Screw you," said Cutter.

"We gotta make this look good." Aquan winked at Cutter.

"Holy shit, is it you?"

Aquan smiled and raised her arm to shoot. "On a count of three, I shoot past you and then you fall down," she said in a low voice. "1,2,3."

Her shots whizzed past Cutter's head twice and he pretended to drop dead at Diablo's feet. Stepping portside, she seized Chunk's rocket launcher and waited as their dinghy got closer to Diablo's powerboat. Looking through its scope, she aimed for its rear engines and squeezed its trigger. A rocket whistled through the air and slammed into their boat. Its fuel tanks exploded sending a fireball into the night sky. Its impact knocked Chunk and Blanco out of their tender and into a burning pool of oily water.

Aquan stepped over Cutter and headed below deck.

"Hey, how about untying me first?" yelled Cutter.

She tossed a sheathed dive knife up to Cutter. "Do it yourself. Unleash Gypsy quick. We gotta get out of here before the Mexican Navy shows up."

Jumping into Cutter's pilot chair, she turned on *Calusa*'s engines and hit its gas pedal. Glancing back, she continued to blast past Tulum's majestic cliffs.

Cutter slid down his boat railings with Gypsy dancing behind him.

"Thanks," he mumbled, entering his pilothouse.

"Huh?" she said.

"Thanks."

"For what?" she asked with a smirk.

"Thanks for saving my ass, again."

"And your dog. And your boat. And probably your world."

"Yeah, those things, too."

Cutter stood close to her and rested his hand on her shoulder. She unexpectedly felt a few butterflies in her stomach.

"I'm glad you made it out alive."

"Me, too," she replied.

"But don't go getting a big head," he added. "After all this, did you get it?"

Aquan pulled two amulets on her chain out of her wetsuit.

"Was she still wearing it?"

"Yes, a very brave Ophion. She gave her life to safeguard it. I offered her your thanks."

"Good. Now where to?"

"I don't know. But we ought to lay low and think about next steps. You lived here before, any suggestions?"

"I've got an old research buddy in Belize who owes me big. Gus Harper. We can crash there for a couple of days."

Chapter 35

With hundreds of deserted or sparsely settled islands off Belize's coast, there were plenty of places for fugitives to hide out from authorities. Cutter's boat rumbled into a peaceful cove where morning sun glinted off a turquoise sea like millions of gleaming blue diamonds. Sea gulls, red-footed booby birds and scarlet-breasted frigate birds covered its rocky shores. Their squawks and screeches filled its air. Thick green fronds of swaying palm trees rustled in soft ocean breezes. Tiny sea birds scurried away as Aquan and Cutter pulled their tender on to a quiet beach alongside a battered eighteen-foot skiff.

"Does your friend, Gus, know we're coming?" asked Aquan.

"I didn't want to chance hailing him in case the Coast Guard's monitoring open radio channels. A nutty little Brit, but he'll be fine with it. I brought along an old friend." He held a bottle of Jack Daniels in his hand. "Besides, he's probably dying to talk to someone."

"He lives here alone."

"Yup, pretty self-sufficient. Picks up supplies every few months from the mainland. But mostly it's him and his birds. He's an expert on all kinds of sea birds. Never met a feathered creature he didn't like. But humans, that's another story. Watch yourself. He can be a little crusty."

"So he shares your people skills," said Aquan.

"Yeah, he and I are kindred spirits," replied Cutter. "We get along much better with animals." He patted Gypsy's back.

His dog barked and chased two seagulls. Weathered clapboards of a rustic camp on stilts stood alone on a rocky outcrop above pure white sands. Long fishing rods leaned against its driftwood porch railings. Solar panels blanketed a thatched roof beach hut and a satellite dish was fastened high on a tower. Sudden gusts of wind sent dozens of hanging bamboo and shell wind chimes thumping and clacking. A cluster of wooden whirligigs of jumping dolphins, casting fishermen, and swimming mermaids frantically sawed back and forth in blustery airstreams. Three camouflaged wind turbines, their bases painted elephant gray to blend in with palm bark, spun fiercely behind Harper's home. A tang of saltwater and a charcoal aroma of fish cooking on a grill wafted in the air.

"Seems like we're here in time for lunch," said Cutter. He yelled out "Gus Harper," two times and then threw several stones against Harper's wooden house. "Get out of bed, you lazy old fart."

A shirtless man with wild tufts of gray hair and faded blue board shorts tottered out barefoot on to his front porch. Like a grizzly bear waking up from a winter's hibernation, he rubbed his eyes and scratched his tanned barrel chest. An unlit stogie hung out of one side of his mouth.

"Look what low tide washed in to Little Moon Island," he said.

"Kiss my arse, Gus."

In unison they said, "Not on the right cheek, not on the left cheek, but right in the groove." They both laughed at some inside joke that baffled Aquan.

"You must be in heaps of trouble if you came here, muffin head."

"Absolutely, an all points alert for murder through Interpol."

"Bugger me," he exclaimed. "I should probably radio our local Coast Guard. But I see you brought me a present, so I guess they'll have to wait." Gus yawned and his stogie fell on to his porch floor. He picked it up and stuck it right back into his mouth. "Who's your little lady?"

"Kirra, a friend from Australia," said Cutter.

"Lots of short-tailed shearwaters and fairy terns nesting on those Aussie coasts," replied Gus. "You a wanted killer, too?" he asked, nodding to Aquan.

"No, Gus. Just hitching a ride on *Calusa*."

"Expect you're both hungry with all that murdering and hitching. Come on in. I got brekky grilling out back."

In Gus's hut, high stacks of open books and copies of journal articles covered nearly every spot in his front room floor. Charcoal sketches and color photographs of sea birds were plastered over every inch of his walls. A laptop computer blinked next to a digital camera and scrawled handwritten notes covered a shabby wooden desk in its corner. Aquan glanced at an unmade bed with a bamboo headboard and a half-size fridge crammed into a tiny second room. Its shutters propped open, two Piping Plovers flew into his shack and chased each other out a back door. Gus took three scratched up plastic plates and forks and jelly jar glasses out of a small cabinet and handed them to Cutter. In a moment, they were outside his shack. A jumble of lobster traps spilled out of an unpainted shed with a noisy generator inside. A fat grouper fish crackled over coals on a rough-hewn stone grill.

As they ate grouper, Gus encouraged Cutter to start pouring some whiskey.

"It's tea time somewhere, mate," he said.

Cutter poured amber liquor into each of their glasses. Aquan pretended to take sips but drank little of it. As whiskey flowed, Gus spoke animatedly about his sea bird research, his tracking of their migrations for over thirty years and his sorrow at seeing their numbers continually plummeting.

"Every year, fewer and fewer birdies come back to nest, to breed. Between collapsing fish stocks and all those pollutants, I'm afraid some morning I'll wake up and not see a single bird. We're killing this planet," he said. He took a sip of whiskey and looked a bit sad. "I hope I never live to see it. I'm glad I'm getting old. Your generation better act fast before we completely trash this place and become as extinct as the dodo bird."

"Here's to our generation kicking ass and cleaning up your generation's mess," said Cutter.

They clinked their glasses and Aquan joined in to be polite.

"So what have you been up to that's got you running?" asked Gus.

Cutter told him about Papandreas's conference and that fateful night on his yacht witnessing Candelaria's tsunami. Gus listened intently as Cutter spoke about Tuttleberry hounding him after Rodrigo's death and how that pesky insurance adjuster ended up murdered on *Calusa*. Avoiding any details of his escape, he explained that a police investigation would exonerate him once they checked his whereabouts with locals he hung out with that night.

"Remind me never to take holiday with you two," said Gus. He slung back a shot of whiskey. "I'm sure your old man is as proud as ever of you. Has he tried to contact you, mate?"

"No, I'm bad for business. We don't talk much." Cutter fell silent for a moment.

"Not that anybody will really mourn one less insurance adjuster in this world, but any idea who mucked up your boat with his bloody body, Cutter?"

"I don't have a clue. Not even sure why he was on my boat. Probably trying to gather evidence of some grand plot to defraud his company."

Aquan realized that she hadn't told Cutter about a Sea Monk's scent on his catamaran or discovering Tuttleberry's audio recorder and cell phone. She had stuffed his recorder into her canvas bag and his phone was likely still wedged in a crevice under Jenn's lab table. As the two friends talked about old times, Aquan excused herself to take a walk with her backpack resting on her shoulder. She seized a long fishing rod from Harper's porch before heading to the beach.

Sitting down on warm sand, she pulled out Tuttleberry's recorder. She listened to several mundane audio clips of his daily observations of Cutter and his vessel until she reached his final day of investigation.

"August 7, 8:25 p.m. Fraudster has exited his ship and marina. Based on past observations, should be gone for several hours. Surveillance of marina gate will continue until I gain entry. Will search his vessel for evidence of life insurance fraud in Case #300758."

His audiotape ended and there were no further recordings. Aquan left her canvas bag ashore and took Cutter's tender back to *Calusa*. She stuck a slender tip of Harper's fishing rod under Jenn's work bench. It took several whacks to poke his cell phone out from under it. Fortunately, his cell phone wasn't locked. She rolled a track ball over a camera icon to check his photo folder. He dated each folder containing a cache of mundane photos of *Calusa*, Cutter, Dr. Ortiz and Emerson. She rolled through to the date of his murder. In that folder, there were numerous pictures of Cutter coming and going on his boat. But this folder contained a series of short video clips, too.

Aquan played one clip of Tuttleberry taping his own trespass on to Cutter's boat. The initial one bounced around as he shot video of Tenerife Marina and *Calusa* docked in its slip.

"Santa Cruz Marina. Canary Islands. August 7, 8:45 p.m. Contraband ship, *Calusa*, slip #64." That clip ended.

Another jangling clip started as Tuttleberry climbed aboard Cutter's vessel, breathing heavily. He ran his cell phone camera across *Calusa*'s deck, stopping at its radar tower and satellite on strapped to its mast.

"New equipment, possibly from illicit funds," he whispered.

In a third clip, he's creeping down steps to *Calusa*'s lower deck. His cell phone camera briefly sweeps across Cutter's lower deck. It catches Emerson removing a clutch of sealed water samples and putting them in a small container. Surprised, Emerson quickly turns around.

"What are you doing here?"

"I told you and Dr. Ortiz already. Life insurance fraud. You're up to your ears in it."

"Who is this man? Get him out of here." Aquan recognized Countess Daimonakis's voice on Tuttleberry's clip.

"I'm not going anywhere," he replied. "Until I get some answers."

"You'll be sorry you ever asked any questions," she responded.

His video ended abruptly. Aquan recognized that Emerson must have been a Drowner, an Exori mole on *Calusa*. A flash of relief passed over Aquan realizing Cutter hadn't betrayed her. Yet she recalled Jenn opened her locked specimen box and found her research samples intact that night. Perhaps Emerson stole L11 samples and replaced Ortiz's research vials with bogus ones. But why? Aquan didn't know for sure, but feared for Jenn's safety if Exoris wanted more of her microbes back in her Key West lab. No way for Cutter to show his face in Florida right now, she thought. She scrawled a quick note to him and left it on Jenn's lab bench. Changing into a speedy Commerson Dolphin, Aquan hoped she wasn't too late to rescue Dr. Ortiz.

Chapter 36

Late on Saturday afternoon, Aquan squeezed through a ridiculously small hole in the Institute's rear delivery door as a mouse. She scurried across a cement floor in its delivery area and snooped around its hallways. With a mouse's powerful sense of smell, she rapidly picked up a metallic scent of blood exposed to air. Wrinkling her whiskered nose, she darted along a main corridor and saw blood drops on its tiles. Renewing her Kirra form, Aquan tiptoed along this blood trail. Motion lights popped on as she reached each new section. She glanced into windows of each deserted lab. Blood stains turned into wide, long streaks of an injured person dragging their body toward a front lobby. She ran hoping she wasn't too late to spare Dr. Ortiz.

Up ahead, Aquan saw a silhouetted body lying across a reception area floor, a pool of blood thickening around this figure. She stepped on a pair of eyeglasses before kneeling over a figure dressed in black. She touched his neck, his pulse weakly sputtered. Faint breaths expelled from his lips. It was Emerson, not Dr. Ortiz. Several bullet holes riddled his black windbreaker.

"Who did this to you?"

His eyes rolled back into his head, his lips moving, but no audible words came out.

"I can't hear you. Try to say it again, Emerson."

Aquan bent over him, getting her ear as close as she could to his lips.

"Right in the nick of time," he boomed.

Stumbling back, she recognized the Margrave's voice, projecting himself through Emerson's nearly lifeless form as he had done with Chappelle's body in Paris.

"I'm glad you made it before this human shell expired," he added. "I do need a spark of life to talk to you."

"Why do you want to speak to me at all?"

"It's lonely and boring down here. I know you can appreciate that. Roaming around the globe reporting on for those water-logged Elders."

"Where's Dr. Ortiz?"

"If I told you, then our little game of hide-and-seek would be over. Even if you're not as good as I am at it."

"Not much of a boast. You've been looking for those amulets for centuries. I've only had a few weeks."

"Don't be mad at me. I didn't make those rules. But I'm ahead 2-0 and I still want to play."

Clearly he could not see her wearing two amulets, an important advantage over him.

"To keep you up-to-date, our score's actually 2-1."

"Ah, you discovered that western Sentinel. You're so lucky to be able go wherever you wish. I'm stuck here working through witless puppets, relying on others to carry out my plans."

"Maybe if you behave yourself, you'll get a reprieve from exile."

"I doubt it. How about you plead my case to Mopsus and all those good Elders in Quartz Hall?"

"I'm not sure how good they are." Aquan frowned as she thought about their decades of cruel deceptions.

"That's the spirit. Finally questioning those deceitful Archigens."

"Did you keep your word and free Queen Chione's sister?"

"Of course. Nobody will cooperate with me if I don't make good on my promises."

"If you release Dr. Ortiz, I promise to say nice things about you."

He sighed. "Not a very good exchange. Besides I can't do that. I don't have her."

"No, but I'm sure you can persuade your pal Papandreas to free her."

The Margrave let loose a deep laugh. "You're catching on. He'll keep her safe. For a little while. But don't go looking for her or you might get her killed."

"You better tell him to protect her if he wants to stay alive."

"Sadly, I can only project my thoughts and images through lesser beings such as Sea Monks, Hydromorphs and greedy

Drowners, like Emerson. I can use my mind to communicate with my fellow Archigens, but I can't make them do anything. Otherwise, you would've already given me that amulet by now."

"I'll never give it up."

"I wouldn't be so sure about that." He remained silent for a moment, letting his taunt sink in.

"You'll have to kill me to possess this one."

He huffed. "Not that again. I can't take them from you. You must choose to give them to me."

"Then I choose for you to give me back that amulet your Sea Monk stole at Shore Temple."

"Sure, but you'll have to come and get it."

Mopsus warned Aquan about traveling beyond Obzula Ridge. Yet she knew the Margrave needed her alive and capable of handing over her remaining amulets.

"Is this a formal invitation or a nasty trap?"

"Come and find out. Once you meet me you might realize how likeable I am. Have you given any thought to my earlier offer to join forces with me?"

"Not a second thought. I've been too busy looking for amulets to prevent global cataclysm."

"Love your sarcasm. But I'm actually trying to save our world from complete destruction."

"You're no savior. I witnessed your cruelty at Candelaria, your horrific massacre of my House of Triton in Bliss Valley."

"I told you before that it doesn't serve my interests to destroy your House. Triton females are my only hope for future Emissaries to support my cause, to reset Concordia. Ask yourself who benefits if there are no more Emissaries. It's not me."

She knew that he was right. Protosian hopes for triumph rested with Triton females surviving to give birth to new Emissaries.

"I'm trying to set Eternal Concordia to save our Earth from decimation by those Surface Dwellers."

Aquan thought of Gus and his observations about declining sea bird populations and his toasting Cutter about future generations stopping global pollution.

"Earth's demise has been forecast for millennia, but it keeps rotating on its access. They've done great harm. Yet they'll keep learning from their past mistakes. We must give them time to change their ways."

"You don't understand. There is a war coming between Surface Dwellers."

"Wars are nothing new. Mopsus taught me about human wars throughout history. It doesn't mean our planet is doomed."

"Not just any war." She could hear real frustration growing in his voice. "Not those usual human squabbles over power or territory. This time it will be over water. An essential resource for our intermingled survival."

"There is plenty of water. Two-thirds of our Earth is covered with it."

"Not clean drinking water. In seventy-three years, a third world war will erupt amongst nations over drinking water. Nation against nation, brother against brother, parents against their children, in a fierce battle for their continued existence. They will annihilate each other with biological and nuclear weapons. Leaving a dead shell, a toxic spinning orb. Poisoning all fresh and saltwater, killing our oceans that we need to continue to exist."

"That's a good story. If your claims were true, then Mopsus and our Elder Council would favor another Great Flood. But they don't. "

"They cling to a blind faith in an Infinite Dreamer. Believing they must uphold the Dreamer's oath to Surface Dwellers to never destroy Earth by a flood again. But at what cost? And where is the Dreamer now? Long gone birthing new worlds. Abandoning us, if she ever existed."

"You speak heresies."

"No, I speak hard truths. Wiping out Surface Dwellers spells our only hope for preserving any life on this planet. I plan for our peoples to survive for many more centuries, even if humans must die for that future to exist."

"How can you even guess what will happen in a distant

future? You didn't even know I possessed this amulet from a western Sentinel until today." She touched her necklace dangling from her neck. "So much can happen in seventy-three years."

"Your mother predicted it, Aquan. Mopsus saw this same vision, too. When she gave birth to you, Evadne hoped you would reset Eternal Concordia, call forth the Vanquishment before our mutual destruction."

"You know nothing of my mother or what she wanted me to do. You never met her."

"That's true. But Phorcys spoke of her often and I feel like I know her."

"You knew my father?"

"Yes, Phorcys was a great warrior who fought many glorious battles. He never lacked for mates. He fathered many offspring with Triton females in hopes of creating another Emissary. He mated with your mother, Evadne and other Tritons. Even after that ban on their unions."

Aquan remembered Clarissa's words to her about centuries of civil strife and Triton females who refused to abandon their mates.

"For many decades, he warred with my father, Bythos. Until your father realized his mistake and joined forces with him."

"You lie and dishonor Phorcys."

"No, it was only natural for them to quarrel but eventually they came together to fight for their family, cousin."

"Don't call me 'cousin'. You're not my kinsmen."

"But I am. I am Skeiron, son of Bythos and Aello. Bythos was your father's eldest brother."

Aquan gasped.

"You can't expect me to believe that the seeds of two brothers, created an Emissary and her sworn enemy, the Margrave."

For once, he didn't spit back some pithy comeback. Silence opened up between them.

"I'm sorry you don't know this fact already, cousin." His tone became more serious, more somber. "My father was the first Margrave in exile. For centuries, your father stood by his brother in exile. Until Phorcys died nearly a hundred years ago in battle."

"What combat?" stammered Aquan.

"In a fight at Rapture's End. Trying to rescue his mate, Evadne, and her infant daughter from death sentences. The Elder Council wanted to kill both of you. Your mother for violating their mating ban and her only child for being born an Emissary."

His charge hit her like a harpoon thrust through her heart. Clarissa had told her about debates over her mother's mating with an Archigen.

"No, no," whispered Aquan. Her mind raced with contradictory thoughts. "My father is buried in Memorial Grotto..."

"Buried alongside your mother?" he asked.

She paused for her mother's grave was but an empty marker. Evadne's frequent trips to his grave were likely symbolic efforts to memorialize her exiled mate.

"On his deathbed, Phorcys begged my father to make a pact with Archigen Elders to remain in exile in exchange for your continued protection. He hoped you would someday reset Eternal Concordia and release your people from banishment. My father agreed to his brother's dying wish. Upon his death sixty years ago, I took over Exori leadership during my third season."

Shuddering with disbelief, Aquan felt the lobby beginning to spin around her. No one ever told her any of this history. Not Clarissa, not Mopsus, not Aunt Sofronia. She couldn't conceive that Mopsus would train her for almost a century to hate and to war against her uncle and her cousin, kinsmen of a father she never knew, a father who suffered and died to spare her life.

"I was born in exile with my father. Neither he nor Phorcys ever rejected their Protosian roots. As my father lay dying, I made an oath to him to continue to fight for the House of Proteus, our true House."

Letting out a pained whistle, Aquan collapsed on to

a reception area couch, her thoughts bouncing between feral anger and wild confusion.

"Do not despair, cousin. Fight back with me." His voice reverberated with fierce rage. "Together we can destroy those who imprisoned your mother, who destroyed our fathers."

Aquan struggled to control her fury, to regain her composure. She knew to remain skeptical since the Margrave would weave any tale to help his cause.

"I'm sure these charges are all lies. You would say anything to capture these amulets and escape your exile, to reign supreme."

"Go to Mopsus. Ask him. He won't be able to deny it. Then join me to avenge our fathers, your Triton people."

Emerson groaned. Blood trickled out of his left ear, his shallow breaths ceased. Aquan checked and found no pulse. The Margrave's channel of communication was cut short.

Aquan dug out her magical mirror and ran her fingers over its engraved words. Staring into it, she recited, *"Amor vincit omnia."*

Her essence split, one version returning to *Calusa,* another vaulting to Rapture's End, each bearing a single amulet. She needed to hear the truth from Mopsus's own lips.

Chapter 37

Aquan heard familiar thwacks of Mopsus chopping thick stalks in remote kelp fields. It made her wonder if she had awoken from a frightening nightmare. Yet two amulets clasped around her neck reminded Aquan of her painful reality. She darted from stalk to stalk until she could almost reach out and pull on one of Mopsus's sea worms.

"Was it all lies?" she asked.

Mopsus didn't seem startled or stunned to see her.

"Hand me that pruning tool, will you?" he asked calmly. "These stalks need to be thinned out."

His calm demeanor only roiled her rage growing inside. "I'm not here to garden."

He grabbed his tool and removed dead branches from a stalk.

"You don't seem surprised about my visit, Mopsus."

"It was inevitable," he said. "A day I feared would come for nearly a century." Mopsus continued to prune his kelp.

"Stop, Mopsus." She yanked his tool from his hand and tossed it away. "Look at me."

He halted his trimming and looked somberly at her. Dark blue circles ringed his eyes, his skin a pale blue from exhaustion.

"I want answers. Honest ones this time."

"What do you want to know, Aquan?"

"Is my mother dead?"

"Dead to her people."

"You still play word games with me. Even now. Give me straight answers for once." She wanted to shake him, but something within her still restrained her worst impulses toward her mentor.

"Clarissa told you already about your mother. Evadne disobeyed our laws and threatened our security by mating with Phorcys. Her pregnancy delayed her sentence to stasis until she weaned you."

"And what about my father, Phorcys?"

"He was exiled with other Protosians beyond Obzula Ridge."

"Was his brother Bythos, the Margrave?"

Mopsus looked down and nodded his head "yes".

"Phorcys was a tremendous warrior, half-Archigen, half-Protosian, widely respected amongst both peoples. There have always been wars amongst our diverse Houses. At first he fought for Archigen values, but over time his brother preyed upon his vanity. Convinced him to mate against our laws to create an Emissary who would restore the House of Proteus back to power with another Great Flood. In his last military campaign, thousands of Archigen lives were lost and he was exiled. As a natural leader, he quickly became the Margrave's military commander of exiled Protosians, the Exoris."

"Did my father ever mount a direct attack on Rapture's End to spare my life, my mother's life?"

"Yes, he led a battle and died hoping to reclaim you."

His reply hit her like a sudden blow to the head and she staggered back from him.

"Did—did he do it because I was his daughter?" she stammered. "Or because I was an—an Emissary who might fulfill the Vanquishment?"

"I can't know for sure. After Phorcys died, Bythos didn't want to provoke his Archigen enemies to rise up and kill you while Eternal Concordia might still be reset. Ultimately, there was a pact between our warring factions. The Margrave would remain in exile as long as your life was spared until the next Sequencing."

"And what about you, Mopsus? For decades you taught me, cooked for me, joked with me, listened to me. You became my dearest mentor and friend." She took a deep breath as her voice quavered with anger and hurt. "Was that only because I was an Emissary?"

"That's how it started."

Aquan looked away from him as her head pounded and her wounded heart sank into the pit of her stomach.

"But that's not how it ended, Aquan. All the time I spent as your tutor and friend were some of the greatest moments of my many seasons. I couldn't help but love you as my own child, my own daughter."

He reached out to gently touch her arm, but she pushed his hand away.

"Would you send your own child on a risky mission without telling her what she needed to know to complete it, to protect herself? Like the meaning behind these gemstones? Or the identities of the Sentinels hiding them?"

"I can only confirm facts you already know, I can't tell you about anything that is to come. Our Sacred Songs reject any interference in this process, in the Sequencing. Your decisions must be independent ones."

"So you won't tell me about any Sentinels that remain alive?"

"I cannot identify them."

"Or any details of your prophecy about a future global war over water?"

"I cannot even confirm whether there is any prophecy."

"Or if those Exoris or my own people slaughtered the Tritons?"

"I wish I could, Aquan. But I cannot."

"Cannot or will not!" She exploded in rage, tearing apart kelp stalks Mopsus had gathered with her bare hands and teeth. "Even if following these sacrosanct rules put my life and the lives of others at risk?"

"Yes," he replied. "It would be wrong to influence any outcome of the Sequencing. Our holy texts demand that you make your own choices as a judgment on our people and their stewardship of Eternal Concordia."

Quaking, Aquan felt tears welling up in her eyes. She had never cried before, not after her sudden loss of her mother, not after the Triton massacre, not even for a father she never got to know. But to think her lifelong friend and mentor would so easily and so coldly wash his hands of her let loose a torrent of bitter tears.

"Once the Sequencing ends, I remain a liability for another hundred years. Plus I always create a risk of a birth of another Emissary." She sobbed, choking on her words. "When I have completed my mission, what will become of me?"

"I don't know," he replied.

"Does Raynord know that the price he pays for commanding his Timarchs? Bottling me up in eternal stasis or exiling me beyond Obzula Ridge. Or will he only have to kill me?"

"Raynord has stepped down as Commander."

Aquan knew her answer. The Elder Council planned to kill her either way.

"I will argue to my last breath to spare your life again if you preserve Eternal Concordia, saving our people from eternal darkness. But I hold little sway over our Elder Council anymore."

"So if I retain Eternal Concordia, I'm doomed and if I reset it, I'm equally doomed."

"I'm sorry, Aquan. If I could change your destiny, I would," whispered Mopsus.

Once more, he reached out to her, but she cringed and turned her back on him. She couldn't bear to hear him speak his shallow sympathies for another second. In a moment, she rocketed away to rejoin her other essence in Belize.

Chapter 38

As she gulped back salty tears, Kirra stopped watching her essence in Rapture's End through her mirror. She breathed her essence back in, experiencing the crushing weight of her despair. Shoving her mirror back into her jeans, Aquan looked out over a vast sea. Suddenly, she felt tiny and hopeless, wondering if she possessed enough strength to continue on. Cutter strolled down Harper's beach toward her, throwing sticks for Gypsy to catch along a sunset shore.

"Hey, where have you been hiding?" He plopped down beside her in a mound of sand.

She quickly wiped lingering streaks of tears from her dark cheeks.

"Did I miss something?"

Aquan got up and waded into the surf in her shorts and T-shirt. Cutter followed her.

"Are you okay?"

She buried her face in her hands, her shoulders shaking. "No," she whispered.

"What's going on?"

Aquan could barely form any words at first and then they tumbled out. "I feel like my whole world has been turned upside. For so long, I blindly followed these rules. Trying to do the right thing. Training endlessly as an Emissary. Waiting for my big chance to do something really worthwhile. Now that time has come. And it turns out everyone I trusted has turned against me. Everything that I once knew was a lie. No matter what I do, my life is over."

At first, Cutter said nothing, only sounds of slapping waves responded. He stepped closer and put his arm around her shoulders. She trembled at his warm touch, a stark contrast to Mopsus's icy detachment.

"I don't know what happened. Probably couldn't even guess. But I felt the same way a few years back. I had always been a good son. Did all the right things. Followed in my Dad's footsteps with a serious marine biology career. People told me

I was a golden boy, destined to be director of his Institute one day. But that's not what I really wanted. I woke up and decided to go my own way. Once I came back talking aquatelligence, everybody called me nuts, turned their backs on me. My own Dad disowned me. Booted me out of my job. Even Jenn didn't speak to me for a while. I pretty much thought my life was done, too."

"What did you do?" asked Aquan, blinking back tears.

"I decided, screw them. I'm gonna write my own rules. Live by my own standards. Follow my own path. Things got really rough for a while. I thought my life was over, but it was actually just beginning."

"Thanks," she said. "That helps a little."

"Besides, you're like a hundred years old," he said, smirking. "It's about time to make your own decisions, Granny. Blaze your own trail before you're hobbling around in a walker."

He splashed water on her and she couldn't help but laugh and battle him back. Soon they were whooshing water at each other harder and harder until Aquan was churning up a whirlpool that nearly sucked Cutter underwater.

"Truce, truce," he said.

She stopped splashing him and the surf settled back into its normal rolling pattern.

"Sorry about that. I got a little carried away, Cutter."

Under a pink sky, they swam and bodysurfed in foamy waves. At one point, they caught a cresting wave together and got tangled up as it pounded the shore. Catching their breath, they laughed and lounged on the sand. Cutter reached over and brushed a strand of seaweed from her cheek. He stroked her dark cheek several times. Aquan tingled with his touch. On impulse, she kissed his fingertips and he pulled her close to him. As his warm lips gently pressed against hers, Aquan trembled with this first kiss and hungered for more. Running her fingers through Cutter's blond hair, she placed her lips over his and softly kissed him. He ran his tongue over her lips and kissed her again, and then they rained a torrent of supple wet kisses upon each other. Crashing cadences of waves were punctuated with their puckered squeaks of their kisses.

"I want to be with you," he said.

"Come and truly be one with me."

She reached for her canvas bag and pulled out her last vial of green Olivine mixture. It was forbidden but she didn't care. It was time to make her own rules and Aquan wanted her first time to be as a Protosian. Taking Cutter's hand and they waded into the surf. He didn't question her as she broke open her vial and sprinkled it on him. She retained his pleasing appearance from the waist up except that gills sprouted behind his ears and his skin turned gray. He laughed as his legs gave way to the powerful steel gray tail of a male of the House of Proteus. As a diver, swimming and breathing beneath the surface came naturally to him. Cutter swam beside her as she transformed into her Triton body.

They plunged deep into the Caribbean Sea where they traded kisses, their tongues caressing each other's. She quivered as his right hand brushed across her breasts and firmly ran his hands across her slender rainbow tail. Every cell of her body prickled with desire. They shared the sheer joy of tenderly exploring each other's contours as sea creatures. Purple fan corals swayed as their bodies intertwined making love in undulating ocean currents.

*****

Aquan awoke with a start on Harper's beach and thought she heard someone whispering her name. Bathed in moonlight, she glanced over at Cutter who slept deeply in his human form by her side. Closing her eyes, she cuddled up to him. Quick bursts of visions interrupted Aquan's peaceful reverie. She saw a young Triton woman struggling against two Archigen males in an underwater wreck, murky water shrouding their faces. Her squeaks and whistles were silenced by one of the males pulling her hair back and covering her mouth. Scratching one Archigen's face, she drew blood. In anger, he struck her with a piece of sharp coral. Black blood hemorrhaged from one side of her head.

Dizzy with pain, this Triton wobbled and cried out for help, "Aquan, Aquan."

Awoken, Aquan looked around and didn't see anyone, and heard only whining ocean breezes and distant cawing of sea birds. She gently stroked Cutter's back, but a moment later her name softly floated in the air, and then again she heard her name being called more loudly. This voice became more piercing, more strident. This urgent chant came from the sea, not this beach, luring her into the bay. She took several darts and her amulets with her, placing them in her pouch.

Following these repeated utterances, Aquan in Triton form swam toward the Atlantic Ocean. As she approached the Mid-Atlantic Ridge, something glistened above a deep underwater volcano. Its currents pulled a rectangular ice tomb like those she saw at Queen Chione's castle. Aquan darted over and found it smashed open, its prisoner no longer in stasis. She sniffed this deserted chamber, searching her memories for her mother's scent. Did it smell of her mother's presence or did her wistful hopes cloud her beliefs? Those same visions appeared again. Yet this time, the besieged Triton female turned and looked at her. First, it was her mother's face tortured face.

"Mother," called out Aquan. "Mother."

Turning toward Aquan again, the female Triton's bloodied visage was now Aquan's own face. There was no reply and the image vaporized. She examined this empty stasis cube and found no further clues. She wondered if at long last her mother had been freed and might return to her House of Triton or seek refuge somewhere else.

"Help me, Mother. What should I do?" she called out. "What should I do?"

Rushing sounds of whirling eddies were her only reply. She swam back toward Little Moon Island, her questions remaining unanswered.

Chapter 39

Under an early morning sun, a glassy sea belied further troubles awaiting Aquan. When she arrived in Little Moon's cove, *Calusa* was gone. She hurried to Harper's shack and found him glued to his computer screen.

"Bloody hell, we looked all over for you. Thought you flew the coop."

"Where did Cutter go?"

"Heading back to Key West." He chomped on a cigar.

"That's crazy. He's still a fugitive."

"I told him that, but no stopping Cutter once he gets riled up."

"What happened?"

"Dr. Ortiz called by radio about two hours ago. Sounded real upset. She's in some kind of trouble," he said. "He bolted out of here. Been under power for over an hour."

"Did he say where in Key West?"

"Yeah, he's going to that Institute."

Right on time to be framed for Emerson's murder, thought Aquan. Before Harper could say another word, Aquan ran to the shore and dove in as a speedy Swordfish racing after *Calusa*. She caught up with Cutter's vessel outside of Lighthouse Reef in the Caribbean Sea, skipping off tops of waves at high speed. Gypsy hid under a galley table as his boat bounced wildly in ocean currents.

"Cutter," she called out. She raced toward his wheelhouse and he barely looked at her. "Are you insane? You're going to wreck *Calusa*."

"Jenn's in trouble, so I gotta get there fast."

"Take it easy," said Aquan. "You're gonna blow your engines."

Clinging to his lever, he continued to strain his vessel to its maximum speed.

"Stop, it, Cutter."

He tightened his grip as his boat roared ahead. Aquan tried to wrest his boat throttle from his hand, but she couldn't loosen his clenched fist. *Calusa* banged hard against an onslaught of waves and skimmed erratically across each ocean swell.

"Ease off, ease off," yelled Aquan. "You're gonna flip her. Kill us all."

Yet Aquan saw Cutter bearing down harder, intensifying his grip. She stopped shouting and then gently placed her hands over his fist.

"It's alright. Jenn's safe," she said, calmly in his ear. "She's safe, Cutter."

Exhaling deeply, Cutter relented as Aquan clasped her hands over his and methodically geared *Calusa* down to a reasonable speed. His catamaran boat rolled over each wave in low gear. For a few moments, they said nothing to each other.

"Are you sure she's okay?"

"Yes." She hoped the Margrave was right.

Sweat trickled down his forehead. "Jenn sounded so frightened. She'd been kidnapped. Something to do with those microbes."

"Papandreas and his crew. They killed Emerson over them."

"What?"

"I found Emerson dying in the Institute's foyer. He told me Papandreas took her." Aquan didn't speak of the Margrave's role, this explanation was sufficient for now. "They would love you to show up there and pin another murder on you."

"I don't see why anyone would get killed over her microbe research."

"It's hard to know for sure." Aquan didn't want to alarm him further. "*Athena* is a large vessel so she couldn't have gotten that far from Key West. Can you hail his ship on your radio? I have a proposition for Papandreas."

*****

Calusa looked like a gnat compared to *Athena* as Cutter pulled his vessel alongside it, not far from Cuba.

"Give me your, gun. They're bound to search you."

As Kirra, Aquan strapped his gun to her inner calf and secreted away several darts into her jeans pockets and socks.

Countess Daimonakis waited for them on deck along with two of Papandreas's security officers.

"This is a different look for you," she said to Aquan. "What is he doing here?" The Countess pointed her long thin finger with its sharp red fingernail at Cutter.

"My bodyguard," she replied.

"Check him," ordered the Countess.

A security guard patted down Cutter and found nothing. One of them tried to search Aquan but she turned into an albino python and they jumped back.

"Not her. It's pointless."

Countess Daimonakis escorted them to Papandreas's luxury cabin where Aquan had viewed his restored bridle.

"Take a seat. He'll be with you in a moment."

Neither of them sat down.

"Have it your own way," she said with a frown before exiting.

Aquan couldn't hear a soft hiss of his oxygen tank.

"Keep your eyes peeled." She looked around and handed Cutter his gun. "Papandreas can turn into a python, too." She yanked two darts out of her pockets.

Seconds later, a center flat screen TV flickered on and Papandreas's face filled its monitor, plastic tubes of oxygen inserted in his nose. His skin appeared more pallid, his cheeks more hollow since their last meeting.

"Security must be slipping in my absence," he said, his voice barely audible. "Thank you both for coming."

"Not like we had any choice," replied Cutter.

"Dr. Cutter, I should also thank you for being so instrumental in locating an amulet from our western Sentinel."

"Save it. Where's Dr. Ortiz?"

"Not to worry about Dr. Ortiz. She's fine."

"I won't exchange an amulet for her without proof that she is unharmed. And *Calusa* and her crew must also get safe passage out of here," said Aquan.

He inhaled deeply, wheezing loudly.

"All I need is your word that you will release an amulet to us. Then she will be returned to *Calusa*. Your ship may leave without incident."

She still possessed two gemstones, enough to stop another Great Deluge. Since he could see her, she didn't want Papandreas to think it was an easy decision to forego her claim to this talisman. Aquan hesitated for a moment, furrowing her brow.

"You will receive one amulet provided my conditions are met, too." Aquan removed an amber gemstone from her pocket and held it up. "Is the Countess your mail carrier?"

Papandreas smiled, his lips quivering. "Thank you, Aquan. But you need to make a special delivery. We must speak privately about it." He coughed and coughed.

Two attendants suddenly appeared at his cabin doorway to escort Cutter out. He hesitated.

"I don't like this."

"It's okay. Go to your boat, Cutter. Make sure she's there. I'll be right behind you."

Once Cutter left, Aquan sat down on Papandreas's couch.

"You have shown great loyalty to your friends. I admire that."

"Does Dr. Ortiz know about us?"

"There was no need to disclose that fact to her." He brusquely shooed away a nurse trying to untangle his oxygen lines.

"Aren't you worried she'll go to authorities?"

"I doubt our good doctor wants to spend the rest of her life looking over her shoulder. Especially since I have so many friends in high places."

"Why did you have her kidnapped and Emerson killed over those L11 microbes?"

"Emerson was disposable once Dr. Ortiz showed up in Key West. She possesses much greater knowledge about these microbes and how they might be manipulated." His breathing became more labored. "It isn't often that a new bioweapon is discovered. There are many political factions that would pay a great deal of money for it."

"You mean terrorists."

"One man's terrorist is another's freedom fighter. You

should know that by now."

"I can't believe this exchange is all about money."

"Money is not important; power and influence are."

"It seems like a waste of time considering your plans to wipe out the human race in the next thirty-six hours."

He laughed hoarsely. "I am confident that you will free your Protosian people, Aquan. To stay alive as long as I have, it's necessary to always have a back-up plan. In case you let us down."

"I plan on it," she replied.

"The hubris of youth." He shook his head and then his tremulous hand adjusted his breathing tubes. "Your decision was enough to spare your friends for a little while. But to finish this deal you must agree in person to deliver this gemstone to the Margrave, face-to-face."

"Why?"

"Because he wishes to meet you in person for this exchange to be fully honored."

"And if I don't?"

"Then I can't promise Ortiz and Cutter will remain alive for very long."

He coughed and took a series of shallow breaths. Aquan knew there had to be more to this demand, but she didn't have much choice at this point.

"How will I be able to find him?"

"Go beyond Obzula Ridge and descend down to the sea floor, then swim with southerly currents and his escorts will be waiting for you. He'll have another important proposal for you to consider."

"What is it?"

"I wouldn't want to ruin his surprise." He let loose a hacking string of coughs and Aquan saw blood on his lips. "Go now and keep your mind open to what the Margrave has to offer. It will be of great value to you."

"I have to make sure that my friends are both secure before I'll travel anywhere."

"Do so if you must. But know that the final phase of a full moon begins tonight. If you don't arrive before the moon rises to its apex tomorrow night, then this deal is off. And your friends are as good as dead."

His screen flickered off and went black.

*****

Aquan returned to *Calusa* and found Dr. Ortiz sitting at a galley table looking tired, but relieved. Gypsy sat at her feet, softly whimpering.

"Thank you for helping me. I don't understand what's happening," she said.

Cutter handed Jenn a cup of tea and her hand shook as she took a sip.

"He wanted those L11 microbes for a bioweapons for a black market deal," said Aquan.

"But they're not dangerous to humans."

"Dr. Ortiz, I need you to explain to me in the most straightforward way possible about your L11 microbes."

"It's complicated. But I'll try."

"I still have slides from your conference presentation," said Cutter. "Hang on a minute."

He disappeared into his quarters and came back with a paper copy of Jenn's slides from Papandreas's maritime conference. Jenn walked them through her theory about L11 microbes causing mass strandings and pointed to key slides in her presentation.

"There are millions of microbes in our oceans at any one time. Through taking water samples at these beachings, I found a few constant strains of microbes in water currents when there were unusually large numbers of animals in a single stranding event. Most were harmless, but L11 microbes seemed to be a type of toxin."

"How does it work?" asked Aquan.

"Whales, dolphins and squids are expert navigators. If microbes become concentrated in certain waters, perhaps through currents, they contaminate these creature's natural navigation systems, causing them to lose their sense of direction." She motioned to a slide detailing their sonar systems. "L11 may likely cause brain lesions or other disruptions that infect their radar. Their malfunctioning sonar abilities might trigger beachings since they can't distinguish between ocean and land. They end up careening on to shore and dying. It could infect them all or merely a pilot or leader of these social groups." She sipped her tea.

"Is there any way it could be used against humans?"

"No, they have no impact on humans."

"Jenn, what did they want from you on *Athena*?" asked Cutter.

"They didn't ask me much. Mostly inventorying my water samples and skimming through my laptop files on my L11 research. They've still got them. Asked about how long these microbes could live and if I knew how to multiply them."

"What did you tell them?"

"I have a few ideas about how to multiply them or how long they last, but no solid proof. So far, they seem to be able to remain alive as long as they remain in sea water. They can divide themselves into multiple microbes organically in sea water where there are high concentrations of sodium and potassium. They made me test a few samples with active L11 microbes in crates I shipped home."

"Is there any antidote to them? Something that can kill the microbes."

"I'm not certain. But I did some initial observations with water samples taken from seaweed patches near strandings. Seaweed naturally tends to draw out sodium and potassium from nearby sea water. It seems to weaken or absorb toxins in L11 microbes."

"Okay, that helps," replied Aquan. "How many samples did you send to the Institute?"

"Over two thousand vials of microbes. I still have a few dozen samples here."

She pointed to her specimen safe next to her lab bench.

"I think they're gone."

"No, I checked them myself back in Tenerife. After Tuttleberry's murder."

Jenn got up and opened up her locked container. She pulled out several samples and showed their unbroken seals. Cracking one tube open, she put several drops on a slide and looked at it under her digital microscope, appearing in detail on an attached computer monitor. She tossed this slide and split open another vial and displayed it, and then a third. Jenn pounded her fist on her work bench.

"They're gone. These are all plain sea water. How did you know?"

Aquan handed her Tuttleberry's cell phone.

"It's right on Tuttleberry's video. The night he got murdered on *Calusa*. He caught Emerson stealing them, replacing them with sealed vials of normal saltwater. Tuttleberry paid for it with his life."

She played his video.

"It will clear Cutter of Tuttleberry's murder," said Jenn.

"Great, let's head back to Key West and get matters resolved," said Cutter.

"Actually, I think it might be a good idea for you to go back to Little Moon Island. At least for the next couple of days."

Aquan knew the Sequencing was beginning tonight, fulfilling itself at the apex of a full moon and high tide tomorrow night.

"Why?" asked Cutter.

"Papandreas won't know where you are and that's a good idea. Just get there and stay onshore. Don't get back on *Calusa* until I return." Aquan thought of her visions of *Calusa* in her amulet. "I've got to go."

Cutter took hold of her shoulders. "Where are you going?"

"Someplace where you can't go with me."

"You can always change me..." He stopped, looking over his shoulder at Jenn. "Using that stuff," he whispered.

"I don't have any more of it and it won't work for such a long journey." She looked him squarely in his eyes. "Please do what I say. Anchor your ship and get off it as fast as you can. Don't get back on it, no matter what."

They gave each other one long last kiss before Aquan raced up to his main deck, diving into an open ocean. She had no time to waste as the hour drew near for her to finally confront the Margrave.

Chapter 40

In raging Pacific Ocean currents, Obzula Ridge stretched north of Rapture's End. Aquan carried biolumens light sticks to mark her trail as she swam in utter darkness beyond this trench. Her pouch hid lethal and paralyzing darts and Mopsus's *Santa Maria* mirror. From a distance, Aquan easily spotted jagged crests of a towering range of cooled magma mountains stretching for miles like a meandering backbone along the ocean floor. This trench's sheer cliffs plummeted into cavernous ocean valleys capable of swallowing any surface mountain peaks. At its mouth, Aquan snapped a biolumens stick in two and she dropped it into a deep, black gash. Following its streaks of blue-green light, she descended about seven miles down into frigid waters in this gaping crevice. Constellations of blue, white and red lights of bioluminescent fish twinkled in this bleak void. Odd screeches and sporadic grunts echoed in this canyon of eternal night.

Aquan avoided an elegant tangle of ghostly hydromedusa jellyfish, their long, wispy tentacles pulsating under their transparent domes. Several dozen ugly angler fish, their bioluminescent lures hanging in front of their open, spiky-toothed jaws, patrolled for unsuspecting shrimps and sea worms. Transparent comb jellyfish with rippling rainbow lights, like colorful chaser lights on a Las Vegas marquee, floated past her.

Swimming deeper, rows of underwater volcanoes spewed fat mud balls from grinding serpentine tectonic plates, burping thumps and splats of slimy ooze. Once she smelled sulfur, Aquan knew his exile lay nearby. Bubbling sulfur cauldrons spit up superheated water from Earth's molten core into colder sea water. Aquan clasped her hands over her ears to dampen incessant roars of sulfide gases and scalding waters disgorging thick, black steam clouds through porous smokestacks. Aquan choked on noxious fumes and felt her skin blistering from scalding discharges of hypothermal vents. Thousands of ruby-tipped Giant Tube Worms danced around these black smoke plumes, sucking in sulfide bacteria for nourishment. She tried to change into one of them, but discovered she could not transform. Trying to shape-shift into a mottled brown and white flatfish which thrived alongside these smoldering vents, Aquan once more was unable to turn into another creature. Perhaps geomagnetic anomalies near the Earth's crust were blocking her transformative powers. The Margrave's exile might have been chosen, in part, to limit his shape-shifting abilities. Without touching any churning muck of the sea floor, she moved with southern currents to the outskirts of Obzula Ridge.

About one mile farther south, a Sea Monk stood with six Hydromorphs near a sooty rock chimney, beckoning her with his claw to follow him. He led her past several roiling vents and toward a jagged wall of cooled magma with a three-story boulder sealing a soaring entryway. Hundreds of Hydromorphs hung like lifeless puppets in sea water surrounding its entrance. Six guards groaned as they struggled to yank two thick ropes of twisted seaweed on each side of an enormous boulder, rolling it away from a narrow entryway.

Several Hydromorphs remained behind as the Sea Monk escorted her through a long, dark channel and then into a dimly lit chamber. It glowed red as bioluminescent worms crawled along its pock-marked molten rock walls. Black smoke contrails swirled in and out and a stench of sulfur clung to this compartment's walls. This room shook with a series of short rumbles from grinding plates at the Earth's crust. Loose gravel rained down on Aquan. Brushing off this soot, she sensed movement behind her. Spinning around, she squinted at a figure lurking in a rock cavity.

"Forgive my humble surroundings, cousin. I have so few visitors."

He remained in the shadows. His quiet, raspy voice sounded so different from his earlier booming communications with Aquan.

"This isn't a social call."

"It is for me. We could communicate through our thoughts, but I seldom have an opportunity to undertake a real conversation with anyone."

"You have your Sea Monks and Hydromorphs to speak with anytime you want."

"They merely reflect my own thoughts. I've been talking to myself for decades. Not knowing what your replies would be, I've so enjoyed our verbal sparring, Aquan."

"I've come only to exchange the amulet for my friends' safety."

She pulled an amulet out of her pouch and held it out in his direction. His Sea Monk snatched it with his lobster claw and quickly exited. In silence, Aquan could hear air fluttering unevenly through the Margrave's gills.

"I'm pleased to have this gemstone. Strangely, I don't sense any fear or fury that I expected with this handover."

Aquan felt fortunate that he could not read her thoughts.

"The moon is not yet full and there is still another talisman yet to be found. So nothing is finally decided in our match."

"I hope our talk will soon finalize this matter."

The room quavered with vibrations from minor aftershocks.

"Show yourself to me, Skeiron. I won't talk through a shroud."

"It is best that I remain hidden."

"Why?"

He paused and Aquan sensed his unease. She noticed him momentarily shrink back into his dark nook.

"If you see me, I should be able to see you."

"I cannot see you, cousin. Only dark and light, certain colors, but nothing else. My mother, Aello, was exiled when she first learned of her pregnancy. She spent her gestation period here and gave birth to me in this hostile environment. It resulted in nearly total blindness and other anomalies that you may find unpleasant."

"I've seen thousands of Surface Dwellers killed in a tsunami, my Triton kinsmen butchered. Murdering innocents is far more disgusting than any physical limitation or distortion."

"True enough," he said. But I needed you to understand the power of these amulets at Candelaria. Perhaps my method was

269

too heavy-handed for you."

Skeiron slowly emerged from his hiding place. Aquan squelched a gasp as he moved under crimson lights. His lifeless white eyes stared blankly from a misshapen skull with odd tuffs of black hair dotting his head. Sallow skin clung to a skeletal chest, his right arm shriveled without a hand into its socket and his gray-blue tail missing half of its fluke. For a moment, Aquan felt a twinge of compassion for him, deformed physically from birth in this hellish darkness, warped emotionally from life in a cloistered exile.

"I'm sorry for your suffering," said Aquan.

"Don't pity me. My physical limits pushed me to expand my other senses, my mental powers. I have a tremendous sense of smell and hearing, too."

"Can you transform?"

"Sadly, I'm not an Emissary. So Father taught me how to use my intellectual abilities to project my thoughts and manipulate lesser life forms. I can project my will through Hydromorphs and my Sea Monks can regenerate three times. I excelled beyond Father's wildest expectations, his own capabilities. You possess this power, too. I can teach you how to access this ability."

"I can't stay to learn more. I must continue my search for that final amulet. While you delay me here, your allies are certainly scouring our southern hemisphere for its final prize."

"They located it already."

"Then why am I here? Shouldn't you be preparing for a global chariot ride?"

"The Sentinel who possesses it won't release her amulet to anyone but you."

Aquan smiled thinking of Kadru's fierce defense of her gemstone.

"Then our game of hide and seek is done. At least for another hundred years."

"We don't have a hundred years. Only seventy-three years."

"That's your claim. For me, our game is over now."

"Not yet. You will change your mind."

"I doubt it." Aquan turned to leave his chamber.

"You will if it spares your mother's life."

She stopped and thought of that empty stasis chamber.

"You can rescue her if you hand over your last amulet to me."

"I won't betray Kadru or renounce her sacrifice to protect it for a century."

"You imperil a remaining Sentinel if you don't give it to me. Your mother is the Sentinel who bears a final amulet for our southern hemisphere."

"My mother?" exclaimed Aquan. "Impossible. Our Elder Council wouldn't ever let her participate in the Scattering once she violated their mating ban."

"Evadne was chosen before she knew of her pregnancy. Once given an amulet, the Elders can't take it away from her, only an Emissary. Her unborn daughter possessed that authority. Keeping her away from you prevented Evadne from persuading you to give your amulet to your father or his brother."

"You can't know any of this information since you've been in exile since your birth."

"Yes, but I have an ability to communicate with my fellow Archigens using my mind. Certain members of your Elder Council have been communicating with Father and me for years."

"Queen Chione told me that Elder Camulus moved my mother from a Borean prison. He always beat the drum loudest for your destruction."

"The best ally is the one no one suspects."

"I don't believe it."

"It is true. Camulus despises ponderous deliberations and shared power in Quartz Hall. He longs for full authority over his people in the House of Hadros."

"I can't believe any of this story until I speak directly with my mother."

"She recovers from decades in her debilitating imprisonment in stasis. I will take you to see her now."

The Margrave motioned for her to follow him through a

series of concealed arches burrowed into volcanic rock. Aquan picked up a female Triton's scent and searched her memory for her mother's distinctive fragrance.

Skeiron pointed to a small entryway. "Go to her."

Aquan hesitated wondering if she was walking right into a trap. She carefully examined its entrance for signs of hidden gates or metal pens, but found none.

"After you," she replied.

Skeiron entered and she trailed him. Inside, a Triton female gripped a slab of smoothed lava, her back to them. Her sandy hair cloaked her narrow shoulders and cascaded down her glacier blue torso. Her rainbow tail twitched as she moaned in pain. This compartment shook as tectonic plates, in constant motion, chafed against each other. Aquan approached her and tenderly placed her hand on her shoulder.

"Daughter."

She turned to reveal Evadne's ashen face. Her turquoise eyes glazed over in a trance-like state.

"Mother," cried Aquan. She threw her arms around her mother's limp body and listened to her slow beating heart. "Are you alright?"

"Daughter," she repeated, offering a wan smile.

"She is exhausted and still fighting narcotic effects from her long captivity in stasis fluids," said Skeiron.

As Aquan embraced her mother, Evadne's trembling hand reached into her pouch and removed a final amulet. She pushed it into Aquan's hand before falling back into a dazed state. The Cartographer had been right all along, Aquan realized. She gently rocked her mother.

"The choice is yours, Aquan," he said.

"You turn my mother into bait. How can you be trusted to honor your word to free her?"

"I don't wish to harm you or Evadne. But it seemed the only way to convince you to give me your final amulet. Not just for me, but for you and Evadne's future. Cousin, we're meant to be great rulers of this planet, reborn as a sea water orb. You owe nothing to that Elder Council. They lied to you and manipulated you, and will discard you when your mission is complete."

Aquan's face burned scarlet knowing he was right.

"I envision a world where we are no longer subjected to their cruel punishments, their callous deceptions. Where we are free of destructive whims of ignorant Surface Dwellers. Together none can overcome us. Our dominion will be supreme."

Aquan remained reluctant to give him this final amulet, to offer him even a symbolic victory. But as with Surface Dwellers, deception came with her territory.

"Brother, I don't wish for power, only a chance to be free. My final amulet is yours if you promise us our freedom in this world."

Skeiron smiled. "You have my word as your Cousin and as King of the Houses of Proteus and Archigen."

Aquan pressed her mother's southern hemisphere amulet into Skeiron's left hand. Broad smile crossed his face.

"Thank you, Aquan. You will not regret this decision."

"Skeiron, I must leave and take my mother to mineral springs of Grannus to revive and heal her."

"Go, Aquan. No Exoris will stand in your way. I need to prepare my bridles and Hippocampi for tonight's journey." He held up a vial of olivine mixture in his hand. "Mopsus is not the only one to create transforming sands. With a full moon and king tides, I should be able to transform for many hours once I leave this dead zone. Our House's dream of another Vanquishment will be fulfilled at last."

Cradling her mother in her arms, Aquan rushed out of the dreary chamber.

"You and your mother will always have a place in my royal court," he called out.

*****

Instead of heading north to Grannus, she headed southeast to more remote mineral baths at Cortonis. Aquan knew these caretakers would watch over Evadne's recovery during the Sequencing. She assessed what items remained; two paralyzing darts, four lethal ones, her diver's watch with one minute and three seconds remaining, and Mopsus's *Santa Maria* mirror. It wasn't much but it would have to do. She split her darts up and decided to send her diver's watch along with her eastern essence, keeping her mirror in the hands of her southern twin.

Looking into this mirror one last time, she spoke its incantation, "*Amor vincit omnia.*"

Aquan split herself with one essence remaining in the eastern hemisphere and her primary essence journeying to the southern hemisphere, awaiting an inevitable battle.

Chapter 41

Aquan sang her special trill, her call to Thalassa to play hooky when they were children. It didn't take long for her friend to appear at a rear entrance to their favorite shortcut.

"I've been so worried about you."

Thalassa hugged her several times.

"I'm surprised you had a moment to think of me during those mating rituals."

Aquan smiled thinking of her own lovemaking with Cutter.

"There were lots of gorgeous males. But none of them really pleased me. Their silly flirtations were so pointless. I couldn't keep my mind on it. Especially when I found out my best friend was in trouble."

"How did you know?" asked Aquan.

"Raynord, told me. He stepped down as commander, blaming his injuries. But I know he had a falling out with our Elder Council. Polemus's son, Mestor, has taken charge. Nobody likes him at all."

"I need you to give this message to Raynord."

She handed a small rolled up scroll to Thalassa.

"Why can't you tell him in person?"

Her friend tugged her towards their shortcut entry.

"Because I must return to Obzula Ridge before the moon rises tonight."

"No, Aquan. You shouldn't have gone there at all. It's too dangerous."

"I don't have a choice. Neither do you. Now go, my friend."

They embraced each other and Aquan started her journey. She hated to cloak herself as Camulus, but it meant she had no difficulties leaving Rapture's End's fortified borders.

As a full moon approached, Aquan returned to Mariana Trench to await Skeiron's departure. Shore Temple's eastern amulet would create a series of tsunami waves sufficient to submerge Asia and Australia. She surmised that Skeiron would begin in the eastern hemisphere when a full moon reached its apex first. It would improve his chances of completing his global chariot route before the Sequencing concluded in the western hemisphere.

Aquan heard muted squeaks and grunts of Hydromorphs and distant shrieks and squawks of Pterons echoing in this abyss. Their cacophony grew louder as they ascended from its depths. Hundreds of Pterons and Hydromorphs swirled in a frenzied saltwater funnel. As each creature reached the top it shot south, heading for Rapture's End. When this spout became depleted of creatures, the trench became still once more.

Looking into this gaping ravine, she watched bioluminescent fish streak away from an enormous black dust cloud pushing toward the surface. Sea quake tremors rocked volcanic mountains as water currents churned violently. Aquan backed away from this ridge as black gas clouds exploded out of it. Deafening sounds of clattering hooves and piercing horse whinnies resounded within this chasm. In an instant, four white Hippocampi yoked together leapt out. Each wore a golden bridle on their crown, with an amulet in each center brow band. Their ivory manes flowed and their serpent's tails were adorned with green and blue biolumens. A handsome Protosian male, likely Skeiron transformed with his olivine blend, flew out piloting a golden chariot and grappling with thickly-woven jellyfish tendrils, serving as reins. He wrapped them around his left clenched fist and forearm. A half-dozen Hydromorphs trailed him. Aquan transformed into a Hydromorph blending in with his pack.

Skeiron journeyed west toward Australia and Asia as sea floors rumbled under his chariot's path. Aquan chased him as he prepared to soar skyward to direct tsunamis to overwhelm these continents. She heaved forward as a tiger shark and sunk her serrated teeth into his tail. He shrieked and lost his grip on his reins. Galloping Hippocampi tore away from his chariot's control. Skeiron willed one of his Hydromorph's into a hundred foot long Blue Whale. Swatting Aquan with its enormous tail, she spun around like a pinwheel into an oncoming pack of Hydromorphs. His whale liquefied and Skeiron turned another Hydromorph into a white and gray bull shark.

His shark bared its teeth ready to attack a momentarily

Aquan. As it whirred toward her, she zigzagged away from this aggressive hunter. It pursued her, nipping at her tail. It lunged for her dorsal fin and clipped off part of its tip. Aquan suddenly changed into an Orca whale, letting loose a series of high-pitched whines. Skeiron's bull shark tried to evade its fierce predator, but she clamped her jaw around its body, ripping it in two. It collapsed into sea water. As another Hydromorph shuddered about to shape-shift, Aquan pitched a lethal dart at its throat and it also was instantly liquefied.

Aquan spied Skeiron regaining control over his underwater steeds. He regrouped his team and renewed their rush across the sea. Aquan whisked past them and then turned into their path as a Ladon, a hundred-headed sea serpent with dozens of rows of sharp black arrowhead teeth in each set of jaws. Skeiron's Hippocampi reared upon seeing a huge serpent. One of his sea horse's pointed tail accidentally slashed Skeiron's chest and he cried out in pain. He angrily transformed another Hydromorph into a Ladon as well.

Each Ladon snapped fiercely at each other. Aquan heard Skeiron's creature gnashing a set of its serrated teeth as it whizzed near her serpent heads. As these two Ladons battled each other, Skeiron's horses rumbled across the sea creating a series of increasingly strong sea quakes. Aquan kept dodging away from the other Ladon's striking serpent heads. Reverting to her Triton form, she then pressed her diver's watch and Skeiron's Ladon froze still in the sea. She grabbed a lethal dart from inside her pouch. As ocean currents pulled her toward it, she wriggled along its body and plunged a deadly barb directly into its heart. Her watch clicked to zero and Skeiron's Ladon twitched and kicked before falling dead underwater.

She realized that Skeiron had once more breached the water's surface. In collaboration with a king tide and a full moon, Skeiron and his team conjured up a gargantuan tsunami to flood the eastern hemisphere. Unfortunately, Aquan must let Skeiron escape for now and continue on his journey while she battled the destruction he had unleashed.

Aquan pierced ocean waves and could hear hundreds of screaming sirens signaling tsunami alerts across Asia and

Australia. She turned into Airavana, an enormous winged white elephant of Hindu mythology, a creature capable of draining water from Earth and drenching land with rain. Flying high above the ocean, she observed a bulging series of tsunami waves. Sticking her trunk into the sea, she sucked in these tidal waves. Her body grew more bloated as she vacuumed up ocean swells. Extending her trunk, she then released collected sea water tropical rainstorms over both continents. Aquan repeatedly siphoned off water from these tsunami waves, converting them into salty showers. Once sirens ceased blaring, Aquan continued to drain Pacific waves until the ocean settled down into its normal rhythm. By then, Aquan collapsed exhausted. It was now up to her primary essence to prevent destruction in the southern hemisphere. Falling into a trance-like state, she hoped Raynord heeded her warning.

Chapter 42

Harper sat with Cutter and Jenn beachside under a nearly full moon, a small campfire at their feet. Despite a clear, starry sky, he knew weather conditions were changing for the worse.

"Do you hear that, mate?" he asked.

"I don't hear anything," replied Cutter. He blew a smoke ring from one of Harper's Cuban cigars.

Jenn poked at their campfire with a stick. "It's beautiful. So quiet here."

"Too quiet," said Harper.

Harper's beloved sea birds had fallen completely silent. He jumped up and hurried to his shack. Turning on his crackling marine weather radio, he heard a monotone hum of an emergency broadcast alarm followed by a robotic taped message.

"Emergency weather warning from Belize National Meteorological Services. Category five hurricane alert. ETA three hours. Sustained winds of 133-155 miles per hour forecast. Seas thirteen to twenty feet above king tide levels. Mainland citizens in low lying areas cautioned to seek higher ground or refuge in emergency shelters. Residents of barrier islands urged to evacuate immediately to mainland. Emergency weather warning from Belize National Meteorological Services. Category five hurricane alert. ETA three hours...."

This announcement continued to repeat. Harper ran out to his porch and called out to Cutter and Jenn, waving his arms over his head. Crashing surf swallowed up his words. Heading back into his shack, Harper rummaged through his bureau for an air horn from his Manchester United fan days. He blasted his horn several times and continued to signal wildly to them.

"Something's going on. We oughtta get up there, Jenn."

They jogged along Harper's beach with Gypsy in tow.

"What's happening?" asked Jenn.

"We gotta pack up and head for the mainland. A Cat five is coming and this bloke's rolling up on us fast." He snapped down his laptop and quickly collected his papers from his desk.

"Cutter, your boat ought to be our fastest and safest refuge in case things get squirrely out there."

Cutter remembered Aquan's admonition to stay off his boat.

"I'm not sure that's a good idea. Maybe we should just hunker down here."

"A Cat five is no tea party. Expecting a storm surge twenty feet higher than a king tide. This whole island will be under water in no time," said Harper. He tossed a stack of notebooks and computer CDs into an old sailor's trunk.

"She told me not to get on *Calusa*," said Cutter.

"Who?"

"Acqua...I mean, Kirra warned me to stay off my boat, no matter what."

"You mean that crazy bird who bailed on you. Hardly a reliable weather source."

"Normally she's not wrong about these things."

"Hey muffin head, this is Belize, not Australia." Harper playfully smacked Cutter's cheek a couple of times. "Wake up, Lover Boy."

"Can I help?" asked Jenn.

"Sure, grab any water bottles and canned food you can find in those cabinets. Candles, flashlights and batteries, too, in case my power goes out."

Cutter remained torn as he helped them gather essential items from Harper's shack. Climbing the satellite pole, Cutter removed its dish while Jenn helped Harper shut down his wind turbines and generator. All three gathered lobster pots and lounge chairs and put them in an outbuilding. Harper picked up a hammer and tossed a second one to Cutter as they nailed down his wooden shutters.

"It's probably a fool's errand, but it might keep a few things from blowing away," said Harper.

In a short time, evening winds picked up dramatically, blowing strong and hot. Blades on Harper's wind turbines and assorted whirligigs spun faster and faster. His collection of wind chimes clanged loudly on his porch.

"Might as well take these with us." Harper grabbed his

fishing poles. "We may need to catch our dinner until things settle down."

They loaded a cart with fat buggy wheels and pushed it down a sandy hill to the beach. It started to drizzle. Wading into an angry green surf, Cutter released his tender's anchor and pulled it close to shore. Suddenly, sheets of rain soaked them as they piled Harper's sea trunk and emergency items into it. Buckets of water sloshed inside Cutter's dinghy as it rode a roller coaster of choppy waves. Gypsy howled as Harper looked back somberly at Little Moon Island.

"Hope it's still here tomorrow morning," he muttered.

"Don't worry. It's been here for centuries." Jenn smiled and patted his hand as rain streaked down her face.

Calusa bounced up and down violently as Cutter hitched his tender to its rear diving platform. Jumping out, he fought to keep his balance as Harper and Jenn passed up boxes to him. They groaned shoving Harper's sea trunk aboard while Cutter yanked on its side handle to get it on to his ship's upper deck. Jenn lashed down Cutter's tender while Harper and Cutter lugged items below. Rain pelted his vessel as Cutter fired up its engines. He punched in GPS coordinates for Belize's mainland.

"Visibility really sucks, but tonight's full moon should reflect off any channel markers. Gotta watch out for rocks at its mouth," said Cutter. "We should be in port about an hour or so."

"Where are we going to anchor?" asked Jenn.

"Harper, you know locals. See if you can hail them and try to find us a slip. I'd hate to leave her on a mooring ball if it's gonna be a Cat five."

While Harper radioed area marinas, Jenn and Cutter looked out the pilothouse windows over roiling white caps glistening in moonlight. Incoming waves were rapidly getting higher.

"Hang on folks, it's gonna get really bumpy out here," said Cutter.

Calusa shook as its hulls banged over increasingly menacing waves. Harper braced himself and grabbed a hand hold while he called various harbor masters. After a couple of big jolts, Harper got knocked to the floor and Cutter and Jenna almost fell out of their pilot chairs. Only Gypsy with her webbed feet kept roaming around Cutter's pilot house with ease.

"You alright, Harper?"

"Kiss my arse," he said.

"Not on the right cheek, not on the left cheek, but right in the groove," Cutter and Harper sang out in unison. This time their laughter had a tense edge to it. *Calusa* creaked and moaned as it struggled against roaring waves.

"What the hell?" said Cutter.

"What's wrong?" asked Jenn.

"Either my radar is screwed up or something enormous is coming right at us."

"I don't see a single thing out there," said Jenn.

"Take the wheel for a minute. I gotta check out my radar."

Cutter threw on a green slicker and headed topside. He clutched lifelines attached to railings along his boat. Looking at his radar arch, it didn't appear to be dented or damaged. A white radar bar on his open-array antenna continued to spin, scanning all directions for objects. Cutter stared toward a moonlit horizon as rain cascaded over him. He squeezed his eyes shut to clear his view.

"Oh my God," he said.

In the distance, he spotted a mammoth black and red creature with colossal bat wings filling the night sky. Each flap of its wings blew a stronger gust of wind across his vessel and Cutter struggled to cling to a soggy lifeline. Its eyes glowed like fiery yellow orbs and its pointy ears jutted out of a thick mane of jet black hair. Its muscled arms gave way to hundreds of wriggling snake heads instead of hands. Rather than legs, two gigantic spotted serpents split from its thighs, their tongues slithering in and out. As its massive chest heaved in and out, its lips spewed out flames, thick black smoke poured out of its nostrils. Throwing its head back, it let loose a deafening string of guttural shrieks and growls before spitting out missiles of hot coals.

The fearsome creature straightened its body and stretched

out its wings covering both moon and stars. Like a velvet curtain dropping over a sunlit window, the evening sky instantly went pitch black. Cutter could no longer distinguish between sea and sky, shore from surf. A moment later, he spied a white streak bursting out of the sea which suddenly froze mid-sky. Squinting his eyes, he made out a team of enormous white sea horses with serpent's tails flickering with green and blue light pulling a glittering golden chariot. Panicked neighing followed as this entire group fell back into the ocean, creating an immense splash.

Cutter rushed below deck where he found Jenn tapping on a radar screen as she tried to maintain control over his catamaran.

"Your radar screen is totally messed up. It's one big splotch. Can't tell where we are. Any luck with that radar arch, Cutter?"

"Grab something we're gonna get hit by a huge wave."

Within a few seconds a gargantuan wake from the fallen horses struck *Calusa* pushing it up toward a cluster of rocks. A high-pitched squeal followed as one of *Calusa's* aluminum hulls scraped against sharp-edged rocks. A second wave smacked his ship hard again and a front section of hull became wedged in a rocky fissure. Cutter took the wheel and tried to reverse *Calusa* out of this crevice.

"Come on, baby, you can do it."

Cutter revved his ship's engines. As twisting metal of a portside hull screeched, *Calusa* wouldn't budge.

"Lousy timing, muffin head," said Harper. "Do you want to put out an SOS on your radio or should I do it?"

Cutter thought for a moment about the entire Belizean Coast Guard coming upon this scene. They might put Aquan in danger. If she was willing to jeopardize her life for them, he needed to put their lives on the line for her. Holding pat for now made sense to Cutter.

"No may days," said Cutter. He took a radio microphone out of Harper's hand. "She might break free as these swells increase."

"You're nutty, mate. These waves are going to tear her

and us with her."

Harper tried to take grab a radio receiver out of Cutter's hand, but he wouldn't let go.

"I'm captain of this ship. No SOS."

"Harper's right. We can't wait here, Cutter. There's a hurricane barreling our way. If *Calusa* takes on water, your tender's no match for this storm."

A strong wave slammed *Calusa*'s port side and it shook. All three of them were knocked to Cutter's pilot house floor. The radio microphone fell out of Cutter's hand and Harper seized it. Before he could call for rescue, Cutter yanked its cord out of his marine radio.

"I said no may day and I mean it," said Cutter. "We've got a blow-up survival boat in the starboard hull with an emergency beacon if we have to use it."

"If? We're certainly are going to need it, you damn muffin head."

Harper stormed out to find it and Jenn looked at Cutter with complete bewilderment.

"What's wrong with you?"

"It's too much to explain right now. You wouldn't believe it even if I did."

As he left, Jenn tried to figure out if she could reconnect the torn cord enough to send out an alert. Cutter hurried to Aquan's borrowed quarters and searched around for her spear gun and lethal darts. Finding them hidden under her bunk mattress, he headed back to his main deck. He unlocked a fuse box near his galley and flicked power off and then locked it.

"Put those lights back on," yelled Jenn. She sat crossed-legged on the floor trying to get his radio to work.

Climbing steps headed topside, he slid open the main bulkhead door.

"Where are you going?" said Jenn.

"Out," replied Cutter.

Gypsy trailed behind him. He slammed this bulkhead shut, locking Harper and Jenn below deck. In a few moments, he could hear them hollering at him and pounding their fists. Bashing waves overwhelmed their shouts as he latched on to a safety harness and shimmied his way up *Calusa*'s mast. With each mighty wave, Cutter was knocked off its mast and hung suspended in the air, then swung back and clambered up a bit further, like a rock climber on a sheer stone wall.

Aquan kept her Typhon wings spread out across the sky until the full moon slipped past apex and started to descend, assuring that Skeiron's bridles no longer retained any power. As she relaxed her enormous bat wings to her sides, Skeiron rocketed out as a Hydra, a huge nine-headed serpent, eight mortal and one immortal. His Hydra slammed into Aquan sending her spinning across the sky. She flapped her huge bat wings to create forceful winds pushing Skeiron back as he tumbled over whit tips of cresting waves. Spitting out hot coals, she scorched large black pockmarks in his Hydra body as it hissed and writhed in pain. Two burning coals engulfed one of Hydra's mortal heads in flames and it ducked beneath the sea to extinguish it. Rising out of swirling surf, this charred head remained lifeless. Aquan sprayed searing flames at two other Hydra heads, burning them into charcoal cinders.

"You deceived me cousin," howled Skeiron. "Only two of those amulets were real."

"You couldn't think I'd give in so easily to your demands."

"You will pay for your lies with your life and your friends' lives, here and at Rapture's End."

Flying above him, Aquan's serpent legs battled two more Hydra's coils, they nipped at each other trying to strike a deadly blow. A third Hydra serpent leapt up and bit off twenty snake heads from Aquan's wriggling left hand and she screamed in pain. Skeiron bellowed with pleasure and tossed half of Aquan's snake heads into another Hydra serpent's masticating jaws. As Skeiron's hungry serpents tore through Aquan's snake hands, her remaining eighty wriggling hands attacked them landing hundreds of lethal snake bites. Two more of Skeiron's serpent heads shriveled up dead.

As Skeiron's serpents nipped at her wings, Aquan snorted out black smoke and he briefly lost sight of her. Aquan's snake heads attacked another of Hydra's coils, their sharp teeth and powerful jaws tearing off its head, but two more grew in its place. Her snake hands struck again, snapping off both of them. She roared out scorching flames on each stump preventing their regeneration.

One of Skeiron's three remaining coils wrapped itself around one of her serpent legs. Aquan beat her wings feverishly but couldn't fly away. One of her serpentine legs hissed back at Skeiron's choking coil and they landed alternating strikes at each other. Skeiron's immortal serpent head took a chunk out of her flapping right wing. Aquan shrieked and careened into the waves. Another coil wrapped itself around her Typhon chest and wings so Aquan was unable to fly. As she struggled against him, Skeiron pulled her above the ocean's surface and exhaled his Hydra's toxic breath, knocking her into a daze. Barely conscious, she could feel Skeiron communicating with her through his thoughts.

"You will die, cousin. But not until you see your friends die first."

A whizzing sound of a lethal dart pierced the air and struck him from behind. Another Hydra coil squirmed and then drooped dead by his side, unwrapping from Aquan's leg. Angered, Skeiron turned and spied Cutter clinging to his boat mast with Aquan's spear gun. Skeiron's Hydra swam toward *Calusa*.

"Holy shit," said Cutter. His hands shook as he tried to quickly reload her spear gun. "Aquan, a little help here. Aquan!"

In a foggy haze, she saw Skeiron's immortal serpent head reach out to strike Cutter, but he swung away from his mast using his safety harness. Cutter shot a lethal dart but it flew past Skeiron's head. Like a cat trying to paw a dangling ball of yarn, Skeiron waited for Cutter to sway back, its mouth open wide.

"Aquan," yelled Cutter.

She awoke and her serpent jaw clamped shut on a Hydra coil wrapped around her wings, wrenching it from its base. She spit out a series of hot coals into Skeiron's open mouth and he choked on her fiery volley. Skeiron tipped backwards and Aquan's serpent legs attacked him and their fangs sank into his Hydra neck, delivering lethal poisons into his remaining head.

Dark green blood spurted from this giant reptile. As Skeiron jerked back, his immortal head burst into flames from the inside out. Cutter crashed through its smoldering immortal head raining down black ash and glowing embers on to his boat deck. Aquan sealed every stump with bursts of blistering flames to insure that none of this creature's Hydra coils would be able to revive themselves. A sooty Cutter whooped and laughed, swaying back and forth on his safety harness. Gypsy barked and raced around Calusa's upper deck.

Aquan beat her wings so hard she covered the rocky outcrop in sea water releasing *Calusa* from its grip. Cutter's boat slid back into an open channel. She flew skyward and flapped her mighty wings beating back an oncoming hurricane. Her enormous wind gusts knocked the hurricane off its course as it sped off into an open ocean, away from land masses.

As Aquan collapsed back to her Triton form, she felt sharp pains and noticed black blood spilling from wounds on her torso and back from her battle with Skeiron. Although weakened, something within her sensed that her battles were not quite over yet. She must rejoin her essence and help Raynord to defend Rapture's End from Skeiron's forces. As Cutter clambered down from the mast, he looked out over the glassy sea for her. Under a starry sky and full moon, he called out her name. Only the plaintive cries of sea birds replied.

Chapter 43

As she breathed in her waiting essence, Aquan expected to hear sounds of war when she returned to her home. Instead at the outskirts of Rapture's End, she found Timarch soldiers clearing away a few dozen bodies of dead Hydromorphs. Having lost a great deal of blood, she shuddered as pain shot through her body. Raynord swam toward her with a spear, its tip sheathed in seaweed, clasped in his hands. He gathered her up and took her to the House of Triton and into her Aunt Sofronia's care. Raynord's troops guarded her Triton compound. Thalassa and her mother aided Sofronia as she ministered to an unconscious Aquan with Mopsus's most powerful healing elixirs. For two long days and nights, Aquan straddled a thin fragile line between life and death. On a third morning, she opened her eyes and jolted up. Her aunt and Raynord bowed before her.

"Why do you bow to me?"

"You bear our sacred amulets of victory over the Margrave around your neck," said her aunt.

Aquan touched her hand to her throat and found four amulets hanging from her chain. Returned once more to Rapture's End in anticipation of a future Scattering.

"You retained Eternal Concordia and restored honor to your Triton House." Aunt Sofronia smiled proudly.

She shrank from her aunt knowing of her cruel deceptions about her Protosian roots. Instead Aquan turned away from her and motioned to Raynord to look up.

"Rise, my loyal friend. You never have to bow to me. I'm grateful that you believed in me and fought simply because I asked you to do it."

Raynord stood up. "You know I can't deny your wishes, Aquan." He tenderly touched her arm. "I thought we might lose you these past two days. But thankfully Mopsus's medicines revived you."

Wincing at his name, Aquan felt no desire to see or thank Mopsus.

"What happened in your battle, Raynord?"

"At full moon, hundreds of Hydromorphs massed on our borders. But only several dozen launched themselves at us. Our seaweed tips killed them without any contamination of our troops. They liquefied instantly."

She wondered if Skeiron merely used them as a test run or as a diversion from their battle near Little Moon Island.

"Have you found Elder Camulus?"

"No, he must have allies amongst us. We can't find him anywhere within our territory, but we'll continue to search for him."

"Our Elder Council is waiting for you in Quartz Hall to hear about your success in defeating the Margrave," said Aunt Sofronia.

She hesitated and looked warily at her aunt, uncertain if the Elder Council still meant to kill her now.

"Don't worry, Aquan. I'm coming along with a dozen of my hand-picked troops. You don't have to fear for your security."

Aquan doubted she could ever feel safe or at home in Rapture's End ever again. She needed to speak with her mother and decide what to do next. Unfastening her chain from her neck, she gave three gemstones to Raynord.

"I don't report to the Elders any longer. Give these three amulets to them for safe-keeping until the next Scattering. Let them know that I'll be serving as Sentinel for this one."

Retaining this talisman insured her safety from both Archigen and Protosian enemies alike. She didn't have to worry about another Sequencing for at least another hundred years. She gazed into her amber stone and saw *Calusa* anchored in a sleepy Belizean port. Cutter stood on its deck, looking out to sea. Once her mother was fully recuperated and securely relocated, Aquan planned to return to him.

"I must go to see my mother who recovers from stasis."

"Where? My warriors and I will protect you on your journey."

She smiled. "It's best that this moment be a private reunion."

"Will you return to us?" Raynord grasped her hand.

"Thalassa would be heart-broken if you stayed away too long."

Aquan noticed a slight tremble in his lower lip. She knew he asked for both of them.

"I hope so. Tell Thalassa that you will both be close to my heart while I'm gone."

She embraced Raynord and kissed him on his cheek, then darted away before he could respond.

*****

Aquan swam toward rich healing waters at Cortonis. Upon her arrival, her mother's caretakers insisted that she let them further tend Aquan's wounds before taking her to see her mother. When they finally escorted her to Evadne, her mother drifted placidly in a picturesque coral garden.

"Speak in a low voice and be gentle with her. She remains weak from her time in stasis."

Aquan rushed over to her mother who looked at her blankly.

"Mother, I've so missed you," she whispered.

She touched Evadne's cheek. In an instant, her mother's figure reverted to its actual form, a cloaked Hydromorph. She grabbed the creature and shook it.

"Where is my mother? What did you do with her?"

"Our game isn't over yet, cousin," Skeiron's voice taunted. The Hydromorph liquefied in her hands. "It has just begun."

ABOUT THE AUTHOR

As a kid, Bridges tortured her eight siblings by writing and directing annual family plays. Starting with a pad of paper, then moving to an orange Smith Corona typewriter, and now to her trusty laptop, she has always enjoyed the puzzle of finding the right word, phrase or plot twist. Her published works are both non-fiction and fiction. She has published two non-fiction books and numerous articles, manuals, and editorials in the legal, travel and business fields and short stories in the science fiction, fantasy and mystery genres. *Bridles of Poseidon* was chosen as a finalist in the 2012 Royal Palm Literary Awards (unpublished fantasy) from the Florida Writers Association. Her legal mystery, *Deadly Sacrifices*, set in Boston, won a 2012 Royal Palm Literary Award (unpublished mystery—2d place).

Her short story, *Clair de Lune*, based on the Celtic myth about Selkies, is published in *Mother Goose is Dead, Modern Stories of Myths, Fables and Fairy Tales* (Damnation Books 2011) and *Chasing the Moon*, about a werewolf with Parkinson's Disease who revels in his monthly transformation, is published in *Tails of the Pack: A Werewolf Anthology* (Sky Warrior Books 2013). Her non-fiction essay, *Brick*, honoring her late father, Joseph, and his love of words is published in *Living Lessons* (Whispering Angels Books 2010). She is also a member of Sisters in Crime, Inc. and the Florida Writers Association.

When she is not writing, she teaches law courses, creates educational game apps, and lives happily in sunny Central Florida. To learn more about Bridges DelPonte and her writing, please visit:

Author web site: *http://www.bridgesdelponte.com*

Amazon Author Central page:
http://www.amazon.com/Bridges-DelPonte/e/B00BW7BZYU/ref=ntt_athr_dp_pel_pop_9